I Know Where You Live

by

Pat Young

First published in 2018 by Bloodhound Books

www.bloodhoundbooks.com

Print ISBN 978-1-912604-01-2

Also by Pat Young

Till The Dust Settles

This book is dedicated to my children who light up my life and to my husband whose encouragement has brought me this far.

Chapter 1

Penny searched the departures board. Their flight was still delayed.

She sighed out her disappointment, her shoulders sagging, and touched the back of her neck. Same spot she always felt the tingle – when she was being watched.

No, not here.

He *couldn't* be here. It wasn't possible.

She turned, scanning faces.

And caught him staring. She looked away, expecting him to disappear like that time in the shopping mall. There one moment, vanished the next, as if she'd imagined him.

When she looked again, he was still there. Still looking at her. She stared back, taking in his dark hair, pale face, his slim build and his height, taller than average. Mentally noting details, gathering evidence. Doing what she should have done before.

He dropped his gaze, guilty. Pushed back the cuff of a business jacket and checked his wrist. He was too far away for her to see his watch, but she imagined a Rolex.

He fixed his sleeve and looked up again. Straight at her.

Something snapped, like an elastic in her head. How dare he?

Penny walked towards him, concentrating on his face, not knowing what she was going to say, but hoping she'd sound brave and serious enough to scare him off. For good.

She'd had enough fear. Enough hiding. Enough running away.

He saw her coming and smiled.

She stopped. Held her ground as he approached. She decided what she'd say. 'Back off. Leave me alone.'

He swerved around her, brushing past with a quiet apology. 'Pardon me, ma'am,' he said.

Oh, he was cool, she'd give him that.

She turned, prepared to follow. Saw him open his arms. Noticed the woman, running towards him, her face full of love. They collided, embraced, and hurried away towards the departure gates.

Penny deflated as if all the breath had left her body at the same time. She started to laugh, more manic than amused. People passed, not noticing her, or choosing not to see.

She looked around for somewhere to go till she composed herself.

Seth had told her to take her time, grab a coffee or a glass of wine, a break from the kids who were bored by the long delay and grouchy. Wine was tempting but unwise before a transatlantic flight, so Penny chose coffee and settled at a table where she could keep an eye on the departures screen.

She felt free in a way that made her want to smile at everyone. No more fear. She'd been terrified for months, convinced she was being watched. When all the time the only thing stalking her was her own terror. Why couldn't she see that before? Or tell Seth, so he could convince her she was being silly?

She would have told Janey, without hesitation. Because Janey would have cared. Janey had protected people like them for more than twenty years. In the early days, Penny used to lie awake worrying about how she'd cope without Janey. And then, suddenly, she'd had to.

A replacement had been appointed. Marcus. Young, flash, on his way up. Eyes on a higher goal. Not really interested in her and Seth, she felt. They'd been part of the Witness Security program for almost ten years, after all. Expected to need 'minimal' support.

She knew he had more interesting cases. High-risk witnesses. Running from murderous gangsters who had connections everywhere. Not like you, he seemed to imply, dismissive of her fears.

'How often have you seen this guy?' he'd asked, when she'd plucked up enough courage to share her fears. He leaned towards her, smooth chin cupped in his manicured hand. She caught a whiff of cologne.

'I'm not sure.'

'Ball park?'

'A couple of times.'

'A couple being? Twice, three times?'

'Don't know. I've seen him twice. But before that I had, you know, the feeling I was being watched.'

'The feeling?' He had leaned back in his seat at this point and balanced for a second on its hind legs. Then straightened as if he'd remembered to take her seriously.

'Yeah,' said Penny, 'like when you just know someone's staring at you? But you look round and no one's there.'

He'd shuffled some papers. A message, she felt, that he was a busy man with more important work to do.

'One day in K-Mart, for example. I was picking out a dress for my daughter's birthday party and I just had this feeling – that someone was watching me.'

'Was someone watching you?'

'I'm sure he was. But when I looked round, he was gone.'

'How do you know it was a "he", if "he" was gone?'

'I saw him another time. At the school. I'm sure I did. When I went to fetch Angel.'

'What did he look like?'

'I don't know. Kind of medium height? Yeah, not that tall.'

'Anything else? Young? Old? Gimme something to work with, please.'

She couldn't. It was like trying to conjure up her mum's face in the months after she died.

'Was he black, white …?'

'White. Definitely.'

'Well,' he sighed, 'that sure narrows it down.' He had the grace to smile, which relaxed her a bit.

'Sorry, I'm not much help, am I?' It was like being back in that scary place when she was being prepared by the FBI lawyers to give testimony. Frantic in case she'd get it wrong and Scott Millburn would go free. Free to come after her again. Or to send someone to kill her like they'd killed Charlotte.

Her confidence deserted her, just like it had in those months before the trial.

'You're doing okay,' he said, checking his phone as he spoke, as if something or someone more important needed his attention. 'Sorry, I was just checking your notes.'

'You carry them around on your phone?' Great, something else for her to worry about.

'I *access* them, that's all. It says here that you're a writer.'

Penny gave him an embarrassed smile. 'Who told you that? Seth? I would *like* to be a writer, as in, I've got a book in my head. Unfortunately, small kids don't leave too much time for Mommy to become a bestselling author.'

'I hear you,' he said. 'It's just, I went out with a girl once who was a writer. Man! She just about drove me crazy. Talk about hyperactive imagination.'

'Did she go, "What if the plane crashes? What if a hurricane hits?" Catastrophising all the time?'

'What if someone's watching me?' he said, with a sly grin.

'Okay,' said Penny. 'I take your point. Seth would probably agree with you. Poor guy, he's had ten years of this. He's always telling me to chill.'

'Seth's right. You should try to lose the fear. You don't have to worry.'

'How often do you say that in a day?'

'Many times. But it's true. You're a brave lady. Not everyone would agree to be alone in her apartment with a felon, wearing a wire to record his every word. Even with the FBI waiting outside the door. Then you testified in court. That takes courage.'

He'd paused, as if waiting for her to agree.

'Penny, Scott Millburn is in high-security prison. He'll be there for a very long time for what he did. And his contact with the outside world is minimal. Trust me, he is no threat to you.'

She had heard this so often she barely listened anymore. She laughed, for his benefit, as if she hadn't a care in the world, and squirmed at the sound of it. 'Oh, I'm just being silly. This isn't the first time I've been convinced someone was watching. I don't suppose it will be the last.'

Penny had known then she couldn't stick around to find out. 'Say, I wanted to ask you something.' She'd tried to sound casual. 'Could we move away, d'you think?'

'From Texas?'

'Yeah.'

'I'm pretty sure you could. But I'd advise you to avoid a knee-jerk reaction to this guy you "think" is watching.'

When Seth had come home a few nights later and mentioned he'd been offered the chance to go and work in Toulouse, Penny had thought her prayers had been answered.

'The aerospace industry's huge there,' Seth had explained. 'And they're offering a six-month exchange opportunity to highly qualified workers.' He'd thumbed his chest in mock pride.

'We should go,' Penny had said. 'Why not?'

'Why not?' He looked at her as if she'd gone mad. 'You know why not. Small matter of our identity?'

'It's almost ten years. Surely it's okay for us to leave the country now?'

And it would be okay, if the damn plane ever took off. Penny drained her coffee mug and went to relieve Seth.

Ethan was squirming in his daddy's arms, his little face red and streaked with tears. He was crying in a grizzling, exhausted way that tore at her and demanded she do something to comfort him.

Seth looked up as she approached. 'Hey,' he said, with his usual grin. Nothing fazed this man.

She still thought of him as Dylan sometimes, although she never, ever said his real name in public, or in front of the kids. Except for that once, yesterday. They'd made a whistle-stop tour of New York City, the first time either of them had been back. Penny had been keen to visit the 9/11 memorial because it felt the right thing to do. She wanted to say a private goodbye to the person she used to be, all those years ago. In that place of sanctity, she had felt completely safe and his old name had simply slipped out. 'I love you, Dylan.'

'You okay, Peanut?'

Penny smiled. His many versions of her new name always had that effect on her. 'Yeah,' she said, nodding. 'Sorry I was away so long.'

'Look pretty worried there. Bad news?'

'More delay. No word of how long. Some guy says it's an air traffic control dispute. Apparently, the French are guilty of striking at short notice. "At the drop of a baguette" was how he put it.'

'And the rest of the world can go hang? Nice one! Remind me, whose idea was it to go live in France?' His grin told her he was teasing and she smiled in return.

'Poor Ethan. Shall I take him for a bit?' she asked.

Ethan had stopped whining and was watching his sister, who was on the floor building an impressive pyramid of the playing cards they'd brought for Go Fish.

As Angel carefully positioned the top card, the PA system announced a flight that was about to board and a large man bustled out of his seat and gathered his belongings. He swept off, creating a draught in his wake that demolished Angeline's creation. The child looked astonished. And then appalled. Penny knew what would come next.

Angeline inhaled a lungful of air, her mouth distorting into the perfect square that every parent dreads, but, before a tear had fallen, a young woman dropped to her knees beside the child and began to pick up the cards. Like a conjuror, she made the first card flip over in mid-air and caught it. Then a second, then a third. Angeline seemed mesmerised.

'You wanna try?' asked the young woman.

Penny's well-trained child looked to her for reassurance that it was okay to engage with this stranger. Habit made Penny want to gather her children to her, but she reminded herself: no more fear. She nodded to her daughter and watched as Angel mastered the simple trick. Ethan, quiet now, climbed down and stood, leaning on his daddy's knee, eyes on his sister.

The young woman noticed Ethan. Taking a handful of cards, she made one pop up and down out of the pack. Each time the card popped up, she said, 'Peek-boo!' and Ethan giggled on cue.

Penny stood, shaking her head. It never failed to amaze her how quickly kids could go from inconsolable to enchanted.

'You're a lifesaver,' said Penny. 'You should get a job here, hire yourself out by the hour. People like me would pay you to entertain their kids. Look at these two. You'd never guess how long they've been cooped up waiting for a plane that might never take off.'

Angeline, always listening, piped up, 'Aren't we going to France now, Mommy?'

'Course we are, sweetie. In a little while.'

Ethan scooted round and sat himself down next to Angeline's new friend who said, in a mock-astonished voice, 'Fra-ance? Wow! Amazing! That's where I'm going!'

Angel laughed and Ethan copied his sister, then said in an excited voice, 'Big airplane.'

'Wow! Amazing! I'm going in a big airplane too!'

'Mommy, can we sit beside her on the airplane? Can we, Mommy?'

Penny leaned forward and tucked a stray lock of Angel's blonde hair under her favourite pink Alice band. Smiling, she said, 'See what you've gotten yourself into?' She held her hand out in a gesture that might prompt the young woman to reveal a name. It worked.

'Sophie,' she said, '*enchantée*.'

'Hi, Sophie. This is Angeline, usually known as Angel, though she doesn't always live up to her name.'

Sophie took Angel's hand in hers and shook it, very formally, saying, 'Hello, Miss Angeline. I'm very pleased to meet you.'

Angel giggled and Ethan held out his hand towards Sophie.

'His name's Ethan,' said Angel. 'He's my little brother.'

'Our kids are showing us up,' said Seth, reaching across to offer his hand. 'I'm Seth Gates and this is my wife, Penelope.'

'Most folk call me Penny.'

'Daddy sometimes calls her another name,' said Angel, then clasped both hands over her mouth, as if she shouldn't have said anything. Penny's heart stopped. Had the children overheard her and Seth in bed some night when everyone ought to have been asleep? Could Angel have been listening yesterday and caught Penny's slip of the tongue?

'Ooh,' said Sophie. 'I wonder what that can be?'

'Daddy calls Mommy ...' Angeline paused and looked at her mother, clearly trying to gauge her reaction. Penny felt frozen. She tried hard to smile, which was all the encouragement Angel needed.

'Peanut!' she screamed and burst into hysterical laughter. At the nickname or, more likely, the fact she'd been naughty enough to reveal a family secret to a stranger.

'Someone's getting a little bit overexcited, Sophie. I'm sorry.'

'Please don't apologise. It's a pleasant diversion. My Kindle battery's dead so your kids are, like, doing me a favour. Anyway, I need the practice.'

'Oh, yeah?'

'I'm hoping to find work as an au pair, ideally in a family with children. I'm kinda counting on it, to be honest, cos I'm not too keen on earning my keep by doing bar work or waitressing.'

'Speak any French? Apart from *enchanté*?' asked Seth, voicing one of his main concerns about their plan to live in France for a while.

'I grew up bilingual. American mom, French dad. They met when my dad came to the States to study Louisiana French for his thesis. He swept her off her feet apparently. Then swept himself off out of our lives.' She shrugged. '*C'est la vie*. How about you folks?'

'Don't speak any French at all. I've heard they all speak English, at least that's what the guys at work said. Still, we're hoping to take some lessons while we're over there and Penny's particularly keen for the kids to learn. We plan to send Angel to school and see if she likes it.'

'That's a great idea. They'll soak French up like little sponges. Watch this.'

Sophie showed them a game of counting cards in French and within minutes Angel knew the numbers one to ten, and Ethan could say, '*Un, deux, trois.*'

'Boy, I wish we could learn that fast,' said Seth. 'Are you a teacher, Sophie?'

'No, but I'd like to be. Just not ready to go straight from college into teaching. I want to see a bit of the world first, starting with Paris. Where are you folks heading?'

'Few days in Paris and then right down to the south. We're doing a house exchange for six months.'

'That's amazing. My dad came from the South of France. You don't think it could be the same town, do you?'

'We're heading for a place called Carcassonne.'

'I've heard of it. Isn't that where they filmed that Kevin Costner movie?'

'That's right. *Robin Hood: Prince of Thieves*. Angeline is very excited about living near a castle, aren't you, kiddo?'

The child nodded. 'I want to see a princess.'

Penny became aware of people around them stirring. 'Is it worth checking the board again?' she asked Seth.

Before he could answer, passengers on Air France flight number FR543 to Paris were invited to proceed to the gate for immediate boarding. A cheer went up and Seth said, 'Guess the strike's off.'

'Looks like it,' said Penny. 'No going back now.'

Chapter 2

Sophie checked her watch then moved it forward to Central European time. The flight was scheduled to take seven and a half hours, which meant they should be landing in Paris mid-morning, all being well. Although the delay had been a pain in the ass, it might work in her favour. Sitting around the departure lounge had allowed her to indulge in her favourite pastime of people watching. It had also given her the chance to get to know that lovely family. The two kids were so cute. Sophie knew she would love to spend more time with them. She planned to wait until the flight was well under way then have a walk around the aircraft to see if she could spot them.

'Something to drink?' Sophie looked up at the flight attendant and said, 'Yes, please. I'll have a glass of white wine.' May as well get into the French lifestyle. 'Actually, sorry. Do you mind if I just have a diet soda instead?' She didn't want anyone to smell alcohol on her breath.

Dinner had been served and cleared away before Sophie got the chance to stretch her legs. Queues of passengers had formed outside the restrooms and, as Sophie squeezed apologetically past, Seth hailed her.

'Hey, Sophie. How you doing? Pen's right over there with the kids.' He pointed a few rows back to four seats in the centre. 'The little guy's tuckered out. But Angeline's wide awake.'

'Should I go say hello?'

'Yeah, they'll be glad to see you.'

Penny, clearly pleased, greeted her like a friend and invited her to sit in the empty seat near the aisle. Seth's, presumably.

Angeline, in the next seat along, hugged Sophie's arm when she sat down.

'Angel, why don't you go see Daddy up there by the restroom?'

'But Mommy, I said I don't need to go to the bathroom.'

'I know you said that, but soon the lights will go down and everybody is meant to go to sleep. Be a good girl and go ask Daddy to take you.'

'Will you wait right here till I come back, Sophie?'

Sophie laughed. 'Sure, right here, and I might even show you another magic trick.'

'Promise?'

'Cross my heart.'

The child clambered over Sophie and ran off down the aisle.

Penny leaned towards her, as if she were about to share a secret.

'This might be way out of line, Sophie, but Seth and I have been talking. We're wondering if, by any chance, you're planning on staying in Paris for a few days?'

Sophie knew it would be better to appear a bit wary, so she said nothing.

Penny blustered on. 'Sorry, I shouldn't have asked. I'm sure you've already made plans. It's just that, with your fluent French, and you're so good with the children. Sorry, I've embarrassed you.'

Sophie smiled and touched Penny's arm. 'You haven't embarrassed me. I'm, like, a bit surprised, that's all. What did you have in mind?'

'No wonder you're surprised. You don't know a thing about us. You probably think I'm a complete madwoman. I mean, we've only just met. In an airport lounge, of all places. Sorry, forget I mentioned it.'

Sophie felt a rush of sympathy. 'Mentioned what, Penny?'

'I'm not quite sure how we're going to find our way around Paris. I'm worried.'

'Can I let you into a secret?' Sophie whispered.

Penny nodded.

'To tell you the truth, I'm scared shitless.' She clamped her hand over her mouth, exactly like Angeline had earlier. 'This seemed like a great adventure when I was planning it. Now? Not so much.'

Penny laughed. 'Me too. The reality of dragging my family halfway across the world is beginning to kick in. What on earth was I thinking? How will we ever survive in a country where we don't speak a word of the language?'

'You'll manage. Everyone does, eventually. Apparently.'

'Could you *be* any more encouraging?'

Both women laughed and little Ethan stirred on his mother's lap. He opened his eyes, said, 'Sophie,' and went back to sleep.

'I think my kids are a little bit in love with you. Oops, here comes trouble.'

Angeline climbed over Sophie back into her seat, then rummaged in her little backpack and produced the playing cards.

'Will you have a think about meeting up in Paris, Sophie? Doing a bit of sightseeing together?'

'Say yes, Sophie,' squealed Angeline. 'Then I can learn more tricks.'

'It's okay, Penny. I don't need to think about it. I'll make us a plan. Right after I've taught this kid my favourite card trick.'

'Maybe we can talk again when we land?' said Penny.

The lights dimmed as Sophie returned to her seat. She reclined it as far back as it would go. In economy, that wasn't much. She unwrapped a little blanket from its polythene bag and plumped up the tiny pillow she'd been allocated. It was important she grab a few hours' shut-eye. She'd need to be alert tomorrow. She wondered what the little family was thinking about, back there in row fifty-one. If the parents were still awake, they were probably thinking how perfect she was and how meeting her was going to make their life so much easier.

If only they knew.

Chapter 3

By the time she was in a position to ring, Sophie was about eight hours late in making the agreed phone call. She hoped Miss L would be okay about it. She didn't want to lose this job, especially now she'd met the family. They seemed like great people. The wife might indeed be a bit neurotic, as Miss L had suggested, but no wonder. What woman wouldn't be nervy, making the changes they had planned? With two small kids. The husband was so laid back he would probably make up for it.

They'd seemed genuinely delighted when Sophie told them she'd love to meet up the next day, visit some sights together. They were kind people, she was sure of it. They had even insisted on giving her a ride from the airport in the oversized cab they'd booked in advance.

'See why we had to go for a large cab?' asked Seth, as he retrieved bag after bag from the conveyor belt and piled them on a luggage cart. 'Why do kids always need so much stuff?'

They'd paid off the taxi at their budget hotel and insisted she keep it for the rest of her journey to the 'hostel' she'd booked 'somewhere near the Arc de Triomphe'. The driver hadn't batted an eyelid when she told him her destination was the plush Concorde Lafayette at Porte Maillot.

Sophie's room was on the twenty-second floor. She dumped her bags and drew back the pale gauze curtain, gasping at the view. Way over the rooftops the Sacré-Coeur Basilica sparkled on its hilltop. Sophie had done her homework and had a fair idea of how this city was laid out, as well as a clear plan for how much she could see in a few days. She'd wanted to visit Paris for as long as she could remember and Miss L's offer of an all-expenses-paid trip had been enough to tempt her.

She dragged herself away from the window and flopped on the bed. Eyes closed, she fought sleep as she fumbled in her bag for the new mobile phone she'd been given. It had been topped up with a staggeringly large amount of money, designed to cope with many transatlantic calls. The first of which she knew she ought to make right now, dog-tired though she was.

It was answered on the first ring.

'Oh, my sweet Lord! Thank goodness. Whatever happened?'

'Hi, I'm sorry. The flight was delayed because of some strike threat. I was worried for a bit that it might be cancelled.'

'That would most certainly have been inconvenient, not to say disastrous.'

Sophie loved this woman's voice. Her breathy delivery and tinkly laugh always made her think of Scarlett O' Hara in *Gone with the Wind*, Mom's all-time favourite movie.

'Yes, we were all, like, pretty relieved when they suddenly announced the flight was boarding.'

'I'll bet you were. Did you get a chance to make contact?'

Sophie smiled to herself, sure her employer would be pleased with her progress.

She wasn't disappointed. The tinkly laughter showered over her like fairy dust and the compliments came thick and fast. 'Oh, you clever little thing! How smart you are! All I'd hoped for at this stage was that you'd find out more about their eventual destination so you might be able to follow them.'

'It was so easy. Maybe because I told them my dad was French? I think that made them, like, trust me? Anyway, you were right, it's Carcassonne.'

The laughter stopped. 'When you say "it was so easy", I hope you didn't give them cause to be suspicious?'

'No. I didn't.'

'Not even the tiniest reason? It won't take much. I hope you're sure?'

The word sounded like shoo-ah and made Sophie smile again. 'It's fine. I'm sure.' She was confident the family trusted her. Why wouldn't they? 'Penny practically begged me to join them when they go sightseeing tomorrow. I didn't jump at the offer. To tell you the truth, I was a bit shocked myself at how quickly it all happened, so it was easy to sound surprised and, like, indecisive.'

'What did you do? How did you leave it with them?' Sophie noticed the note of panic that had crept into the voice. This wasn't the first time she'd heard it.

'I'm boxing clever. I told Penny I'm scared, too. Not sure this big adventure is such a good idea after all. That's exactly how she's feeling, by the way. She told me so.'

'You haven't arranged to see them again? Oh, my Lord! What if you lose contact, or they change their minds?'

'I won't. And I'm sure *they* won't. Please don't worry. I'm meeting them tomorrow at the Eiffel Tower and we're going to spend the day together. I've got an itinerary all planned out. I want to appear, like, totally trustworthy and reliable. Also, I intend to get those kids on my side.'

The line was quiet for a few moments, as if the woman on the other end was thinking, considering the points Sophie had made. She held her breath. She wanted this job to work out.

'Fine.'

Sophie relaxed.

'I think you're handling this well, Sophie, by the sound of it. Did you remember to bring the references I prepared for you?'

'Yes, I did.'

'I don't imagine they'll ask for them at this stage. You don't think it will seem a little odd, spending the day with complete strangers?'

'Maybe strangers isn't the right word. We chatted in the airport lounge, on the flight, in baggage reclaim, and during the cab ride all the way into town. We hit it off so it's natural to want to spend more time together. By the way, I mentioned that I'm here to look for a nanny's job. Just like you said I should.'

'Well done. I knew I'd made a wise choice when I picked a Louisiana girl.'

'Thanks, Miss L. I won't let you down.'

'You'd better not, for all our sakes.'

Sophie shivered a little. At those words? The tone of voice? Or just because she was jet-lagged and desperate for a shower?

'Anyway, tell me, how are my sweet grandchildren?'

This was a more comfortable topic and Sophie grabbed it. 'Oh, they're adorable! So cute, and such bright little buttons.'

'Bright, you say?'

'Absolutely. Particularly Angeline. The little boy isn't saying very much, yet.'

'Just as well, for what we have in mind.'

'Yeah, guess so.'

'Do you know when they're heading for Carcassonne?'

'In a couple of days. We didn't discuss it in detail. I thought it best not to seem too curious.'

'Is their hotel the one we were expecting?'

'Yep, and it's not nearly as chic as mine, thank you.'

'You're very welcome, my dear. Try to get a French bank account set up as soon as you can and I'll arrange for your allowance to be transferred. As I explained before, the larger sum will be deposited into your Internet bank account on completion.'

'Thanks, Miss L.' Sophie felt the same awkwardness she always did using the name she knew was false. Once they'd reached a point in their relationship where her employer had gained enough trust, she'd explained to Sophie that the 'bilingual nanny job' she'd applied for was not quite as advertised. She'd shared more details and wasted no time in telling Sophie that the name Mouche-Chamier was false. She'd made it clear to Sophie that the situation was extremely delicate and for that reason she chose to protect her real identity. She went on to add that she expected Sophie would Google Miss Louise Mouche-Chamier. 'Isn't that what you young people always do these days? Save yourself the time, my dear. You'll come up with nothing.'

She'd been right on both counts.

'Why don't you get some rest now, Sophie? You must be completely worn out after that awful journey. I know I would be. You're going to need your wits about you tomorrow. Let's speak again once you have a clearer picture of their plans, yes?'

'Yes. And thank you.'

'Y'all take care now.'

Perhaps it was the southern drawl of her homeland, or perhaps the kind tone of voice, but Sophie believed Miss L was genuinely concerned for her welfare. That's what had drawn her into this intrigue in the first place: the woman's kindness and a desire to help her. That, plus an irrepressible curiosity she'd had since childhood. Although the sensible side of her brain was telling her to be careful, Sophie liked to think of herself as a free spirit, ready to grab every adventure life might offer. Unfortunately, being a free spirit meant she had no one to turn to, except her mother, when she needed advice on something like this. As far as her mom was concerned, going to be a nanny in France was as good a career plan as any.

Sophie's mom had met, married and produced two kids to another man when her dashing Frenchman had dashed off back to France and deserted her. Sophie had been eight, old enough to speak two languages fluently, but not nearly old enough to understand how grown-ups can fall in and out of love. She had been hard to convince, no matter how much her mother tried, that Papa still loved her, even though he had packed his bags and gone while she was at school. He'd left her nothing but a *billet-doux*, one of the little love letters he'd written since she was old enough to read. She used to find them in her lunchbox with her sandwiches. '*Bon appétit, chérie.*' Or tucked under her pillow. 'Golden slumbers, my precious one.'

Sophie had also been hard to convince that her mom still loved her, given how little attention she gave Sophie, compared to her cute half-brothers. Many a time she'd wished someone would just take them away so that she could have her mom's undivided attention. Her stepfather was kind enough, and generous to a fault, putting her through college, buying her a car and, she supposed, trying hard to be a good dad to his stepdaughter. But no matter how much effort John made, Sophie longed for the handsome Papa of her early childhood.

Maybe she'd look him up. She could start her research while she waited for the next step of their plan to work itself out. She knew Papa and his family came originally from the Aude, but it was a big area. She imagined the joy of meeting her father again after all those years.

Sophie woke from a deep, dreamless sleep, fully clothed and feeling grim. She glanced at her phone, hoping she hadn't slept too long. The last thing she needed was jet lag. Tomorrow would be a challenging day. The first of many.

Chapter 4

'Why are you eating your fingers, Mommy?'

Penny hid her nibbled fingernails. Sophie was late.

'Can we have another ride on the carousel, please?' Angeline took her hand and dragged her towards the pretty vintage carousel that was gently turning behind them, its music evoking the belle époque from which the guide book said it dated.

'If she doesn't come soon, we'll have no spending money left,' muttered Seth under his breath. 'Think everywhere in France will be as expensive as Paris?'

'I think these are the best children in the world and they deserve a few treats.'

'In that case, come on, kids, let's go get some cotton candy.'

'One each?' begged Angel.

'No, let's share. Look, they're humungous.'

The giant pink cloud of spun sugar was half gone when Sophie appeared from nowhere. With a quick, 'Sorry I'm so late,' she knelt in front of Angeline and looked longingly at the candy floss. '*La barbe à papa! J'adore la barbe à papa!*'

'*La barbe à papa,*' repeated Angeline in a perfect French accent.

'You'll be speaking French in no time, Angeline. Bravo!' Sophie offered her upraised palm and the little girl high-fived like a pro footballer.

Penny's hopes soared ridiculously. 'Do you think it's okay sending her to a French school, Sophie?'

Sophie nodded. 'I think she'll do great.'

'Wouldn't it be wonderful if Sophie could come live with us and help us all learn to speak French?'

'But I already speak French, Mommy,' said Angeline. '*La barbe à papa* – that's French for cotton candy. Isn't it, Sophie?'

She looked adoringly at Sophie who nodded and said, 'And do you know why it's got such a funny name?'

Angeline shook her head, very serious.

'It means daddy's beard, cos it looks like a big fluffy beard. Don't you think?'

Seth grabbed a chunk of the spun sugar and stuck it to his chin. '*La barbe à papa*,' he said, pointing to his face and sounding proud of himself.

Angeline immediately copied her father and stuck some candy to her own face and then, before Penny could stop her, to her little brother's. The children roared with laughter, as if this was the funniest thing they'd ever seen. Although she normally insisted that food wasn't for playing with, Penny joined in and gave herself a cotton candy beard.

'You too, Sophie,' shrieked Angeline, jumping up and down.

When they all had their beards in place, Seth asked a passing tourist if he'd take a photo of the five of them.

'Now we'll never forget our first day in Paris,' said Penny. 'Are you planning to stick around here for a while, Sophie?'

'Pen,' said Seth, 'sorry to interrupt, but the kids seem to have forgotten about the carousel. Why don't we go find someplace where we can have a coffee and you can talk with Sophie about her plans?'

'Shouldn't be too difficult to find a café in the country that, like, invented the word,' said Sophie.

'Café,' repeated Angeline, as if she were under a spell.

A café near the Eiffel Tower was harder to find than they'd thought and they settled for some little tables beside a street vendor's coffee stall. The children amused themselves by throwing crumbs to the tiny sparrows that clustered around their feet and the adults were free to chat.

'Do you have particular things you want to do in Paris, Sophie?'

'Yes, a whole list. Montmartre and Sacré-Coeur, you know, the white basilica that sits sparkling on the top of the hill?'

'Isn't that where the artists all gather in a little square and paint portraits?'

'La Place du Tertre? That's the one.'

'Then there's The Arc de Triomphe and the Louvre and Notre Dame. Oh, Seth, I'd love to see all those iconic sights. I wish we could stay on a few days.'

'When are you thinking of leaving?' asked Sophie.

'The house will be available from Monday, so we'd like to be there by the afternoon. No point paying for a place in Paris when we've got a house sitting down there waiting for us,' said Seth.

'Always one eye on the dollar, my husband. Sorry, Sophie.'

'Seth's right. It makes sense. And listen, Paris will always be here. You can come back another time. Maybe just the two of you, for a romantic break, next time?'

'Ooh la la!' said Seth, laughing. 'Hey, you never know, Penny. If you play your cards right.'

'Who's playing cards?' said Angel. 'Can I play with Sophie?'

Penny shrugged. 'She doesn't miss much, this one.' She grabbed Angel and tickled her till the child squealed for mercy.

'You were saying about your dad being French. Is he living in France right now?' asked Seth.

'As far as I know. He left me and my mom when I was about the same age as Angeline.'

'Oh, I'm so sorry,' said Penny, feeling for the girl.

'That's okay. Mom remarried and I have a nice stepdad who's extremely good to me, and two half-brothers. We get on well enough. I can't complain.'

'Won't you miss them when you're over here?'

'I might, from time to time, but I've been away at school for a while now. I've kinda got used to being, like, independent.'

'That's good.'

'I guess I should be polite and ask about you folks.'

Penny and Seth looked at each other. Penny waited for him to speak, just as they'd agreed, prepared to tell only the absolute minimum. Giving away as little as possible.

'Sophie! Come see the birdies!' called Angeline, breaking the silence.

'I think it's time to go,' said Seth. 'If we don't move soon, the Eiffel Tower will be closing for the day and I really want to get up there and take in the view.'

'You're on your own there, bud,' said Penny. 'I've got a phobia about heights, Sophie. Okay inside a building, behind glass, at a push, but something open like that?' She pointed to the latticework in the distance. 'Not a chance.'

'Oh, that's a pity. I was hoping to go up. Maybe in the evening. It's open till late,' said Sophie.

'Oh, is it?' said Seth. 'Been doing some research?'

'I'm a walking Michelin guide.'

'This girl could come in handy in more ways than one, Pen. I think we got lucky.'

Chapter 5

P aris seemed like little more than a dream now. They'd decided to stay a few days, seeing all the major sights that were accessible with two small children. Having Sophie along had helped and by the time they were ready to say goodbye, it felt like they'd all known each other for years.

The children had cried to leave Sophie but going on the train ride cheered them up. They'd finally gone down for the night, although Angeline had stayed awake long after her brother. Her first sighting of the mediaeval citadel of Carcassonne and the excitement of exploring their new house had kept her buzzing till way past her normal bedtime. Penny stood in the room her children had insisted on sharing and watched them as they lay fast asleep. She wished she could slow time. Ethan was losing the cute, clumsy mannerisms of a toddler and Angeline was growing so fast her summer clothes already looked like last year's.

The day she and Seth brought Angeline home from the hospital was still a vivid memory. Penny had expected euphoria. Bringing home a perfect baby girl was a privilege she'd never been granted the first time she'd been pregnant, to Curtis. She'd expected to be so happy she'd forget the past and move on, serene as a Madonna. Instead the enormous shock of motherhood hit her like the dust cloud of 9/11. All encompassing, taking her breath away, leaving her lost and inadequate. Knowing that tiny creature would be her responsibility for the rest of her life had made Penny feel sick with fear. Thank God for Seth.

She tucked the covers under her son's chin and leaned over to kiss his forehead. Wary of waking Angeline, Penny dropped the lightest of kisses on her soft hair and patted her shoulder. A wave of love washed over Penny and her eyes filled. Time to get downstairs and join Seth, before she got overemotional.

He was sitting at the old wooden table in the centre of the kitchen. He raised his wine glass. 'Come and join me, sweetheart,' he said. 'You've had a long day.'

Penny took a sip. She was concerned about how much she had to do the following day, and wanted a clear head in the morning.

'Are you sure you'll manage on your own tomorrow?' asked Seth.

'I won't lie to you. I'm a bit concerned about how I'll cope with no French.'

'Where are you going? School, bank?'

'Doctor, dentist too, I hope. Don't know how straightforward it will be.'

'Ah, you'll be fine. Can you imagine a doctor that can't speak English? Or a teacher?'

Penny woke to the smell of aftershave and toothpaste. She opened her eyes and reached out to put her arms round Seth's neck.

'I've got to go now, honey,' whispered Seth. 'You have a good day.' He kissed her and slipped from her embrace. 'See you about seven or eight, okay?'

Penny stretched like a contented cat and contemplated the day ahead. Priority was getting Angeline enrolled in school in time for the start of term. Staying on in Paris had seemed a great idea at the time, and it was fun, but it had cost them the few days they'd set aside for seeing to the business of living in France.

The kids woke cheerful and bursting with energy, as usual. Penny could hear the enthusiasm in Angel's voice as she held on to the stroller and provided her little brother with a running commentary. 'Look, Ethan. Look at the fairy-tale castle, up there on the hill. A princess lives there, you know. In one of those big towers.'

At the school they were asked to wait. It was still the holidays and no one, it seemed, was available who could speak fluent English. Finally, after much confusion, Angeline was enrolled for the new term.

At the bank they were also asked to wait. There was some embarrassment when Penny thought they were about to be seen, at last. Instead, she found herself being ushered towards the door. Come back in two hours, she was told. Why, she asked, not understanding. Lunchtime, someone said with a shrug, as if that explained everything.

Fighting back tears of frustration, she pushed Ethan and dragged Angel back to the house. Too wound up to eat anything herself, she fed the children and put Ethan down for his nap. When they ventured out again, it was after three and Angel was in no mood to walk all the way back to the bank. Not even a sighting of some ducks on the river, or the old cobbled bridge that crossed it were enough to distract Angel from moaning. 'But why do we have to go to the bank? We've already been.'

When Seth finally breezed in the door it was closer to nine than eight.

'Hi, honey,' he said, dropping onto the sofa. 'I'm pooped. Any chance of a beer before dinner?'

'In the fridge.'

Seth sat up and looked at her. 'Bad day?'

'Mm, well, I guess that depends on how you define a bad day.'

'Kids okay?'

'They are.'

'Asleep?'

'Now, yes. Fifteen minutes ago, no.'

'Let me grab a shower. I'll be right back.'

Typical. Shower, cold beer and all would be well in Seth's world. Penny sat and waited, recalling a line from a Burns poem: 'Nursing her wrath to keep it warm.' A smell of burning drew her to the oven. Smoke billowed out when she opened the door. She slammed it shut, coughing and cursing.

'Hey,' said Seth, 'what's going on?'

'The fucking dinner's incinerated! I set the stupid oven to two twenty like I always do, and look at it.'

'Oh, honey, they don't use Fahrenheit here, that's American.'

'How the hell was I supposed to know? What should it be?'

'About a hundred, maybe?'

Penny opened the fridge and took out the remains of last night's wine. She emptied the bottle into a coffee mug and drank. Seth looked at her as if she was a stranger.

'Wow,' he said. 'That bad? Wanna tell me about it?'

By bedtime, Penny had cried herself out and left Seth in no doubt about how bad her day had been. He'd been surprised that she hadn't managed to open an account at the bank without his presence and amused that she failed to find the doctor's surgery and gave up on the dentist. By contrast, his day had been wonderful from start to finish, he said, and it was clear he couldn't wait to go back in the morning.

'I don't think I can cope, Seth,' she said, as they got into bed. 'It's crazy to think we can just slot in here when nobody speaks our language. I wish we'd never come.'

'It was your idea, honey, remember?'

'A stupid idea. I know that now.'

Seth switched out the light and wrapped his arms around her. 'Sleep, sweetheart. It will be better in the morning.'

But Penny had too much on her mind. 'Seth,' she whispered, eventually, rolling over to face him. 'I need to tell you something.'

Seth's gentle snoring told her this wasn't the time for confessions.

Chapter 6

'Hi, Sophie, it's Penny.'
    'Penny! How you doing?'
    'I'd love to say great, but I'd be lying.'
'Oh no, it's not the kids, is it?'
'Kids are fine, thanks.'
'Seth okay?'
'Seth's gonna love it here.'

And he might be mad when he knows I've made this call, thought Penny, but too bad. She wondered for a moment if she was making a mistake and rejected the notion. What harm could it do to ask the question?

'What about you? Found a job yet?' Penny's fingers seemed to have crossed themselves without her noticing.

'Not that easy.'

'Oh, I'm sorry to hear that,' said Penny, trying to keep the glee out of her voice. 'Well, here's one out of left field for you. How would you like to come work for us?'

'Seriously?'

'Think of it as a humanitarian act. You'll be saving my life.'

Sophie laughed. 'What's happened?'

Penny told her how awful the past two days had been and how worried she was about her lack of French. 'It's all very well when things are going fine, but what would I do in an emergency? Say one of the kids had an accident?'

'Don't go there.'

'I have to, Sophie. I couldn't even call an ambulance by myself. I've never felt so helpless and scared in my life.' That was a lie, but she could hardly tell Sophie about the time she sat with a killer, wearing a wire so the FBI could catch his every word.

'What do you have in mind?' said Sophie.

'I guess the first thing I should say is, we can't afford to pay you very much.'

'Okay.'

'But we will provide full board and lodgings and lots of erudite conversation.'

Sophie giggled. 'Mm, not sure you're selling this to me.'

'How about I throw in two cute kids?'

'Now you're talking.'

'Help me with the kids, deal with any issues that need a French speaker, teach me a few words so I can at least be civil and courteous, that's about it.'

'What if I were to take Ethan out in the afternoon so you can get on with that book you mentioned?'

'Oh my God, that would be unbelievable. Sophie, you're a star. When can you get here?'

'Day after tomorrow? Say, is Seth okay with this?'

'Leave Seth to me. I'll tell him tonight.'

'You want to have a think about it, wait and see what Seth says?'

'I've had two sleepless nights to think about nothing else, while his lordship snored at my side. Seth will be fine with it. He'll help me work out how much allowance we can give you. If you're good.'

'Good? I'll be the best goddamn au pair this side of the Atlantic. Trust me!'

Chapter 7

'Miss L? I'm in.'

'Already? How in the name of all that's holy did you manage that so quick?'

'Penny just called.'

'She called you?'

'She sure did. I start the day after tomorrow.'

'Well done, sugar.'

'That's not all. I've arranged to take Ethan out every afternoon to let Penny write. Looks like you'll be meeting your grandchildren even sooner than you'd hoped.'

Chapter 8

Seth was at the sink, washing dishes. Dinner had been a jolly affair, the children excited to see Sophie. Penny had finally got them settled.

'Missing the dishwasher, honey?' she asked, as she picked up a drying cloth.

Seth raised his hands out of the soapy water and in a high female voice from a detergent commercial said, 'Just look at the state of my poor hands. I wish I had some nourishing cream to soothe and protect.'

He'd always been able to make her laugh, even on her darkest days. He took the cloth out of her hand and steered her to a chair. 'Sit. Relax. Finish your wine.'

Penny allowed herself to be pushed down onto the woven straw seat and took a mouthful of rich, velvety wine.

'Don't these chairs cost a fortune back in the States?' said Sophie.

'Boho chairs sell for four hundred dollars apiece at Joss and Main.'

'We should go round the house totting up.'

'Ship the contents stateside and sell the lot.'

Seth let the dishwater drain away. The ancient plumbing made a rude noise as it swallowed their waste and the three of them laughed.

'My mom would love this house. It has so much character,' said Sophie.

'It sure does, especially compared to our place back home.'

'Where are you from?' said Sophie.

'Texas. Small town near Houston.'

'But y'all don't have Texan accents,' said Sophie, drawing up a chair.

'Hell, yeah, we do!' said Seth with a swipe at his thigh worthy of a stage musical star. Penny almost expected him to burst into song.

'Hell, no, you don't. I'm good at accents.' Sophie considered for a moment. 'At a guess, I'd say, New York.'

Neither Penny nor Seth spoke.

'Am I right?'

Seth, his voice serious now, said, 'We're from Texas, Sophie, like Penelope said. I work in the aviation and aerospace industry and that's how I got the job in Toulouse for six months.'

Penny didn't like Seth's tone. This wasn't the first time someone had asked about his New York accent and it wouldn't be the last. She tried to make her own voice sound particularly warm to make up for him. And particularly Scottish. 'If you're good at accents you can probably tell where I'm from originally.'

'Ah, I thought I heard a trace of something non-American. Now, let me think, what is it?'

'Guess.'

'It's either Scottish or Irish.'

'That's cheating. Come on, Sophie.'

'Irish.'

'Wrong.'

'Okay, Scottish.'

'Too late!'

Seth said, 'We chose Carcassonne because we didn't want the kids to have to live in Toulouse, it's too big. I'll be commuting and staying over sometimes. That's one of the reasons it will be nice having you around, Sophie. To keep Penny and the kids company.'

'Thanks. I'm going to love it here. How cool is that citadel? Fifty-three towers. No wonder Angeline thinks a princess lives there. I could almost believe it myself.'

Seth topped up his wine glass and offered the bottle to Sophie.

'No, thanks, I'm good.'

Penny, putting her hand over the top of her own glass, was pleased to hear the girl say she'd had enough to drink. The wine was delectable but Penny wanted a good night's sleep and too much alcohol made her anxious, filling her nights with scary dreams of falling. 'I won't have any more either, thanks. In case one of the kids wakes in the night.'

'How's the jet lag?' asked Sophie.

'The children seem to have got over it much faster than us.'

'Do you think their little body clocks are easier to reset?'

'Could be,' said Seth, stifling a yawn. 'Speaking of, I don't know about you ladies, but I'm whacked. Think I'll turn in.'

'I'll be up in a minute, honey.'

Penny waited until she heard Seth go into the little WC at the top of the stairs. There was a separate bathroom and it was obvious both were late additions to this ancient stone house. 'I think I'm going to love living here,' she said. 'This house must have seen so much history.'

'I know what you mean,' said Sophie. 'Don't you just, like, sit here and imagine all the women who must have worked in this kitchen over the centuries? You can almost feel them in the room.'

Penny made a face. 'I think you may have overdone the red wine, girlfriend.'

'No, I've just got a bit of an overactive imagination at times, sorry.'

'Maybe you're the one who should be writing a book.'

A rumble of distant water rushing through metal pipes was followed by some ominous thunks before the system quietened again. Penny heard the bedroom door open and close.

'Sophie,' she said in a quiet, serious voice, 'there's something you should know about us.'

Penny paused, choosing her next words carefully. 'Sophie,' she said again and coughed to clear her throat. It was important she get this right. Say too little and she'd make the girl curious, say too much and she'd risk compromising their whole situation. 'You're right about the accents, although I think Seth sounds quite Texan some days, especially if he's spent long hours at work.'

'It's okay,' said Sophie. 'I didn't mean to pry. I was just, like, making conversation.'

So she *had* picked up on Seth's tone. She was astute, this girl. 'You weren't prying. I know that. The thing is, well, we left New York for a reason. Something we'd rather not talk about, if you don't mind. It's kind of upsetting for both of us.'

Sophie blushed. Penny cursed inwardly. She'd overdone it. Better to have said nothing.

'I'm sorry. I won't be nosy again. Mom always used to tell me that curiosity killed the cat. I never understood what she meant, but I knew it was a warning to mind my own business.'

Penny regretted starting the conversation, but she smiled. 'No harm done. You're a lovely girl and we're lucky to have you.' Time to change the subject. 'Do you think your room's okay? It's a little on the snug side.'

'Compared to my room at college, it's vast. And I love those wooden beams in the ceiling and the tiny little windows at floor level. It's so, like, quaint.'

'I'm glad we got this instead of a modern apartment in the newer part of town, or a place way out in the sticks. Pity we don't have a garden, but hey, you can't have everything.'

'I'll be happy to find a park and take the kids there to play. And we do have the roof terrace.'

'I'm not keen on heights.'

'You'll be okay up there, surely? I can see you, sitting out there in the morning, at that little wrought-iron table.'

'Lingering over a croissant and a cup of coffee? Flicking idly through a glossy magazine? Yeah, right. Have you met my children?'

'But now you have an au pair. Where's your nearest *boulangerie*, by the way?

'*Boulangerie*? That's a nice word.'

'You know, baker's shop?'

'*Boulangerie*? I've no idea.'

'What? You've been here four or five days and you've not found the baker's?'

'I've not found anything. And I'm in no position to ask a neighbour or a friendly passer-by, am I? I'm terrified if anyone speaks to me half the time. It's been horrible.'

'We'll soon fix that. And first thing in the morning, I'll shoot out and fetch some freshly baked croissants, all flaky, golden and buttery.'

'My mouth's watering.'

'Cool. When should I get up?'

'Why don't you have a lie in? I'll get up when I hear the kids. Sharing a room is such a novelty, I imagine one will wake the other.'

'Does little Ethan sleep through?'

'Oh, yes, thank God. He's like his daddy. Once he's asleep you could set off a bomb under the bed and he wouldn't wake. He's been like that since he was weeks old.'

'Lucky you. What's your secret?'

'I have none. Angel was so awful at nights we considered changing her name to Devilla. That child just would not sleep. Why do you think there's a four-year age gap?'

Sophie laughed loudly then stopped abruptly. 'I'd better be quiet. Wouldn't want to wake her.'

'Not unless you want to be reading fairy tales at four in the morning.'

Chapter 9

Sophie had set the alarm on her phone, wanting to make a good impression on her first day as an au pair. But she'd been sleeping so lightly she was able to silence the alarm on its first chime. She hadn't slept well. Still feeling the effects of her transatlantic journey, perhaps, or just nervous at the reality of the job she'd taken on. After all, she had no experience of working with kids, despite her glowing references. There would be a big difference between amusing Ethan and Angel for a few minutes at a time and being responsible for their welfare for hours. She hoped she hadn't overestimated her own abilities.

Maybe the strange bed was to blame for her restlessness. Take the pillow for example, a long, thin sausage of a thing. Quite unlike any pillow she'd ever slept on before. She assumed it was traditional. It was certainly uncomfortable. She might have to invest in a proper flat pillow. She gave the offending object a few punches and lay back looking at the aged wooden ceiling above her head. She wondered idly what scenes it had witnessed over the years. Lovemaking, certainly. Childbirth, probably, and more than likely, a few deaths. Sophie shivered a little at the thought. The room was still quite dark, its tiny window shuttered for the night.

Sophie was speculating on the ghosts that might haunt her bedroom when the door gave a bloodcurdling creak. Sophie shot up in bed and watched as the door crept slowly open. Like a scene from a horror movie, it edged, inch by inch, from its threshold. Sophie hardly dared breathe.

'Mommy?'

'Angeline! Phew, what a fright you gave me.'

'I'm looking for Mommy.' For some reason the child was whispering and Sophie found herself doing the same.

'I think Mommy's asleep. I'm wide awake though. You wanna come on an adventure with me?'

'Mm. I don't know. Maybe I should ask Mommy.'

'I'm sure Mommy won't mind. Do you think you could find some clothes to put on?'

The child nodded. 'Mommy always puts out my clean clothes for the next day before I go to sleep.'

'That's clever. She's a very good mom, your mommy, isn't she?'

Angel nodded. 'Should I go put them on?'

'Yeah, why not?'

'What if I wake Ethan? He'll be grumpy and he'll want to go on our adventure too.'

'Tell you what,' Sophie whispered like a conspirator. 'Why don't you sneak back through and fetch your clothes. You can dress in here and I can help you, if you like.'

Angel shook her head. 'I'm a big girl. I don't need help.'

Sophie nodded. 'That's excellent. Scoot through, then, and I'll see you downstairs, okay?'

'Okay,' whispered Angeline. She tiptoed towards the door and grimaced theatrically as it creaked again.

Sophie was putting on her Converse when the child appeared, fully dressed and hair brushed. She was a good kid. That was going to make Sophie's life so much simpler.

Sophie picked up her backpack and held out her hand to the child. 'Shall we go explore, Angel?'

'Can we go to the castle, please?'

'Maybe not right now.'

As they walked through the narrow streets of the old town, stopping every so often to let Angeline stare up in wonder at the ramparts and the towers, Sophie began to wonder if they had gone in the wrong direction. So far there was no sign of a bakery. Also they seemed to be heading up towards the castle, which had not been her intention.

Chapter 10

Penny woke to silence. Gradually she recognised the bedroom with its shapes of antique furniture and beamed ceiling. The room was still in semi-darkness, making it difficult to guess the time. One sliver of light, sharp as a stiletto, pierced the old wooden shutter. It was morning. And it was sunny. Life always seemed so much easier with the sun shining.

Beside her Seth snored gently, his back turned to her. They had never been the sort of couple who slept glued to each other all night and Penny was still grateful for that. When she was married to Curtis, he always insisted on lying like two spoons in a drawer. That may have been okay at the start, although Penny preferred her own space, but towards the end she had found it unbearable. His touch made her skin crawl and to lie there trapped in his arms all night made for poor sleep. Penny often thought it was his way of controlling her every move, even while she was asleep.

She shook off thoughts of Curtis. He had no place in this house. She'd come here to escape negative thoughts.

She made a conscious effort to think of something else, something good and positive, just like Dr Johannsen had taught her. Her thoughts immediately went to the children. She'd learned a lot about her kids on this trip. They were resilient, taking each big change in their stride. Unless they were hungry or tired, they'd been good-humoured and excited by the whole experience. Taking them to New York was a risk, but she'd been keen to go see the memorial. Dr Johannsen had thought it might do her good, help her to move on. He was right. Seeing her name among the victims of 9/11 had been weird, no other word for it, but it had also been healing. Could there be a more emphatic example of closure than seeing your own name on a memorial?

The long, delayed flight from one major city to another hadn't fazed the kids at all. Sure, Ethan had been a bit grizzly for a while, but what toddler wouldn't get bored sitting around an airport? That delay was the low point of the trip, when Penny had found herself wishing they could just go home and forget the whole crazy idea. Then Sophie had appeared with her magic tricks. And things had gone smoothly ever since.

Penny threw her arms over her head and stretched. She felt filled with optimism, for the first time in months. Seth turned, slid one long bare leg over hers and raised his arm till his fingers met hers. Barely touching her skin, he ran the tip of one finger slowly along the length of her arm. He paused at her armpit, tantalising her for a moment, then traced a line down the side of her breast. When she sighed, he slid his hand inside her vest top and touched her gently, just the way she liked it. Seth knew how brutal Curtis had been and was the opposite. Their lovemaking wasn't always slow and sensual, but one of the things she'd grown to love about this man was the way he could read her moods and respond to her needs. He hardly ever got it wrong and this morning was no exception.

When Penny came back from her shower she expected to find both kids climbing all over her husband but he'd gone back to sleep. Maybe they were all still a bit jet-lagged. She wasn't surprised by Ethan, but for Angel to sleep this long was unheard of.

Wondering whether she ought to wake both kids so they'd get back into a regular sleep pattern, Penny took her time getting dressed, enjoying having her own space again. All four of them in one hotel room had been a bit of a challenge, but at New York and Paris prices, they'd had to economise. Living out of suitcases had also been challenging so Penny was glad to have the chance at last to smooth out her clothes and hang them up. The wardrobe was a sarcophagus of a thing with a heavy wooden door that swung open with a squeak when she turned the key. Penny inhaled a mixture of old wood, lavender and something vaguely unpleasant and chemical, maybe mothballs. A bunch of metal coat hangers clanked in discord, as if they were annoyed at being disturbed. Penny grabbed a handful and hung up the few items she'd brought that needed hanging. Most of their luggage space had been for the kids' stuff, so she and Seth were travelling light.

Penny placed underwear, socks and T-shirts in the drawers of a tall armoire that sat below the window, then opened the shutters and pushed them back. The citadel, bathed in sunlight, dominated the skyline. Its stone turrets, some tiled in red, some grey, rose high above the ramparts. Penny felt as excited as Angel. Who was still sleeping, it seemed.

Penny lifted Seth's watch from his bedside table and checked the time. It was gone ten. No way. Even given the seven-hour time difference between France and Texas, those kids should not be asleep. It didn't make any sense. And besides, it was days since they'd left the States. They'd had time to acclimatise.

Penny stepped across the landing and opened the door to the room the kids were sharing. All was quiet and dark. In a sing-song voice, she said, 'Time to wake up, sleepyheads,' and threw open the shutters.

Ethan stirred, groaning, sounding like his father when he was wakened too early. Penny rumpled his hair and bent to kiss him. 'Morning, my precious. You're a sleepy boy this morning.'

'Mommy,' said Ethan, with a smile that made her heart soar every single time. He reached up for a hug. She lifted him into her arms, surprised as always at how heavy he felt.

She nuzzled his neck, enjoying the morning smell of him and whispered, 'Come on, let's wake that old lazy bones Angel.'

Penny turned to her daughter's bed, expecting an indignant response, but Angel wasn't there. Had she gone downstairs by herself?

Penny made for the landing and called, 'Angel, where are you?'

At the foot of the wooden stairs the house was still dark and shuttered. Penny switched on the light but the kitchen and living room looked just as they'd been left the night before.

Panicking in case her six-year-old had stepped out into the street, Penny flew to the door. It was unlocked.

She put Ethan down, told him Mommy would be right back, then took the stairs two at a time, her bare feet slipping on the uncarpeted wood.

Seth woke as she raced into the bedroom, shouting his name. He darted out of bed and grabbed her. 'What's wrong?'

'She's gone, Seth. Angel's gone.'

Chapter 11

Sophie was trying to stay cheerful. She didn't want to frighten the child. But there was no doubt about it, they were lost. The citadel was bigger than it looked from below the ramparts and was made up of more streets than Sophie had imagined. It was a rabbit warren and no matter how many times they walked around, Sophie found it impossible to identify the street that led back to their house. Somehow, she'd expected one way in and one way out, but that wasn't the case.

They'd followed a long, cobbled street and eventually found an exit – or an entrance, whatever – with a proper drawbridge, the kind of thing that she would normally have found exciting. This morning it seemed more threatening and sinister, as it was probably intended to all those centuries ago. They came out onto an open area with a clear, beautiful view across the plain towards the distant mountains. Which confirmed what Sophie suspected: they were well and truly lost.

Angeline's little legs were getting tired and she'd begun complaining that she was hungry and wanted her breakfast. Sophie had promised her a delicious flaky pastry and the child had cooperated for a while, practising the new words and rehearsing her request to the baker: '*Un pain au chocolat, s'il vous plaît.*' The fun of that had soon worn off when there was no bakery to be found, and Angel had started to whine, saying the bumps in the road were hurting her feet. Sophie explained about cobbles, but she could tell Angeline was too fed up to listen.

'Tell you what, Angel, why don't you sit here for a moment?' Sophie led Angeline to a wooden bench by a low wall, safe from the road. 'I'm going just over there to ask that nice lady a question.' She pointed to a uniformed woman who seemed to be controlling traffic.

'Excuse me, ma'am,' said Sophie, 'Can you direct me to the other side of the citadel?'

A complicated instruction in rapid, accented French made Sophie none the wiser. She'd have to break it to Angel that they had to go back the way they came. Except that Angel was nowhere to be seen. Some scruffy kids were running around amongst the chestnut trees that shaded the benches, but there was no sign of Angeline. Sophie felt a surge of nausea.

She spun round, eyes scanning the broad esplanade. Two large tour buses were disgorging their passengers and the space that had been wide open and empty began to look busy and crowded. Beyond those, another two coaches were waiting in line, ready to drop even more tourists. Sophie had to find Angel fast, before it became impossible to spot her.

'Angeline!'

The coach passengers were staring. Sophie didn't care. She shouted again, her voice louder and shriller this time. She told herself not to panic. Angel was bound to be here somewhere. Where else would she be?

The answers to that question flooded into her imagination and the sick feeling in her stomach got so bad she thought she might throw up. Jesus, she had to find this kid. The alternative didn't bear thinking about.

She started to grab at passers-by. All of them looked curious, some sympathetic, a few alarmed. 'Have you seen a little girl, six years old?' she asked, time after time. No one answered her.

Sophie turned away. This was pointless. These people had just got off a coach. Of course they hadn't seen the child.

Sophie shouted again, 'Angel, where are you?' and looked helplessly around. 'Angel!'

An elderly man leaning on a walking stick gestured to her to approach him. Sophie ran over. He asked if she was looking for a little blonde girl.

Sophie nodded, scared to trust her voice.

The old man pointed to a white stone monument amongst the trees. '*Voilà*,' he said, with a toothless grin.

Sophie ran to the monument, praying, 'Please, please, please.' Behind the stone stood Angel, her eyes covered. She was quietly counting. 'Ninety-eight, ninety-nine, one hundred.' She opened her eyes and smiled. 'Sophie! Can you help me find the boys?'

Sophie grabbed her by the shoulders. 'What the fuck are you doing?'

Angeline looked shocked. And frightened. Sophie tried to hug her, saying, 'Sorry, sorry,' but the child pulled away and started to howl.

A little group of boys about the same age gathered around, watching with accusing eyes. Sophie shook her head and tried to take Angel's arm, but again the child squirmed away from her wailing, 'I want my mommy.'

'Come on, Angel. It's okay. Let's get you home.'

A small crowd had started to form. Where were all these interested citizens when she was desperately hunting for a lost kid?

A woman, toddler on a rein, knelt by Angel and said, 'Are you okay, *chérie*?'

Sophie explained she was the child's nanny and that Angel's family had just arrived in town. After a few questions the woman, and the spectators, seemed satisfied that the little drama was over and drifted away, leaving Sophie with the still sobbing child.

Sophie knelt as the woman had done and took Angel's hand. This time the little girl didn't draw away and allowed herself to be drawn into a hug.

'I'm so sorry for shouting at you. That was naughty of me, but you see, I thought I'd lost you. Didn't you hear me calling your name?'

The child nodded.

'Then why didn't you come?'

'Because I had to count to one hundred. We were playing hide and go seek and Daddy says you have to count to a hundred without stopping or that's called cheating.'

Sophie could see the kid's logic. 'But Angel, I couldn't see you. You were hiding behind this big stone and I thought …' Sophie decided against telling this little child what she'd thought might have happened to her. 'I thought you'd gone back to the house without me and your mommy and daddy would be cross.'

'Because we didn't get the croissants?'

Sophie smiled. 'No, honey, not because of the croissants. Because they'd think I wasn't taking good care of you.'

Angel nodded, as if she understood what Sophie was saying. She was about to tell the child off for straying when she reminded herself that she was the one at fault, leaving a small child unattended in a public place.

'Let's go find something cool to drink, and then we'll see if we can finally get those croissants, shall we?'

She held out her hand and said a silent prayer of thanks when Angel took it and walked alongside her. The ragtag bunch of boys followed for a bit, then got fed up and wandered off to start a new game.

Sophie blew out a long sigh of relief. Thank God that was over. Nevertheless, the experience, horrendous though it was, had taught her a few things.

And given her some ideas that might please Miss L.

Chapter 12

'Gone? What do you mean, gone?'

'She's gone, Seth. Not in her bed and not downstairs.'

'Isn't she with Sophie?'

Penny let out the longest breath of her life and buried her face in her hands. 'Oh God, I'm so stupid!'

Seth laughed. 'Don't tell me you forgot about Sophie?'

Penny felt her face glow. 'Sorry. I'm an idiot! A neurotic, panicky idiot.' She smacked her forehead with the flat of her hand. 'What a fool!'

Seth flopped back onto the bed. 'So? Panic over?'

'Yip,' said Penny, her lips making a loud smack on the p. Saying no more she turned and left.

On the landing, she listened outside Sophie's door, expecting to hear Angel's excited chatter or Sophie reading a story. Nothing. She knocked on the door. Knocked again, louder this time. Feeling like an intruder, she murmured an apology as she opened the door. The room was filled with sunshine and the bed was empty. Sophie's suitcase lay open on the floor, a few clothes scattered around it.

Of course. She'd gone to fetch croissants for breakfast and taken Angel with her. Probably to stop her waking everyone at dawn. How thoughtful of the girl to let everyone else sleep on.

'They've gone to the bakery, Seth. Can you get up and make the coffee, please? I'll see to Ethan.'

At the foot of the stairs her little boy was running a toy car back and forth over the stone flags of the kitchen floor. 'Hungry, Mommy,' he said.

'Potty first, and then how about a drink of milk? We'll get your clothes on and we'll all have breakfast when Angel gets back. Good boy.'

'Angel, Mommy?'

'She's gone with Sophie to buy some yummies for breakfast.'

'Sophie.'

'Ethan likes Sophie, don't you?'

Ethan nodded his head, smiling. 'I like Sophie too,' said Penny, hugging him tightly, 'and I love Ethan.'

'Daddy?'

'Daddy's still in bed. He's being a lazybones. Shall we go and bounce on his tummy till he gets up?'

Seth allowed his son to bounce and giggle till he got bored and then Penny bathed and dressed him while his daddy showered.

Together they set the table, opening cupboards and drawers until they found plates and cutlery. In a big dresser by the window, Penny found stacks of table covers and napkins. She selected a red-checked set that looked typically French and laid the table. From the fridge they took the orange juice, milk and butter they'd bought the night before and added a jar of local jam that had been left in the cupboard with a handwritten sticker that said 'Please use'. When he could wait no longer they sat Ethan at the table, perched on a cushion, and helped him eat some cereal. Seth worked out how to use the coffee machine and they got it going. It gurgled away to itself, making Ethan laugh and filling the kitchen with the most delicious aroma of fresh coffee.

'Where on earth have they got to?' asked Penny.

'Third time you've said that. Did you realise?'

'Sorry, no. But I don't understand where on earth they can have got to.'

'Four!' said Seth, holding up four fingers.

'Sorry. I'm starting to get worried. I can't help it.'

'You? Worried? Never!'

She knew he was trying to cheer her up and she smiled, just to please him, but inside she could feel the old familiar anxiety creeping up on her.

The coffee machine went quiet and Seth said, 'I can't resist any longer. Let's take a cup of coffee up to the terrace while we wait for them to bring the croissants. Isn't that where you fancied sitting this morning?'

'Yes, but then I thought it would be nicer for the five of us to have breakfast together down here.'

Seth lifted Ethan down from the table and said, 'Come on, little fella. Let's go see if we can spot your sister coming. Will you bring the coffee, Pen?'

Penny tried to still the fear that was growing inside her. She tried to apply the lessons she'd learned in therapy. Think of something nice. Do something to distract herself.

She took Seth his coffee. 'How about that for a view?' he said, pointing towards the citadel. 'We couldn't afford to rent a place like this so close to the mediaeval city with views to die for. Aren't you glad we were able to arrange a house swap?'

Penny nodded. 'I just hope they're looking after our house. Oh Seth, what if this turns out to be a huge mistake?'

Seth touched her cheek. 'Cheer up, kid. Sophie and Angel will be back soon.'

'Oh, Seth, what if they won't?' She wondered if she ought to tell him how scared she'd been for weeks on end.

'Hey, remember Dr Johannsen banned those words – what if. A recipe for worry.'

'I'm sorry. It's just that I got such a bad feeling when I couldn't find Angel this morning and it's getting worse by the minute. What do we know about Sophie, really? We only met her a few days ago, in an airport lounge, for God's sake. She could be a maniac, and I let her just walk off with my child. In a strange town. In a foreign country.' Penny could hear hysteria creeping into her voice and tried to keep herself under control.

'Penelope, listen to me,' said Seth. 'Look at me.'

She obeyed. She knew that tone.

'Sophie came with a bunch of glowing references.'

'Which we didn't phone to check. We ought to have phoned, checked her out.'

'Why would Sophie take our daughter? Ask yourself, logically.'

'To sell to child traffickers? Hell, I don't know. It's just that, Seth, I don't think I could bear it if anything was to happen to one of the kids.'

Seth put Ethan down and said, 'Sorry, L'il Buddy. Mommy needs a hug.'

While he hugged her tight, Seth asked, 'Have you called Sophie?'

'No.'

'Then why don't we do that? Right now?' He fished in the back pocket of his jeans, took out his phone and dialled. Directly under their feet, in the room that should have been Angel's but was now Sophie's, a jolly ringtone jangled. Seth hung up.

'Okay. Next suggestion?'

'Well, I think the fact that she's left her phone is a good sign. She wouldn't leave that behind if she was planning to disappear, now would she?'

'No.'

'Did you have a nosey in her room to check if she's taken anything?'

'No.'

'Why don't you go and do that?'

'What, rummage through her personal stuff? That's not very nice, is it?'

'Neither is accusing her of being a child trafficker, Pen.'

Penny felt bad, but the nagging worm of worry was still squirming around deep in her belly, despite Seth's reassurances.

Reminding herself that she was supposed to have given up being afraid, Penny began tentatively picking through Sophie's suitcase. She had no idea what she was hoping to find.

Chapter 13

On the way home, Sophie found a bakery that sold the most mouth-watering pastries. She and Angel scoffed one each as they walked. When they got back the child was no longer grumpy and complaining about her legs. She just seemed genuinely glad to see her parents and keen to tell them all about the castle on the hill.

Penny came downstairs looking flustered and red in the face. She looked hard at Sophie. 'You guys were gone an awful long time.' She picked Angel up and gave her a hug. 'Well, did you see any princesses?'

'No, Mommy, but I played hide and go seek.'

'Was it fun?' asked Penny.

Angel looked at Sophie. She smiled. Nodded. And held her breath.

'Yes,' said Angel. 'And we saw the drawbridge and everything.'

'Wow,' said Seth. 'I'm not sure I know what a drawbridge is.'

'It's, like, a big heavy bridge that lifts up and keeps the baddies out of the castle.'

Seth looked at his wife and a funny looked passed between them. 'See, Penny. Angel was learning from Sophie all the time they were gone.'

Sophie felt she ought to say something. 'Sorry, we walked further than we meant to. We wanted to surprise you with croissants.'

'Daddy, I know how to, like, ask for a chocolate pastry all by myself.'

'Shh!' said Sophie. 'Secret. Remember?'

Angel looked confused for a moment and then giggled.

'Sorry, Mommy,' said Sophie. 'I bought Angel a pastry. She was getting a bit peckish.'

'You had one too, Sophie, and don't forget I asked for it all by myself.'

'Yes, you did. Angel. In the most beautiful French.'

'In that case,' said Seth, 'I reckon she deserved a pastry.' He pulled out a chair and offered it, like a waiter, to his daughter. 'Does Princess Angel still have room for some OJ and cereal?'

And so Angeline getting lost seemed to be forgotten.

Still, days passed before Sophie could even begin to relax. She lived in constant fear, wondering every morning if Angel had told her mom the night before. Maybe in those precious moments after the goodnight kiss, when most kids would do anything to hang on to their mother just a little bit longer.

Eventually, when there were no questions or accusations from Seth or Penny, Sophie began to believe that Angel had forgotten the whole thing, or at least the getting lost part.

If Sophie had loved the kid before, she loved her even more now. She was fond of the little boy too, for Ethan was a sweet-natured and easy-going child, but it was Angel who had stolen Sophie's heart.

Soon it was time to give Miss L her second weekly update.

'Hello, Miss L. How are you?'

'I'm good, bless your sweet heart for asking. Are things progressing well at your end? Got that family of mine trusting you one hundred per cent?'

Sophie hadn't mentioned her first day disaster to Miss L. Couldn't think why she should. 'Seems like it. They had a look at the references you gave me, but when I said they could call any of the numbers to check, they just laughed.'

'I was expecting a call. That's very trusting of them.'

'Oh, I almost forgot to tell you. Angel goes to school now and she's settled in already.'

'A regular French school?'

'Yes. She's real bright.'

'Oh my, that's a big step for such a little girl.'

'If Angel's going to get the best out of her time here, it makes sense. She could be pretty much bilingual by the time they head back to the States.'

'She sounds like a great kid. I can't wait to get to know her.'

'Not long now.'

Chapter 14

Sophie had gone out for a walk and the kids were asleep. Penny was free to indulge herself in a second glass of wine.

She reached for Seth's glass. 'Top up?'

'Better not. I've had two already. But you go ahead, please.'

'Don't mind if I do,' said Penny, already halfway down the stairs to the kitchen. That would be her only criticism of this house, the fact that their outside space was two floors up, at roof level. It meant that she hadn't breakfasted al fresco as often as she'd imagined because of the hassle of carrying everything upstairs and down again on trays. And somehow, something always seemed to get forgotten, little things like teaspoons. And a second pot of coffee was out of the question.

Tonight though, it was worth the trek. Penny liked her wine chilled. Just like her men, she always joked, although that was a lie. Curtis may have seemed the very essence of cool when she first met him, but there was nothing chilled about him by the time she'd finally managed to escape. Her memory flashed back to him lying on that kitchen floor, dead or alive, she didn't know at the time. Worse than that, she didn't care at the time, although it became a big deal later. Penny flicked a little switch in her brain, a trick she'd learned, like changing channels when you see something upsetting on TV.

She looked around this quaint room, so different from their modern, bright house in Texas, and felt at home. There were kids' toys lying about and a line of shoes by the front door, from Ethan's tiny boots to Seth's giant trainers. Just like back home.

Full glass in hand, she took the stairs carefully. As she stepped out onto the tiny terrace, she gasped at the view. It got her every time.

'Isn't it amazing?' said Seth, pointing up to the towers. The sky was darkening and the mediaeval walls looked gilded in the floodlights. 'I'd never get tired of that view. Ever.'

'Me neither,' said Penny, tucking herself under her husband's shoulder. He hugged her to him, spilling a little wine.

'Hey, watch it, buddy,' she scolded. 'It's a long walk for a refill!'

'I wondered why your glass was so full. You developing a little problem?' He tickled her. 'Something you wanna talk about?'

Guarding her wine, she squirmed out of his arms and sat down. 'As if.'

'I guess Curtis did us both a favour, putting us off too much alcohol.'

'That's funny. I was just thinking about him –' she tapped the side of her head '– before I switched channels.'

Seth never asked why she would be thinking of her ex. They didn't avoid the subject of Curtis, or anything else from the past that haunted her, but they didn't often revisit those times. They tried to keep their focus firmly on the future, just like they'd been advised.

'Are you happy here, Seth?'

Seth turned away from the view and looked at her. 'What makes you ask?'

'Well, it's just that I am, but I know you were never a hundred per cent convinced this was a great idea.'

'Hey, what can I say? I was wrong.'

'Really?'

He came and sat beside her, moving the little wrought-iron chair, whether to be closer to her or to maximise his view of the castle, she wasn't sure.

'What's not to like?' he said. 'The view, the house, the wine.'

'That's not what I mean.'

'I know what you mean, Pen. And I'm glad you're happy.'

He leaned in close and kissed her, very gently. She loved the way Seth would kiss her for no other reason than he wanted to. The only time Curtis had kissed her was if his mind was on sex. There was no such thing as an affectionate, no strings kiss or a friendly reassuring hug. Every physical contact had an ulterior motive and a predictable outcome. When she'd been pregnant, he'd never laid a finger on her, although she had craved the reassurance of a loving touch. The pregnancy had cost her all contact with her parents, for God's sake, and yet he kept his distance from her when she needed him most. And then she'd lost the baby, too.

Why so much thinking about Curtis tonight? Damn him. She made herself concentrate on Seth's kind face; the failing light made it hard to see his eyes, but she knew how blue they were, and how guileless. She touched his cheek. His skin was soft and clean, his beard a soft rasp against her palm. Everything about this man was gentle and easy to love.

'I *am* happy, and I can't quite work out why. The house just seems to have opened its arms to us, somehow. I feel safe here. Does that sound crazy?'

Seth shook his head and his fair hair flopped into his eyes. He swept it back and put his hand on her shoulder. She considered telling him about the guy who'd been watching her.

'And running into Sophie like that,' said Seth. 'As if it was meant to happen.'

The moment had passed. And she didn't want to spoil the mood. 'She's so good with the kids.'

Seth nodded. 'Yeah, she's terrific. Angel idolises her.'

'Doesn't she? Have you noticed how she's taken to sticking the word "like" into every sentence?'

'I had noticed. She probably thinks it makes her sound, like, cool.'

'It makes her sound, like, precocious. I'm going to have a word with them both about it.'

'Still, credit where it's due. Sophie's taught her an incredible amount of French in a short time.'

'Have you forgiven me for taking her on without asking you first?'

'Yeah, if it gives you time to write, and helps with the language, that's great.'

'I was kind of wondering, if it all works out with Sophie, I mean, I was thinking I might, well, maybe, stay the night in Toulouse some time?'

'You mean it? You ready to leave the kids?'

Penny thought what it would be like to spend a night away from her children. Scary, no doubt about it. But the thought of a night on their own, in a hotel room, was exciting. No interruptions for 'bad dream' or 'can't sleep'.

'I think so. Almost. They'd be fine with Sophie, don't you think?'

'Of course they'll be fine.'

'Seth, by fine, I mean safe.'

'Why wouldn't they be safe, Penny?'

'You know.'

He hugged her. 'I know, but we asked all those questions before we applied for the transfer to France, didn't we?'

She nodded. 'I guess.'

'Pen, it's been ten years. Let it go. We're different people now. Try to stop looking back.'

Penny debated with herself again whether she should tell him how scared she still felt at times.

'Remember what we say? Mind in the present …'

'Eyes on the future,' she added, completing their mantra. They *had* asked all the questions. WITSEC had told them that they couldn't be *guaranteed* safety if they left the United States, but that, after ten years in the program, witnesses could travel abroad if they wished.

Seth said, 'Remember how many good folks have been kept safe by the Witness Security Program?'

'Thousands.'

'Yeah, over eighteen thousand.' Seth paused as if to let the number sink in. 'And not a single participant following the program's guidelines has ever been harmed.'

'There's always a first time.'

'Oh, come on, Penny. We've been over this. What's with the negative thinking? You've just told me how happy you are here.' He tapped the side of her head, just above her temple. 'What's going on inside that head of yours?'

'Well, we broke the rules, didn't we? Going back to New York City when we weren't supposed to?'

'For one night. Less than twenty-four hours.'

'Yeah, I know, but maybe we should have stayed away.'

Seth shook his head. 'You were the one who was adamant we should go. You said you'd get closure if you could see your old name on the 9/11 Memorial.'

She'd ruined the lovely mood of the evening with her stupid neuroses. Why couldn't she just keep her mouth shut? Seth deserved better than this.

Downstairs the front door opened and closed. 'Hi, anyone home?'

'There you go, Pen.' Seth tapped his watch. 'She said she'd be back before nine and it's three minutes to. I think you should come to Toulouse one night. We couldn't leave the kids in a safer pair of hands.'

Chapter 15

Sophie could hardly believe her good luck. The Gates family had welcomed her so warmly she almost felt as if she'd known them for ages. Days passed and all five of them fell into a routine. Seth went early to work, often before the kids woke. She and Penny had a coffee then got the children up and dressed. After breakfast, Sophie walked Angeline to school. Sometimes she took Ethan in his stroller and sometimes he stayed with his mom. After lunch, Ethan had a nap and when he woke, Sophie took him out until it was time to fetch Angel.

Twice she and Ethan had met up with Miss L in the afternoon.

The first time had been by the river. Ethan loved the ducks and would sit entranced while Sophie threw stale bread. The bolder ducks would come out of the water and waddle right up to them. When Miss L had arrived, Ethan was giggling with delight.

For a long moment she just stared at the child, her eyes filling with tears. 'He's so darling,' she whispered to Sophie. 'Such a beautiful child.'

'I can't believe you've never met,' said Sophie.

Miss L shook her head sadly. 'Nor can I. Better late than never. Should I speak to him, do you think?'

'Of course. The whole idea is for you to get to know each other, isn't it?'

Miss L had nodded, her face serious. 'I'm not quite sure what to say to a two-year-old, to be quite honest.'

'Why don't you just smile and say hello? We'll take it from there.'

'Em, hello, Ethan,' said Miss L, as if she were speaking to royalty.

'Relax. You're doing fine. Ethan, say hello to the nice lady.'

Ethan seemed engrossed in the ducks.

'Ethan?' Sophie shook his arm a little. 'Ethan?' she sang.

Ethan turned huge blue eyes first on Sophie and then on Miss L.

'Oh, my good lord,' she said, 'those eyes. Hello. Are you Ethan?'

The little boy nodded very solemnly.

Miss L smiled. 'My name is Mawmaw.'

The child smiled back.

'Can you say "Mawmaw", Ethan?'

'Mawmaw,' he said, and Miss L leaned on Sophie, as if to steady herself.

'I never thought I'd live to see this day. Thank you, my dear. Thank you so much.'

'Ethan, can you say "Hello, mawmaw"?'

'Hay-o, Mawmaw.'

'Oh, Sophie, he's just too adorable.'

'Isn't he? And he's such a sweet-natured child. Hardly ever cries or makes a fuss.'

Ethan had turned his attention back to the ducks.

'Why don't you give him some bread to throw?' said Sophie.

Miss L took the bag of crumbs and said, 'Would you like to give the nice ducks some bread, Ethan?'

'Ess, peese.'

'Oh, my goodness, you're so cute.' Miss L handed the bread to Ethan, one chunk at a time and Ethan, still too young to throw, dropped it by the stroller. Several ducks pounced at the same time, making him laugh.

'Even his little laugh is charming.'

'I think you're smitten,' Sophie said. Miss L hadn't disagreed.

On the second meeting they had fed the ducks then gone to the Place Carnot to buy ice cream. Ethan was too small to manage a cornet by himself, so Sophie had suggested Miss L help him.

'Are you sure, Sophie? I've never done anything like this before.'

'Trust me, there's nothing to it. Put a little ice cream on the spoon, hold it to his lips and Ethan will manage the rest.'

'Ethan, would you like some?'

'Ess, peese,' he said, his eyes lighting up.

When it was time to say goodbye, Miss L had been quite emotional. 'Sophie, I will never be able to thank you enough. Without your help, I'd never have met this precious child and my life would have been so much the poorer.'

'Oh, don't be silly,' Sophie had said, embarrassed. 'Ethan, we have to go and fetch Angeline now. Can you say bye-bye to Mawmaw, please.'

Ethan waved his hand and said in his cute, little-boy voice, 'Bye-bye, Mawmaw.'

Miss L had looked like she might melt, right there on the sidewalk.

It was all going really well. When Sophie got back to the house, Angeline in tow, Penny was in exuberant mood.

'Sophie, how can I thank you? With the house to myself, I'm easily writing a chapter a day.'

Sophie felt warm inside. Making other people happy could become addictive. 'At this rate you'll be ready to publish before we head back to the States,' she said.

'Well, you never know. It's looking good.'

Later, when Penny had put the kids to bed she said, 'Why don't you grab a glass of wine, Sophie, and come join us on the terrace?'

'Sure you don't mind?' Sophie usually tried to give them some space in the evening, once the kids were asleep.

'Why would we mind? We like your company,' said Seth. 'Reminds us of when *we* were young.'

Penny thumped him on the arm and Seth yelped.

'Thanks. Just let me dump my stuff.'

Sophie closed her bedroom door and leaned against it. At their meetings in the States, Miss L had been insistent she not get too close to the family. 'Do you hear me, Sophie? They're not your friends. You'll be there to do a job. Please do not forget who is paying you. And how generously.'

'I know.'

'There's far too much at stake for me to take any risk that you'll change your mind or do something silly.'

'I won't.'

'You'd better not. You know how much it means to me to see those grandchildren.'

Sophie needed the remuneration Miss L had promised her. Plus, she wanted to help reunite the children with their grandmother. So far, so good. Ethan seemed to like Miss L and it was clear she adored him. A few more visits and it would be time to take Angeline along to join the fun. Sophie had planned the trip already. On the Place Gambetta she'd found an old-fashioned carousel just like the one they'd seen in Paris. She knew Angeline would love to ride it with her newly found Mawmaw.

Sophie's only concern was that Miss L could be a bit too controlling. Why shouldn't an au pair enjoy a drink with her employers? It wasn't as if anyone was going to get hurt at the end of the day. If Seth and Penny ended up mad at her for bringing Miss L and her grandkids together without their knowledge, too bad. What was the worst that could happen? Sophie sprayed her wrists with a defiant spritz of perfume, brushed her hair and whispered to her reflection, 'What harm can a glass of wine do?'

After a bit of chit-chat about the kids and the funny things Angel had said or Ethan had done, Penny and Seth went quiet.

Sophie concentrated on her wine glass.

Seth reached out and took his wife's hand. 'We've got a favour to ask.'

'A big favour.'

'Anything,' said Sophie, shrugging. 'Whatever I can do to help you guys.'

'Well, there's nothing certain yet,' said Penny.

Seth gave his wife's hand a little tug. 'Come on, Pen. I thought you were up for it.'

Penny took a deep breath. 'Okay. Sophie. We were wondering how you'd feel about something.'

When Penny said no more, Sophie spread her hands wide and raised her eyebrows.

Seth burst out laughing. 'Oh, for pity's sake, Pen, spit it out!'

In a rush of words, as if she was scared she might lose her nerve, Penny blurted, 'We were thinking we might stay a night in Toulouse some time and we're wondering how you'd feel about having the kids overnight. On your own. By yourself. All night.'

'Stop, Penny, please,' said Sophie, holding up her hands in surrender. 'I get it.'

'And?'

'And I'm flattered to be asked. But the answer's no.'

Seth and Penny abandoned the high-five they were about to do and turned to look at her.

'Seriously, Soph?'

She nodded her head gravely.

Penny took a gulp of wine and tried to speak before she'd swallowed it. 'Sorry,' she spluttered, 'we shouldn't have asked. It's too much.'

Seth patted his wife on the back until he seemed sure she was okay then said, 'You don't have to, of course, Sophie, and obviously, we'd pay you for the extra hours and the added responsibility.'

Sophie shook her head. 'It's not that.'

'What is it, then?'

'Drop it please, Seth,' said Penny. 'It doesn't matter. I wasn't sure about it anyway.'

'No, Pen, I'm just curious to know why Sophie said no. You seem so confident with the kids, Soph, we didn't think you'd mind.'

'Are you guys for real?' Sophie waited just long enough to see the shock on their faces.

Then she smiled. 'Why would I want to spend one minute longer than I have to with those adorable little kids? Why would

I want to have them all to myself at bath time and bedtime, and first thing in the morning when they wake up? The best-behaved, smartest, sweetest kids on the face of the planet? It's a joy to look after them.'

Penny looked confused.

'Is that a yes?' asked Seth.

'I'd love to.'

Seth blew out long and loud. 'You had me going for a minute there, kid.'

'Me too,' said Penny, laughing now and rising for a hug.

'I'm sorry. That was mean, but you were, like, so serious. As if you were asking some enormous favour of me. I couldn't resist.'

'You're forgiven,' said Seth, 'but only if it's a definite yes.'

'Definitely, positively, absolutely, yes. When are you thinking of going?'

'In a couple weeks, maybe?'

'You think the kids will be okay? Have you ever left them overnight before?'

The look Penny gave her husband told Sophie the answer.

'Not once? They've never slept at Grandma's? I used to love going to stay with my grandma when I was Angeline's age.'

Penny shook her head.

'She's never been to a sleepover?'

Another unambiguous shake.

'What, never?'

'I'm not a big fan of sleepovers, to be honest. I mean, letting your little girl go and sleep in a stranger's house. I'm not sure that's such a good idea.'

'I get that, but Grandmas are different.'

'The children don't have any grandparents,' said Seth. He sounded weird. Sad, or something.

'Oh, I'm so sorry. My mom used to say, "Sophie, engage brain before putting mouth in gear." Sometimes I forget.'

'It's okay. No harm done.'

Sophie didn't know what to say.

Penny filled the silence. 'Tell you what. It's early days. Why don't we wait and see how things go over the next couple weeks?'

Seth said, 'Yeah, make sure Angeline is happily settled in school first.'

Sophie nodded. 'Maybe you two could go for a stroll one bath time? Then disappear another night and let me put them to bed?'

'That's clever,' said Penny.

'On the third night,' said Sophie, warming to her suggestion, 'you two could go on a date. Have a drink, grab a little dinner. There are loads of chic bistros in the new town. Not so touristy over there.'

'I'm liking that idea. Whaddaya say, Mrs Gates? Gonna let me take you on a date some night?'

Penny blushed like a ninth-grader being asked out for the first time.

'You're cute,' said Sophie, 'for an old married couple.' Then she ran for the stairs.

Chapter 16

'But when will Mommy and Daddy be back?'

'Shh, I already told you, Angel. They'll be back later.'

'Where are they?' the child whispered.

'I told you that, too.'

'Why have Mommy and Daddy gone on a date? That's just silly.' Angel giggled and Sophie touched a finger to her lips.

'Why is it silly, Angel?' Sophie knew Angel could probably keep this conversation going all night, given the chance.

Penny's approach was to say, 'Last kiss, Angel,' so she'd get the message, and then say, 'Goodnight,' and leave the room.

While she totally respected Penny's style of mothering and admired the loving but firm way she handled her children, Sophie didn't want to adopt her last-kiss-and-leave strategy. This was the first time these kids had been put to bed by anyone but their mom and Sophie thought that was a pretty big deal. Also, if Penny came back and found her children upset, she was likely to abandon any idea of a trip to Toulouse.

Angeline caught hold of a strand of Sophie's hair and was trying to wind it around her finger. The imagery was not lost on Sophie. 'Shouldn't you be sleeping now, Angel? Listen to your little brother.'

Ethan was snoring gently in the twin bed across the room. He sounded like a kitten, purring in contentment. The little boy had fallen asleep while his big sister was reading him a story. His eyes had closed just before the end and Sophie had to stop Angel from waking him up to hear how the fairy tale finished. Sophie was keen for him to remain asleep. She had no way of knowing how the child might react if he woke looking for his mommy and found her gone.

For that reason, despite knowing she was encouraging bad habits, Sophie continued to indulge Angeline by answering one whispered question after another.

'Do you think mommies and daddies should go on dates?'

'Of course. Why not?'

The child giggled and pulled the covers up over her face. 'Because dates are for kissing.'

'Well?'

'Well, Mommy and Daddy are married, aren't they?'

'You know they are.'

'Well then.'

Sophie decided it might be wise to leave that one right there and change the subject.

'When I was a little girl, my mom and dad went out on dates. I used to go stay over at my grandma's.'

'I don't have a grandma.' The child's voice was matter of fact. 'My grandmas both went to heaven before I was born. My grandpas too. Mommy says my grandma's an angel.'

Sophie was lost for words. Finally, she managed to whisper, 'Just like you. You're an Angel.'

'Yes, but not a real one, like Grandma.'

'Right, Miss Angel, last kiss.'

As she closed the bedroom door, she heard a plaintive, 'Sophie, I need to pee.'

When she was sure both children were sound asleep, Sophie rang Miss L. She had a question she needed to ask, or at least an answer she wanted to hear.

'Sophie! This is an unexpected pleasure. Everything okay?'

'Everything's fine, thanks, Miss L. I just wanted to, like, touch base.'

'Always happy to hear from you, my dear, although I don't have all that much time to talk right now. I'm in the most darling little bistro and I just ordered up some foie gras.'

Sophie had a sudden picture of Penny and Seth in the same 'darling little bistro'. 'In Carcassonne?'

'No, I'm meandering my way south, you might say. Enjoying this Indian summer weather.'

'Hasn't it been beautiful? Typical of this time of year, according to the locals.'

'Sophie, while it is always nice to talk to you, I'm sure you didn't call me to discuss the weather.'

The way she said 'weatha' made Sophie feel homesick. She longed to chat some more, but the message was clear, however enchantingly spoken. Miss L did not have time for small talk.

'What is it you want to tell me, my dear?'

'Just that things are going well and it looks like Penny and Seth will be spending the night in Toulouse soon. Provided tonight goes according to plan.'

'What's happening tonight?'

'They've gone out and left me to put the kids to bed.'

'And how did that go?'

'Fine, they're both sound asleep.'

'I sure hope so. Wouldn't want any small ears eavesdropping on our conversation.'

Sophie panicked for a moment, replaying the conversation in her head. She hadn't said anything suspicious, had she? And anyway, the children were asleep. She'd double-checked.

'Miss L, there's no easy way for me to say this so I'll come straight to the point.'

'Please do.'

'Angel says she has no grandmas. Both her grandmas died before she was born, apparently.'

In a Southern Belle voice, more saccharine-sweet than Scarlett's ever sounded, Miss L trilled, 'Why, I do declare, that foie gras looks mouth-watering. Thank you most kindly. Could I trouble you to bring me just the tiniest sip of Sauternes to go with it, please?'

The line went dead.

Chapter 17

Penny and Seth had been home by eleven. Penny had practically sprinted up the stairs the minute she walked in the house. She claimed it was to get out of her 'posh clothes' but Sophie heard the door to the kids' bedroom and knew she'd gone to check on them.

According to Seth, she'd checked her phone every five minutes in the bar. She even refused dessert at the restaurant, which Seth said was a first.

'It was included in the price,' he'd complained to Sophie. 'I asked them to put it in a doggy-bag so we could bring it home and share it with you. You should have seen the waiter's face. He made me feel like I had no right to ask. I love a doggy-bag. Half the fun of going out to eat is bringing some home to snack on later.'

'It's a different culture here, Seth.'

'You're right about that. There wasn't enough food on my plate to feed a mouse.'

'Do you think that might explain why most French people are slim while the US has an obesity epidemic?'

'Maybe, but he still ought to have given me that dessert as take-out. I'd paid for it.'

Seth had seemed genuinely aggrieved, but they claimed to have enjoyed themselves and the children had slept through the night and woken unscathed by their experience, so the proposed outing to Toulouse was still on the cards.

The next morning, she rang Miss L. Her employer wasted no time in getting to the point.

'Are you alone?'

'Yes, Miss L. I've just dropped Angeline at school and Ethan is at home with his mommy doing kindergarten stuff. Did you know Penny used to teach preschool in the states?'

'Why, of course I knew. Just because I don't see my family doesn't mean I know nothing about them.'

'Sorry.'

'I would like to meet in Narbonne tomorrow. I want to treat you to a nice meal.'

Sophie was reminded of her mum's favourite saying. No such thing as a free lunch.

'We need to talk. Let's say twelve, shall we? The French eat early and when in Rome, if you catch my drift. Trains run at least once an hour from Carcassonne. Take a cab to the restaurant. I'll reimburse you.'

'I'll have to ask Penny for the day off.'

'I'll be at Le Saint Georges. The maître d' will bring you to my table if you ask for me by name. Do not give your own name. It won't be necessary. Tomorrow, you are my niece.'

'What should I wear, Miss L?'

'Oh, my dear girl, I've no idea. As long as it's not jeans and those awful sneaker things you had on last time we met. Try not to be late.'

Sophie couldn't get the conversation out of her mind. She'd asked what the meeting was about and been met with a curt response to wait and see. She couldn't help feeling she ought not to have mentioned the grandma thing. Would she never learn to hold her tongue?

What would she do if Miss L was calling this meeting in Narbonne to tell her the whole scheme was off?

Sophie wasn't ready to go home to the States yet, but without Miss L's money, she'd have to revise her plans, big time. There would be no grand tour of Europe for her. No seeing places she'd dreamt of. Places whose names had fascinated her since she was a child. The Acropolis, the Trevi Fountain, the Bridge of Sighs. Further afield, the Blue Mosque, the Alhambra, the Fjords. Sophie had no idea how feasible it might be to visit all the places her heart desired, but Miss L had suggested she'd be paying enough to make them a possibility.

The way things were looking, Sophie might have to go home without ever finding her long-lost father.

And yet, why would Miss L go to the trouble of meeting for lunch, if she was planning to abort the mission? And why change her mind when things were going so well with Ethan? As little as she knew about the woman and her long-term plans, it was clear to Sophie that Miss L was desperate to spend time with those kids. She'd been planning this for some time and had gone to great lengths to find an 'accomplice'. Once, when Sophie had referred to the two of them as partners in crime, Miss L had been quite scathing. 'This is no crime, Sophie,' she'd said. 'I am simply righting a wrong, that's all.'

It seemed to Sophie like a complicated way to go about things, so it must be a very big wrong, but hey, it had got her an all-expenses-paid trip to Europe. She wasn't going to complain.

On the way back to the house it occurred to her that perhaps she ought to have asked Penny for the time off before she'd agreed to have lunch in Narbonne, but it hadn't crossed her mind to say no to Miss L. Sophie had the impression she was the kind of woman who was used to everyone saying yes.

Penny and Ethan were making play dough when she got back. Ethan was up to his elbows in blue goo.

'Making pay-doh, Sophie.'

'Wow, looks like the best fun.'

The little boy nodded and held a clump of gloop up for her inspection.

'Mess is always fun for a preschooler,' said his mom.

'Always. Say, Penny, can I ask a favour?'

'Sure thing.'

'Would you mind if I had tomorrow afternoon off? I'll take Angel to school, same as usual, but then I'd like to take a train ride down to Narbonne. See the Mediterranean. Would that be okay?'

'Oh, shoot! We should have offered. I forgot you wanted to look up your dad while you were over here. Is that where he's from?'

Sophie realised she'd just been provided with the perfect excuse for her day off. She'd be mad not to grab it. 'Maybe. I'm not sure yet. That's what I want to find out.'

Chapter 18

While Sophie waited to be seated, she scanned the restaurant. Her dining companion was nowhere to be seen. When the maître d' approached, Sophie told him she was here to join her aunt but thought she hadn't arrived yet.

'Ah, Miss Mouche-Chamier's niece. Would you like to come this way?' He swept away. Confused, but not wishing to argue, Sophie followed.

It wasn't quite midday and yet the place was already busy and full of the tantalising aromas of good food. The maître d' led her to the furthest corner of the dining room and stopped beside a small table set for two.

'Hello, my dear. I'm so glad you can join me.'

The voice was the real deal, but Sophie would not have recognised Miss L in a lifetime.

The waiter pulled out a chair for Sophie. The moment she was seated, he flicked a white serviette in the air in front of her face. Like a parachute it floated onto her lap.

'Would mademoiselle like an apéritif?'

Sophie looked at Miss L in disbelief while the waiter poured some water into two glasses.

'Sophie?'

'What are you having?'

'I'm having a kir royale. Champagne and crème de cassis. You know what that is, don't you?'

Rising to the challenge, Sophie regained her composure and turned to the waiter to order, in flawless French, the same drink as her employer, but with raspberry liqueur, not blackcurrant.

Miss L smiled. 'I thought I told you not to draw attention to yourself?'

'Sorry. What did I do wrong?'

'An American who speaks perfect French? That makes you stick out like a sore thumb right away.'

Sophie had no idea whether to laugh, apologise or say thanks for the compliment. She covered her discomfort by taking a sip of her drink. It was divine. Cold, sweet and bubbly with a tang of ripe fruit. 'Mm, this is delicious.'

'I thought you'd like it.'

'Miss L, you look wonderful. I didn't recognise you.'

'I think I look pretty good every time you see me.'

'No, I mean yes. Yes, you do. It's just that, well, I guess I'd got used to you with grey hair.'

'You mean my grandma look?' Miss L's girlish laughter tinkled around them. Did she take a delight in making Sophie feel gauche and awkward? It sometimes felt that way.

Miss L leaned across and touched Sophie's hand. 'Sorry, my dear. Thank you. Whether your compliment was for how I look or how good my disguise is, I accept it, graciously.'

'But your hair?' Miss L had gone from steely grey to a sun-streaked blonde.

'A wig. A very expensive wig, may I say?'

'It looks fabulous.'

'I have a collection. All real hair, all professionally toned to suit my complexion. Nothing worse than a cheap wig, I always say.'

Sophie would have loved to ask if Miss L wore her wigs by choice or out of necessity, but she didn't have the courage to ask and anyway, that was a pretty personal question.

Lunch was as delectable as the cooking smells had promised. Miss L chose foie gras, clearly her favourite. When Sophie gently asked how she felt about the rather unethical methods of production, Miss L laughed and said, 'Someone close to me used to say, "Ethics are a luxury I can't afford." When it comes to goose liver, I agree.'

72

Sophie dropped the subject and wondered who the someone close might be and why he 'used to say'. Sounded like the guy was dead. Did that make Miss L a widow? Again Sophie longed to ask, but didn't dare.

Dessert was the best lemon meringue tart Sophie had ever tasted. As she pushed her plate away, Miss L thanked the waiter who seemed to appear from nowhere to clear the table. He brushed up the crumbs and smoothed the starched linen cloth, offering coffee, which Miss L refused for both of them. She waited until he was out of earshot.

'Earlier you mentioned ethics, my dear Sophie,' she said. 'That brings us neatly to our business.'

Not knowing where this was going or what to say, Sophie simply smiled and hoped that was the appropriate response.

'Do you recall the meeting we had after your interview, when I told you what this job entailed?'

Sophie nodded. 'Helping you spend some time with your estranged grandchildren.'

'Do you remember we agreed how vitally important it would be to trust each other? Implicitly?'

'Yes.'

Miss L drained her glass, taking her time to savour the last mouthful of wine. Or maybe to let her words sink in.

'You say yes, and yet I had the impression the other day that I may have lost your trust.'

Oh dear. Didn't sound good. 'I'm sorry if I made you feel that way.'

'It is vitally important that you trust me enough to do as I say. At all times. Without questioning. Am I making myself clear?'

The charming way she said 'cle-ah' and left the question hanging made her sound harmless. Anyone passing the table and catching her delicate voice and rising intonation might imagine she was offering Sophie another drink or insisting she let her doting aunt get the check. Only Sophie was close enough to see the steel in the blue eyes or pick up the menace hidden in the words.

A long pause indicated that Sophie should say something. But what to say? While her mouth waited for her brain to click into gear, a little voice in her head ran through the pros and cons of her job.

The pros were many. Money, tick. Chance to travel, tick. Opportunity to look for her dad, tick. Valuable experience as a nanny, tick.

Cons? Just this dark feeling that something about their arrangement was wrong.

'Miss L?'

'Yes, Sophie?' The smile was back, the words warm and sweet as summer honey.

'That was the most delicious lunch I've ever eaten.'

Sophie pushed back her chair and the waiter appeared at her side, ready to help her. Sophie rose to her feet and smiled at him.

'Thank you so much, Auntie. For everything. You've been more than generous. But please don't deposit any more allowance in my bank account. It's time I stood on my own two feet.'

Chapter 19

'Are you okay, Sophie?' asked Penny, looking up from giving Ethan his lunch. The girl looked like she had a world of cares on her shoulder.

'Sure.'

The response had been automatic, too fast to mean anything.

'You can tell me if something's troubling you.'

'It's fine. I'm just a little worried about money.'

'Things are more expensive here than back home, aren't they? We've noticed that too.'

'Yeah, I guess they are.'

'I wish we could afford to pay you more. You're worth your weight in gold.' She handed Ethan an apple stick and wiped a stream of juice from his chin. 'Isn't Sophie wonderful, Ethan?'

'Underful,' said the little boy through a mouthful of fruit. When they laughed, he did too, and a dollop of half-chewed apple dropped out onto the table.

'Oops. What a mess!' he said, and beamed at them for approval.

'It's just that, when we budgeted to come here, a nanny wasn't in the equation. Don't get me wrong, I'm so glad we met you and frankly, I'm not sure I could cope without you and your fantastic French.' She tailed off then added, 'But you know what I'm saying?'

'I know,' said Sophie, 'and I wouldn't have missed this opportunity for the world.' She ruffled Ethan's hair and said, 'Meeting this little guy and his sister has been one of the best things that ever happened to me.'

Penny lifted Ethan and held him close. 'I hope you're not about to tell me you're leaving, Sophie?'

'No, I'm not. But to be honest, I may need to think about it.'

Penny came and gave her a hug. Sophie could feel Ethan's little arm go around her neck.

'Family hug!' he said.

'He's right, you know, Sophie. You feel like part of our family and you've been so good for the kids.'

'Thanks, Penny.'

'No, seriously. Look at Angeline, going off every morning to a French school, happy as a clam at high tide. That's way beyond any expectations we had of our stay in France.'

'She's a clever cookie. Like this one.' She tickled Ethan under his arm, just the way he liked it, and was rewarded with a giggling fit. 'That's all down to you.'

'I couldn't have taught her French.'

'Please don't worry, Penny. I'm just, like, considering my options. That's all.'

'I wish we could afford to come up with a bit more spending money for you.'

'It's okay, seriously. Sorry if I sounded grumpy.'

'Gwumpy,' said Ethan, breaking the tension.

'Is it still okay for me to go to Toulouse?' asked Penny. 'That will bring you a little extra cash.'

'Oh no, please. There's no need.'

'We promised. You can't do all those extra hours for nothing. You've already put in a few long shifts making sure these two will be okay with Mommy and Daddy being away overnight.'

'I don't mind.'

'I insist. In fact, if you refuse to take some extra payment, then I refuse to go.'

Sophie shook her head and smiled, as if she knew there was no point in arguing. 'Okay, then. Thank you.'

'Don't thank *me*, Sophie. I'm the one swanning off to visit a new place and spend the night in a hotel while you stay and look after my two monsters. You've drawn the short straw, kiddo.'

Sophie went up to her bedroom. She'd come to love this room with its beamed ceiling and low window, its creaky door and ancient furniture. She'd even grown used to the big old bed, although the bolster pillow now lay banished to a corner in the eaves. It would be hard to leave. And where would she go? Home to Mom's where her two half-brothers seemed to fill the entire house with sports gear and testosterone? And what would she do there? She couldn't imagine her stepdad forking out to keep her living like a lady of leisure for what remained of the academic year. But how would she support herself if she didn't move back in with them, sweaty jocks and all? At best, she'd pick up work in a call centre, at worst she might get some shifts in a bar. Neither would bring in enough for her to rent a decent place. Not without a substantial top-up from Mom and 'Dad'.

And then there was her real dad out there somewhere, maybe only a few kilometres away from where she was sitting right now. If she went home she'd never get the chance to track him down, she knew that in her bones.

Staying with Penny and Seth – working for pocket money – would allow her the time and space to trace her father, but she'd have no cash to go looking for him. The trip to Narbonne had left her short. She wished now she'd got the train and taxi fare from Miss L before making her dramatic exit.

Had she been too hasty?

It was the 'without questioning' that had tipped her over, although she'd been having some doubts before then. Sophie's nature was to question, always had been. To be informed that she must do as she was told, *without questioning*, had just seemed too much.

She'd come this far on trust, believing Miss L's story. All the woman wanted was the chance to get to know Angeline and Ethan. If this was the only way she could get to spend time with her grandchildren, Sophie felt sorry for her.

When Sophie had asked why they had to go all the way to France, Miss L had explained that in the States, taking a child – even for a short visit – without the permission of its parents was a crime, period. Child abduction laws were strict. Get convicted of a felony and you could face four years in state prison and a ten thousand dollar fine.

Sophie could see how organising an opportunity to see the kids here was a safer option for Miss L. It was also, potentially, a lot more cost effective. Beyond that, Sophie had sought no further explanation, until she found out that the kids had no grandparents.

Sophie didn't blame Penny and Seth. If the estrangement was permanent, it would be easier to tell the kids that granny and gramps had gone to be with the angels or some other such crap.

She wondered what had caused such a catastrophic rift in the family. Penny could be a bit overanxious at times, but she had a good heart. And Seth was just a darling man. Hard to imagine him falling out with anyone. However, Miss L wouldn't be everyone's idea of a perfect grandmother. She was strong medicine.

Mom always said, 'Never judge a man till you've walked a mile in his moccasins.' Who knew what had happened? Mom was right. It wasn't Sophie's place to judge.

Still, something about this didn't feel good. If Sophie wasn't allowed to ask any questions, her instinct was to get out while she could.

From the foot of the stairs she heard Penny's voice, reminding her it was time to go fetch Angel from school.

'Be right there,' she called, grabbing her backpack and a sweater.

Angeline was waiting for her at the school gates, surrounded by a bunch of little girls, all with fat schoolbags on their backs.

'Sorry I'm an itsy bitsy, teeny weeny bit late, Angel.' It was a game they played.

'It's okay. It was only a tiny winy bit.'

'Let's see if we can think of a new one, shall we?'

The challenge kept them going all the way home and the best they could come up with was ickle pickle. Angel wasted no time in trying it out on Ethan. She hugged him and said, 'Hello, ickle pickle brother.'

'Penny, I meant to get something at the pharmacy.'

'I want to come,' shrieked Angeline.

'No, sweetie. You stay here with me and tell me all about your day.'

Penny seemed to sense that Sophie wanted some time alone. She did. Just enough to walk to the end of the street and make a phone call.

Chapter 20

Miss L wasn't at all surprised to hear from Sophie. But she *had* been a little shocked at the girl's demands. Not for more money, as might have been expected. That, she'd have given willingly.

What Sophie wanted was something much more difficult to give away.

'I need the truth,' she'd said.

Such audacity for a young thing.

'Trust works both ways, Miss L.'

Yep, got to hand it to her. The gal had some nerve.

'Very well, Sophie. In a spirit of mutual trust, I shall tell you the truth. Angeline and Ethan's parents made a choice, for reasons they chose not to share with me, to move all the way to Texas before those sweet babies were born.'

'Let me get this right. Penny's Scottish. That makes you Seth's mother, right?'

'Seth has no mother. He chose to make a new life for himself. Clearly I have no part in it.'

'That's so sad.'

A pause for effect, a sniff, and a delicate nose blow. Just enough to suggest tears. 'Perhaps now you can understand why I prefer not to talk about it.'

'I'm so sorry, Miss L. I didn't mean to upset you.'

Another sniff to seal the deal, then her most fragile voice. 'That's okay. Now, let's put all this behind us. Tell me, Sophie. When can I see that charming little grandson of mine?'

'Tomorrow, if you like. Penny is heading for Toulouse, to stay over. In fact I'll be glad of some help with Ethan.'

So it was arranged. Sophie would see the girl off to school and then bring the little boy, in his stroller, up into the old town.

'I'd love to buy him a small gift, if you think that would be okay?'

'Sure, we'll just pretend I bought it. For being good while Mommy's gone.'

'I was thinking a toy, something to remind him of his time in Carcassonne?'

'I know exactly what he'd like. A little plastic sword.'

'Where on earth would we get such a thing?' She knew the answer of course.

'You know the little souvenir store near the Porte de Narbonne? The one with all sorts of stuff in plastic buckets in the street? Ethan sticks his hand out every time we pass, trying to grab a plastic sword. I think he'd love one.'

'Is that the shop with the full-sized suit of armour by the door?'

'That's the one. There's always a traffic jam of pedestrians stopping to pose for photos.'

'Shall we meet there?'

'Yes, let's.'

'Perfect. Till tomorrow then.'

Sophie was a great find. Intelligent, caring and completely trustworthy. More than could be said about some of the dizzy airheads who'd applied for the job. She reckoned some of them had seen 'work in Europe' and not read beyond that point.

An astonishing number of hopefuls had responded to the ad. The first day she'd gone to check her PO box, she'd been expecting half a dozen letters. The box had been almost full although she'd chosen one big enough to take 'two shoeboxes and ten to fifteen letters.'

She'd smiled to herself at the mention of the two shoeboxes, imagining the set of circumstances that might force someone to hire a PO box to take delivery of shoeboxes. Some downtrodden little housewife out in the boonies who scrimps and saves nickels and dimes in a jelly jar till she's got enough to send for some fancy shoes. Shoes she can't wear anywhere for fear of her redneck husband finding out and asking where she got the money. She'd pictured that poor woman trying on those gorgeous high heels and strutting her stuff around the post office lobby. Then packing them lovingly in their tissue-filled box and locking them away till the next time she came into town for groceries. Or a big, rough farmer with a secret cache of women's clothes, picking up his newest man-sized stilettos and sneaking them off back to the barn. She imagined his thrill when he went out, late at night, lantern in hand, and slipped his huge feet into their pointed toes. She saw him mincing around happily while his wife and children slept on, innocent as the Waltons.

She'd gone back twice to empty the box, ending up with so many applicants it had taken her days to go through them. The first triage had been simple and fast. No males. None need have applied, but she couldn't put that in the ad for legal reasons. No one over twenty-two. Anyone who couldn't spell or hadn't taken the time to check for mistakes was out. Like Jemma Louise who'd spelt her middle name Lousie. Just like her chances of getting the job.

Miss 'Mouche-Chamier' was looking for someone smart, ruthless, ambitious and willing to please. Not all of which she could put in the job advert which had simply sought 'Young person to work in Europe as an au pair for family with small children. Must speak fluent French.'

She'd eventually narrowed it down to six. She could have interviewed a few more, based on their applications, but time was precious and the fewer who knew anything about this venture, the better. The interviews were enlightening. She met a lovely girl who spoke fluent French. Pity the same couldn't be said for her English. Then there was the Goth who looked like she slept in a coffin and avoided daylight. One girl seemed ideal until the interview had switched into French and faltered to a stop.

'I thought I could pick it up when I'm over there. I'm a real fast learner.' Not fast enough. Next.

Candidate number five was a no show and she'd been on the point of abandoning the whole plan when Sophie walked in. Perfect in every way.

She had arranged a few more meetings, always in different and very public places, getting to know more and more about the girl while giving away the absolute minimum about her own situation. As far as Sophie was concerned, Miss Mouche-Chamier was recruiting on behalf of a friend who wanted an American girl to help look after the kids and teach the whole family some French. She'd centred her search around New Orleans, a university town with a long and strong French tradition, and been glad to hire a Louisiana girl like herself.

Well, not quite like herself. The very idea that she'd ever have to apply for a job! Daddy would have sold his soul to the devil to prevent his darling girl having to work for a living. Had she wanted to go to France or Switzerland it would have been to a finishing school, no expense spared, but she hadn't been interested in that. Instead, she'd shadowed her daddy, learning how he made his millions, and investing wisely when her turn came.

The only unwise investment she'd ever made was in a husband. But because Daddy had liked him so much she'd allowed herself to be wooed by this *beau* and had, for her sins, grown to love him. Love him, but not entirely trust him. Her daddy always said, 'Trust nobody but yourself. And me, of course.' Wise words.

She'd applied that wisdom to every relationship she'd ever had, and never regretted it. Even though it meant she didn't have many friends, and no one she'd call close. Thank God she'd never fully trusted that charming husband of hers or she'd be penniless today.

She gave her head a little shake to rid herself of things she'd rather forget and touched her hair to make sure it was undisturbed.

She trusted Sophie wholeheartedly, but still she never forgot what Daddy said.

Chapter 21

The next day dawned bright, the sky an unblemished blue. She was pleased the beautiful weather was holding up; the gods must be on her side. Far fewer people would be likely to visit Carcassonne on a cold or a wet day, although an umbrella was great for hiding behind. She knew that.

She lingered outside a nearby nougat shop, as if she were trying to decide what flavour to buy. Every so often she glanced towards the souvenir shop, unwilling to approach it until she knew Sophie was there. She wondered if she ought to buy some sweeties for Ethan while she waited but didn't want to go inside for fear of missing Sophie. The girl was late.

She watched the crowds swirling around a suit of armour near the doorway, jostling to take photos. It was the right shop. She'd chosen well. Both place and time. There was a hectic period each day when all coach passengers had been offloaded but few had started to wander back to their pick-up point. Although it was late season, Carcassonne was always busy, it seemed, and even on quieter days the narrowness of the little streets concentrated the visitors and made the town appear crowded. It was ideal for her purposes.

She spotted the girl working her way through the tourists towards her, pushing the stroller and looking as if she was finding it tricky to make progress on the cobbles.

Sophie stopped and scanned the faces around her, then knelt down and spoke to the little boy.

'Hello, Sophie, hello Ethan.'

The girl, hearing her name, looked up. 'Hi, there. Isn't it a lovely day to go feed the ducks?'

'It is. Say, why don't you go buy Ethan his gift? I'll wait here with him. It's far too crowded to take the stroller inside.'

'Okay. Won't be long, Ethan.'

'Take your time. In fact, could you pick out something for me to give Angel when I meet her?'

'Sure. How much should I spend?'

'Here, please take this fifty. Buy something nice. I've never been allowed to spoil them. And don't you worry about us. We'll be just fine here. Won't we, Ethan?'

She watched Sophie disappear into the shop and waited for a throng of tourists to approach.

'Okay, kid,' she said to Ethan. 'Let's go.'

The child giggled with every bump of his stroller as she hurried away over the cobbles towards the Porte de Narbonne. Progress was slower than she'd have wished but the crowds of tourists all around would make it so much more difficult for anyone to remember her. In any case, she was just one grey-haired lady amongst so many others.

Once they reached the esplanade the stroller moved smoothly over the blacktop and it was easy to go fast.

'Whee,' said Ethan, clearly enjoying himself. She was glad she'd got to know the kid beforehand. It would make life much simpler in the days ahead.

She turned right and hurried up the hill towards her car. Pushing Ethan with one hand, she took out her phone with the other and dialled Sophie's number.

'Hi, Miss L. Sorry I'm taking so long. Believe it or not, I can't find the swords. I haven't even started looking for something for Angel.'

'That's okay. Take your time. Change of plan. Ethan asked to go potty. Isn't he a clever little thing? I know it's important to let them go when they need to at that age, so I've headed down to the restrooms just outside the Porte de Narbonne. You know, on the right-hand side? And he performed. Isn't that amazing?'

Sophie laughed. 'You're turning into such a proud grandma. Listen, I'm on my way. We can come back later and buy toys when it's quieter. I'll see you in a moment, by the restrooms.'

'You know what, I've got this covered. Ethan's back in his stroller and he seems quite happy. He knows me now, which is so lovely. Why don't you take some time off? Go grab a coffee and read a magazine for a while. This could be a long day for you on your own with two small kids.'

There was a long pause, as if Sophie was trying to make up her mind what to say. 'Are you sure?'

'It's no trouble and I'd just love to have him to myself for a while. We could meet later and buy him that sword. Maybe choose something together for Angel?'

'I'll be honest with you. It's very tempting. Ethan should be fine with you for a few hours. I've put his little cup and some cookies in the bag under the stroller. I've also packed some lunch. Trust me, that kid likes to eat. Oh, Hoppy is in the bag too, by the way.'

'Pardon me?'

'Hoppy, his rabbit. Ethan goes nowhere without Hoppy. It's hilarious.'

'Sounds like you've thought of everything. Bread for the ducks?'

'In the bag.'

'Sophie, how will I ever repay you for this? It's like a dream come true. I'm taking my grandson for a walk and a little picnic by the river.'

'Hope those cute ducklings will be around so you can throw them some crusts. Have fun and I'll see you later. Call when you're ready to hand him over.'

Chapter 22

Ethan smiled as she lifted him out of the stroller. 'Mawmaw,' he murmured, putting his arms round her neck. Something tugged deep inside her, in a place she'd thought long dead. She hugged his little body for a moment then placed him carefully in the car seat.

He looked up into her face. 'Sophie?'

'No, Sophie's not here, Ethan.'

His eyes widened, his lower lip trembled, and he started to whimper like an abandoned puppy. Diane felt her own eyes fill. A single teardrop ran down his face and dripped off his little puckered chin.

'It's okay, Ethan,' she said, trying to keep her voice reassuring and soothing. Difficult, considering the struggle to fasten him into the car seat.

The single tear became a flood and Ethan howled. More loudly than she'd ever expected. She was glad she'd foreseen this possibility and had made arrangements. It was also fortunate that she'd chosen to avoid the car park so there was no one nearby to hear him. She offered him his drink bottle, which he refused to take. She tried a cookie, putting it to his lips, but he turned his face away and pushed at her with his hands.

'Okay, Ethan, have it your way,' she said, closing the car door and wondering what the hell she was doing.

She took a few minutes to calm herself, slow her breathing and consider all the consequences, real and possible, of what she was about to do. This was not the first time she had contemplated the ramifications of her plan. She had been over it so often that she could recite her pro and con lists from memory. She knew exactly how serious this was and, up until now, this very moment, she had been sure it was the right thing to do. For so many reasons.

But there was a big difference between sitting on one's porch on a balmy evening, glass of wine in hand, mulling over the possibility, and this. An apoplectic toddler writhing and kicking in the back seat of your car.

'Ethan, it's okay,' she said in a sing-song voice. She looked round and smiled. The kid was in a world of his own, caught up in his own distress and not seeing or hearing anything or anyone. She knew nothing about kids, but instinct told her this was not the time for conversation.

Diane turned around and looked through the windscreen. Across a wide plain, mountains faded into blues and greys. All she needed to do was start the engine and drive.

Or, she could call Sophie, put the kid back in his stroller, wheel him up the cobbled streets of the Cité and hand him over. Sophie would be there, waiting. She probably wouldn't even be surprised to see them back.

Diane could park the stroller and say, 'He's all yours.' And leave. Walk away. Go back to her old, uncomplicated life where she need concern herself about nothing more than how her stock was performing.

The screaming stopped. Ethan was sobbing, but in little bursts, snuffling and hiccupping in the pauses.

Diane sat and listened, not daring to look in case she'd start him off again. The sobs became less distraught. The snuffling more intermittent. Quieter. He sounded like a little engine running out of steam. Apart from the occasional hiccupy catch of breath, which was quite cute in a way, there was silence. Diane turned her head ever so slightly, just enough to allow her peripheral vision to focus on the child. He was asleep. Unbelievable. She'd heard the expression "crying oneself to sleep", but she'd thought it was no more than a line from a country song. It really happened. How about that?

She looked at the time. She'd lost a bit, but not that much. And with the kid asleep, she could make it up.

She put the key in the ignition and started the engine.

Chapter 23

The waitress, eyebrows at her hairline, pointed to Sophie's empty glass. She had made a mineral water last a world record amount of time. When she'd decided to wait here for Miss L, she'd forgotten that cafés in the Cité liked a quick turnaround. Someone like her, hogging a table with the cheapest item on the menu, was not good for business. It was not the custom in France to share a table, so that meant she was taking up the space that four or even five customers might fill, each with a hefty appetite and a wallet to match.

Sophie looked at the group of tourists hovering hopefully nearby and nodded. The waitress snatched the glass.

Sophie had been thinking of leaving anyway. All must be well or Miss L would've come back looking for her by now.

As she stood to go her phone vibrated in her pocket. Speak of the devil.

'Hi! Everything okay?'

'Relax, my dear. Everything's just perfect. What a darling little boy.'

'Isn't he? You two getting along okay?'

'Like we've known each other his whole life. The way it should have been.'

'That's fantastic. I'm so happy for you.'

Sophie picked up her book and, still chatting, made for the door. She was stopped in her tracks by the torn-faced waitress who looked as if she'd been expecting her to slip away without paying. Sophie fumbled for money, handed over a ten-euro note and dashed out, muttering an apology.

'What's going on?'

'Almost left the café without paying. The waitress wasn't loving that idea.'

'I thought you might be glad of an update.'

'Thanks, that was thoughtful. Did you see the ducks?'

'Yes, we did. Did we see the ducks, Ethan?' After a pause, she said, 'He says yes.'

Sophie laughed, imagining Ethan's grin. 'Did he do his duck impersonation?'

'He sure did.'

'Where are you now?'

'We're having a seat at a café in the Place Carnot. I've just had the most delicious cake and coffee and Ethan's polishing off an ice cream. He's a bit messy. Hope that's okay?'

'It's fine. Sounds like you two are having the best fun.'

'Oh, we are, my dear. Thank you so much.'

'What's that noise? Sounds like traffic. I thought Place Carnot was pedestrianised.'

'Some kid at the next table, playing a video game on his phone. Darn things ought to be banned in public.'

'You tell 'em!'

'Anyway, thought I'd let you know we're all good here, so you can relax and enjoy your free time.'

'Cool. Say, if you're in the new town, I could come and meet you there. Save you schlepping that stroller all the way back uphill.'

'Thanks, Sophie, but I'd rather stick to the plan. Less room for confusion that way and I want to get this little munchkin back to you in time. See you in the café near the toy shop.'

'If you're sure.'

'I'm sure. We'll see you later. Say bye-bye, Ethan.' Another pause, then, 'He's waving. Bye.'

Chapter 24

Sophie picked up a half baguette to go with the local pâté she'd spotted in the fridge at breakfast time. She counted her small change. She had just enough to treat herself to a trashy magazine. Sophie couldn't wait to have money. Soon, thanks to Miss L's generosity, she should have enough to finance her grand tour.

Sophie took her lunch and a small glass of rosé up to the terrace. She flicked through the magazine, enjoying the warm afternoon sun. She leaned back and closed her eyes, just for a moment.

Somewhere, far away, a phone was ringing. Why didn't someone answer? It stopped. Thank goodness. It started again. She recognised the ring tone just as the vibration dragged her back to the surface.

'Hello,' she muttered, her throat dry.

'At last.'

'Penny! It's you.'

'Of course it's me. You okay?'

'Sure.'

'Were you asleep?'

'Sorry, yeah, I sat down after lunch. Think I must have dozed off.'

'What's Ethan doing? Can you put him on?'

'He's snoozing right now.'

'Oh no, he's asleep. You were asleep. Does that mean you were all up in the night?'

'They slept like babies.'

'Did Angel go off to school okay?'

'She did. And don't worry. They both slept all night. Seriously.'

'Did you sleep all night?'

'Not so much!' They laughed. 'How's Toulouse?'

'Oh, it's heavenly. I've taken so many photos. It's got all these old buildings built of red clay bricks. Not the least little bit like Paris or Carcassonne. You have to come see for yourself.'

'I'd like that.'

'Well, we're gonna catch the train just whenever Seth finishes work so we shouldn't be too late home. Will you keep the kids up till we get there, please?'

'That's my plan. I thought it would be okay for Ethan to have a late nap today so he'll be full of beans when you get home.'

'I can't wait to see them. I know it sounds silly, but I've been missing them.'

'What time do you think you'll be back?'

'Depends when Seth finishes. The train takes about three quarters of an hour. We should be home no later than eight, I expect. Anyway, I'd better go. Don't want to make you late for picking up Angel.'

'What? Is that the time?'

'Better run.'

Penny rang off and Sophie stared at her phone in disbelief. She had less than half an hour to find Miss L, collect Ethan and pick up Angel at school.

Sophie ran all the way to the café. Her favourite waitress was still working, looking no more charming than before. Sophie asked her if a woman with a stroller had been in. The waitress shook her head. Service with a shrug. Sophie decided to wait outside. She'd no time to drink a coffee anyway.

The little street was busy as ever. Outside the souvenir shop a bunch of Japanese kids were taking selfies. No sign of Miss L and Ethan.

Angel would be getting out of school any minute. With no one there to pick her up, any weirdo could go off with her.

Fingers trembling, Sophie brought up the school phone number. It rang for ages. 'Come on, come on,' Sophie urged. 'Answer the goddamned phone.'

Finally. 'Hi, can someone please tell Angeline Gates, the little American girl, that Sophie's got held up, but I'll be there soon?'

'How long till you get here?'

Sophie thought for a moment. What was the best way to deal with this? Wait here till Miss L arrived then go to the school? It would be faster to run there by herself, unimpeded by Ethan and the stroller. Miss L was sensible. She'd wait for Sophie to come back.

'I'll be right there. I mean, I'll run. I'm at the Cité, so … ten minutes?'

The voice on the other end didn't sound delighted. Sophie said, 'I'll be as quick as I can, sorry.'

The crowds made it impossible to run, and she stopped once to text Miss L.

She made it to the school in twelve minutes. The yard was deserted. The only sign that kids had ever been there was a garish painting, lost or discarded, near the gate.

Sophie pushed open the door and ran in, calling, 'Angel?' Her voice echoed. She tried again, this time calling Angel's full name the way the French did, 'Angéline!'

At the end of the corridor a bright red door opened and Angel appeared. She sprinted the full length of the hallway and jumped into Sophie's arms.

Sophie swung her round, hoping to avoid tears, but Angel was bubbling with excitement.

'Mademoiselle Darcy let me help her tidy the classroom and I sorted all the felt tips and threw out the ones that were dried up and they were mostly the reds and the blues and the yellows cos everybody likes to draw with red and blue and yellow and nobody likes brown and then she let me open all the new packets and put the pens in the jars so that every table got the right colours and I didn't get mixed up once or make a single mistake.' She looked at the teacher for approval.

'That's right. She did a superb job,' said the delightful Miss Darcy, seizing the opportunity to get a word in while Angel took a breath.

Sophie thought it a good time to apologise and get going.

They were at the gates before Angel asked the question Sophie had been dreading.

'Where's Ethan?'

Chapter 25

The journey had gone well, considering.

She'd allowed herself over seven hours to drive a distance that the app on her phone had told her would take five. Looking at the route across the Pyrenees on the map, the timing seemed impossible. But Highway A64 was amazing and the app had been right. Including stops, she made it in less than six.

When the satnav told her she was within twenty kilometres of her destination, she pulled off the motorway and soon found a minor road that passed a few tall farmhouses then rose steeply into the mountains. She parked in a layby under the trees and got out to stretch her legs and shoulders before facing the tiny demon in the back seat. It was cool here under the trees and more than a little spooky. Diane was not keen to hang around any longer than necessary.

She opened the rear door and waited for Ethan to open his eyes. Long eyelashes, glued into clumps by his tears, rested on his pink cheeks. He looked hot. She hoped he wasn't running a temperature.

A sick child. She hadn't considered that possibility. A fresh rush of panic hit her, similar to the one she'd had when they'd stopped at a service station. Diane felt awful about it now, but she'd been tempted to simply abandon him and drive off. She'd even gone so far as considering the best place to leave him. In the restaurant? Pretend to go looking for cutlery and walk on out? Or take him into the restroom, sit him on a toilet and close the cubicle door as she left? It was only when she thought about dropping him off in the car park and driving away that her moral code kicked in. The vision of the little boy stepping in front of a moving vehicle was so horrifying it brought her to her senses.

So here she was. Up a track in the middle of nowhere. Terrified of waking a two-year-old in case he started screaming. To be fair to Ethan, he'd been pretty good for most of the journey. Once the car was moving smoothly along the motorway he'd slept for a while and when he woke he seemed happy enough. Perhaps he forgot who was driving, or, more likely, he was tuned into the CD of children's songs she'd brought with her from the States.

While she waited for him to wake, she prepared a drink for him. The blackcurrant juice that she knew he liked plus three drops of the special elixir she'd ordered off the internet and had delivered to her PO box. She'd spent many hours looking for ways to make a child sleep. It was shocking how much was on offer. Stuff that was easy to get from the drugstore or health food shop, like melatonin or Benadryl. And stuff that was much scarier, but alarmingly easy to get. Diane had bought a preparation that the suppliers claimed to be effective, fast-acting and harmless. She sure hoped they were right. On all three counts.

Ethan opened his eyes and looked around him. 'Mommy,' he said. Said, not screamed. That was progress of sorts.

Diane knew she had to get the next bit right or all hell would break loose.

'We're going to see Mommy real soon. Going in the car. Does Ethan like riding in the nice car?'

The little boy nodded and Diane felt so weak with relief she had to steady herself against the door.

'And we'll listen to the music. Ethan likes the music.'

He nodded again.

'Would Ethan like a little drink now?' She'd been withholding fluids in the hope he'd drink the whole cupful and swallow the full dose of elixir.

Another nod. This was looking promising. She offered his drinking cup and this time the child took it and guzzled noisily.

She felt guilty at how thirsty he must have been. Dangling the cup from his thumb, Ethan held it out to her. 'Mo juice, peese.'

She couldn't help smiling. He was too cute.

She didn't want him to drink a whole lot more, given that she needed him to sleep soundly for some time. But she knew it was important to keep him happy. Food worked for puppies. Kids couldn't be that much different, could they?

'Okay, Ethan,' she said stroking his hair. He didn't even flinch. 'Mawmaw will get you more juice.' Getting the kid to call her Mawmaw, the Cajun word for grandmother, had been a masterstroke. It sounded so close to Mommy that anyone hearing him crying for his mother would be reassured to hear her say, 'Mawmaw's here.'

Pretty soon she was going to have to quit calling him Ethan. Sophie said his dad called him L'il Buddy. That would do for the moment.

Although he'd spent most of the day sleeping, Ethan was rubbing his eyes with his fists. The elixir must be taking effect.

'You sleepy, L'il Buddy?'

Ethan looked straight at her, as if the name were familiar. She hoped he wouldn't start screaming for his daddy now, but the kid just nodded. He was sleepy. Good.

'Shall we see if you can go potty first?' This was something she'd had to look up online. Amazing what you could learn on moms' forums. She reckoned Ethan should be able to pee standing up, according to various posts, although the matter did not seem straightforward. She remembered Sophie saying how smart the two kids were. 'Here goes,' she said as she lifted him out of the car and set him down on the grass verge.

'Big trees,' he said, pointing to the tall firs that marched in ranks up the hill. He seemed oblivious when she pulled down his little shorts.

Ablutions completed, Diane showed Ethan the comfy bed she'd made for him in the footwell behind the front seats. She had placed a thick foam cushion in each space and a cot mattress over the top. There was a little black pillow and a fleece blanket to keep him cosy. Sitting on the pillow was his cuddly rabbit.

As if he'd spotted his best friend, Ethan said, 'Hoppy!' and climbed in. Without bidding, he lay down, grabbing the soft toy and cuddling it tightly.

'There you go,' said Diane. 'Snug as a bug in a rug.' The child joined in on the last word. It must be a family saying. Diane tried again, keen to connect. 'Snug as a?'

'Bug!'

'In a?'

'Rug!'

The child giggled. This was beyond good.

She leaned in and tucked the blanket around him. He kicked it off. She had the impression this was a game he'd played before. She'd be happy to oblige another time, but right now she had to get all the kiddy paraphernalia into the boot, change her wig and get going.

They had a boat to catch.

Chapter 26

'Sophie, I said, where's Ethan?'

Sophie didn't dare answer the question. She still hadn't decided what to say. None of the versions she'd rehearsed during her run to the school would sound good if Angel repeated it to Penny at bedtime.

'Angel, listen, I need to make a quick phone call, okay?'

Angel rolled her eyes like a teenager.

'I'll be quick, promise. Stand there a moment, please, and wait for me.'

Without taking her eyes off her charge, Sophie stepped out of earshot and selected Miss L from her contacts. Straight to voicemail.

'Hi, it's Sophie. Had to pick up Angeline. I'll be right with you. Wait for us in the café.'

She took Angel's hand. 'Right, Teacher's Pet, let's go.'

Angel tugged on her arm. 'Sophie?'

'Mm?'

'Is he with Mommy? Is Mommy home already? Has she bought me a present?'

Answer the easy one first. 'I'm sure she's bought you a present. What do you think it could be?'

When they'd exhausted every possibility starting with puppy and pony and ending with candy, Angel asked again where her little brother was. Sophie played the same guessing game about Ethan's gift from Mommy's trip to Toulouse. It didn't last quite so long and they still had a long way to go.

'Where are we going, Sophie? I want to go home and see Mommy and get my present.'

'We are going to buy you a pastry for being such a good girl helping Miss Darcy.'

'Why were you late, Sophie?'

'I was chatting on the phone to your mommy and forgot the time. Look, we're almost there. Have you decided what kind of pastry you want? And do you remember how to ask for it in French?'

The pastry bought Sophie a bit more time, but Angel insisted in knowing why they were going up to the Cité. 'These bobbles in the road hurt my feet.'

'You mean cobbles. Those stones are called cobbles.'

'I don't care. My feet hurt. Can we go home now?'

'You know the shop that sells all the soaps with the nice smells?'

'Right at the top of the hill?' She dragged her feet in an exaggerated display of exhaustion.

'That's the one. I thought we'd go buy Mommy a welcome home gift. Isn't that a nice idea?'

It was a favourite pastime of Angel's to go along the whole line of handmade soaps and sniff every single sample. She never tired of saying, 'Smell this one, Sophie. Guess what it's made of.'

'Mommy doesn't need any soap. She told me that the last day. I wanted to buy one that smelt of daffodils.'

Sophie urged the kid on, hoping they'd pick up Ethan before Angeline became impossibly grumpy.

'I'm too tired to go shopping, Sophie. I want to go home and see Mommy and Daddy and Ethan.' Angel was starting to whine. Never a promising sign.

'Look, we're almost there.'

Just one more corner and they'd make it. She would just have to introduce Angeline and Miss L to one another and make up some story about bumping into her. The plan was for them to meet the next day anyway, so where was the harm? Except that Angel, in this mood, was unlikely to make a good first impression on the grandma she'd never met.

Sophie hoped Miss L wouldn't be mad at her for being late, then reminded herself that her employer was the one who'd caused all this drama by not bringing Ethan back when she'd promised. She had promised Sophie she'd be there ten minutes ahead of schedule and she was at least half an hour late. The moral high ground, were there to be any fault finding, was all Sophie's.

'Here we are,' said Sophie, relief making her voice much louder and jollier than necessary. Angel gave her an odd look, as did a couple of elderly tourists.

Sophie ignored them and scanned the narrow street for Miss L. No sign. A sick feeling that she'd been trying to ignore was getting worse by the minute. Like a bellyache that starts off mild and builds.

Angel was hauling on her arm now, whinging about going home to see Mommy.

'Shut up!' Sophie wrenched her hand out of the child's grasp. Angel looked at her, stunned, then burst into tears. Sophie knelt and took Angel into her arms. While she whispered words of comfort into the child's ear she searched every face in the passing crowd.

'Let's go in the café,' said Sophie. 'We'll get you some hot chocolate.'

'I don't want hot chocolate. I want to go home.' The last word rose in a wail that echoed up the high walls of the little street.

'Let's go,' hissed Sophie, and dragged the kid by her sweatshirt. A woman tutted in disapproval and Sophie glowered back.

The café had chairs upturned on most of its tables. Only one was occupied – by a man reading the newspaper.

'We're closing,' said Waitress of the Year, as much for the man's benefit as for Sophie's, she thought.

'Has there been a grandmother in, looking as if she was waiting for someone?'

The waitress's face was blank and uninterested. Sophie grudged her generous, if accidental, tip of a few hours earlier.

'The woman has grey hair,' Sophie stopped, realising she'd no idea what else she could say about Miss L.

The waitress had already turned away towards the lone customer.

'Sophie?'

Angel's tear-stained face looked up at her. 'Please can we go home now?'

'Course we can. Sorry.' She got down on her knees and said, 'Climb on. You deserve a lift.'

'Yay, piggy back,' said Angel, swiping at the last few tears.

Sophie set off at a trot, Angel bouncing on her back. Between giggles she said, 'Why are we going this way, Sophie?'

'I thought maybe we'd go check out those cute ducklings on our way home.'

She couldn't tell the kid why she was taking a circuitous route, but it wasn't because she fancied a walk. Angel was much heavier than she looked and Sophie wasn't sure how far she could carry her like this. The child had already walked much further than she normally would and Sophie didn't want to force her. But they couldn't go home until she'd searched for Ethan.

What if something had happened to Miss L and the child? So many things could go wrong. Innocent folks got hurt all the time. A driver losing control of his vehicle and killing pedestrians. She'd heard of that happening. Or Miss L could have taken ill, a stroke or something horrible like that. Something that meant she couldn't communicate and tell people she had a little boy to look after. Crazy thoughts raced through Sophie's mind. Maybe Miss L had decided to keep Ethan? Now, that was beyond crazy.

Chapter 27

As she waited in a queue of cars Diane checked her paperwork, again. Every detail had been double- and triple-checked before she left the States. She'd invested a lot of time in the planning of this project and the anticipation of success had kept her sane.

As a US citizen she'd need to complete a landing card, but she'd been assured there would be no problem, even travelling on a US passport in a French car. A bonus was that all the admin would be dealt with before she boarded the ship. Maybe that meant she'd be able to relax a little. If she made it on board.

Only one car ahead of her now. It stopped at border control and the driver handed over a bunch of passports. They were handed back almost immediately. The barrier rose and the car pulled away.

Diane swallowed and allowed her car to creep forward to the kiosk.

The man behind the glass looked up from his mobile phone, glanced at her passport and waved her through. Seemed the Spanish authorities didn't care who was leaving the country.

She caught up with the car in front and waited till it passed through British immigration. A young woman who seemed far too young to be official, even with her hair scraped back into a severe ponytail, gazed at Diane.

'Passport?' she said. No smile, no hello.

Diane handed over her paperwork. The woman looked at it, checked a screen and said, 'You'll have to complete a landing card on board and hand it in at the purser's desk.' She studied Diane's photo and gave her a long look. Diane crossed her fingers that she'd worn the same wig for the photo as she'd put on this morning. She decided it was time to play her trump. Touching her hair, she said, 'I know what you're thinking and you're right.'

There was no official response.

'It's a wig,' said Diane.

The young woman looked mortified, just as Diane had hoped.

'Not cancer, at least we don't think so.' She waited a moment to let that one sink in, then leaned forward a little as if she were letting the young woman in on a secret and said, 'Alopecia. Completely bald. Thank the good Lord wigs are allowed in passport photos or I'd never travel again. And that would be my bucket list ruined.' She laughed and, to her relief, the woman laughed too.

'What's the purpose of your trip?'

'Well, you see, I've never been to Britain before. Decided it was time to put that one right. Such a lot of breathtaking places to visit.' Diane started to recite her fictitious itinerary.

As she'd anticipated, the immigration officer cut her short halfway through the sights of London. 'Tourism, then?'

Diane smiled her most charming smile and said, 'Sorry, I get so excited. Yes, tourism.'

The young woman hit a key on her keyboard, handed over Diane's papers and fluttered her fingers in a tiny goodbye. 'Have a good trip, madam.'

She was through.

No one gave her a second glance as she carried her bundle of fleecy blanket from the car deck to the cabin. The few people that were around were too busy seeing to their own overnight luggage and finding their way.

She laid the little blanket-wrapped body on the lower bunk, closed the heavy metal door to their cabin and locked it behind her. As she hurried back to the car for the rest of her things the smell of trapped exhaust fumes stung her throat. The car deck was filling up now and a large four-by-four was parked so close behind her own vehicle, she struggled to raise its tailgate. She cussed quietly to herself in a most unladylike manner. Then she squeezed herself like a contortionist into the small space and grabbed what she needed.

When she'd dumped everything on the lower bunk at Ethan's feet, she looked at the child and carefully pulled the cover away from his face. All the bright pink had gone from his cheeks and he lay pale as a doll. Perfectly still, no sign of life.

In a panic, she put her face close to his. Nothing. She gave him a shake but he didn't stir. She knelt on the floor and touched one fingertip to his skinny little neck, frail as a bird's. She felt for a tiny beat. There it was. A flutter of life. Or did she imagine it? She bent towards his face. The faintest breath touched her cheek. Then another and another. Gradually her heart stopped racing. She sat on the bunk and blew out all the tension she'd been feeling since she first put the child in her car.

What on earth she was doing?

She still had options.

No one knew she'd brought a child on board. She could leave him asleep in the cabin, drive off at the other end and no one would be any the wiser. She could get the first flight home and she'd be back in her beautiful house as if none of this had ever happened. A pang of homesickness jabbed at her. The temperatures would have cooled some with the time of year, but it would still be warm in the daytime and cool enough to sleep at night. Right about now, early evening, was her favourite time of day. She'd sit on the porch with a cocktail, smell the late roses and wait for the sun to go down before dinner.

Deep below her she could hear the throb of the great engines warming up to take them away from here. Other than that, nothing. She knew there were passengers in both neighbouring cabins. She'd seen one grey-haired, beige-clad couple go in next door, bickering about who would have to take the top bunk. On the other side, while she'd seen no one, the cabin door had been propped open when she was looking for her own and closed when she came back from her second run to the car. And yet there was no sound of voices. This would be an ideal place to make her phone call. If she could get a signal.

'Sophie, my dear.'

'Thank God! Are you okay?'

'I'm better than okay, thank you.'

'What about E?' There was a pause and then a few words, presumably to the little girl. Sophie's voice sounded muffled, as if she had her hand over the phone when she spoke again. 'What about you know who? Is he okay? I've been worried.'

'He's sleeping like an angel, don't you worry.'

'I *am* worried. What kept you? Where are you?'

'Which question would you like me to answer first?'

'I don't know. Where are you, I guess. I need to come and pick up the item you have belonging to me.'

'Strictly speaking, my dear, he doesn't belong to you, does he?'

'No, of course he doesn't, but you know what I mean. Listen, I don't know what's going on here, but I do know that you have to get that item back to me within the next hour, or I'm in deep trouble.'

'That's why I'm making this courtesy call. To let you know that won't be possible.'

'What the hell are you talking about?'

'Ethan won't be coming home tonight. Or any time soon. You'd better start thinking about what you plan to tell his parents when they get back. I expect a smart girl like you to be quite imaginative when it comes to explaining what happened today.'

There was a silence at the other end. She could hear a little girl's voice saying Sophie's name over and over in a most unattractive whine. She was glad she'd chosen the boy, for so many reasons.

'Is this some kind of a joke?' She could hear the shake in Sophie's voice. Could tell she was trying to keep it under control.

'No joke.'

'Have you taken leave of your senses?'

'I won't dignify that with an answer.'

'But you can't do this. You can't just take a, you know what.'

'I just have.'

'You're fucking crazy! I'm gonna call the police.'

'One, that is entirely inappropriate language to use in front of a small child. Two, think very carefully before you call the police, Sophie. And three, please Google the penalty for conspiring to abduct a child and for aiding and abetting child abduction.'

'Are you completely mad? I'm not guilty of conspiring to do anything. You told me you were a grandma who couldn't see her grandkids. I thought all you wanted was a chance to meet them, to get to know them.'

'And I travelled all the way to Europe to do that? Have you any idea how insane that sounds, Sophie?'

'You're fucking insane!'

'Language, language.'

'Where are you? I'm coming to get him. Right now.'

'Don't think so. Anyway, Sophie, it's been lovely chatting with you but I must dash. Oh, just one more thing. Check the balance on that internet account we set up. I don't think you'll be disappointed.'

Chapter 28

'Hello-oh! We're home! Where's my best girl?'

Angel sprinted to the door and jumped into Penny's arms. Penny hugged her tightly and whispered, 'I've missed you so much. Wait till you see what I've got for you.'

'Where's Daddy?'

'He's paying the cab. He'll be right in.' She put Angeline down and the child ran out to greet her father. Penny looked around. 'Where's Ethan? Is he asleep already?'

Seth came bustling in with one bag in each hand and his daughter hanging from his neck. 'Boy, that's some welcome,' he said. 'We should go away more often. Where's the little guy?'

'He's on a play date,' said Angeline, kissing her father's chin.

'A play date?' said Penny, looking at Sophie for an explanation.

'Yes, with his new friend,' said Angel. She let go of her dad, dropped to the floor and ran to her mother. 'Mommy. Can I see my present?'

'In a minute, Angel,' said Penny. 'First I want to hear about Ethan's new friend.'

'Penny,' said Sophie, 'we need to talk.'

Something in Sophie's voice made Penny's stomach curdle. She instinctively gathered Angel into the protective circle of her arms.

'Is this about Ethan?' said Seth.

Penny said, 'Apparently he's on a play date. With a new friend. I'm not sure how comfortable I feel with that idea.'

Seth came and put his arm round her shoulder. 'Loosen up, Penny. It's great that the little fella has made a friend. I'm sure he'll be back soon. Is he being dropped off, Sophie, or do you have to scoot and collect him?'

'Seth. He's two years old. He doesn't have any friends. Does he, Sophie?'

Sophie shook her head.

Seth's voice turned serious. 'What's going on here, Sophie?'

'I think Ethan's lost,' said Angel.

Penny and Seth stared at their daughter.

Seth said sharply, 'Don't be silly, Angeline.' He looked at Sophie's face and said, 'Penny, why don't I take Angel upstairs and get her ready for bed? Leave you and Sophie to talk.'

'But I haven't had my present yet.'

Penny unzipped her overnight case and pulled out a plastic carrier bag. Her eyes on Sophie she said, 'Here, sweetie. Go on upstairs with Daddy. You can open this once you're in your PJs.'

'Can't I open it now?'

'You heard Mommy. PJs first.' Seth made a move for the stairs. 'Come on,' he said, 'I'll race you.'

Penny felt as if time had slowed down. Seth and Angel seemed to take forever to reach the top of the stairs.

Finally, the two women were alone.

'Penny, I don't know how to say this.'

'Just tell me what's happened. Is he in hospital? Please tell me he's okay. Is he okay?'

Sophie shook her head.

'He's not okay?' Penny could not put her next question into words. Could not utter her worst fear.

'No. Yes! I don't know. I've lost him.'

'Lost him? What are you saying? Lost him where?' Penny, suddenly understanding what was going on, smiled. 'I get it,' she whispered. 'He's hiding, isn't he? Angel used to love this game when she was his age. She'd stand behind the curtain with her little legs sticking out the bottom.' Penny walked in circles around the room, saying theatrically, 'Oops. Ethan's lost. Now, let me think. Where can he be?'

She listened for his giggles, expecting him to toddle out from the sofa.

She looked behind it, shouting, sing-song, 'Ethan. Come out, come out, wherever you are.'

From upstairs, Angel called, 'Ethan's not here, Mommy. Just me.'

Penny continued to shout, but with less fun in her voice, 'Ethan! Come to Mommy. Come here, baby.'

'Mommy! He's not here. Daddy, tell her.'

Seth appeared at the top of the stairs. 'What the hell's going on?'

Jovial again, Penny said, 'Sophie says Ethan's lost. Now that's just silly. How can he be lost? He must be hiding. Help me find him, Daddy. He must be here somewhere. You look under the stairs.'

Seth gave Sophie a long look. She shrugged, which made Penny want to slap her. Why the shrug? What did that even mean?

'Is Ethan here, Sophie?' asked Seth, his voice sombre.

'No.'

'Then you have to tell us where he is. Right now. Was there a play date?'

'No.'

'A friend?'

'No.'

Seth smacked his forehead. 'Jesus, Sophie. Why couldn't you have told us this right away?'

'Seth, please tell me this isn't happening?' Penny could hear her voice rising, remembered Angel upstairs and told herself to calm down. She took Sophie's hands in hers and spoke quietly. 'Look at me, Sophie.'

She could see the girl was in agony. Shouting at her would not help. 'Sophie, you need to tell me what's going on, because right now I feel like I must be dreaming. So, please, let's sit down and, whatever it is that's happened, just tell me. Okay?'

Sophie nodded and Penny led her, like a child, over to the big wooden table and drew out two chairs.

The girl seemed reluctant to speak. As if she were afraid.

'Seth, honey. Can you see to Angel, please?'

'No way. I need to hear this.' He prowled behind the two of them, head down, hands in pockets.

Sophie seemed unsure what to say, or perhaps where to start. Penny wanted to give her a shake and say, 'Get on with it,' but she used all her self-control to stay silent.

Sophie started to speak but seemed to have lost her voice. She cleared her throat and began again. 'Ethan and I went for a walk.' She gestured round the room. 'I'd done all the housework. Wanted the place to look nice for you getting back.'

Penny nodded, trying to look more encouraging than impatient.

'Ethan fell asleep in the stroller.'

As usual.

'He's been so good while you were gone, I, like, wanted to buy him something?'

Penny nodded again, no idea where this was going, but in a hurry to get there.

'You know the souvenir shop in the Cité? The one with the suit of armour, and all the plastic swords and stuff?'

Another nod.

'You know how it's always such a crush inside? I parked the stroller, like, just by the door?'

'With Ethan in it?' Penny shook her head over and over as she spoke. 'Please tell me you didn't.'

'It was just for a moment.'

'You left my baby in his stroller outside a shop in a crowded street?'

Sophie dipped her head, broke eye contact. Penny grabbed her shoulder and shook. 'Then what?'

'I came back out. And he was, like, gone.' The girl spread her hands, as if she'd just completed one of her magic tricks.

'What do you mean, gone?'

'Just gone. Like vanished. Disappeared.'

Penny got to her feet. Raked her hands through her hair and held on to two handfuls. 'The stroller? Or just the baby?' Her voice broke on the word.

'Both.'

'And you're sure you took him with you?' Penny realised what a stupid question that was. The look on Sophie's face confirmed it.

'Have you called the police?' asked Seth.

Sophie shook her head. 'I wanted to wait till you got home.'

Penny started pacing the floor. Back and forth, trying to decide what to do next. Incredibly calm. In control. Aware that she had to keep that steely composure in place.

'Go and get Angeline ready for bed. Tell her nothing.' Penny searched for a topic that would interest a child whose little brother had gone missing. 'Talk about the gift we brought. Distract her. Then somehow get her to sleep.'

'She'll be tired. We walked a long way today.'

'Looking for Ethan?'

'Yes.'

Penny shook her head, disgusted. 'Go see to the children. I mean, child.'

She turned to Seth. He looked ten years older than the carefree husband who'd walked in the door. Toulouse seemed like a lifetime ago. Penny wished with all her heart she'd never heard of the damn place.

'Come over here, babe,' said Seth. He crushed her in his arms. It felt good, for a nanosecond. Then she pulled away.

'Oh, Seth,' she said, looking at his stricken face. 'Where is he?'

'He's been taken. No wonder. That fucking idiot abandoned him in the street.'

She'd never heard him so angry. He rarely swore. She understood his need. 'What are we gonna do?' she asked.

'We're gonna call the police.'

'No, Seth. We're not.'

Chapter 29

After her phone call to Sophie, Diane had stayed on deck until mainland Europe disappeared into the distance and her cashmere wrap could no longer keep out the chill of the evening sea air. She couldn't quite believe she'd got away with this, but apart from one terrifying moment, when a police car raced along towards the terminal, lights flashing and sirens screaming, all had gone according to plan. The police had sped on by, in pursuit of some other criminal, and Diane had known she was safe. For the next twenty hours at least.

A criminal. That's what she was. Dress it up every which way, she was still a criminal. Just like her husband. No, not quite as bad as him. She hadn't killed anyone. Yet.

Diane swung by the cafeteria and picked up some snacks to take back to the cabin. She would eat a proper meal later, in full view of everyone. Resplendent in red wig and make-up. Someone would be bound to remember a striking woman travelling alone.

Although the company claimed their ship offered a cruise experience, it was like no cruise she'd ever been on. Entertainment seemed to be restricted to the mediocre duo in the corner who were crooning a poor cover version of a song from the seventies. A look around the bar suggested the decade represented glory days for most of the clientele. She'd never seen so much grey hair in one place. As she ordered a gin and tonic an old boy at the end of the bar gave her a lascivious wink. Was he coming on to her? Seriously? She looked away, horrified, and smiled at the young barman. Much more to her taste.

Diane had no desire to go back to the cabin. She had planned to sit for a while and people watch, but the geriatric Lothario at the bar still had his eye on her and she couldn't bear to have to speak to him. Further along the deck was a quiet lounge that was surprisingly empty. She found herself a club chair with a small table and settled down.

How on earth had it come to this? She could not imagine a scenario further from the idyllic retirement she had planned ten years ago. Before the Twin Towers crumbled into ruins and her life with them. Scott had always talked about leaving New York and finding a 'real ritzy place' in the Hamptons or on the Cape. When they had enough money. And that was the root of the whole sorry mess. Scott never believed he had enough money.

If only she'd told him about her private fortune, the one he still didn't know about. Maybe she could have prevented those awful things he did. Many a night she'd lain awake till dawn, doubt gnawing at her brain like a scavenging rat. Was she responsible for Charlotte's death?

In daylight, she could tell herself not to be ridiculous. She had nothing to do with Charlotte's death. That was all down to Scott. Charlotte's death and the others. Maybe not *all* down to Scott. If Charlotte had kept her hands off another woman's husband, none of this would have happened. Scott wouldn't be in prison and Diane wouldn't be a fugitive on the high seas with an abducted child in her cabin.

She reached for her glass. The ice cubes chinked merrily and the bubbles tickled her nose as she took a deep drink. The cold liquid slid over her throat, refreshing and calming.

No, she would not blame Scott or Charlotte for *this* situation. It was of her own making and her own design, and in fact she was rather proud of how well it was all going. She had planned well.

Originally her dream of revenge had been just that, a dream. An initial flurry of invitations had dried up and she'd been forced to accept that they'd been spurred by curiosity and not support. Suddenly *all* their friends were 'busy' when she tried to organise a dinner party. Time was, most folks would have killed for an invitation to their beautiful home. She and Scott had been famed for their hospitality. Scott was the most charming and generous host, welcoming and genial. And they had always made a point of including single guests, even if it meant an odd number at table. My goodness, just because someone was unfortunate enough to be widowed or divorced, didn't mean she or he became persona non grata. Seemed not everyone shared her point of view. A husband in prison made her different from the poor widows and divorced philanderers. She became what her mother would have called a 'social outcast'. One friend, well-meaning, perhaps, had tried to explain when Diane had called her up and burst into tears.

'You see, Diane, it's not just that Scott's in jail. It's why he's in jail that we're finding difficult to come to terms with.'

'I understand that. Even though he's my husband and I still love him, I'll be the first to say he deserves to be in jail for what he did. But Scott's the criminal here, not me.'

'I *know* that, sweetheart, but ... oh, maybe I shouldn't say this.'

'Say it, please. I need to know what's going on, what people are saying. You're the only one prepared to even take my call, bless your heart.'

'Well ... it's just that, you know how it is ... some of us don't understand how you could know nothing about Scott's plans. There. I've said it.'

Diane had struggled to find first the breath and then the words to answer.

'How can you even suggest that, May-belle? We've been friends since third grade. Do you really think I could have known what Scott was up to and allowed him to go ahead?'

Diane had let the silence at the other end last for ten seconds. She counted them in her head. Then she quietly laid the phone back in its dock. May-belle hadn't called back.

Diane didn't visit Scott. No one visited her. She had no reason to remain in New York.

She moved back to Louisiana. Became a recluse. Her hair began to fall out, first in clumps on her brush, then in handfuls.

Even if she'd had somewhere to go, she wouldn't have dreamt of leaving the house.

The house. The beautiful big house. Built by her great-grandfather. Extended and modernised by her father. Her pride and joy. She'd loved that house right from childhood. Thank the good Lord she'd kept it in her name. And now it too was gone. No point in keeping a house that size. Far too big for one person, even with live-in staff. And far too full of memories. Each day she rose to the reminder of all she'd lost.

Her thoughts had gradually turned darker, despite the medication. Vengeance had become not a dream but a project. It had given her something to live for. Giving shape to her days and a purpose to her existence. She had started to feel well again and for a while her hair had even made a reappearance, although nothing she'd ever want to be seen in public with. She had her standards. On her darkest days, when she never crossed the threshold, the only person who saw her poor, pathetic scalp was Emmeline, the most loyal maid a woman could ever have.

Emmy was more like a mother to her than Diane's had ever been. Convincing Scott to keep Emmy on, once they were married, had been difficult but Diane had stuck to her guns. And Emmeline had moved with her to their mansion in New York State.

'No lady should ever be without a lady's maid,' Diane had said in her best spoilt-princess voice. The one she'd always used on her daddy. And she'd got her way. Scott never could say no to that voice.

She smiled as she thought of Emmy, way beyond retirement age, but still looking after Diane when the world crashed around her. She hadn't been able to do much, but Diane paid other staff to cook and clean for her. Anyway, that had never been Emmeline's role. She was a confidante, an advisor, a sorter of underwear and tidier of closets. Not to forget her most important role in recent times, keeper of the wigs. It was Emmeline who first suggested Diane wear a wig.

'What else you gonna do? Stay locked up till your hair grows back? And what if it never grows back? Get yourself a wig, Miss Diane. The best that money can buy. Ain't nobody 'cept me will ever know anything about it. Look at Dolly Parton. Wearin' a wig ain't done her no harm.'

Emmy had quoted Dolly's famous line about her wigs. 'People always ask me how long it takes to do my hair. I don't know, I'm never there.'

Emmeline just loved Dolly. Knew all the words to all the songs and would sing them as she went about the house. She liked to quote the woman she considered the greatest philosopher of all time.

'We cannot direct the wind, but we can adjust the sails,' she'd said the day Diane first wore her wig. 'Go on, get out there. Whole lotta your life still waiting to be lived.'

Emmy would live out *her* life in the comfort of the little house Diane had bought for her on St Ann Street, just off Orleans Avenue in Tremé.

Diane wished Emmy was with her right now. She could sure use one of her pep talks. 'Come on, now, Miss Diane,' she'd always say. 'Ain't no use lying in bed all day, just frettin' yourself to a shadow.'

Emmeline knew nothing of Diane's plan, other than she was going on a trip to Europe, finally getting to visit Paris. Scott had always refused to leave the States. 'Why would you want to go all that way, Diane?' he'd say when she suggested a vacation or a cruise. 'We have everything here – mountains, seas, deserts, canyons.'

'I'd like to see some history.'

'History? We have history here. I'll take you to Boston. Do you know, they have a house there built in 1661? Go figure!'

She'd given up trying to convince him that by history she'd been thinking of the Acropolis in Athens, dating from fourteen centuries BC. Scott, gifted though he was with numbers, didn't get it. Dollars he could reckon in billions. Years, not so much.

The last time she'd seen Emmy, they'd gone to Café du Monde and sat amongst the tourists, eating beignets. As the icing sugar floated around them like mist, Emmy had sighed, deeply satisfied. 'I been longing to come here since I was five years old.'

'Oh, Emmy, I wish you'd told me that before.'

'The old Miss Diane would never have been seen dead in here, now would she?'

Diane had smiled, knowing Emmy was right. 'Never mind that. Was it worth the wait?'

'Sure was. Best beignets I ever did taste.'

'Should we order some more?'

'No, thank you. I'm already fit to bustin', but I could sure use another coffee.'

Later Diane had taken Emmeline home and hugged her on the little front porch. Diane had never been inside the house. When it was time to say goodbye she'd been so emotional, Emmeline had said, 'Why the tears? You know somethin' I don't know? Think I won't be here when y'all come back?'

At that point, Diane had thought her plan too wild to succeed. How could you abduct a child in broad daylight and then smuggle him out of the country? Impossible. And yet, she'd just done it.

'Mind if I join you?'

Diane looked up into a pair of pale rheumy eyes. Under a canopy of ginger-grey eyebrows they stared at her hopefully.

Taking her silence for consent, he sat down.

Diane stood so quickly the last dregs of her cocktail spilled over the glass and splashed onto the table.

'Can I get you another drink?'

'No. No, thank you. I'm feeling rather seasick. I think I need to go to my cabin and lie down.'

Chapter 30

'Go to sleep, Angel.'

Sophie tucked the covers under the child's chin and patted her gently.

'Sophie?'

'Yes, pet?'

'Where's Ethan?'

'Didn't Daddy tell you?'

'Daddy said to go to sleep. Will Ethan be here when I wake up?'

'Is that what Daddy said?'

The child nodded, her face solemn.

'It must be true, then. And the sooner you go to sleep, the sooner you'll see your little brother.'

Sophie felt the words catch in her throat.

'You know my Ballerina Barbie?'

'Yes.'

'It's my very favourite in, like, all the world.'

'I know.'

'I'm going to give it to Ethan tomorrow.'

Sophie couldn't speak. She leaned over and kissed the child on the brow, wishing she could turn back time.

'Sophie?'

'Yes?'

'Why were you saying bad words?'

'When?'

'Earlier. On the phone.'

Shit! Had the kid overheard? Sophie frantically tried to remember what she'd said. She'd been guarded, she thought. Hadn't mentioned Ethan by name. Or had she?

'I don't remember. I suppose I was angry. Sometimes grown-ups say bad words when they're angry.'

'Were you angry 'cos we couldn't find Ethan?'

Sophie didn't answer.

'Is that why Mommy and Daddy are angry? 'Cos you lost Ethan?'

Downstairs Seth and Penny were arguing about the police. Sophie wanted to tell them to lower their voices. Angel heard a lot more than they thought.

'We're *not* going to the police,' shouted Penny. 'Anyway, what's the point? We can't even talk to them.'

'Sophie can talk to them. She can speak French.'

Sophie hadn't thought of that. The French police would want to talk to her. She'd better get her story straight.

'We have to get her down here.' Seth's voice rose from the foot of the stairs. 'Sophie!'

'Oh dear,' whispered Angel. 'You're in trouble.'

Sophie went and stood on the landing. 'Angel's still awake,' she said.

'Can you come down here, please? We need you to call the police. Explain what's happened.'

'No, Seth, wait! We have to think about this.'

'There's nothing to think about.'

'Seth, we are *not* calling the police.' Penny's tone was harsh. 'Put the phone away.'

He turned his back on his wife. 'What's the number for the French police, Sophie?'

'I don't know. I can Google it.'

'Don't you dare! We don't need the police, Sophie. We haven't even looked properly ourselves yet. You can't report your child is lost and then say you haven't even looked for him. What kind of parents does that make us?'

There was a certain logic to her point, but Sophie had already looked everywhere she could think of. Also, it was no good looking in Carcassonne. Ethan was gone. But she could hardly tell them that.

Seth put his phone back in his pocket. 'Alright, Penny. I think this is a mistake, but I can see your point.' He grabbed his jacket. 'What are we waiting for? Let's get going.' He made for the door.

'Wait! We can't all just dash off. What about Angel?'

'What about me?' asked a small voice. The child appeared on the top step. It was clear she had been eavesdropping. 'I want to go look for Ethan too.'

Penny burst into tears. Seth took her in his arms and soothed her. He looked at Sophie over the top of Penny's head.

'I'll take Angel,' he said. 'That way we can all go searching, cover a bigger area.' He smiled up at his child. 'Go put some warm clothes on, Angel. On top of your pyjamas. It'll get cold later.'

Sophie ran up the stairs. 'I'll help her.'

'No,' said Penny through her tears, 'I'll go. You should tell Seth where to search. Where you last saw our son.'

Seth gave Sophie a look that was a lot more sympathetic than she deserved. If only this man knew how she'd betrayed them, he'd have his hands round her neck right now, squeezing the life out of her.

Seth took a kid's drawing pad from Penny's preschool corner. As he flicked over the pages, Sophie caught sight of Ethan's drawings, wild swipes of crayon filling sheet after sheet.

On a fresh page, Seth drew two felt-tip lines from top to bottom. At the top of each of the three columns he wrote a name. He paused and looked at Sophie. 'Where do you want to start?'

'I don't know. I already looked all around the Cité. In fact, I already looked everywhere I could think of.'

Seth put the pen down and leaned back in his chair. He ran his hands through his hair and raised his face to the ceiling.

At the end of a long exhalation he said, 'Sophie, are we wasting our time here? Shouldn't we be calling the police, if you've already looked everywhere you could think of?'

She didn't know what to say and shrugged to show him that. She was way in over her head. Her priority had become self-preservation.

'I'm ready, Daddy,' said Angeline. 'Can we go?' Sophie thought the child sounded as if this was a big adventure and to her it possibly was. Heading out into the night with her daddy, helping look for Ethan. As casually as they might search for a stray kitten.

'Sorry, Angel, we're not going.'

'What do you mean?' said Penny. 'We're not going? Seth, of course we're going.'

He gave his wife a hard look. 'No, we're going to phone the police.'

Penny put her hands on her daughter's shoulders and moved her away from her father's side. 'Sophie,' she said, 'can you come and stand by Angel for a moment while I have a word with Seth, please?'

Penny leaned over the table but managed to keep her face turned away from Sophie and the child, so lip-reading wasn't a possibility. Penny's voice was low and desperate. While trying to distract Angel with a book, Sophie strained to hear the conversation at the other side of the room. She could hear it, but she couldn't understand it.

'Seth, what are you thinking? We *can't* call the police. They're gonna need our names. What are we gonna do? Give them false identities? Think about it for a minute.'

'There's nothing false about Ethan's identity. He's little Ethan Gates, our son. He's two years old and he's out there somewhere. Lost. You think about *that* for a minute.'

'I have thought about it. Calling the police is a risk we can't take at this stage. We might find him. At least let's look and then if, God forbid, we don't find him, we'll call the cops. I promise.'

'And what if we've wasted valuable time by then?'

'We're wasting valuable time right now.' She tapped the drawing pad. 'Come on. Draw up a quick plan of action and let's get going.' She turned from the table. 'You girls good to go?'

Sophie nodded, astounded at the woman's cool head. A minute ago she sounded hysterical.

'Then come on over here and tell us where we should start looking, Sophie.'

Seth lifted the pen and removed the cap. 'You've got two hours, Penny. Then I'm calling the cops.'

Chapter 31

Diane ate the snacks she'd bought earlier. She couldn't face dinner on her own, at the mercy of every lonely old Romeo who might be aboard. Besides, it made sense to be with the child, just in case he woke up. She hadn't decided what she would do if and when he did.

For the briefest of moments, she considered taking the little bundle up on deck and throwing it overboard. The kid would feel nothing. If the fall didn't kill him the icy cold water of the Atlantic would do the job within seconds. The shock of hitting water that cold might even do it instantly. Or he'd soon drown, dragged down by the black fleece blanket, invisible in the dark waters.

Then she could drive off at the other side, free to get on with her life. Ethan's mother would never find out what happened to her kid. She'd spend the rest of her life looking, watching, waiting. Praying for a miracle to bring him back.

No, that wasn't enough. Diane had a plan and she wasn't going to abandon it that easily. Also, when it came to the nitty gritty, Diane didn't know if she was capable of throwing a child to his death. Even Lucie Jardine's child. But she might find out. If Lucie failed the ultimate test.

While she'd been gone, Ethan had cast off the fleece cover and it lay in a tangle about his little legs. She pulled it free and folded it up. The cabin was warm. With its metal walls and bare floor, it resembled a prison cell, not unlike the one Scott had described to her in a letter one time. Diane had no wish to know what the inside of a cell looked like and certainly had no intention of finding out.

She stroked Ethan's bare leg where his trousers had bunched up. The skin was softer than anything she'd ever touched before. And his face, so innocent and sweet.

Diane looked away, as if she might be smitten with some emotion she'd rather not name or feel. The upper bunk caught her eye. How on earth was she going to get up there? She had to sleep. She had a long drive ahead of her. Provided there were no police waiting for her in Portsmouth docks.

The parents must be back by now. Must know the kid was gone. She wondered what Sophie would have told them. Knowing what she did about human nature, she would bet her entire fortune that Sophie had not confessed to her part in the abduction. Diane had set it up so that Sophie might genuinely feel she had not done anything too awful. Helping reunite a grandmother with the grandchildren she was prevented from seeing. When she found out there was no family relationship between Diane and the Gates family she might feel differently, of course. But she'd only find out if she came clean. That was unlikely. Sophie was an intelligent young woman. She wouldn't have been hired otherwise. Right now, she would be running through all her options. Confessing to his parents that she'd left Ethan with a woman he didn't really know would not be her favourite, Diane was sure of it.

What she would give to be a fly on that wall. To hear whatever tale Sophie had made up to explain losing a toddler. To see his parents' reaction to the situation, whether they were blaming and accusing Sophie or being tolerant of her mistake and blaming each other. She hoped the little girl wasn't too upset. She would have taken them both if she could, but that was a logistic impossibility. As it was she was dreading Ethan waking up.

She watched him open his eyes and close them again. He blinked a few times as if he were trying to make sense of his surroundings. There was nothing familiar for him to see. Not a single thing. He seemed to register this fact and his face crumpled in preparation for a howl.

'Hello, Ethan,' she said. 'Mawmaw's here. Did you have a nice sleep?'

She had expected the child to recognise her, then remembered she was wearing the red wig. He'd only seen her with grey, granny hair. She snatched the wig off and the child's face registered his surprise. His puckered features smoothed out again and he watched her, apparently fascinated. Diane stuck the wig roughly on her head and then, with a flourish and a 'Ta-da!' pulled it off again. Ethan smiled uncertainly. She wigged and de-wigged herself a third time, complete with silly sound effects. The child sat up to get a better view. She plonked the wig on his head. It fell over his eyes, but he smiled at her. She pulled the wig off and he looked less certain, so she stuck it back on. 'Funny Ethan,' she said. 'Look in the mirror.' She pointed to the full-length mirror opposite the bed and the child looked, at first a little shocked and then amused. He pulled it off, then tried to stick it on again. The kid was playing dress-up with a thousand-dollar wig, but what the hell. When he giggled, Diane felt as if she'd achieved something marvellous. Maybe this wouldn't be so tricky after all.

Then Ethan said, 'Mommy?'

'Mommy's not here right now, Ethan. We'll see Mommy soon.'

'Daddy?'

'Daddy too. Real soon, okay?'

'Angel?'

'Yes, and Angel too. Don't you worry.'

He seemed to accept her promises and went back to admiring himself in the mirror. Diane offered him a piece of the sandwich she'd picked up earlier.

'Is Ethan hungry?'

The child took it eagerly and stuffed so much into his mouth Diane was worried he'd choke. She wished she'd taken a course in childcare before she'd embarked on this malarkey. But she hadn't wanted to arouse suspicion and it was too late now.

After what seemed like ages, Ethan finally swallowed and said, 'More peese.' This time she broke off a smaller piece and he popped it into his mouth, chewed and swallowed.

'More?' she asked, hoping he wasn't too hungry. She didn't have a lot of food in the cabin. He nodded and said, 'Ess, peese.'

He polished off every scrap of sandwich and then a banana. What an appetite for a small child.

Suddenly he scrambled off the bed.

'Go potty!'

Diane had no idea what to do. She opened the door to the toilet and helped him over the metal threshold. Ethan stood by the toilet bowl, clearly in need of help. 'Pants off,' he commanded. Diane knelt in the tiny space and pulled off his trousers and underpants. 'Up,' he said. She lifted him onto the seat and supported him under his arms. He grunted for a bit then sighed and, just as she was about to lift him down, a fountain of pee sprayed all over her skirt. She tried to move out of the way, but couldn't let go of the child. Ethan saw what was happening and laughed as if he had just fired off the world's best water pistol. As the front of her pale skirt darkened, he said, 'Oops, what a mess!' then giggled some more. Diane couldn't help joining in.

She got them both cleaned up and washed her hands and his. His face could wait till morning. She didn't want to push her luck. 'I think it's time for Ethan's pyjamas,' she said, and produced a brand-new pair from her bag. She'd had to guess the size and had gone for too big rather than too small. The trousers hung off the ends of his legs and the sleeves covered his hands, but Ethan didn't seem bothered. 'Like a story, Ethan?'

'*Dear Zoo*,' said Ethan, 'Daddy read.'

Diane had never heard of *Dear Zoo*. She produced the books she'd brought and said, 'Look, Ethan. *Little Blue Truck*. This one?'

'*Dear Zoo*,' said Ethan, sounding more determined. 'Daddy read.'

'*The Wheels on the Bus*. Look. Shall we sing?'

No response. Ethan crossed his arms and did a very good impression of sulking. Oh dear, this was not looking good.

'What about this one? *Doggies*. It's a counting and barking book. That will be fun.' She turned the pages, saying and barking the numbers and, glory be, the kid responded.

Diane checked her watch. It was only nine o'clock and she was completely worn out. She couldn't keep this song and dance routine going all night. After the fifth time through the book, Ethan lay down. Diane said, 'Want to jump under the covers?' She was amazed when he did.

She pulled the sheet and blanket up to his chin and was wondering whether it would be a good to give him a goodnight kiss, when Ethan said, 'Hoppy.'

Hoppy the rabbit, Ethan's favourite. Diane was sure she'd tucked it in the blanket with the kid when she'd lifted him out of the car. Trying to pretend it was a game, she searched for the toy. Wherever he was, Hoppy wasn't in the cabin.

'He must be in the car,' she said, as if that explanation would mean anything to a toddler. 'We'll get him tomorrow.' Did kiddies Ethan's age have a grasp of the concept of tomorrow?

Apparently not. His crumpled face was back. He took a huge in-breath and Diane braced herself for what was to come.

Ethan wailed, 'Want Hoppy.' Then, as if he'd suddenly thought of his mother, he changed to a heartbroken, 'Mommy.' Diane was filled with a mixture of guilt and sorrow.

Ethan was building up a head of steam. His cries echoed in the small cabin, amplified by the metal walls. Or so it seemed to Diane. How could other people possibly *not* hear such a racket. She tried saying, 'Shh' and 'Hush' and any other word or comforting sound she could think of. She tried to hug him and he fought her off, pushing her away with surprising force for a small boy. Adrenaline flooded Diane's system, making her nervy and anxious. Not ideal for calming a distraught child.

She'd have to give him some drops. That wasn't the plan, but what option did she have? Ethan, as well as being abducted, was also a stowaway, and Diane couldn't risk some other passenger calling the steward. She put the dose of elixir into his cup and swirled the juice around. What if he was too upset to take a drink? Then what would she do? And how was she going to get through the next fifteen or sixteen hours if she couldn't get him to stop screaming?

Chapter 32

Sophie was glad to get away from the others. They'd agreed to split up and go to three separate starting points then work their way into the Cité like spiders on a web. The plan was to meet in two hours at the shop where Sophie had last seen Ethan. Or call when one of them found him. As if.

She had almost blurted out that Miss L and Ethan had been at a café in the Place Carnot. Keeping vital information to herself was already proving to be a strain. Sophie wasn't sure how long she could last.

As she made her way towards the new town, Sophie knew in her heart that this was a pointless exercise. There was no way Miss L would have stayed in Carcassonne. She'd have fled to Narbonne, or Paris – or anywhere. In fact, she could be somewhere over the Atlantic on a flight home. Sophie wished herself inside a plane, flying home to the States. She'd never complain about her life again.

She had chosen the busy area in the town centre and Seth had agreed that it made sense for a French speaker to ask in the cafés and restaurants that filled the square. He and Penny would take the surrounding streets and the riverside. Penny had burst into tears at the mention of the river and Sophie understood why. She had a picture of Ethan feeding the ducks, stretching out towards a duckling. Miss L wouldn't know how tightly you had to hold on to him. Perhaps she hadn't taken him at all. Maybe something awful had happened and rather than confess that Ethan had drowned, she was pretending to have kidnapped the child.

No. Sophie would not allow her thoughts to go down that dark, scary road. Ethan couldn't be dead. Not on her watch. Miss

L had taken him, but Sophie believed Miss L would not let Ethan come to any harm. He was her grandson, after all. She would give him back eventually. Sophie had to believe that.

And tonight, no matter how futile she knew it to be, she had to carry out this search to the best of her ability.

Although the summer season was over, it was Friday night and the Place Carnot was buzzing. Trees, starting to lose their leaves, were strung with lights and music blared from open doorways. The unseasonably warm weather meant that extra tables spilled over from the restaurants into the square and every single one seemed to be occupied. It was dinner time and waiters dashed back and forth, some of them running. Sophie's mouth watered as she caught rich garlicky smells from a passing plate.

She started at the first table. 'Excuse me.'

The couple did not look pleased to have their meal interrupted.

'I'm looking for a little boy who has gone missing.'

Sophie expected the woman's face to melt in sympathy. Perhaps she'd ask Ethan's name or his age.

The woman turned her face away and moved her shoulder forward so she could lean on the table and look at her companion. Not at Sophie.

She moved on to the next table, a family group, with children. She tried again. This time one of the women put her arms around the children as if Sophie might mean them harm.

At the third table, she started by describing Ethan but got no further than his hair when a haughty waiter hissed at her, 'What are you doing here? Get lost.'

He turned to his customers and made an oily apology. Sophie picked up the word *tsigane*. Was that what these good citizens thought of her? That she was a gypsy begging her way around the square? Using some sob story of a lost kid to get sympathy? She didn't know whether to laugh, cry or scream with fury. She didn't get the chance to make up her mind as the waiter put his hand on her back and firmly suggested she leave or he'd call the police.

Sophie looked down at her clothes. Converse, jeans, and a sweatshirt. Hardly the garb of the Roma girls she'd seen around the town.

She moved away, conscious of the waiter, and others, watching her. She'd try the opposite side of the square. Perhaps her mistake had been to speak directly to the diners. She could see their point.

At a busy pizzeria, she tried to catch the attention of the waiting staff. Apart from a brusque, 'We're full,' called to her in passing, no one spoke to her. She moved to the bar. The young barman looked harassed but good-natured. He glanced at Sophie as he selected three bottles from the gantry and prepared to make a cocktail.

'Hi, what can I get you?'

'Nothing, sorry. I'm looking for a little boy.'

'Good luck with that.'

'No, seriously. A toddler's been abducted and I'm trying to find him.'

The barman shook the cocktail mixture in the air and looked straight at her. 'Is it your kid?'

'No, I'm his nanny.'

'And you've lost him? Man!' He rolled his eyes. 'You're in deep shit.'

'You could say that.'

He poured the cocktail into a special glass and tipped the remainder into a plain tumbler which he slapped on the bar in front of her. 'On the house,' he said. 'You're gonna need it.'

Sophie drank it like a shot and coughed. The barman laughed. 'Hey, that was meant to be savoured, not downed in one like a cheap tequila slammer.'

Sophie nodded while she tried to get her mouth to form words. 'I thought I could ask around the square if anyone had seen him.'

'Tonight? In the Place Carnot? Are you kidding?' He waved a bottle of mineral water towards the crowded square then deftly flipped the cap off.

'The waiter over at the big swanky place accused me of being a gypsy.'

The barman scowled. 'Man, they really distrust those gypsies.'

'Yeah, he wouldn't let me near his precious customers.'

'Why don't you call the cops?'

'We thought we'd look for him ourselves first, me and the family.'

A waitress came up to the bar. 'That cocktail ready yet, Marc?'

'Got it right here.'

'I need a Perrier and a carafe of house red too.' She rolled her eyes at Sophie and hurried off.

'Marc, three beers,' shouted a waiter as he passed with an enormous pizza in each hand.

'Want some free advice?'

Sophie nodded.

'Go to the cops. They're bastards and everyone hates them, but hey, take a look out there.' He pointed to the bustling square. 'What chance have you got of finding him on your own?'

'Thanks for the advice,' said Sophie, 'and the drink.'

'Hope he turns up.'

Sophie walked out into the cooling air. She'd try one or two more places, maybe on a side street, then head for the Cité. Time to make up her mind what she was going to tell the police.

Chapter 33

Penny saw Seth before he saw her. He was at the souvenir shop leaning against the wall, his head on his forearms. The little street was dimly lit, but she knew it was him. As she got closer she could see his shoulders shudder. She wiped her own tears on the soggy scrap of tissue she'd been clutching for the last hour and told herself to be brave.

'Seth,' she said gently, leaning against him. He didn't react at first. Then he took one arm off the wall and she stepped into his embrace. His face was wet.

'Nothing?' she asked.

She felt the shake of his head.

'Me neither. Not sure what I expected, but it wasn't nothing.'

'Penny, how did it get to this? We were so happy in Texas. Why did we ever have to leave?'

Penny had never heard Seth sound downbeat about anything. He could see the best in everyone and the potential for good in every situation. He'd been her rock, her anchor, the wind beneath her wings for so long. All those corny words that people overused because they were good words to describe strong, dependable, inspirational characters like this man. He'd stuck by Curtis long after his other friends had walked away, and he had stuck by her. She couldn't imagine how she'd have made it through without him. He had literally given up everything for her – his whole life, his mother, his friends, his home, everything. For love of her. Even though he'd known from the start that she didn't feel the same way.

She couldn't tell him why she'd been so keen to leave Texas. Not while he was like this. She'd only make him mad as well as sad.

'Oh my God, where's Angel?' she said, pushing him away.

'Shh ...' Seth pointed to his feet where their daughter lay wrapped in his jacket, sound asleep. 'She's exhausted. Fell asleep on my shoulders.'

Penny's tears flowed unwiped as she knelt on the cobbles and stroked her child's face. Angel didn't stir. Poor little thing.

'How the hell could she lose him, Pen? I mean, who leaves a two-year-old outside a shop?' He gestured to the street around them. 'You've seen this place in the daytime. It's so mobbed, anyone could have taken him. Nobody would even notice.'

As if the thought had suddenly occurred to him he said, 'Didn't you tell her to never leave the kids unattended?'

'It never crossed my mind.' Nor had it. Sophie had seemed so competent and confident, they'd never discussed anything so basic. Maybe Seth was right. It was her fault. For bringing them here. For trusting a stranger with her kids. For not laying down the law.

A pool of light from an old-fashioned lamp illuminated Sophie as she walked underneath it and came towards them.

'Anything?' asked Seth.

'Sorry.'

'Oh God,' said Penny, fighting hysteria, 'he's really gone.'

'It was impossible to ask people if they'd seen him. It was so busy. And the waiters wouldn't let me speak to customers. One of them even threatened to call the police.'

'Which is precisely what we ought to have done hours ago.' Seth stooped to pick up Angel. 'Come on, let's get this kid to bed.' He strode off without waiting for them.

'Penny, I am so, so sorry. I don't know what to say.'

Penny touched Sophie's arm but she had no words of comfort to offer.

'I can't believe this is happening,' said Sophie. 'It's like a bad dream. I keep hoping I'll wake up. How's Angel doing?'

Penny shrugged. 'She's sleeping.'

'You must be exhausted too.'

Penny searched her pockets for a drier tissue and made an effort to pull herself together. 'Well, this day's a long way from over. Come on. Let's go. Tell me again what you know that might help the police.'

Chapter 34

'Inspector Morand says you must have a photograph of Ethan.' Seth and Penny looked at each other then back at the policeman. They shook their heads.

'Not a single photo?'

'Sure, we have photos. In boxes, back home in the States.' Sophie translated.

The policeman exchanged a look with his colleague. It wasn't hard to interpret.

'He wants to know if you could get one emailed.'

'Tell him no. There's a family in our house while we're gone. Our stuff's all in storage.'

This time the cop did not even try to hide his frustration. He muttered his opinions to his colleague, a young, college-grad type who was saying very little. Sophie had the impression from the apologetic smile he gave her that he didn't share his boss's views of foreigners.

'And you insist you want no publicity?'

'Correct,' said Seth.

They'd been over this several times already. Sophie was so tired she could hardly focus. The effort of telling her own story had been trying enough but translating every question and answer for Penny and Seth was too much. Sophie was surprised the police were accepting her version of what Penny and Seth said. She suspected the younger cop could understand every word of English, but Topcop Morand insisted on conducting the interview in French.

Penny and Seth looked as tired as she felt. Penny was on a roller coaster of emotions. One moment she was calm and controlled. The next, she would wail like a banshee in pain.

Sophie's overwhelming emotion was one of disbelief. Disbelief that the whole crappy thing could be happening to them and disbelief that she had brought it about. If only she hadn't applied for the job. Common sense told her that Miss L would have found someone else. The Gates family would still have ended up right here, just with a different nanny.

The hardest thing to believe was that Penny and Seth were lying. Sophie knew they had photos of the kids. Loads of them. She even had some herself, on her phone. Taken for Miss L's benefit. Sophie had almost offered to share them then Seth said, 'No publicity.' How could they hope to get Ethan back without some help from the media?

That was precisely what the two cops were talking about right now. Youngcop agreed with his boss. Media could play such an important part in finding a missing child. Topcop turned to her. 'Please ask them again to consider making an appeal on television.'

'He really wants you on television, appealing to the public for help.'

'No way,' said Penny, shaking her head to make her opinion clear.

'Are you sure they understand what I'm talking about?' asked Topcop. 'Are you translating it accurately?'

Sophie might have been offended were she not too tired to care.

'Ask him where it will be broadcast,' said Seth.

'Worldwide.'

'Ask if it can be restricted to France.'

They didn't wait for her to translate. Topcop said a word that needed no translation. His colleague examined his fingernails.

With a final disgusted complaint to his sidekick, Topcop scribbled a few words, snapped shut his notebook and stood. 'There's nothing more we can do here tonight. Give them the papers. All we can do is hope they'll see sense by the morning.' He waited for his colleague to sign in triplicate the paperwork that he'd been filling in throughout the interview.

Handing a copy to Seth, he said wearily, 'Please tell Mr and Mrs Gates that I am very sorry. We shall do all we can to find their son and return him to his family. Starting with the paperwork which we will now go back to the station and file. Before we go off shift, we shall inform our colleagues all over France that a little boy answering the description you have given us is missing. Perhaps by tomorrow morning he will have been found safe and well.'

As she laboriously translated all he'd said, Sophie couldn't help thinking that he hadn't sounded terribly optimistic, despite the rather forced smile he gave as he shook their hands.

'Sophie?' said Penny, as if she'd just thought of something. 'Was Hoppy with you?'

Youngcop looked interested. Sophie was right. He understood every word.

'Of course. Ethan won't go anywhere without him.'

Youngcop said, 'Sorry, who is Hoppy?'

'Ethan has a favourite cuddly toy. It's a rabbit. A glove puppet.' Sophie noticed her hand miming Hoppy's favourite poses as she spoke. 'Ethan takes him everywhere. He loves that rabbit, doesn't he?' She looked at Penny and wished she hadn't. The tears were streaming down Penny's face and suddenly Sophie wanted to join in. 'Sorry,' she said, wiping her eyes. 'It's just, you know, Hoppy.' She didn't bother trying to translate the last sentence. It made no sense. She'd been dry-eyed all day and now the thought of a cuddly toy was cracking her up.

She sobbed out a description of Hoppy, which Youngcop, to his credit, noted in his book with as much gravity as he had the description of its owner.

'And the child definitely has this toy rabbit with him?'

'Definitely. Thank goodness. He won't sleep without it.' She couldn't finish.

Penny was weeping inconsolably now. The thought of her child crying himself to sleep was obviously too awful for her to contemplate.

'Thank you,' said the policeman. 'These little details can often be the key to solving a case. If you think of any more, don't hesitate to get in touch.'

'Ask them what we do now, Sophie,' said Seth, pumping the hand of the younger policeman.

In perfect English the young officer replied, 'Try to get some sleep, sir. In the morning we will ask you to come to the station to make a more formal report. We can provide an interpreter.'

Penny and Seth looked at each other.

'Fine by me,' said Seth.

Penny tried to smile, her lip trembling. In a shaky voice that sounded nothing like her own, she said, 'We don't need another interpreter. We trust Sophie.'

Chapter 35

Diane felt bad about drugging the child again, but how else was she meant to survive this journey? It was naïve, she now realised, to think the kid would forget so quickly or that he was too young to understand what was happening.

Even if he had been fine with her and not crying for his mommy or his rabbit or whatever the hell he'd been crying for, how on earth had she imagined she might keep a toddler entertained for endless hours in this tiny cabin?

She looked around, grateful that she'd never again have to climb into, or out of, a bunk bed. Thank goodness no one had been here to see the indignity of that particular challenge. Once she'd mastered the ladder and made a final effort that reminded her of early attempts to mount a horse, she had slept surprisingly well. Although she'd heard horrendous stories about the Bay of Biscay, all she'd felt was the thrum of the engines and a gentle rocking. Just enough to lull her to sleep and keep her there, dreaming of surreal landscapes filled with toy rabbits, none of them Hoppy.

On waking she'd been beset by worries. Was the child still alive? Would he wake hysterical? Was she turning him into a junkie? Would they get caught when the ship docked? Would Interpol be waiting to pick her up?

When she was sure Ethan was safely under, she dressed quickly and put on her wig, a different one this time. Red was not appropriate for this foray. She wanted to be forgotten, not remembered.

She left the cabin, locked the door and waited for a moment, in case the noise of the door closing had disturbed Ethan. An elderly man approached from the end of the narrow passageway. She recognised him as her suitor from the night before. She prepared to say a polite 'Good morning', but the man passed her with no sign of recognition. Whoever said a grey-haired woman was invisible got that one right.

She followed signs for the car deck, taking far more stairs than she remembered climbing the night before. Blue Stair. Garage Deck Five. This should be it. She tried the door. Locked. A sign informed her that access to the garage was strictly forbidden during the crossing.

Diane trudged back up the stairs, wondering what she could do. If she asked to be allowed on to the car deck to look for a cuddly toy she'd be told no. That was clear. And if she reported the rabbit missing, she was as good as revealing that she was smuggling a small child. There had to be another way.

Lost property enquiries were to be made at the purser's desk, apparently. The same place she had to take care of the landing card business. Convenient. The purser turned out to be a pretty young woman who didn't bat a heavily made-up eyelid when Diane told her she'd lost her 'lucky charm'. Looking suitably embarrassed for a middle-aged woman seeking a soft toy, she explained that she never travelled without him.

'A sort of St Christopher rabbit?' asked the young woman with a smile that suggested this was not the most bizarre item she'd ever been asked to find.

'Exactly. Silly superstition, I know.'

'Nothing silly about good-luck charms.' She was checking a screen while she spoke. 'I'm sorry, nothing has been handed in so far.'

'I think I may have dropped him on the garage deck.'

'Ah. That could be tricky, but if one of the men finds him, I'm sure Chris Rabbit will be kept safe. He'll probably be sitting on your car waiting for you when you go down to disembark. Check back later, if you like. Or leave me your name and a forwarding address?'

With her most gracious smile, Diane declined, then, on a whim, asked the way to the gift shop.

Unfortunately, there were no Hoppy lookalikes for sale, but Diane bought a furry elephant, a cuddly dinosaur, of all things, and a dog that looked alarmingly lifelike. Surely one of those would appeal to Ethan.

He was still asleep when Diane got back. She stowed the new toys under the bunk for when he woke up and went to grab some breakfast. She hoped she could smuggle a sausage or two out of the restaurant. Something to distract Ethan when he woke ravenous. And looking for Hoppy.

Chapter 36

When Sophie woke, Ethan had been missing for twenty-four hours.

Officially, he was missing from 9.14 p.m., which was when the Gates family contacted the police. The police who, incidentally, were not at all impressed by the parents' decision to delay.

Penny believed Ethan was asleep in his bedroom when she'd rung from Toulouse. Sophie had told her she'd decided to run up into town to buy him a toy for being good, just before she was due to collect Angeline from school. As far as his parents were concerned Ethan was missing from late afternoon.

After a night of tossing and turning and begging for sleep, Sophie had made up her mind to come clean. She planned to tell the true story, or part of it, first to the police and then to Seth and Penny. The reason for that order was one of self-preservation. She was genuinely scared of what Ethan's parents might do to her when they heard she was the reason their son had been abducted. Okay, Ethan was with his grandmother, but they must have had a pretty good reason for cutting the woman out of their lives.

Sophie reasoned that, if she told them about Miss L at the police station, in front of the police, someone would protect her when Penny or Seth tried to kill her. With police officers restraining Ethan's parents, Sophie could explain everything. She would look like a stupid, naïve liar, but once the police knew who they were looking for, Miss L would be picked up. Ethan would soon be back safe in his mommy's arms.

Sophie felt like a weight had been lifted from her shoulders. Relief made it hard to behave appropriately. She'd felt like singing in the shower but caught herself mid-warble. Just as well the house had thick walls.

On the way to the police station, she had trouble keeping the skip out of her step as she walked hand in hand with Angel. She chatted inanely to the child, trying to distract her from watching her parents.

Penny looked ghastly, her eyes red-rimmed and weary. She hadn't slept at all, she said. She refused breakfast. When Seth had encouraged her to have a coffee, she'd run gagging to the toilet. They'd heard her being sick.

Seth was steering his wife along the street now, his arms around her. They looked like a couple of survivors staggering from a collapsed building. In a way that was what they were, except it was their life that had collapsed around them. Sophie felt guilt stab at her like a sharp pain in her stomach. She massaged it away with the thought that soon she'd come clean and Penny's nightmare would be over.

'I want to catch up with Mommy and Daddy,' said Angel suddenly.

'That's a good idea. I think Mommy could use a hug.' Sophie called out Seth's name and watched him turn.

'Wait for me, Daddy,'

It suited Sophie to have a few moments alone. She wanted to do as Miss L had suggested and check her bank balance. She opened the banking app she'd installed at Miss L's suggestion. One hundred dollars had been deposited weeks ago to open a web-based bank account in Sophie's name. Miss L had pledged to credit the account with a generous, but unspecified amount at the end of their agreement. Sophie cleared security and selected the current balance option. A line of figures appeared. Sophie gasped and read it again. That couldn't be right. Like a child learning to count, she touched each tiny zero with the tip of her fingernail, fighting the urge to throw up.

When Seth gave his name at the reception desk, he was asked to hand over his keys. A team of officers was waiting to search their house. Seth tried to complain about his property being searched in his absence and was told, 'This is the way we do it.'

'If they tried that in the States someone would sue their ass,' he muttered to Penny.

'I suppose it stops people hiding evidence,' said Sophie, thinking out loud. Seth gave her a look that made her feel sorry she'd spoken.

Penny seemed to have no opinion on the subject. She stood there, wraithlike, wringing her hands and saying nothing.

They'd been instructed to take a seat. At first Penny refused, insisting they were here to talk to the policemen who'd promised to find her son, not to sit around and wait. It soon became clear they had no choice. Penny sat and talked non-stop, as if her tongue, now loosened, couldn't lie still. She pointed to a poster on the wall. Sixteen stark photos of missing children. 'Is that why they wanted Ethan's photo? So he can be up there with all those other little lost souls?' Suddenly she went quiet and sat absent-mindedly gnawing on her fingernails.

The older officer they'd seen last time appeared behind the counter.

'Inspector Morand,' said Penny. She stood up and grasped at the man's sleeve. He took a small step back.

Penny let go of his shirt. 'Did you find him?' she asked, her face full of hope.

Morand shook his head.

Penny seemed to fold in on herself like a paper doll. She dropped to her knees, an animal keening for her lost young. She'd been counting on Ethan being found by morning, it seemed. Handed over the desk like a lost umbrella.

Seth put his hands under his wife's arms and helped her to a seat.

Sophie gave Angeline a tight squeeze and whispered to her, 'Why don't you go give Mommy a hug?'

The child, eyes wide, shook her head. 'I don't want to.'

Morand explained in passable English that today's interview would be conducted by different officers who would take each of them, one at a time, into an interview room. Despite Penny's request that they speak through Sophie, an interpreter had been provided. Seth, Penny and Angeline would have no choice but to use the interpreter but Sophie insisted she speak for herself. Angeline would be interviewed with her mother present, but Penny was not allowed to prompt the child.

When she came out, clinging to her mother, Angeline seemed dazed by the whole experience. According to Penny, Angel had found the DNA swabbing particularly unpleasant.

'Did she tell them anything?' asked Seth.

'What could she tell them?'

Angel could tell them the hide and go seek story and reveal that Sophie had lost her too. Angel could tell them about her nanny's potty-mouth. A nanny who used the F-word in the hearing of her charges was not the squeaky-clean young woman Sophie claimed to be. Maybe Angeline would even tell them about the conversation she'd overheard. Sophie had replayed the scene countless times, trying to recall her own words. Something like, 'You're fucking crazy! I'm going to call the police.'

'She was a very good girl, Daddy. Really helpful to the nice police lady, weren't you, honey?'

Angeline nodded her head and looked pleased with herself. What the hell had she told the cop? Sophie put her hands in her pockets and crossed her fingers till Youngcop came through and said they could leave.

'Boy, am I glad that's over,' said Seth the moment the police station door closed behind them.

'Me too,' said Penny. 'I know I'm innocent and yet they managed to make me feel guilty. As if I'm the one to blame for losing my son.'

She looked at Sophie and blushed. 'Sorry, Sophie. Didn't mean that the way it sounded.'

Better to say nothing. 'Is it okay with you guys if I stay in town for a little bit? I need to get some, like, personal stuff.' She gave Penny a look only a woman could interpret.

Seth's face turned a shade pinker than usual. Guess some men knew what that look meant.

Penny said immediately, 'Of course. I'd stay out if I could. I'm dreading going back to the house and seeing what kind of a mess the police have made.'

'Oh, sorry. I forgot about that. Would you prefer me to come and give you a hand clearing up?'

'We'll be fine,' said Seth. 'Go ahead and do your shopping.'

Sophie didn't need any stuff, personal or otherwise. All she needed was some time to think.

A woman walked by with three kids. Sophie found herself studying the two smaller ones. She wondered if Penny had done the same. She pictured Penny and Seth, old and grey, scrutinising middle-aged men, searching for some resemblance to the son they'd lost when he was two. She tried to erase the image from her mind before it got embedded there.

It was a ridiculous thing to imagine. Ridiculous because Miss L would not keep Ethan forever. That wasn't part of her plan. Sophie didn't know how she knew that, but she did. She tried hard to remember exactly how Miss L had put it. 'He's not coming back tonight,' or 'You won't see him tonight.' Something like that. Oh yes. 'Ethan won't be coming home tonight.' That was it. Implying he wasn't gone for good. Then she'd added something. Like an afterthought, an attempt to clarify. Think, Sophie, think. What was it?

Miss L's voice had been honey-sweet as she crooned 'Au revoir' at the end of their last phone call. Au revoir didn't mean goodbye. It meant till we meet again. Sophie was sure that was a deliberate choice of words. It meant the Gates family would be reunited.

And Sophie would be rich. Thirty pieces of silver, current value a hundred thousand dollars, were sitting in a bank account with her name on it. Why wasn't she singing and dancing, rebel-yelling and punching the air? This was wealth beyond her greediest dreams. She could see the world, all of it, if she wanted. Not in squalid hostels and backpackers' hotel rooms. She could travel in comfort, live in style, and still have money left over to see her through grad school, without going cap in hand to her stepdad. She'd have the wherewithal to find her own dad, to stay on in France while she looked for him.

'Hey, gypsy girl!'

Sophie turned.

'Gypsy girl, wait!'

A tall guy in a black tee and slouchy jeans was jogging in her direction. His face was familiar. The young cop from the night before? Off duty?

'You don't recognise me?'

Sophie hedged her bets. 'Maybe I do.' Damn, he'd think she was flirting with him. A policeman.

'Sex on the Beach?'

'Pardon me?'

'The cocktail? Last night? Pizza place?'

Had the cop been there? Sophie was confused.

'Sorry, can we start again?'

'That would be good.'

He held out his hand. Waited for her to take it. As they shook he said, 'Marc. Barman in the pizza restaurant on the Place Carnot.'

They were still shaking hands when he said, 'I gave you the dregs of a cocktail called Sex on the Beach.'

Sophie remembered.

'What did you think?'

She couldn't answer that. Instead she looked down at her hand, still clasped in his.

'Sorry. A bit of an over-shake going on there.'

He had the most amazing smile and Sophie could sure use a smile.

'Wanna go grab a coffee?' he asked.

'No Sex on the Beach?'

He gave her a look that was impossible to misinterpret.

'Like, in your dreams, buddy,' she said.

They both laughed.

'How about we start with coffee?'

It was wonderful to sit there having a laugh with a guy. As well as being clever and witty, Marc was very easy on the eye.

'Always good to meet a fellow American,' he said. 'Especially one with an accent like yours.'

Sophie smiled.

'Where y'all from?' he asked, sounding like a Nashville country and western singer. 'Sounds like Mississippi to me.'

'Close, but zero cigar.'

'Atlanta, Georgia?'

'Nope, much prettier than that.'

'Louisiana! Nawlins?'

'Yeah, and wherever *you're* from, it sure ain't the deep south.'

'That's where you're wrong, Missy.'

'Well, it must be the deep south of California.'

'Got it in one. Huntingdon Beach.'

'You a surfer boy?'

'Used to be.'

'Don't look much like it. What happened to the waist-length dreadlocks?'

'Not a great look for a law graduate.'

'You're a lawyer?' Sophie had a sudden urge to ask him how many years she'd get for aiding and abetting a kidnap.

'Will be soon. I've been taking a year out to see the real world before I join the corporate one.'

'Sounds like a plan. What brought you here?'

'I did two semesters of mediaeval European history. Became a bit fascinated by the Cathars.'

'You've come to the right place then. My boss is writing a book about them. Well, she was, until all this shit happened.'

'Shall we talk about something else and try to take your mind off it?'

As she drained her cup Sophie realised she hadn't felt this relaxed for months.

Her anxieties had started while she was waiting for Miss L to offer her the job. Then she worried the Gates family might not take her on. Add the stress of looking after two small children. All that drama about trusting Miss L. The trauma of realising Ethan was gone. Knowing it was her fault. And then today, being interviewed by the cops while an obscene amount of money sat in her bank account. Money that made it impossible to own up to her part in Ethan's disappearance. She felt weighed down under a load she'd expected to shed by now.

'Why the sad face?' asked Marc.

She wondered what he'd say if she slid her phone across the table and showed him the balance on her internet account.

'Feeling a bit homesick,' she lied. 'Must be your accent.'

Marc flashed her that killer smile again. 'Sophie,' he said, leaning forward and slapping his thighs, 'This has been terrific but I've got to go to work. I've been late a few times and the owner is on my case.'

'Go,' said Sophie. 'No worries.'

She watched as he hurried off across the square. Suddenly he stopped and came running back.

'Sorry, meant to ask, did you go to the cops?'

'That's where I've been.'

'What was it like?'

'It was awful. Felt like I'd committed a crime.'

'That's cops for you. Not that I've had anything to do with them, but you know, people talk.'

'Listen, Marc, thanks for cheering me up. This morning's not been a bundle of laughs.'

'I guess not. But hey, sorry. I've really got to go.'

Sophie knew it wasn't cool, maybe not even safe, but she couldn't stop herself. 'Want to swap numbers? We can do this again some time?'

'Why not?' Marc grinned at her. 'Maybe we could even have Sex on the Beach next time?'

A woman at the next table gave Marc a frosty look and Sophie giggled. This guy was fun.

She was still smiling when she crossed the old bridge. She stood for a moment gazing up at the skyline of ancient towers. Something she'd been trying to remember was darting around at the back of her mind, flitting in and out of reach. Something to do with what Miss L had said about Ethan.

'Ethan won't be coming home tonight.'

Yeah, she'd got that. It was the next bit she couldn't remember.

'Or any time soon.'

Sophie's good mood evaporated.

Chapter 37

'Seth, stop. I want to go back.'

'Yeah, so do I, Penny. I wish I'd never set foot in this godforsaken country. We should never have left Texas.'

Penny grabbed his arm. 'No, I mean I want to go back and tell them what we really think is going on here.'

'Penny, we talked about this. We were still awake at five talking about it. We agreed.'

'I know we did, but what if we're hindering the investigation by not giving them a photo and not going on TV to make an appeal?'

'You said you were afraid to let the media know anything about us. In case they find out who we really are.'

'Don't you mean, who we were?'

'You know that's what I mean.'

Seth sounded impatient. No wonder. She'd kept him awake all night, but how the hell could they be expected to sleep anyway? Their toddler son had just been abducted. And Penny had another demon keeping her from sleeping. One he knew nothing about. And that was what she had to get off her chest. She'd kept it to herself long enough. Maybe too long.

'Seth, please, I need to talk to you.'

He pointed to Angeline a few steps ahead. She appeared to be concentrating on avoiding cracks in the pavement. But they knew better. 'Not with you know who listening to every word.'

'Let's go to the park by the river. It's on our way.'

'The Jardin Bellevue?'

'Yes, she likes the play area there. So did Ethan.' Penny felt her eyes fill. How could they possibly still be producing tears?

Seth hugged her to him. 'Hey, it's okay. That's a good idea.' He called to Angel. 'Hey, sweet-cheeks, wanna go play in the park for a while?'

'I've got no one to play with, Daddy,' said Angel, sounding pitiful. Penny suspected she was missing her little brother more than they knew.

They had given Angeline as little of the truth as they could. Last night at bedtime she had asked why someone had 'borrowed' Ethan.

'Is it because he's cute?'

'I suppose.'

'Why didn't they want to borrow me? I'm cute, too.'

There was no answer to that. They'd been given some advice by a woman at the police station that they should attempt to answer Angel's questions, if they could, but not offer any information that might distress a child of her age. So far, she seemed to be coping. The test would be on Monday morning, if they tried to send her to school.

When they got to the park, a girl about seven or eight years old was playing on the climbing frame. Angel asked if she could go and play with her.

'Sure, honey,' said Seth. 'Go ahead. Mommy and I will wait right here.' Once their daughter was out of hearing distance, Seth said, 'Okay, Pen, what is it you want to tell the police?'

'Everything.'

'Why would you want to do that?'

'In case it's relevant.'

'In what way could it be relevant? You think it's someone from the past who's taken Ethan? Penny, you know that's not possible. He's in prison. We'll be told when he gets out. Anyway, he can't possibly find us.'

'Unless we go public.'

'Which we agreed we wouldn't do. At least not at this stage.'

Penny nodded, chewing her lower lip.

'So what's changed?'

'What if it is someone from our old life?'

'Like who?'

'Curtis?'

'Penny, he's in a wheelchair. You know that.'

Penny was so glad he didn't remind her why. She lived every day with the knowledge that she'd almost killed Curtis. 'Yeah, but maybe he could have arranged for someone else to take Ethan.'

'Why would he do that, Penny?'

'Because he's jealous?'

'Of me and you? Penny, he doesn't even know about me and you. All he knows is that we both disappeared out of his life around the same time.'

'Maybe he's worked it out. Maybe he knows we're together and he's found out we have two beautiful children.'

'And you think because he can't have any of his own, he's stolen one of ours?'

'Maybe. Or he's run out of money.'

'Penny, honey, you're not thinking straight. And I don't blame you. This is enough to mess with anyone's head. But listen to me, Curtis has enough money to last his lifetime.'

'What if he's squandered the lot? You know what he's like. Hanging around some bar, acting the big shot. Buying drinks for any loser prepared to listen to his sob story.'

'You're still bitter.'

'Of course I'm bitter. If it hadn't been for Curtis, my path would never have crossed Charlotte's and I'd never have met that bastard Millburn.'

'Come on, Pens, we've been over this a million times. You'd never have married me and there would be no Angel and Ethan.' He stopped. 'Sorry.'

She went on as if he'd never spoken. 'But what if he's drunk it all, or snorted it up his nose?'

'Pens, he's a changed man. The accident changed him.'

Penny noted the word accident. 'You really believe that?'

'I do. Also, that little nurse who looked after him in hospital? She moved in, remember?'

'And you think she'll still be there a decade later? Only if she's a saint.'

'I think she might. Last time I saw them together I was sure it would work out. Curtis needs her.'

Penny knew all this stuff. Seth was right. They'd been over it countless times in the past ten years. Still, it felt reassuring to hear him say it all again.

'I'll let you into a secret. I Googled Curtis, once,' said Seth. He must have caught her look. 'Only the once. I was curious. He and I were friends for a very long time, remember.'

'I know. Since before first grade. You told me.'

'He's made a success of himself – running a business. He won't come after you for money. He has much more money than us these days.'

'Shouldn't we tell the police so they can eliminate him from their enquiries.'

'It's not Curtis, Penny. Ask yourself, what would Curtis want with our kid?'

'Revenge?'

'Say what?'

'I put him in that wheelchair!'

'You didn't do it deliberately.'

'I deliberately hit him with a heavy metal object.'

'Because you thought he was going to kill you.'

'I *knew* he was going to kill me.'

Penny started to cry again. She rubbed her fists into her eyes. She would *not* shed tears for that no-good loser.

'Penny, you're an emotional wreck. Distraught with worry about Ethan and exhausted through lack of sleep. This is not the time to be dredging up all these old memories.'

She sniffed loudly. 'You're right. But what if it is him?'

'Penny, can I remind you why it cannot possibly be Curtis?'

'Please.'

'Curtis thinks you're dead. He believes you died in the dust on 9/11. Doesn't he?'

'Yes.'

'So there's no need to tell the police about Curtis. Agreed?'

'I guess.'

Angel scampered up and they both smiled at her.

'Daddy, can we go get an ice cream?'

'Sure. Why don't we get one for your new friend? You go and ask her mommy if that's okay.'

Angel ran off, excited.

'Maybe it's someone else who wants revenge?'

'Who, Penny?'

This was the moment to tell him. About that day in the mall and those other times when she'd felt someone watching.

'Don't you think we should be looking closer to home, Penny?'

'What do you mean?'

'I mean Sophie. I thought that's what you wanted to talk to me about.'

'About Sophie?'

'We haven't been entirely truthful with the cops, have we?'

'Haven't we?'

'We didn't tell them we'd done no proper background checks. That we didn't even know her before we left the States. That we left our children in the care of a girl we met in an airport departure lounge.'

'But we spent all that time with her in Paris. And we trust her. We agreed she would be an asset. That's why we took her on.'

'You took her on, you mean. And *you* trusted her to look after our children. Look how that's turned out.'

'Oh, Seth, you can't think Sophie had anything to do with this.'

'Can't I? Where is she now? And what about that day she disappeared to Narbonne? What was she doing there? Who was she with? Have you asked yourself that?'

Penny was shocked. 'Of course I haven't.'

'It's time you did.'

Chapter 38

Ethan hadn't been enchanted by the elephant. Nor was he delighted by the dinosaur. He'd not been best pleased to see Diane when he woke up, either. Clearly he was expecting someone else. Like his mother or father. Not an unreasonable expectation for a toddler.

She'd distracted him with food for a little while, but once he'd finished eating, he'd shown no interest in his new toys or in reading a story. All he wanted was his mommy and, by the looks of things, he was prepared to cry till he got her.

Diane had no choice but to drug him again and hope the effects would last till they got off the boat and through immigration and customs. Her internet research suggested that a car with one middle-aged lady driver and no passengers was likely to be waved through. According to one survey, eighty-eight per cent of travellers aged between fifty-five and sixty-four smuggled goods through customs without being stopped. She sure hoped the survey was right. If customs officers decided to turn over her car, searching for illegal cigarettes or alcohol, they were in for a shock if they found a little boy asleep in the footwell.

When it was announced that drivers and passengers could return to their vehicles, Diane was one of the first on the garage deck. She carried Ethan folded over her arm like a particularly bulky blanket. Making sure no one was watching she opened the back door. A few people had come to cars near hers, but they were preoccupied with getting their own stuff stowed away, ready for the onward journey. She gently laid the boy on his little black nest and made sure the blanket was covering him completely. She took care to leave him a clear flow of air then closed the door and locked the car. On her way back to Blue Stair she looked around for Hoppy, but he was nowhere to be seen. She considered for a moment checking with the purser but by the time she had battled her way back to the cabin for the rest of her belongings, she felt like a fish that had swum from sea to source. She flopped down on the lower bunk, banging her head on the edge of the upper bunk as she sat. A flash of pain made her eyes water. It was the last straw. She'd taken on far too much for a woman of her age. She should have done this years ago – kidnapped the girl when she was Ethan's age. When Diane had more energy and resilience. Too late now. She blinked back tears of pain and frustration and gathered up bags and holdalls. How could one small kid need so much stuff?

Laden like a pack mule, she headed for the car deck, eyes searching the floor for Hoppy. She felt a ridiculous sense of disappointment that the rabbit seemed to be gone for good. It would have been nice to surprise Ethan when he woke.

The smell of diesel and petrol fumes was strong as drivers started up their engines in preparation for disembarkation. Diane did not want to linger amongst the vehicles. She placed her bags on the back seat and in the boot and got in. Hoppy was a lost cause.

As the line of cars began to snake forward she caught sight of a flash of pale fur disappearing under the car in front. She stopped, meaning to get out and save Hoppy, but a man in overalls with a Hi-Viz jacket and walkie-talkie waved her on. Keep moving, his hand signals commanded her. She thought it wise to do as he instructed. Stopping the whole line of cars while she climbed out to rescue a soft toy would draw unwelcome attention. She glanced back and saw poor Hoppy disappear under the tyre of the enormous four-by-four that had been parked behind her. 'Bye, Hoppy,' she said, feeling sad. Whether for Ethan or his favourite toy, she couldn't say.

The car bumped across the ramp and along a single-lane bridge that dropped them on the quayside. A blue-and-white sign reminded Diane, in four languages, that she must drive on the left. She was not looking forward to the experience. For now, all she had to do was follow the car in front and hope for a clear run through the docks. Otherwise, what side of the road to use would be irrelevant. She'd be riding in the back of a police car.

Gradually the cars slowed to a standstill. Not another security check. She thought they'd done all that on the Spanish side. Was this where her grand plan would come undone? One zealous customs officer searching for contraband cigarettes and she was a goner. He wouldn't have to be too zealous to discover a sleeping toddler.

How ridiculous to think she could pull this off. The idea had come to her months ago. She'd decided to take the child and had been racking her brain for ways to hide him. A little secret compartment inside the bodywork of the car? Ventilated, soundproofed, safe. And installed by an expert who would want to know why any sane person would need such a thing. In other words, impossible.

She came up with a simpler solution. A little nest on the floor of the car.

Next problem, what if they found him?

Diane realised she didn't care. That was the most liberating moment of her life. Thrilling and scary in equal measure because it meant she'd crossed a line. Some would say she'd crossed the line that divided good people from psychopaths, but Diane knew she wasn't crazy.

The long line of cars began to inch forward, bringing her closer to whatever lay in wait under the huge canopy.

Not caring about consequences meant she was pretty much free to do anything. There was nothing to stop her taking revenge on the bitch who sent Scott to prison. Trapped him, testified against him, then claimed to be so terrified she needed witness protection to give her a new identity. So she could disappear and live happily ever after.

Diane had been determined to find her. Some of the finest private investigators in the world worked out of New Orleans and Diane could afford to hire the best. It had taken him some time but, with a little insider help, J William Pigg had tracked down Mrs Penny Gates, formerly known as Lucie Jardine. And he'd been keeping an eye on her ever since. JW Pigg's services came with a price tag that reflected his status and his skills. Diane felt he was worth every last dime.

Two vehicles ahead of her, a car was diverted out of line and directed into a separate lane. The doors opened and five young men climbed out. Diane didn't care for the look of them and wasn't surprised they'd been pulled over. She hoped to look squeaky clean by comparison. Ironic, really.

A customs officer stepped in front of her car. Diane braked, swallowed hard and rehearsed what she would say. She was winding down her window, smile in place, when he moved aside and waved her through. Like a freeway clearing after an accident, the cars in front accelerated away and Diane followed. Out of the docks and onto the M275 for London and all points north. She enjoyed the freedom of wind on her face for a moment then closed the window. It would be dark soon. She reckoned on having a couple of hours daylight, no more.

Her plan was to drive for as long as she could while Ethan slept. They had a long way to go. Eventually, her bladder demanded she pull in for a comfort stop. She chose a parking place as far from the services as she could. She listened in the darkness to the child's breathing, deep and regular.

She disabled airplane mode and her phone pinged its way back to life. Eight missed calls. Five voicemails. Fourteen messages. All from Sophie.

One voicemail would do. She imagined they all said the same.

'It's Sophie. This is, like, the fifth voicemail I've left. Please, please can you get in touch? I need to speak to you. Urgently. I'm, like, going crazy here.'

It was almost eleven o'clock. Sophie would have to go crazy for a bit longer.

Diane looked across the car park and wished she'd been bold enough to stop in the well-lit section. Back here appeared to be reserved for lorries, the light dim and scarce enough to allow drivers to sleep. Gigantic trucks lumbered in, their air brakes hissing like dragons as they settled to rest for the night.

Diane had heard of atrocities committed in truck parks in the States and had no desire to leave the safety of her car. But she *had* to go to the restroom. Also, she was keen to see if there was any mention of a French kidnapping in the British press. Gathering her handbag and her courage, she clutched both tightly and ran for the first pool of light.

There were no newspapers left in the only shop that was open. Diane bought a book of postage stamps and some chocolate buttons for Ethan. All she needed now was a strong coffee and they could get on the road again.

The motorway was quiet. Most of the traffic seemed to be truckers and they stayed mostly in the slow lane, leaving Diane to cruise the middle lane.

She turned on the radio, real low, hoping for a news bulletin. It was one of those late-night programs of easy-listening songs and she found herself singing along to her favourites. The miles disappeared under her wheels and for a while she forgot about the stolen child sleeping in the back.

Until something touched her face. A dark shape appeared at her shoulder. The child tried to push through the space between the two front seats, screaming in her ear.

She hauled on the steering wheel and the car veered to the left. A mammoth truck blasted its horn, long and loud and far too close. For a moment there was no other sound.

Then Ethan wailed, 'Mommy!' He grabbed for her. 'Mommy!'

Adrenaline flooded her veins. She braked as hard as she dared and dropped in behind the truck.

Steering with her left, she used her right arm to block the boy's path. 'Ethan, you have to lie down.'

He pushed against her, crying as if she was murdering him. She couldn't drive like this. Another huge truck came up behind her, dangerously close, filling her rear view with a wall of metal. She indicated left and slowed until she could pull over. She allowed the car to coast to a halt and then pulled on the handbrake and hit the hazards. Orange light filled the car then plunged them into darkness again and again.

Ethan's little face was stricken. This must be apocalyptically scary to a small child. She gathered him to her and tried to comfort him, but he strained away from her. As she tried to hold him she felt and smelt him simultaneously. His pyjamas were sopping wet. Sophie had sworn he was house-trained or whatever the word is for a kid who no longer wears diapers. She wouldn't have taken him otherwise. What the hell did she know about changing diapers?

'It's okay, Ethan. Mawmaw can see what's bothering you. Let's get you into some nice dry pyjamas.'

Nice dry pyjamas did not seem to be what Ethan had in mind. He stood looking out of the front windscreen, crying. Diane searched in her bag for the candy she'd bought. 'Look, Ethan,' she said, 'Mawmaw's got candy.'

It was gonna take a lot more than chocolate to appease this kid. Still, she offered him the sweetie and was astonished when he stopped wailing and opened his mouth. She popped the button in and waited. Chocolate dribble ran down his chin and dripped off onto his pyjama top.

'Good?' she asked.

He looked at her, lit by the flashing orange lights, and nodded. 'More?'

'More peese,' he said and held out his hand.

Diane was vaguely aware of the flashing lights changing from orange to blue. She heard a car engine close behind her. She looked in the mirror.

Police. Two of them. Getting out of their car.

Chapter 39

Sophie couldn't sleep for worrying. All that money in her bank account. It wasn't just the amount that was freaking her out. It was the fact that, by the terms of their agreement, Miss L had been due to pay the final balance 'on completion'. Rather formal expression, Sophie had thought, to describe a grandmother getting to spend time with her grandkids. She'd pushed the words to the back of her mind, but now they'd come back to haunt her. Big time.

On completion. Did that mean Miss L had no intention of returning Ethan? It did sound very final, as if the job was complete, finished, over. Nothing more to be done.

Penny and Seth had gone quiet. She wondered if they were asleep. Sophie knew she shouldn't be eavesdropping, but the atmosphere in the house had been perceptibly different when she got back from her coffee with Marc.

The walls were so thick it was hard to hear much, but her name had been mentioned a few times and Seth had sounded angry. Penny's voice was soft, as if she was trying to appease or reassure.

Sophie needed to pee. Otherwise she'd never get to sleep tonight, just lie here wanting to go. She got up and opened her bedroom door as quietly as the ancient wood allowed.

The landing was dark. Sophie edged forward, feeling her way along the old stone wall. It was cool to her touch and rough under her fingertips. Stone changed to wood as she passed Seth and Penny's bedroom. All was quiet. They must be asleep.

Stone again. She took two more steps then shrieked as she bumped into something, her own scream echoed by another.

'Sophie!'

'What the fuck?'

'You nearly gave me a heart attack!'

'Right back atcha!'

'What are you doing?'

'Going for a pee! Although it may be too late. I think I just wet myself.'

Penny giggled nervously. Sophie joined in. It was like that moment in a horror movie when the whole audience jumps out of its skin, then dissolves into laughter. There's little distance between laughter and tears and a moment later Penny was weeping quietly into her hands.

Sophie put her arms around her employer, feeling as awkward as a teenager.

Penny wept on her shoulder for a few minutes then said, as if chastising herself, 'Shh, for godsakes, don't wake Seth.'

'What are you doing out here in the middle of the night?'

'Promise you won't think I'm crazy?'

Sophie shook her head then realised it was too dark for Penny to see. 'No,' she said.

'I'm standing here pretending both kids are tucked up safe and sound.'

That was one of the saddest things Sophie had ever heard. She felt for Penny's arm and gave it a rub. 'Sorry,' she said.

'I want to go in and make sure Angel's okay.' Penny's voice broke. 'Maybe kiss her goodnight? But I'm scared to open the door and face the truth. That Ethan's bed is … empty.' Penny sobbed out the last word. 'Oh, Sophie. What am I going to do?'

'You want me to go in with you? Would that help?'

'Not one bit. It's something I have to do alone. But I'm so scared.'

'I get that.'

'Sophie?'

'Yeah?'

'What if we don't get him back?'

'You will. I know you will. He's not gone for good.'

Penny gave her a hug. Sophie smelt unwashed hair and a faint whiff of body odour. 'Sophie?' she whispered, 'just so you know? I don't blame you.'

Sophie bit down hard on her lip. It would be too easy to say, 'I know who took him.'

Chapter 40

Diane lowered her window. Just a little. Couldn't be too careful. Some of the stories you heard.

The first police officer leaned his arm on the roof of the car and spoke through the opening.

'Evening, madam. Everything alright?'

Diane put on her brightest smile. 'Yes, thank you, officer.'

'Has your car broken down?'

'No, sir. It's just fine.'

'Would you mind telling us why you've stopped on the hard shoulder?'

She wasn't familiar with the phrase and his accent was a bit difficult to understand. Also, she needed some thinking time.

'Pardon me?' she said in a southern drawl.

He stood up, the better to indicate the strip of asphalt on which she was parked.

'This is known as the hard shoulder. It's for emergency stops only.'

She noticed the second man had wandered around to the front of her vehicle and was looking at the number plate.

'Oh, I'm so sorry.'

'You didn't know?'

Best to say as little as possible. 'No, sir. I did not. I can only apologise.'

He pointed to Ethan who had climbed onto the front passenger seat and was standing there staring.

'Nice little boy.'

'Why, thank you. My grandson.'

'How old is your grandson?'

'He's two and a bit.'

'Did you know it's an offence to have him in the front of your car?'

Diane pointed to the child seat in the back. 'Oh, he has his own little seat right there. He just climbed over here beside me when I stopped the car.'

'Why did you stop the car, ma'am?'

Diane laughed, as if she were embarrassed. Time to talk. 'He's had a little accident, I'm afraid.'

The police officer was leaning in close again, looking at Ethan with concern.

'His mommy swore he didn't need a diaper. He's such a bright little button, you see. But I do declare, his silly old grandma forgot to wake him up to go potty and he was upset to have wet his PJs. I was just going to slip him into a fresh dry set so he'd be comfortable for the rest of the journey. Do you have kids, officer?'

The policeman straightened up, a pained look on his face. 'Where are you headed tonight, madam?'

'Not much further, officer. This little fella's mommy will sure be anxious to see him home safely.'

'May I suggest you put him in his car seat, fasten him in and wait till you reach the next motorway services before he gets his fresh pyjamas on. Okay?'

'Absolutely. Thanks you so much.'

'Oh, and one more thing.'

'Yes, officer?'

'First chance you get—'

'Yes?'

'Do me a favour and buy a Highway Code. Then do us all a favour and learn it.'

With an abrupt goodnight and an instruction to drive safely, the two policemen got back in their car and drove off. Diane heaved the biggest sigh of her life and said, 'Well now, Ethan, I think we just had a lucky escape. Why don't we get you into your special seat and you can have some more chocolate buttons for being a good boy?'

To Diane's surprise, Ethan held out his arms towards her and allowed her to settle him into his seat. As she tucked the blanket around his legs, he said, 'Buttons, peese.' She handed him the pack and made a mental note to stock up at the first opportunity.

With one of the kiddie CDs in the player, they sped along, listening to the music. From time to time she could hear Ethan singing his own version of the words. He sounded so cute, she couldn't help smiling. Eventually Ethan fell asleep again, this time without the help of any elixir, and Diane pulled in at the next services. She reclined her seat and closed her eyes.

She woke to the sound of truck engines and had no idea, for a few moments, where in the world she could be. It was still dark and it had started raining. Her neck felt stiff and her back was sore. She was far too old to be sleeping in a car. Remembering her reason for being there, she looked at the child. He was sound asleep. She glanced at the time and reckoned she'd been dozing for a couple of hours. Not nearly enough to keep her going, but it would have to do.

She switched on the satnav and checked how far they had to go. Over three hundred miles. In low traffic that would take at least another six hours at the speed she was driving. Add in a few traffic jams and it could take eight or more. She couldn't possibly drive that far without a decent sleep. Diane gave her neck a rub with both hands, wishing she'd taken a hotel near Portsmouth, but she'd wanted to put some distance between them and the boat.

After last night's close call with the traffic cops, Diane did not want to draw attention to herself on the road and if she drove tired that was the least bad thing that could happen. Her encounter with the police had taught her one thing, apart from no parking on the hard shoulder. They weren't on the lookout for an American woman driving around in a French car with a small boy. If the French police were on her tail, they had not yet alerted their British counterparts. She was banking on that to give her some time.

Most of the early-start trucks seemed to have gone and the car park had quietened down again. In the distance, above a line of trees, the sky was showing signs of a new dawn. The deep navy blue had lightened to a purple that promised daylight.

Diane pulled on to the M6 and put her foot down. The sooner she went to ground the better.

Chapter 41

'Can't Daddy take me?'

Penny said, 'Sophie will take you.'

Angeline folded her arms and sat on the sofa, head down. 'I don't want to go.'

'Sweetie,' said Penny, kneeling in front of Angel. 'We spoke about this. I thought you wanted to go to school today.' She put a fingertip under Angel's chin and gently raised her little face. Perhaps it was a crazy idea to send her to school. Seth had called in sick. The police wanted to see them again this morning.

'Mommy, I *do* want to go to school.'

'But?'

Angel whispered, 'I don't want Sophie to take me.'

Usually the problem was Angel's refusal to go anywhere without Sophie.

Penny lowered her voice, aware that Sophie had just gone upstairs. 'Can you tell me why you don't want Sophie to take you?'

Angeline shook her head. What was going on here? Seth and Penny were planning to talk while Sophie took Angel to school. Seth had already voiced his reservations about leaving their daughter alone with Sophie, but Penny had overruled him, feeling it was important to keep Angel's routine as close to normality as they possibly could. Given the circumstances it was difficult, but at mealtimes, bath time and family time, they were trying hard to sound upbeat and cheerfully normal. Only bedtime had changed.

'Would you like to go to school if Mommy takes you?'

Angeline nodded. 'It's Colette's birthday today. Her mommy is bringing cake to school so we can have a little party at lunchtime.'

It had to be a good sign that Angeline was thinking about little girl stuff instead of her missing brother. 'Did we buy her a present?'

'No. Sophie and I were going to buy her something but Ethan got borrowed.'

So she had been thinking about him. It was naïve of Penny to think otherwise. 'I've got an idea how we can give Colette a little gift.'

Angel's face brightened up.

'Why don't you give her one of the presents I brought you back from Toulouse?'

Angel considered the suggestion. 'Good idea, Mommy. I'll give her my drawing book and pencils.'

Penny knew how much Angeline adored a new drawing book. Under normal circumstances the pages would be filled by now, but the stationery gift lay untouched. It was a generous gesture from a small child. She hugged Angel to her and said, 'That's a lovely idea, sweetie and very, very kind. Shall we quickly wrap it up in some pretty paper?'

As Angel raced off to fetch the gift Seth asked, 'What was all that about?'

'Mm. Not entirely sure. I'm gonna go walk her to school and hopefully I'll find out.'

'When will we talk?'

'Later. In the meantime, maybe you could help Sophie with the breakfast things and have a chat at the same time?'

'Pen,' he said, under his breath, 'I can hardly bring myself to look at the girl and you want me to have a "chat". Are you kidding me?'

She shrugged and hollered from the foot of the stairs, 'We need to hurry, Angeline. Sophie! You don't have to rush. I'll take Angel to school today.'

While they walked, Penny encouraged Angeline to chat about Colette and the others who would be invited to the lunchtime cake party. She was pleased to hear the child sound like her old self. Relieved that, on the surface at least, she didn't seem to be traumatised.

When that conversation ran out, Penny talked about school in general and how Angeline was getting on there. This was all stuff she knew, garnered from teatime chats or last thing at night confidences. It was an easy transition to the topic of Sophie.

'Say, sweetie, how about you tell me why you didn't want Sophie walking you to school today. I thought you loved Sophie?'

'I do, Mommy. I'm just scared.'

Well, that was to be expected. 'What are you scared of?'

'I'm scared she loses me again.'

Penny stopped walking.

Angel, like a puppy on a lead, was jerked to a standstill. 'Mommy, you hurt my arm.'

'What did you say?'

'I said you hurt my arm.'

'No, no, no. Before that. About Sophie.'

As if she were explaining something to her brother, Angel said, 'I'm scared she *loses* me.'

'*Again*. Didn't you say you're scared Sophie loses you *again*?'

'Yes.'

'What did you mean, Angel?'

'I'm not sure I should tell you.'

Penny knelt down so her eyes were level with her daughter's. 'Of course you should. It's always okay to tell Mommy. Any old thing. Any old time.'

Angel smiled but stood silently nibbling at the corner of her thumbnail.

Penny moved the little hand aside and said, 'Tell me, sweetie-pie. What is it?'

'Well, Mommy, it was, like, this one time.'

'Yes?'

'Sophie and I, like, went to look for croissants.'

'And?' Penny knew there was no point in being impatient.

'And she lost me.'

Angel must be making this up. They'd been told she might become very attention-seeking while her brother was missing.

That's all this was. Ethan was lost and now Angel had made up a story where she got lost. Penny was unsure what to do. She wasn't keen to encourage this behaviour and yet she'd always believed in letting her kids talk. Listen to them when they're small and they'll talk to you when they're grown.

Penny forced herself to smile. 'Are you sure about this?'

'Cross my heart, Mommy. I was playing hide and go seek with some other boys and girls.'

Penny laughed. So that's what this was about. A game. 'Sophie didn't lose you, Angel. You were hiding. That's different.'

'No, Mommy. She *did* lose me. She left me sitting on a bench all by myself so I, like, asked one of the boys if I could play too. It was my turn to go seek and I was behind the big stone, counting to a hundred, 'cos that's what you do, and you don't peep, not even a tiny little bit 'cos that's called cheating, and I could hear Sophie shouting my name over and over but I couldn't stop counting till I got to a hundred, 'cos that's what Daddy says you've got to do. Count to a hundred, real slow, to give everyone time to find a good place to hide.'

At last Angel stopped to draw breath.

'Then what happened?'

'I got to ninety-eight, then ninety-nine then a hundred.'

Penny screwed her hands into fists. She wanted to scream 'Hurry the hell up and tell me.' Instead she patiently prompted: 'And?'

'And I opened my eyes and Sophie was, like, shaking my shoulders and shouting at me and it made me cry 'cos it hurt and Sophie was angry at me. Very angry.'

Penny knew it was important to get the right end of this stick. 'Did you run away from Sophie to play with the other kids? Tell me the truth now, Angel.'

'No, Mommy. Course not. Sophie wasn't there. That's why I didn't ask her if it was okay. It was naughty. You should always ask a grown-up before you do something. That's what Sophie says.'

'Sophie's right. But you said she wasn't there. So you couldn't ask her.'

'Sorry, Mommy. It was still naughty.'

Penny was torn between telling her child that she was not to blame and reinforcing the message that might one day save her life. She chose the safety propaganda. 'Yes, it was, but you've learned a lesson, haven't you?'

'Yes, Mommy.'

'That's my best girl.' Penny hugged Angel close. Rubbed her face in her child's hair and breathed in the scent of her. A thought occurred. She had to ask. 'Angel, why didn't you tell me this before?'

'Because I didn't want Sophie to get in trouble and she said you'd be really cross with her 'cos you'd think she wasn't taking good care of me.'

Penny didn't know what to say. She needed to choose the right words to reassure Angel that Sophie would take good care of her and she wasn't to worry about a thing. Just because her little brother was missing didn't mean something bad was going to happen to her. How do you convince a six-year-old she's safe, when you're not convinced yourself?

'Mommy? There's something else I didn't tell you about Sophie.'

Chapter 42

Sophie checked her phone. Still nothing from Miss L. She could at least send word that Ethan was okay. Was this why she was so keen for Sophie not to get attached to the kids? So she wouldn't worry? What a joke. Sophie was worried about so many things she didn't know where to start.

She pictured Ethan. Those blue, blue eyes that seemed far too deep for a child and made you wonder what was going on behind them. His dark hair, shiny like a new chestnut and curly like his sister's. Long, too, for a little boy. Every time she had to coax a brush through his curls, Sophie had cursed Penny's refusal to have it cut.

And that smile of his. She'd defy Diane to resist Ethan's smile. Sophie wiped a stray tear. Did Miss L really think she could spend one moment in that child's company and not become attached? Good luck to her.

Sophie walked circles in her room, picking up clothes and putting them away. She was prevaricating and she knew it. She also knew what she was trying to avoid. Or rather who. He was downstairs banging the breakfast dishes and she ought to be down there helping. It was part of her job, but she was scared to face him.

Her phone rang. She grabbed it.

'Hey, Sophie! What's happening?'

'Oh, it's you.'

'Try not to sound so excited, Sophie. You wouldn't want to make a guy feel too good about himself.'

'I'm sorry, Marc. I was hoping it was someone else.'

'I kinda got that.'

'Can we start again, please? Things are tricky around here, yeah?'

'Oh, I'm so sorry. I forgot. What a klutz!'

Now she'd made him feel even worse.

'Any news?' he asked, sounding concerned.

'None.'

'I'm very sorry to hear that. Is there anything I can do?'

'No. All any of us can do is wait.'

'I guess. Look, I just wondered if you fancied a coffee, but forget it. Insensitive to ask.'

Sophie had the feeling he might be the least insensitive guy she'd ever meet in her life.

'No. It's cool. I can do coffee. Later. We've got to go back and speak to the cops today.'

'Okay. How about you text me when you're free and we can meet in town. I don't start work till six.'

If Seth heard her walk into the kitchen, he didn't look up.

'Morning,' said Sophie.

'Hey.'

'Can I give you a hand with those?'

'Sure, grab a towel and you can dry.'

'This is supposed to be my job, you know.'

'Really? I thought your job was to look after the kids.'

Sophie stared at Seth, bent over the sink, as if she'd never seen him before.

'Who was that on the phone?' he said.

Was that really any of his business? Was she even obliged to answer a question like that?

'A friend.'

'Didn't know you had any friends here.'

'I've just met him.'

'You sure about that?'

What the hell was that supposed to mean?

'Of course I'm sure. He works in the pizza place on Carnot. The night Ethan went missing and we were all out searching the town he was kind to me, and helpful. Acted like he actually gave a shit. Then I bumped into him on Saturday when we left the police station.'

'What do you know about this guy?'

'Not very much, to be honest. How much did you know about Penny when you first met her?'

'Don't get fresh with me, Sophie.'

'Sorry, but what is this about?'

Seth turned and faced her. His colouring was always high. Went with his fair, gingery hair, she supposed, but right now he looked like he might burst a blood vessel.

'It's about my two-year-old son who is out there, who knows the fuck where.' He waved his arm wide enough to embrace the world and sprayed her face with soapy water. 'Because *you* lost him. That's what this is about, Sophie.'

'I didn't lose him, Seth. Someone took him.'

'And that's supposed to make me feel better?'

'No, but it's the truth.'

He turned back to the sink and scrubbed furiously at a plate that was already clean. 'What do we know about you?'

'Say what?'

'I said, what do we know about you?'

'Well, you saw my references, you could have called and checked up on me, but you chose not to. So to answer your question, not a whole hell of a lot, I suppose, when you think about it. But then, that works both ways. What do I know about you?'

Winding him up was like poking an angry bull with a red rag on a pointy stick, but she couldn't help herself. He was being so aggressive, as if all the rage that had been buried inside was erupting. She felt his anger flow and burn like lava, destroying whatever friendship had existed between them.

'Meaning?'

'Meaning, I'm not the one keeping secrets from the police.'

Oh God. Did she really say that?

'What are you talking about?'

'All that crap about the police. Do we call them? Don't we call them? I mean, who doesn't call the police the second their kid goes missing?'

'Oh, that's rich. Ethan was missing for hours and you didn't think to call the cops.'

They were shouting. Gloves off. No holds barred. 'I was waiting for you and Penny to come home. To tell me what to do.'

'Really, Sophie? Is that what you were doing? Really?'

The front door opened and crashed shut.

'What's going on?' Penny dashed between them. 'I can hear you right along the street. Isn't it bad enough already? Neighbours having their cellars searched and cops in forensic suits checking our home?'

Neither Sophie nor Seth answered. They just stood and glowered like two boxers ready to beat each other to a pulp.

Penny put her hand on Seth's livid cheek. He drew away as if scorched by her touch.

'Seth, what's the matter, honey? You need to calm down.'

'So does she.'

'Oh, come on, Seth. What are you? Five? Okay, you both need to calm down.'

Sophie said, 'I'm going out.'

'You're going nowhere.'

'What do you mean, I'm going nowhere?'

'Just what I said. You stay here. Where we can watch you.'

Sophie laughed, trying to defuse the situation. 'You're placing me under house arrest?'

'Seth? Seriously?' said Penny.

'Don't worry,' said Sophie, thankful for Penny's intervention. 'I'm not going to run out on you. I'm just going to clear my head a bit before I head to the copshop. Will I see you there?'

Penny seemed distracted. 'Yeah, yeah,' she said, waving a dismissive hand. 'Good idea. Off you go. We'll see you later.'

'I'll collect Angeline from school.'

'No. Don't!' said Penny. '*I'll* fetch her.'

Chapter 43

'Hello to you, my dear,' Diane said, when Sophie answered. 'I can't talk.'

Diane listened to the dead line for a second, wondering what was going on at the other end. 'Sophie just hung up on us, Ethan. Well now, that's a surprise.'

'Sophie?' said Ethan. He was sitting in a high chair holding a fat sausage in his fist and chomping on the end of it.

'Yes. I thought Sophie would be desperate to hear from us, but it seems she can't talk right now. We'll try again later.'

'Later,' Ethan echoed, his mouth full of sausage.

She had planned to get him to say hello to Sophie. Thought it was a neat way of reassuring the girl that he was fine. They'd been practising 'Hello, Sophie' while she carried him into the service station, found a table and got some food. He repeated words like a little parrot. Diane found it real cute. 'Is that a yummy sausage?' she asked.

'Ummy sossy,' he said, nodding and beamed her a ketchupy smile.

Looked like she'd been right about kids and puppies. Keep 'em fed, keep 'em happy.

While Ethan demolished his sausage, Diane consulted the map and route planner on her phone. They had a distance to go yet, but she was feeling remarkably fresh and, with a couple of strong coffees inside her, she felt she could drive for miles.

They'd need to fuel up and do something about clothes, just in case there were CCTV cameras on the forecourt of the filling station. She'd prepared for that, just like she'd brought a wad of British banknotes with her from the States. No one would be following her credit card trail any time soon.

'Ready, Ethan?' she said, when the sausage had gone and all that was left on his plate was a smeary mess of tomato sauce.

'Eddy,' he said and reached out his hands for her to wipe. Sophie was right. He was a smart little thing.

She lifted him into her arms. 'Come on, let's go get you dressed. Mawmaw's bought you some brand-new clothes.'

In the ladies' restroom, Diane chose the stall with the wheelchair sign on its door. It would have more space. There was also a mother and baby room but she was uncomfortable about going in there.

When she pulled on Ethan's new trousers he announced, 'Pink!'

'That's right. My goodness you're a smart one. You know your colours already.'

She popped a pink tee and then a sweatshirt over his head and smoothed them down. She pushed his feet into some tiny high tops and said, 'Look how cool you are.'

Taking a soft hairbrush from its packaging she pulled it through his hair. It caught on the curls and Ethan yelped like a puppy.

'Oh, I'm sorry, baby. Did that hurt?' Hair-brushing was clearly an activity Ethan did not enjoy and he wriggled away from the brush. Diane wondered why his mom kept his hair so long if it meant they both had to endure this trial every day. Still, it served her purpose very well and she was grateful. Gathering his fine hair into two curly bunches, she secured them with pink scrunchies and reflected that a week ago she'd never heard of such a thing.

'Right then, *Bethan*. You look adorable. Now it's time for Mawmaw to spruce up a little.' While the child looked on in amazement, Diane removed her red wig from its bag and pulled it on. She applied some bright lipstick and appraised herself in the mirror. 'Not too bad for an old broad,' she said.

With a pretty little girl in her arms, Diane, the middle-aged redhead, sailed out of the toilets and across the mini-mall, turning a few heads as she went. Exactly as she'd intended.

When she'd fuelled up the car, she took Ethan with her into the kiosk to pay, and let the child pick up a pack of chocolate buttons from the shelf.

As she handed back her change, the girl behind the glass said, 'That lovely pink top's not going to last long once she gets those sweeties opened.'

Diane simply smiled.

In the car she popped a sweet in Ethan's mouth and one in her own. Candy was a treat she'd denied herself all of her adult life. Scott had liked her slim and stylish. The button of milk chocolate melted deliciously on her tongue.

'Know what? From now on Mawmaw's planning to eat however much candy she wants. Nobody loves a skinny grandma, now do they?'

Ethan gave her a chocolatey grin. She caught a dribble before it reached his chin. 'Gotcha!' As she fastened his seat belt she kissed the top of his head.

She slid a CD of Old Macdonald and Other Animal Songs into the player, turned up the volume and drove away. The rain had dried up and a watery sun was lighting up the landscape. The world looked freshly washed. It was only once she was on the motorway again that she realised she'd forgotten to ring Sophie back.

Chapter 44

'What was all that shouting about, Seth?'
'She was winding me up.'
'I could see that.'

'All I did was ask her about this guy she's seeing. I wanted to know how long she's known him. She got fresh with me and I guess I wasn't in the mood to take it.'

'And one word led to another. Because we're all stressed out of our minds. Am I right?'

'I guess so, but she made me so mad, I accused her of losing Ethan. She denied it, said she didn't lose him. Someone took him. As if there's a difference. It all amounts to the same thing. My L'il Buddy's gone.'

Seth covered his face with his hands and made a sound that shattered Penny's already fractured heart. She put her arms around him and patted his back, as if she were comforting a child. The reversal of roles was new for them. He'd always been the strong one.

'Why did you let her walk out like that?' he asked, between heaving sobs.

'Because I needed her gone. So we can talk.'

'Aren't you mad at her, Penny?'

'Oh, I'm mad at her, alright. You just haven't heard the reason yet.'

Seth took his hands away from his face. 'What reason?'

'There's something you don't know. Want to sit down?'

'No, I don't want to sit down. I want you tell me what she's done.'

Penny took a breath. 'She already lost Angel.'

'She what?'

'Sophie lost Angel.'

'When?'

'Just after we got here. Remember that first morning? They went out looking for a baker's shop? That's why they were gone so long.'

'I don't believe this. Where did she "lose" her?'

'The esplanade on the far side of the Cité.'

'The place that's always swarming with tourists? Jesus Christ! This just gets better and better.' Seth stood and stared at her, shaking his head. 'How the hell did that happen?'

'Apparently, Sophie left Angel sitting on a seat by herself. Some kids were playing hide and go seek.'

'Hold it. Lemme guess. Angel went and joined in and Sophie was the one playing go seek?'

Penny nodded.

'This is unbelievable. Do you think Angel could be making it up? Remember what that woman said.'

'I did wonder, but the way Angel told me, it sounds true enough.'

'Why didn't you tell me this before?'

'I only found out this morning.'

'Is that why she didn't want Sophie taking her to school? Is the kid scared her nanny will lose her like she lost her little brother?'

'Something like that.'

Seth grabbed a glass from the draining board and hurled it at the wall. Penny screamed and ducked as shards of glass exploded around them.

'Seth!'

She hardly recognised him as he stood, head down, his shoulders heaving like an enraged bull waiting to charge.

'Seth, you're scaring me.'

He turned to look at her and the rage vanished from his face. 'Oh God, Penny, I'm sorry. This is the last thing you need. Me, behaving like Curtis.'

'I've never seen you like this. I didn't even know you had a temper.'

'Everyone's got a temper. I just keep mine under control. Normally.'

'Nothing about this is normal.'

He apologised again for frightening her. 'But what can you expect? Ethan's gone and now you tell me Angel's been lost too. What kind of a father lets that happen to his kids?'

'You're a marvellous father. None of this is your fault.'

'Whose fault is it, then?'

Penny felt the blame as surely as if the weight of it had been hung round her neck like a yoke.

Seth said, 'We have to challenge her.'

'There's something else.'

'Jeez, Pen, how much more? Can't you just spit it all out and get it over with?'

'Okay, don't get mad. Promise you won't get mad.'

Seth took a deep breath and said, as if it pained him, 'Promise.'

'Angel didn't tell us because Sophie asked her not to.'

His face was like a winter sky right before the clouds burst. 'Seth? You promised.'

'Now she's got the kid keeping secrets from us. What else don't we know about the lovely Sophie?'

'According to Angel, Sophie got so angry with her for wandering off to play she used the F-word.'

Seth laughed. 'She abandoned the kid in a public place then cussed at her for going to play? Unreal.'

'I know.'

'You know?' Seth's tone was mocking. He'd never mocked her before. Only in fun. And this was no fun. 'Pity you didn't know when you left her in charge of my children.'

'My kids too,' said Penny, knowing, as she spoke, how pathetic she sounded.

'Yeah, they are, and we should have taken much better care of them. And stayed in Texas, where we were all safe.'

'That's what you think.'

Chapter 45

The minute she got away from the house Sophie had tried to call back. Miss L wouldn't be happy getting cut off like that, but Sophie could hardly take the call in her bedroom. Not with Seth simmering like boiling oil.

She'd have sworn he was a big softie. Until this morning. Okay, the man must be under impossible stress, but it was like she'd just witnessed a complete personality change. Sophie had to admit she'd been scared. He looked like he might have a heart attack at one point. She was so relieved when Penny came in and calmed things down. But still, she'd been glad to get out before they tied her to a chair or locked her in her room.

She let the call ring and ring, surprised Miss L wasn't picking up. Sophie hoped she wasn't mad at her too. Voicemail.

Sophie waited for the beep then said, 'Sorry if I sounded rude earlier. It just wasn't possible to take your call. Seth was downstairs and I couldn't risk him overhearing anything. Turns out he's already suspicious of me. I'm away from the house now so you can call me whenever it suits you. Actually, I could use speaking to you. I've got to report back to the police station today and I'm scared I might get so nervous I say the wrong thing.' She was about to hang up when some instinct made her say, 'Miss L, please bring Ethan back. I'm sure if you, like, explain the situation, they'll let you see the kids. Now they know how much it means to you. This isn't the way. It's all getting out of hand and I'm scared.'

As she put her phone back into her rucksack, a thought struck her. What if the police asked her to hand over her phone? That would lead them straight to Miss L and they'd both be way up shit creek. No paddles available.

She stood in the street and turned in circles as if she might spot some solution to her dilemma. Suddenly she was deafened and engulfed by a tidal wave of children. All dressed in the same blue sweatshirts, they swept past her on either side. She felt like a rock in a stream. One or two even bumped and jolted her as they went. A teacher, herding them like a poorly trained sheepdog, smiled an apology and harried a few stragglers to move along.

She watched them go and was surprised to see them pile into the cathedral. She wondered if they'd shatter the peace in there too as she heard the same ineffectual teacher hushing them. Although it had been years since Sophie had been inside a church, she felt such a strong desire to visit, it made her check her phone to see if she had time to go in. Staring up at the solid, squat building, she wished for the first time in her life that she had a faith. The thought of going into a little box and confessing all to a stranger was very appealing. As was the thought that someone could pardon her sins and wipe them off the slate.

If she could go back to a clean page, what would she do differently? She'd still want to visit Europe and, if possible, find out about her father. She'd still apply for any job that promised her the chance to do those things and learn some new skills into the bargain. Naturally, she'd try to impress Miss L that she was the best person for that job. She'd think, as she had at the time, that it was a bizarre way for a woman to get to know her estranged grandkids. But life was bizarre. And rich people made their own rules, sometimes. Would she still go along with Miss L's plan, knowing what she knew now? What if she'd been told the job would entail more than just facilitating some meetings? If Miss L had been honest with her about needing Sophie's help to abduct her grandson? Well, Sophie told herself indignantly, she would have refused. Of course. What if Miss L had offered a hundred thousand dollars for Sophie's help? And promised that no harm would come to Ethan?

Sophie felt lost. She'd always believed she was a moral person with a strong, unshakeable sense of right and wrong. Now she wondered. She headed for the vast cathedral doors and stepped into the inner vestibule. It might be worth talking to a priest.

She imagined the conversation she might have through one of those little grilles she'd seen in movies. 'Father, forgive me, for I have sinned.'

'How have you sinned, my child?' the priest would ask. 'What sin have you committed?'

'I handed a child over to his grandmother, Father. She loves him but is not allowed to see him.'

'Where is the sin in that?' the priest might say. 'You've done a kind and loving thing, my child, bringing a family closer to reconciliation.'

'Erm, there's just one problem, Father. The kid's grandma has deposited a hundred thousand bucks in my bank account.'

It was beyond Sophie's imagination to guess how a priest might react to that revelation. 'Give it back at once, my child,' he'd say. Or perhaps, 'Your immortal soul is worth much more than a hundred thousand dollars. But there are many unfortunates in this world. Please give the whole lot to charity and your sins will be forgiven.' He might even tell her to go out there and spend it wisely. Carpe diem and all that.

When she reasoned it all out calmly, she hadn't done such an awful thing, really. Had she?

The priest might well suggest she try asking the child's parents that question.

Sophie pictured the normally gentle Seth with his red, raging face and roaring voice. She could imagine his reaction if she were to say, 'Okay, so I set up this whole thing with a woman I met in the States who tells me she's the kids' grandmother. She said she'd pay me big bucks, I mean, really big bucks, to arrange for her to spend some time with the children. Because you won't let her, apparently. So she wants to take Ethan to feed the ducks. Ethan loves those ducks. Where's the harm in that?'

It got a bit more uncomfortable when she reached the part where Miss L didn't bring Ethan back.

She remembered saying to Seth that morning, 'I didn't lose him. Someone took him.' Thank God Seth had interrupted her at that point. She had been about to shout at him like a spoilt teenager, 'Tell me how that's my fault.'

Sophie rubbed at her chin. Why, if she was innocent, did she have a sick, naggy feeling in her belly all the time?

Maybe it was the bad atmosphere in the house. Sophie had never been good with disharmony.

Or maybe it was just guilt, pure and simple. For if Ethan's disappearance was not her fault, whose was it?

And what was she going to say when the police asked her that in less than an hour's time?

Chapter 46

'Are you going to tell the police she already lost one of our kids?'

'Why would I do that?' Penny thought about dragging a brush through her hair and decided it was too much trouble.

'Don't you think it's relevant to their enquiry?'

Without looking in the mirror, she screwed her hair into a rough ponytail and tied it with an old elastic band. 'I think it's worrying that a nanny should lose sight of the child in her care, but I don't think it means she took Ethan.' As she said her little boy's name, Penny lost control of the tears she'd been trying so hard to hold back. It was awful the way she'd be talking normally one second then weeping the next. She flopped on the bed, as if her spine had melted. 'Oh Seth, what are we going to do? What if we don't get him back? I couldn't go on.' She curled into a foetal position, mother turned baby, and wept.

The bed creaked as Seth sat behind her. Then creaked again and moved with his weight. She felt him curl himself around her, protecting her as he always had.

'Come on, honey,' he whispered into her ear, 'don't think that way. We'll get Ethan back.'

'You don't know that,' she said, her voice harsh with tears.

'No, I don't, you're right. But I *believe* it. And you've got to try to believe it, too.'

She took a deep breath, as she'd been taught, and allowed herself to relax against him. He tightened his hold on her. It felt good, like a whole-body hug, and gave her a little strength. Enough to face the day. She turned her head and he kissed her cheek. 'Right,' she said. 'Lying here crying won't bring Ethan home.' Her voice wavered on the word 'home'. She bit on her upper lip and sniffed loudly.

'That's my girl,' said Seth. He swung his legs off the bed and stood, offering her his hand as if for a dance. She took it and he hauled her into his arms where he held her close and said, 'I'm sorry I lost my temper earlier. I promise you that will never happen again.'

She felt his shame and knew how much he'd hated Curtis's violent outbursts. She also knew how much he regretted letting Curtis get away with years of hurting her. Penny knew Seth was nothing like Curtis and would never harm her. 'Forget about it, please. I already have.'

'You know I'd die before I'd hurt you or the kids, don't you?' He pulled away so he could look deep into her eyes.

She nodded solemnly then smiled. There was no need to speak.

They kissed briefly, as if to seal a pact, then both turned to gather their belongings.

'Let's get this done,' she said.

They were crossing the river before they spoke of it again. Seth brought it up, as she knew he would.

'So, do we tell them she lost Angel?'

'Seth, I don't know what to tell them.'

'You haven't changed your mind about the television appeal?'

Penny thought for a moment, considering her next words. Decided to say nothing and just shook her head.

'Penny, why not? It's clear the police think it's the right approach. Why wouldn't we take their advice?'

'Seth, you know why.'

'What are you afraid of?'

'You know the answer to that one, too.'

Seth caught her arm. Brought them both to a halt. 'There's something else going on here. I need you to tell me what it is.'

'I just don't think these appeals do any good. Look at that Scottish couple whose little girl went missing a few years ago. They made one TV appeal after another. Did they get their kid back? No, all they got was a hard time from the media. The mum didn't look distraught enough. The dad was too calm. For God's sake, Seth, people started to blame them. Even the police treated them as suspects. I couldn't bear it if we were accused of hurting Ethan.' She started to cry again.

Two elderly women shuffled by, examining Seth as if he was the cause of his wife's tears. He gave them a hard stare and they glanced away, only to stop a few steps further on and look back, as if anxious for Penny's safety. She wanted to shoo them away like a pair of old hens.

'See, folk are staring at us on the street already. Can you imagine what it would be like if we went on national television? Or worse, international?'

'Penny, I think we should do what the police tell us. All I care about is getting L'il Buddy back.'

'And you think I don't?'

He put his arm round her shoulder and led her off, to the obvious dismay of their audience. 'Come on, honey. Let's go see what the cops have got to say. I promise we won't do anything you don't want us to do.'

'Promise?'

'Sure. The most important thing right now is that we stick together and work as a team.'

'You and me versus the world, yeah?'

He kissed the top of her head, a gesture that never failed to make her feel cherished. They walked on in silence. Penny was grateful he didn't push her on what else was bothering her. She was overwhelmed with guilt that she hadn't shared her fears months ago. Maybe if she'd told him then, they'd have called off the trip and Ethan would be safe.

How could she tell this good man that she didn't trust him enough to share her fears?

She was ensnared by her own lack of courage. Again. The difference was, this time those fears had put her child in danger.

And this time, she was powerless.

Chapter 47

'Hi, Marc. You know that coffee you mentioned?'

'Where are you?'

'On the Place Carnot. The little place that does the nice pastries?'

'I know it. Listen, I've got a couple of things to tie up but I'll be quick. Buy me a coffee and I'll be there before the froth evaporates.'

He was true to his word. The waitress had just placed the two coffees on the table when Marc slid into the seat opposite her.

'There he is,' she said. 'That was quick.'

'I only live around the corner.'

'From the Place Carnot?' She pointed to the tree-lined square, the pretty little wrought-iron balustrades that adorned the buildings. 'Isn't this prime real estate?'

'Yeah, but affordable when your parents have got well-off friends with a spare room.'

'Handy.'

'Very. Where are you living?'

'Old town. Near the Cité. My employers have done a house swap. Job thing. Aerospace, you know?' She wondered if she'd said too much. This guy was practically a stranger. And yet she felt she could trust him.

'Cool. Were you here in time to catch any of the open-air concerts?'

'Haven't heard any music, so I guess not.'

'Carcassonne Festival. Big names. The Beach Boys played this year.'

'Aw, seriously? I'd have gone to see them. Apparently my dad loved them.'

'Apparently?'

'He left when I was small. Came back to France. Don't know where exactly, but he came from round here somewhere. That's the main reason I took the job, actually. I'm hoping to track him down while I'm here.' She paused. 'Or at least, I was.'

'Before the kid went missing.'

'Precisely.'

His mouth turned down at the corners, like a sad clown. 'Sorry,' he said.

'Yeah, before it all went pear-shaped.'

'Are you French?' he asked, as if keen to change the subject, perhaps to cheer her up.

'Half French.'

'Wow, that must make it a lot easier to mingle with the locals.'

'You seem to do all right. Holding down a job and all.'

'They advertised for an English speaker. I'm picking up the French as I go along. It's tough, but I'm now fluent in pizza toppings.'

Sophie laughed. He was nice. She should go for it.

'Can I ask you a favour, Marc?'

'Oops, serious voice. Should I be worried?'

Sophie decided to ignore the humour and plough on. 'Would you keep my phone for me?'

'Woah! Now I *am* worried. Why would you want me to do that?'

'Bluntly? I don't want the cops to take it.'

Marc raised flat hands towards her face. 'Hang on just a minute. Your phone's hot but you want me to keep it?'

Sophie said, 'One, it's not "hot" and two, it's just for an hour.'

He checked an expensive-looking watch. 'I don't have a lot of time, but, yeah, I guess I can do an hour. But hey, why are you so worried about the police seeing it? You into drug dealing or something?'

Only child abduction, she thought. 'No, nothing like that.' She laughed, trying to sound light-hearted. Carefree. Innocent.

Feeling none of them. 'It's my dad. I've dreamt of finding him since I was a kid. Made it a kind of project, if you like, collecting information.'

'When other little girls were collecting Barbies?'

'Yeah, I was gathering stories, relatives' names and addresses, etcetera. Basically, anything I could find that made him feel real. Maybe I even thought it might lead me to him one day. I've even scanned all the photos Mum had of me and him.' She held up the phone. 'It's all in here. And I couldn't bear to lose it. It would be like losing my daddy all over again.'

'I don't think they'd lose your data.'

Sophie shrugged. 'Not sure I want to risk it.'

'They'll have tech geeks. Experts. They won't scrub your phone by accident. Chill.'

'It's not just that.'

'What is it then?'

'There's a number in my contacts I can't risk them phoning. Under any circumstances.'

His rubbed at his mouth, frowning. 'And you swear it's not a drug dealer?'

'No drug dealers, I promise.' He didn't look convinced. 'Okay, okay, it's a guy I used to know. He got a bit mixed up in stuff he shouldn't have. His number's still in there.'

Marc took in a long, deep breath, and held it, as if he was trying to decide if he should get involved. Sophie held her breath too.

'You should delete that number, you know. And don't mix with bad guys. Okay,' he said at last. 'Hand it over. I've only got about an hour though, seriously. Then I need to get going.'

She switched off the phone and passed it to him. 'Thanks. I owe you one.'

As she walked off, waving her fingers in the air, he called, 'If you're not back here in an hour, it goes in the Canal du Midi.'

She leaned towards the security speaker by the door of the police station and gave her name. A buzzer sounded and she was in. A stylish young woman at the reception desk invited her to take a seat. Was this a deliberate ploy, she wondered, as she watched the minutes click by on a large digital clock. Make them wait, make them sweat? She felt a trickle run down the centre of her back and squirmed for a second, then made an effort to sit still, remembering the three Cs. If anyone was watching her, it would be better to look cool, calm and in control.

A door opened at the end of a corridor and the young policeman from her previous interview appeared. He was smiling. To put Sophie at her ease? Or at a joke someone had just told him? Perhaps to charm the pretty receptionist whose face lit up as if the sun had come out.

'Hello, Miss Picard,' he said to Sophie, opening a small wooden door in the counter. 'Would you like to come this way?' He waited for Sophie, his smile gone, then walked ahead of her down another corridor. Sophie wondered what would happen if she refused to follow him. As if he'd guessed her thoughts, Youngcop hesitated long enough for her to catch up. Automatically, she started walking.

'Come on, Soph,' she whispered to herself. 'Let's get this done. Stay cool.' All she had to do was answer their questions and say as little as possible.

Youngcop stopped at a dark blue door, turned the handle and stood aside to let Sophie enter. When she hesitated, he swept his arm in a gallant gesture, as if he were inviting her to dance, and said, 'Please?'

She forced her feet to move and stepped into a room that felt more like a fridge. She'd never been in a morgue but that was the comparison her brain made.

The sweat on her back ran cold. Someone needed to turn down the air con.

Topcop rose from behind a computer and shook her hand. He gestured to a seat opposite his own. Sophie perched on the edge of it. Youngcop slid into a chair beside his boss and flicked through some papers. Topcop pointed to a woman sitting in the corner. She nodded without smiling when introduced as Madame Robert, an interpreter from Toulouse.

'But I don't need an interpreter,' said Sophie. 'I speak French.'

'She says she doesn't want an interpreter,' translated the woman.

Youngcop appeared to be taking notes.

'Hang on a minute,' said Sophie. 'I said I don't *need* an interpreter. Not that I don't want one. There's a difference.'

Topcop appeared to ignore her remark. 'Are you French?' he asked.

'No, I'm American but half French. My father is French.'

'Do you have dual citizenship?'

'No.'

'Would you say your first language is French or English?'

'It's English, but …'

Topcop looked smug as he announced, 'Very well, we must conduct this interview in English, through the medium of the official translator.'

'But that's ridiculous.'

'She says that is stupid,' said Madame Robert immediately, as if she'd been desperate to get back into the conversation.

'I did not.' Sophie closed her eyes and blew out hard, partly in exasperation and partly so she could take a deep breath and calm down.

'Very well, let us begin the formal interview.' He typed something she couldn't see while Youngcop made notes in a folder that lay open in front of him. When he had finished he pressed a button on a recording machine and said the date and their names.

Madame Robert, sounding self-important, translated his words.

'Seriously?' said Sophie, spreading her hands wide and looking towards the interpreter. 'Do we really have to go through this farce?'

'She says this is a farce,' said Madame Robert.

Sophie raised her eyes to the ceiling then looked at Youngcop for some support. He seemed to be engrossed in his notes.

'Miss Picard, I strongly advise you to cooperate fully with this investigation. You are doing yourself no favours by being difficult.'

Madame Robert opened her mouth, but Sophie held up a hand to silence her. 'I am trying to give you my full cooperation. I am here, of my own free will, to answer any question you may ask, because I want to help you find Ethan as quickly as possible.'

'Excellent. In that case, I am sure you will not mind if we ask you to hand over your mobile phone?'

Sophie delved into her bag and placed her old phone on the desk in front of her.

'Now, can you please tell us how you came to know the Gates family?'

Sophie recounted the tale of the airport meeting, the days spent together in Paris and Penny's subsequent job offer.

'But you knew the family in the United States, yes?'

'No.'

The cops looked at each other. Sophie tried not to read their thoughts.

'Don't you think it a little, how should I say, strange, to be offered a job by people you've only just met?'

'Not really. I needed a job, they needed a nanny. It was serendipity.'

'Ah.' He steepled his fingers and blew air through them. 'Serendipity.' With a shrug of his shoulders he said, 'Perhaps it is the American way.'

Sophie told them about their long days of sightseeing. 'Which means they got to know a lot more about me than if they had advertised for an au pair.'

The policemen did not agree or disagree. Other than the clacking of keys, the room was silent. She tried very hard not to fill the gaps with babble.

'Just a few more questions, if you don't mind.'

Sophie glowered at the interpreter. The woman leaned back against her chair and fiddled with a button on her cardigan.

'Remind me why you went to the souvenir shop. Usually, only the tourists go there.'

Sophie stifled a sigh. They were gonna go over all this again? 'As I said in my statement, I wanted to buy Ethan a little plastic sword.'

'And why did you choose this particular shop, may I ask? The Cité has many shops that sell these things.'

'I've no idea.'

'This was when? Before you fetched his sister from school?'

'Yes, that's why I was in such a rush.'

'Because you were due to collect the older child from school? Is that correct?'

'Yes.'

'If the purpose of the visit to the shop was to buy the child a gift, may I ask why you didn't take him inside?'

'I told you all this before. He was in a stroller.'

'And you couldn't take the stroller inside?'

'Have you seen those shops? We'd have wrecked the place. Also, as I said, I was in a hurry.'

'So you went in alone and bought him a plastic sword?'

'Yes.'

'May we see it?'

Sophie didn't know what to say. She hadn't bought a sword. But she couldn't tell them that. She could say they were out of stock. No, that wouldn't work, not when she'd just agreed to having bought one.

The cop dipped his chin and asked again, 'May we see the sword you bought?'

'I don't have it. It's at the house. Of course it is. Where else would it be? Sorry, if I'd known its importance I'd have brought it with me.' She was babbling.

'Check the notes, please.' His colleague flicked through a couple of pages then shook his head.

'No sword, plastic or otherwise, was found in the house.'

'Really? Well, I guess I must have, like, lost it. In the street. Put it down somewhere in the confusion when I realised Ethan had gone. Some kid must have picked it up. Now I come to think about it, I have no memory of taking it home with me.'

'But you're quite certain you made the purchase?'

'Oh, yes.' Say as little as possible.

'Did you pay with cash or card?'

'Card.' Damn, that was traceable. 'No. Cash, it was cash. I remember handing over a twenty-euro note and laughing with the shop assistant when she gave me all my change in coins.'

'Do you think the shop assistant may remember you?'

God, why couldn't she just keep her big mouth shut? She shrugged. 'I guess she sells a lot of plastic swords in a day. No reason why she'd remember me.'

'Actually, Miss Picard,' he said slowly and left a gap. A very long gap. If it was designed to make Sophie's mind run riot, it worked. 'You'd be surprised what people remember. And the shopkeeper remembers that no plastic swords were sold that day.'

Sophie shook her head. 'That's not true.'

'Shall I tell you how she can be so certain?' He didn't allow her to answer. 'Because she had none to sell. The swords were out of stock. She was waiting for a delivery, which was due that morning, but didn't arrive.'

Giving her a smile that made her insides curdle, Topcop leaned back in his chair.

'I'm sorry to contradict you, and the shopkeeper. But I bought one. I found it right at the back of a shelf, tucked behind some other toys.'

Youngcop rustled some papers and said, 'We asked the owner to check the till receipts. There was no record of any sword being sold that day.' He closed his folder with a snap and looked to his boss.

'Maybe you went to the wrong shop? You said it yourself, every second shop in the Cité sells toy swords.'

He consulted his notes again. 'The souvenir shop nearest the Porte Narbonnaise?'

Sophie could think of nothing to say. At least nothing sensible. All she could manage was a feeble, 'I'm sorry. I don't understand.'

The interpreter started to ask Topcop to repeat what he'd just said. He gave her a withering look and the woman shut her mouth.

'Thank you for your assistance, Miss Picard. That will be all for now.'

Sophie assumed the interview was over and made to rise from her chair. 'So I can go?'

'I expect we will have more questions for you.'

'But I already told you everything I know.'

'An enquiry of this type throws up more questions than it answers. We have a duty to make sure you remain available for questioning.'

Noticing Sophie's puzzled expression, he said, 'Madame Robert?'

The interpreter leaned forward eagerly, a delighted look on her face, but Sophie said, 'It's okay, I understand the words. It's the meaning of your comment I don't get. What exactly are you saying?'

'You were the last person to see the little boy, mademoiselle. That makes you a person of interest, as we say. At the very least an important witness, perhaps more, much more. Time will tell.'

'You don't think I had anything to do with Ethan's disappearance?'

The cop smiled, his eyes cold.

'Am I under arrest?'

Chapter 48

At Abington, the last service station before they were due to leave the motorway, Diane was tempted to keep driving but common sense told her a final stop was necessary. Ethan had been sleeping on and off but he must need a pee by now. As the car navigated the sharp turns of the car park the little boy woke and let out a soft mewling, like a lost kitten.

Making her voice sound much more upbeat than she felt, Diane said, 'Time for a little stop. Shall we see if you need to go potty?'

When she lifted him out of his seat she knew the answer. He was so wet he left a little puddle behind. Wonderful. Another change of clothes required. She was too old for this. Maybe she should have taken the girl instead. At least she was potty trained.

She left the child standing in the footwell and closed the car door while she rummaged in her suitcase for some clean, dry clothes. God, she was tired. She could hear Ethan wailing inside the car. His face was the picture of misery.

She glanced around to see if anyone was watching. The car park was quiet, the hills behind speaking of rural tranquillity. Beyond the filling station she could see the familiar logo of Days Inn. Diane was sorely tempted to run across and see if there was a room available. They could get something to eat, watch the cartoon channel for a while then get a full night's sleep in a proper bed. The very thought of it made Diane yawn and long to stretch out.

She looked at the child, his tear-stained face pressed up against the glass. His tiny nose was leaving a snail trail of mucus on the window. Her first reaction was revulsion, then a few beats too late, pity for a small person in distress. Some mother she'd have made.

She judged the distance to the motel entrance. How long would it take her to run in and ask about a room? She looked back at the kid, who seemed to have increased the volume. She couldn't risk leaving him. Some busybody could have the cops alerted before she made it back out to the car.

And she couldn't take a screaming toddler into a hotel foyer where she might have to stand, exposed to CCTV and the scrutiny of staff and other guests. Even going into the toilets with Ethan in this state would attract more attention than she could afford. Mind made up, she grabbed a towel and closed the boot.

'Sorry,' she said, 'this won't be the most comfortable drive of your short life but I've got no choice.'

She placed the towel on the car seat, where it soaked up the puddle of pee, then lifted Ethan and plopped him on top of it. Shock, or something, made the kid stop wailing for a moment and she took the chance to fasten his harness. The towel made it tricky and by the time she heard the satisfying click of the belt locking into place, Ethan had started up again. Too bad, he'd have to cry for a while.

She got in and started the engine. She could use a toilet trip too but she'd just have to hold it in for now.

Ethan stopped crying, for a reason known only to him, as they left the motorway at the sign for Ayr. Diane heaved a sigh of relief. She was more tired than she'd ever felt in her life. Still, not far to go. Less than thirty miles. The distance between her house and Louis Armstrong airport in New Orleans, give or take a few miles. About fifteen minutes on the freeway.

The satnav was showing forty-five minutes to her destination. That couldn't be right. If she drove just under the UK legal limit of sixty miles an hour they should be there in about twenty minutes.

It took Diane about two miles and the same amount of minutes to work out why there was such a discrepancy in the journey time. No road in the States or Europe could have prepared her for so many twists, turns and bumps. For a moment she thought she must have taken a wrong turning and ventured up a farm track. But a sign saying A70 confirmed her route was correct and besides, there was no imperious 'make a U-turn when possible' from her satnav.

Tight bends and the narrow road meant she had to slow to almost twenty miles an hour in places. Then, when the road finally straightened, a tractor pulled out and putzed along in front of her.

'Come on, come on,' urged Diane. Then remembering her little passenger, she said, 'Look, a big tractor.' She glanced at him in the mirror and the tractor was forgotten.

The kid's face looked green. Must be the light. She looked again, in time to see the little boy vomit. Chocolate-coloured goo spewed from his mouth and the car filled with the sour stench of sick.

Diane gagged as a flood of warm saliva filled her own mouth. She had to stop the car. But where? Goddamn these bends. She banged her palm on the steering wheel in frustration and swerved onto the verge feeling the grass and weeds tangle with the chassis. Diane opened the door and leaned out into the road, expecting her stomach to empty, but nothing. She spat a few times then closed the door and turned to the child. He stared back at her, silent. His blue eyes were wide with shock. Perhaps this was the first time he'd ever vomited. Almost certainly it was the first time without his mom to comfort him.

'Ethan,' she said gently, 'are you okay?'

He shook his head sadly and his lip trembled. Before she could do or say anything, he began to cry. Not the loud, hysterical wails she'd heard earlier but quiet, heartbroken sobs.

Diane felt her own eyes fill. This was ridiculous. She didn't cry. Not really. For effect sometimes, some pretty little tears to make sure she got her own way. Even when her world crashed around her and she found out about Scott's betrayal of her and so many other innocents, she hadn't cried. Anger had kept the tears at bay.

But now?

She staggered round to the passenger side of the car, stumbling into a ditch and snagging her legs on briars as she climbed out again. She opened the door, unclipped the child and ignoring the sight and smell of vomit, she gathered him into her arms and rocked gently from side to side. 'There, there,' she said, through her tears. 'Don't cry, baby boy. Please don't cry.'

Chapter 49

The senior policeman, detective, whatever he was, leaned on the desk and looked straight at Penny. She tried not to squirm under his gaze. He clasped his hands together, a parody of a prayer, and touched his lips to the top of his stubby fingers. He took a deep and noisy breath in. All for effect, Penny thought. He spoke again on the outbreath.

Penny looked to the interpreter, glad to have a reason to break eye contact with this man. She knew he was there to help them, but she found his manner unnerving.

'Why do I feel there's something you are not telling me?' quoted the interpreter.

'I have no idea,' said Penny, evading the issue. Sudden doubt about what was the right thing for Ethan made her tremble.

Seth touched her knee. The weight of his hand felt good. 'You mentioned some CCTV footage.' he said, as if to hurry the interview along. 'Can we see it please?'

'Well, it's not exactly CCTV,' said the policeman, 'we don't have such a thing. The quality is poor, but it may be worth a look.' He nodded to his younger colleague who tapped at a keypad and turned a monitor towards them.

'Okay?' he asked.

Penny nodded and clung to Seth's arm. She could hardly bear to look. Was this the moment they would see who stole their son? Seth took her hand in his and squeezed her fingers. 'Here goes,' he said, with a grimace of a smile.

The screen reminded Penny of the snow globe she had as a child. Flurries of white floated around then gradually dispersed to reveal the scene.

'Look!' said Seth.

'What am I looking at? It's just a blur to me.'

The cop said, 'The picture quality is not the best, I agree, but it's all we've got. Look there.' He leaned forward, stopped just short of touching the screen. 'Sophie. Pushing Ethan in his stroller.'

Penny clasped her hands over her mouth. She couldn't see the baby for the crowds of tourists in the narrow street, but that tiny glimpse of his stroller was enough to rock her world.

They watched Sophie stop outside the souvenir shop.

'She's disappeared,' said Penny, as if watching an illusion. 'Where did she go? Did she just walk off and abandon him?'

'No,' said the young cop, who seemed to be in charge of this part of the proceedings. 'She's there, kneeling by the child. You'll see in a moment.'

A young woman walked across the screen holding an umbrella aloft. A stream of tourists traipsed along behind her, all wearing surgical masks. Penny whispered, 'Come on, come on.' When they kept coming, she lost her last bit of patience. 'Get out of the way!'

At last a space cleared around Sophie and Ethan. The girl was on her knees on the cobbles. Penny tried desperately to interpret Sophie's body language. It gave away nothing.

Penny caught a glimpse of the tiny dark head and thought her heart would burst. When Sophie appeared to touch the baby's hair, Penny heard a choked sob from Seth. He loved to ruffle Ethan's curls. 'Hey, L'il Buddy,' he'd say. Penny stroked his hand, letting him know she shared his pain.

The screen filled with elderly people strolling past, stopping to wait for others to catch up.

'I can't see. It's too crowded,' said Penny. 'Where the hell are they all coming from?'

The police officer tapped a key. Figures froze like statues. 'It's that time of day. Most of the tourists have just got off their coaches.'

'Hang on,' said Seth. 'Did you say, got *off* their coaches?' He scratched the back of his neck. 'What time is this supposed to be?'

'We estimate mid-morning.'

'That's not possible,' said Penny. 'I spoke to Sophie in the afternoon. She said Ethan was having a late nap.'

'Do you remember what time you called?'

'Not exactly, but it was late afternoon. Check my phone. She was due to collect Angel. She said she'd fallen asleep after lunch. I panicked when she said that. I thought she must have been up all night with the kids.'

'How can you tell the time from this?' said Seth.

Youngcop pointed at the monitor. 'These tourists have just arrived. Look at the way they're facing. All walking in the same direction. No carrier bags. They've not hit the souvenir shops yet. It's definitely morning.'

'But,' said Penny, 'there must be some mistake. Sophie wouldn't lie to me. Would she, Seth?'

Seth gave her a look. 'This is guesswork,' he said, waving a dismissive hand towards the screen. 'Don't you have a decent tape with a clock running?'

'I'm afraid not.'

'Unbelievable.' Seth shook his head.

'Are you ready to see some more?'

Penny glanced at Seth. He was chewing the skin on his index finger. 'Yes,' he said, 'of course we are.'

The old people shuffled on, slow as zombies, and for a few seconds the tiny street cleared.

'Stop the tape!' Seth touched the space where Ethan had been. Looked from one policeman to the other. 'He's gone! In those few minutes?'

'I'm afraid so.'

'Take it back to where she kneels by the buggy.'

The tape was rewound and rewound again. Ethan was there. Ethan was gone. Like some sinister magic trick. The Amazing Disappearing Boy.

'Can you slow it? Let us watch it frame by frame?'

'We've slowed it and enhanced it as much as we can.'

'You're telling me this is the best you can do?' Seth's expression was a mixture of disgust and disbelief. 'In this day and age? The quality's terrible. Is this official police CCTV?'

'No, it's from a private video camera, set up by the shop to keep an eye on their suit of armour.'

Seth snorted. 'It's a piece of crap.'

Penny could understand his frustration. 'And this is all you've got to go on?' she asked.

'So far. Would you like to see the moment where Miss Picard comes out of the shop?'

'We have to,' said Penny, 'don't we, Seth?'

'I wouldn't care if I never saw her again, but yeah, I guess so.'

Sophie appeared in the shop doorway and turned to her left. Someone passed the camera and Sophie was hidden. Penny moved in her seat, angling her head as if she was in a movie theatre trying to get a better view.

Sophie reappeared, facing the other way.

'Can't you at least zoom in?' asked Seth. 'So we can read her expression?'

'Sorry. We've tried, believe me. Technicians have been working on this since we got it.'

'Do you have any still photos?'

The policeman passed over a folder. Seth opened it and Penny leaned in close so she could see. The image was blurry but the face was recognisable as Sophie's.

'I knew it,' said Seth.

'What do you know, sir?'

'Look at her expression. Why isn't she shocked? Surprised?'

Penny shook her head. 'Seth,' she said.

He lifted the photo. Stabbed it with his finger. 'Tell me that's an innocent face.'

Chapter 50

'Would you like something else?' asked the waitress, reaching for Sophie's coffee cup. The cup that had been empty for at least half an hour.

'No, thank you. I have to go.'

She rose from the low rattan chair, sighing in exasperation. Or was it disappointment? Worry? Sadness? Sophie had so many emotions battling for control she didn't know how she felt, other than deeply troubled.

She'd been longer at the police station than she'd anticipated, but not that much. Marc had said he'd throw her phone in the canal if she wasn't back in an hour.

That phone was the only line of contact with Ethan.

As more minutes ticked by, Sophie ran through the reasons Marc might be late. There were loads.

Then the reasons why he might not come. Not so many of those.

Maybe he'd lost the phone and didn't want to tell her?

She'd said her phone was full of precious images she couldn't bear to lose. Maybe he'd decided to take a look at her photos, and found none. All that precious information she said she couldn't bear to lose? Had he become suspicious? Maybe he checked her call records and found only one number?

What if he rang it, out of curiosity? Spoke to Miss L? She would know Sophie had screwed up.

What if he was at the police station right now? Handing it over. Telling the cops she'd tried to hide it. Telling them she'd be sitting here in the Place Carnot, waiting.

Sophie scanned the square for uniforms. She'd been planning to go looking for Marc's apartment, ring door bells randomly till she found him, in case he'd simply lain down for a siesta and was still asleep. Or was getting ready to go back to work.

Work. Of course.

Sophie made a beeline across the square to the pizza place.

'We're not open,' called a voice from the kitchen. The wood oven's flames were burning pale yellow as if the fire had just been lit.

'I'm looking for Marc,' said Sophie, trying to keep her own voice bright and friendly. 'When will he be in?'

A flour-covered face appeared at a hatch. 'He won't be.'

'Sorry?'

'I fired him. High season's over. I don't need so many staff. And he was always late so I let him go.'

'I need to find him. It's really important.'

The chef shrugged. 'Did you try his apartment?'

'Where is it?' Sophie knew her voice had lost the friendly note, but she didn't care.

'No idea. Sorry. If he looks in I can tell him you're looking for him.'

'Tell him to leave my phone here.'

'What's your name?'

Sophie headed for the door, ignoring the question. What a fool she'd been. Trusting a total stranger.

Chapter 51

'What makes you think Miss Picard is involved in the disappearance of your son, sir?'

'Apart from the fact she's been lying to us, *and you*, about the time Ethan disappeared?'

'But you had some suspicions before?'

'Yes, and my wife found out this morning that Sophie already "lost" our little girl once.' He held his hands in the air where his fingers had drawn invisible quotation marks.

'When you say lost, what exactly do you mean?'

Seth nudged her arm. 'Why don't *you* tell them?'

Penny cleared her throat, suddenly nervous. What if they agreed with Seth that Sophie was guilty? Taking her on as au pair had been Penny's idea. Seth would blame her.

'When I was taking my daughter to school this morning, she mentioned that, on Sophie's first day with us, she lost her.'

'Go on, please. We're listening.'

'Sophie and Angeline woke early and went out to buy croissants for breakfast, as a surprise. We were still asleep, tired after the journey, I suppose, you know jet lag and everything?'

Both policemen nodded, but said nothing.

'Well, apparently, Sophie left Angel sitting on a bench by herself.'

'And?'

Penny felt her cheeks colour. She spread her hands as if to say, 'Draw your own conclusions.'

No one spoke, leaving Penny to fill the silence. 'Angel wandered off to play hide and go seek with some local kids. According to Angel, Sophie was raging. She said the F-word.'

The younger of the two cops looked as if he was trying not to smile.

'Why is that funny?' asked Penny.

'It's not funny, madame. I understand your concerns. You entrusted her with your child and she left that child unaccompanied.'

'Just like she did with Ethan,' interrupted Seth.

'But she then found Angela.'

'She's called Angeline,' said Penny, wishing she'd never started this.

'So, she didn't actually *lose* your little girl. She left her alone for a moment and the child wandered off by herself, is that correct?'

'Yes, but she *could* have lost her, don't you see? And to make matters worse, she told Angeline to keep the whole thing secret from us. That's not good, is it?'

'No, it's not. But I'm not sure it helps us very much, unless Sophie has asked Angeline to keep other secrets?'

Penny didn't know what he meant.

'Secrets about her plans for Ethan's abduction?'

Inspector Morand said something to the interpreter. His voice was gruff and impatient.

Penny waited for the translation.

'We're wasting time here. And every hour that passes minimises our chances of finding Ethan alive.'

'Finding Ethan alive?' said Seth. 'Jesus, are you seriously telling us you think Ethan might *not* be alive?'

'I don't think that's what my colleague means, but there is strong evidence to support the need to move quickly to trace a missing person within seventy-two hours.'

Penny looked at the clock but couldn't do the maths. Especially if, as the cops were suggesting, Ethan went missing in the morning.

'That's why it's important you don't keep from us any information that might help move the search forward.'

She knew Seth was looking at her but she was careful to avoid making eye contact with him. She also knew what he was thinking.

'And,' continued the policeman, 'it's important to give members of the public the chance to come forward with information.

'Mrs Gates?' He waited till she looked straight at him, like a teacher waiting for his pupils' full attention. 'You realise one of those tourists on that video could have seen whoever took Ethan? Or could, at least, confirm the time.'

'You think someone saw him being taken?' Penny felt a surge of optimism.

'I think there's a very strong chance, but they won't come forward with that information because they don't know the person wheeling your son away had no right to do so.'

'What are you saying?'

'I'm saying if my child were missing, I would use every bit of help I could get.'

'Meaning?'

'Meaning, I would do a television appeal.'

'We should do it, Penny,' said Seth. 'We're crazy not to.'

'We can't,' she whispered. 'You know that.'

'I think we can't *not* do it. We owe it to Ethan.'

They sat and stared at each other, more like combatants than lovers.

Morand sighed dramatically and said, 'Very well. Of course, we cannot force you to make an appeal on television, but I am obliged to ask you why you are afraid to do so.'

'We can't tell you that.'

Another sigh, bigger and louder this time. For effect? Or was he really getting pissed off?

'Penny,' said Seth. 'It's time to tell them.'

She shook her head slowly from side to side over and over again, her eyes never leaving his. She saw him make his decision.

'No, Seth, please don't.'

He looked away, clearing his throat, the way he always did when he was nervous. And she knew. He was going to tell them everything. Their identities wouldn't be protected for much longer.

Chapter 52

It was getting dark by the time she found the cottage. It sat back from the road, surrounded on three sides by tall trees that groaned in the wind. Normally that eerie sound would keep her awake. Not tonight.

The keys were where she'd been told to find them.

Diane set the little boy down on the doorstep. He whimpered and clung to her leg.

'It's okay,' she said. 'Just a teensy, weensy minute till Mawmaw opens the door.' She ruffled the top of his head and smiled down at his little face. He stopped grizzling and reached out for the keys.

'Let's get inside and then you can play with the keys.'

The key turned easily and the door swung open with none of the scary theatrical creaks one might expect from a lone cottage on a dark road.

She picked Ethan up and gave him a reassuring hug, feeling reassured herself when his little arms went around her neck. She hadn't realised how much she'd been missing the touch of another person.

The room she stepped into was small but cosy. And warm. That was a bonus. A grate in the fireplace had been filled with logs, ready to be lit.

She sat Ethan on a plump armchair and handed him the keys to examine. 'Wait here while Mawmaw brings in the bags. Okay?'

He looked up at her, very serious, and said, 'Kay.'

'Back in a tick.'

The car was a mess, the smell of vomit still strong and bitter. She'd worry about cleaning it up tomorrow. She grabbed some of

Ethan's books, stuffed them in her bag and bumped the door shut with her butt.

Car lights beamed towards her from the distance. Diane cringed like a vampire in sunlight and ran for the cottage door. She did not want to be spotted by some curious neighbour who might set local tongues a-wagging.

As she dashed into the room Ethan looked up from his bunch of keys and smiled at her. 'Mawmaw,' he said, and something deep inside her melted. She wasn't sure she liked the feeling and turned snippy.

'Come on, young man. Time for a bath and then bed.'

Ethan started to grumble, clearly not delighted at either prospect. He probably wasn't sleepy. She wondered if he might be hungry. Or needing to use the toilet.

'Want to go potty, Ethan?' she asked, as if inviting him to play a game.

'No,' he said, in a voice that made arguing a waste of time.

She hoped he wasn't going to become difficult over toilet issues, but she sure wasn't going to fight with him about it tonight. 'Okay,' she said brightly. 'Maybe later. Let's go explore, shall we?'

She held out her hand and was astonished when the little boy took it. She helped him off the chair and together they set off to check out their new home.

It didn't take long. An old-fashioned wooden door opened onto a stone-floored kitchen fitted with modern units.

'Wonder if the nice lady has left us some food?' Diane opened the door of a large larder-style fridge. It appeared to be stocked with all the things she'd asked for: fresh vegetables and fruit, orange juice in a bottle, not a carton. She preferred her juice freshly squeezed but had guessed that was unrealistic in Scotland. She opened a carton to reveal six rich brown eggs.

'Eggs,' said Ethan, sounding pleased with himself.

'That's right. Does Ethan like eggs?'

'Omnom,' said the little boy, making her laugh.

'How about some eggs and toast soldiers to dip in? Would you like that?'

He thought about it for a moment then nodded.

'Good. Let's see if we can find a pan to cook them in, shall we?'

Diane opened one cupboard door after another until she found a collection of saucepans. She set a group of them in a semicircle on the floor then took a couple of spoons from a rack near the cooker. Ethan watched intently. He rewarded her with a dribbly grin as she started to bang on the pots. It wasn't musical, but it was fun. She offered him the spoons and watched as he knelt in the middle of the pans and began to hammer them in turn. When she covered her ears with her hands and pretended it was too loud, Ethan laughed and banged all the harder.

Diane left him to his music and went in search of the bedrooms. There were supposed to be two and a box room, whatever that was. A room to keep boxes in, perhaps? She'd not have much use for that.

In fact, the box room turned out to be a tiny bedroom, perfect for a little boy or girl.

Next door was a bathroom, surprisingly well equipped for an old cottage. She looked longingly at the tub and the bottle of good quality bath foam that rested on its rim. She unscrewed the lid and inhaled florals and spices. How she wished she could settle in for a long, relaxing soak in hot, fragrant water. Maybe once the kid was in bed, if she could stay awake that long.

Diane was checking the bedlinen in 'her' bedroom when she realised the drummer had stopped playing. The kitchen was ominously quiet as she approached.

Ethan was standing by the table, his feet surrounded by broken eggs. He looked up at Diane, smiled and said, 'Oops, what a mess!'

'It certainly is,' said Diane, crossly. 'Why did you *do* that, Ethan? Now we've got no eggs to eat. That was very naughty.'

Whether it was her tone, or the look on her face, she didn't know, but the kid's smile faded; his mouth stretched into a square-shaped hole and he started to cry.

She tried to pick him up, telling him to hush, but he twisted and writhed in her arms.

'No,' he yelled, 'no, no, no.'

'Come on, Ethan,' she cajoled, trying to keep calm and avoid upsetting him further. The child was having none of it.

'Mommy,' he wailed, 'Mommeeeeee.'

Suddenly he went quiet and limp. She thought he'd given up, but before she could set him on the floor, he took a gulp of air and started yelling again. She tried to clasp him to her, hoping to reassure and comfort, but his body went rigid. It was like trying to hug a wooden post.

'Stop that, right now,' she said. Even to her own ears she sounded strict, school-marmish. It didn't matter. The child wasn't listening. He was lost in his own misery.

Nothing in Diane's whole life had come close to preparing her for this. She'd never had siblings, nor cute baby cousins to cradle and coo over. Their friends had children and grandchildren but she and Scott had never been ones for hosting child-friendly events. The very expression made her cringe. An invitation to their home was always for adults only and everyone knew that. She'd never seen anyone deal with a toddler tantrum and hadn't the foggiest of notions how to stop a kid screaming. Apart from putting a pillow over his face.

She let Ethan go. Like a stringless puppet he dropped to the floor and lay there on his back, still for a moment. Then he started to flail like an epileptic in a fit. His arms battered the tiles and his little legs kicked at the air then thumped off the floor.

The pillow was beginning to seem like an attractive option.

Time to get out before she was driven to do something she'd regret, if only for the timing.

She retrieved her suitcase from the car, wondering how she'd ended up in a foreign country with a child screaming blue murder.

She was tempted to drive to the nearest airport and leave him to it. If he screamed long enough and hard enough someone would come to investigate. If not, well, what the hell. The owner had said she'd drop by at the end of the week to make sure everything was to Diane's liking. She'd find him. And the news would be round the world in minutes. The mystery of the missing boy would be solved within hours.

Daddy always said *do nothing rash*. He was right; she'd come too far and waited too long to blow it now. But she was just so tired. And that plump armchair by the fireplace looked so inviting. Diane sat down and let the chair embrace her. She leaned her head back and closed her eyes. Ten years she'd waited for this. Ten years since Lucie Jardine had blown her world apart. Diane sat and watched the movie of her life play inside her head. They'd been happy, she and Scott. Rich enough to enjoy every frill life had to offer. And yet Scott was never satisfied. He always had something to prove. To her, or, more likely, her father. 'Stop, Scott,' she'd say, 'what more can we possibly wish for? We already have more money than we'll ever be able to spend.' But Scott couldn't stop. Making money was more than a passion, it was an addiction. They never discussed how he made his money. Sure, she had a vague idea, but when she asked about a new venture, Scott would say, 'Don't you go worrying that pretty little head of yours. It's my job to make the money and your job to spend it.' She'd been only too happy to comply.

Only when they'd lost everything did she realise she'd been spoilt by men all her life. First Grandaddy, then her father. Scott just took over the role of indulging her every whim. Too late she realised that she'd wasted her brain. And that it suited the men in her life to make out she didn't have one. They were wrong. If only Scott had shared his plans with her, she might have been able to counsel him. Warned him away from such a high-risk gamble. Kept him out of the clutches of that Charlotte Gillespie. Strangely, Diane didn't blame Charlotte for what had happened. No point in blaming her – she'd paid the ultimate price for her part in Scott's scheme. And, to his credit, Scott had chosen to stay with Diane. Okay, maybe he and Charlotte had been more than business partners, but so what. He was a man and men had needs. His little affairs suited Diane, so long as they stayed just that. Turned out Charlotte had been looking for more. Scott claimed that was why he had to 'deal with her'.

Diane had not attended his court case. It was fine for Tammy Wynette to stand by her man, but a court of law was no place for a woman like Diane. Her reputation had been tarnished badly enough by the disgrace Scott had brought on himself. She had no desire to see her face splashed all over the gutter press. But just because she'd stayed away from court didn't mean she could avoid the scandal altogether. Whatever had possessed him to act on classified information for his own gains? Greed was the answer. Pure and simple.

The one she felt sorry for was Scott's brother. Okay, he shouldn't have told Scott what he knew, but he was only trying to save his kid brother from harm, as he'd done all his life.

She'd be eternally grateful to Bill. Why, without his help she'd never have found Lucie Jardine.

Chapter 53

Penny woke with a sick feeling, like a bad hangover. They had fought before bedtime. About Sophie, who still hadn't come home by the time they went to bed exhausted. Penny couldn't blame the girl for staying out till she was sure they'd be asleep. While Penny was keen to hear Sophie's explanation, she was sure there was nothing sinister. Seth did not share her confidence in Sophie. And that was what had started the fight.

Penny was caught in a snare of her own making. She couldn't explain her continuing trust in Sophie without telling Seth how, for months, she'd been wary of just about every single person she set eyes on. From that first moment in the airport Penny had felt intuitively that Sophie was someone she could trust with the children. Call it mother's instinct.

Then there was the witness protection thing and the TV appeal. Penny's fear of it had come out as anger towards Seth, even though she knew he believed they had no choice. Time for finding Ethan was running out. The cops said they had to jog the memory of the public before some other tragedy caught their attention.

Penny felt like she hadn't slept at all. Seth continued to snore. What was wrong with the man? How could he lie there, blissfully unconscious, when they were about to go public and tell the world they'd lost their child?

She would be crucified by the press. And even if, for some reason, the mainstream media decided to treat her kindly, Penny knew that on social media she'd be torn apart like a piece of meat thrown to starving dogs. A mother who loses her child is only entitled to so much sympathy, it seemed. Then people start to ask questions. If *they* can keep their kids safe and sound, how stupid does a woman need to be to let hers get snatched?

In her sleepless hours, Penny had imagined every scenario.

Women in coffee shops, toddlers by their side in strollers, serene and happy. Mothers in the park, sitting in circles on hand-knitted blankets, babies gurgling happily on their laps. Moms chatting outside school gates, waiting for kids to run into their arms.

She could hear their conversations.

She what? Let some kid she'd just met look after her children? You can't be serious.

She left them overnight with this girl she barely knew? No way.

You're telling me she didn't check the nanny's credentials? Sorry, I can't believe that's true.

No woman would be that dumb.

What kind of mother …

Maybe they were right, these perfect moms. She'd screwed up big time.

She was dreading the next few hours. She knew it shouldn't matter, and despised herself for even thinking about it, but what was she to wear? Should she tidy her hair that had last seen a hairbrush in Toulouse? Was make-up appropriate? Or would the world respond better to wild, unkempt hair and a haggard, distraught face, blotchy with tears?

She and Seth would appear on TV all over the world. Penny imagined their former friends watching on wide flat screens. She could see poor families clustered round tiny black and white cubes. Working men staring over their beers at screens above bars. She could see their own snug television room in Humble, strangers watching from *her* sofa. She thought of Curtis, sitting in his wheelchair, seeing her and Seth together. He'd call out to his little nurse, 'Hey, come and see this. Lucie and Dylan, man and wife? Hot damn!' Wouldn't he feel he'd been double-crossed? Wouldn't he be mad?

And what about Scott Millburn? They had televisions in prison, didn't they? He'd be watching. He'd know where she was. He'd find out all about her new life. With his connections, he could easily come after her.

Or send someone else to do his dirty work for him.

What was it he'd said to her that night in Manhattan? He didn't like loose ends. Charlotte had been a loose end. Penny had seen what happened to her. She'd fallen over the poor woman lying dead in the street. Wiped out, like she was nothing more than a mistake Millburn needed to erase before she caused him any more trouble.

And Charlotte's sin against him had been nothing compared to what Lucie Jardine had done. She, Lucie, Penny, was the reason he was behind bars. Without her, he'd be living happily ever after, obscenely, immorally, unimaginably rich.

'Seth. Wake up.' She shook his arm.

He flopped onto his back but continued to snore. More loudly now, with his mouth wide open.

'Dylan!' she said, his name feeling strange on her lips.

'What?' he muttered. 'What is it? Why are you calling me that?'

'I need to talk to you.'

'No, you need to talk to *Sophie*. Did you hear her come in eventually?'

'No, did you?' she snapped, instantly regretting the sharpness of her tongue.

He groaned and rolled onto his side, turning his back on her.

She grabbed his shoulder and shook, maybe a little more roughly than necessary.

With an enormous sigh and much heaving of the mattress, Seth rolled over. His breath smelt sour and she turned her face to the side as she spoke. 'Seth, we have to talk.'

'Oh, Penny, sweetheart. What is there left to say? We know what we've got to do today. What time is it anyway?'

'I don't know. Early.'

'How early?'

'Five, I guess.'

'Five?' Seth groaned.

'Maybe it's six. Does it matter?'

'Well, honey, it kinda does. We've got a difficult day ahead of us and we've got to be alert.'

'That's what we have to talk about.'

'Have you slept at all, honey?'

'Not much.'

'Come on, tuck in here. I'm sorry we fought. Forgive me?' He raised his arm so she could nestle underneath. The place she usually felt safe from the world. What a load of crap.

'Yes, of course I do. But we still need to talk.'

'Okay, talk. I'm listening.

'I'm not mad at you anymore. I get it now. The police needed to know who we were before. And why I needed protection.'

'They did. I'm sorry telling them upset you so much.'

'Listen to me,' she said, cutting him off. She had no time for apologies or explanations. 'It's Scott Millburn. He's behind this.'

'Millburn's in prison, Penny. You know that. High-security prison. He's considered an enemy of the state for what he did.'

'I know that, but it doesn't mean he couldn't have taken Ethan, does it?'

Seth laughed for a second. As if she'd said something silly. Maybe she had.

'Well, yes. It kinda does, if you think about it.'

'Well, I don't mean him personally. But he could have paid somebody else to take the baby.'

'Like Sophie, you mean?' Seth raised himself to lean on one elbow. 'Now how could he do that?'

'Don't patronise me.'

'I'm not.'

'Yes, you are. You're speaking to me like I'm about five years old. You don't even speak to Angel like that.'

'Maybe that's because Angel makes more sense than you, right now.'

Penny counted in her head, telling herself to stay silent until she got to ten.

'Okay, I might be talking garbage, but I need you to listen to me, please. This stuff's been going through my head for hours.'

'Sorry, babe, I'm listening. Go ahead.'

'Well, I was lying here worrying about this TV thing. Fretting about Curtis seeing you and me together, as man and wife, and how that might make him feel real mad.'

'Honey, we've talked about this.'

Penny put her hand on his mouth and hissed, 'Shh! You said you'd listen.'

Seth nodded.

'I'm not worried about Curtis anymore. You were right. But thinking about him being mad at me made me think of Scott Millburn. He'll be really ticked off.'

'I guess you could put it that way.'

'So, what if he decided to get revenge?'

'By snatching our kid? He couldn't do that, Penny. The guy's locked up. Don't you remember what you were promised when you agreed to testify? They'd not only lock him up and throw away the key, they said they'd demolish the prison and build a new one before he got parole.'

'He'll have contacts, a guy like him. And I bet he's still got money. Enough money to pay someone to find out where we are. And follow us.'

'To Europe?' Seth shook his head. 'Never gonna happen, Penny.'

'Okay, say it did. What if he's been watching us all along? While we thought we were safe enough to relax. Safe enough to bring children into the world. What if he's been getting regular updates on our lives? "They've gone, Mr Millburn. Quit New York. Living in Texas now. Got new names, new house, new car. Oh, Lucie alert, Mr Millburn. She's pregnant." Can you imagine how that must have enraged him? We're playing happy families while he's holed up in the penitentiary? I think he's come after us. Found the best way to hurt us.'

Penny lost her last little bit of self-control and started to sob. 'Sorry, you must be sick of me crying all the time.'

He took her in his arms and cradled her like a baby. Normally she loved that but she was too tense. She pushed him away. 'Listen to me, Seth. We need to tell the cops right now that we suspect Scott Millburn. They could get the Feds to question him. Make him tell us where Ethan is. Before it's too late.'

'And what about Sophie? Why did she lie about the time?'

'If she did. Do you really think the police would have let her go if that video had proved she'd been lying?'

'Yeah, I guess it's pretty circumstantial, as evidence goes, when you think about it. Everyone walking in the same direction proves it's morning?'

'Sophie's innocent, Seth. Young and naïve, certainly, but innocent. I refuse to believe she had anything to do with this. It has to be Millburn. Why didn't I think of it before?' She pushed away from him and got out of bed. Started to pull on clothes that had spent the night on the floor.

'What are you doing?'

'I'm getting up. So are you. We need to talk to the cops.'

Seth reached for his phone. She thought he was going to call the police but he just checked the time. He lay back on the pillows. 'Penny, it's barely six o'clock. Come back to bed.'

'Are you crazy? There's no time to waste. They said we were to get in touch immediately if we thought of anything.' She was hopping on one foot trying to pull on a shoe.

'I'm pretty sure they didn't mean in the middle of the night. Come on, Penny. This is ridiculous.'

'No, Seth, what's ridiculous is that you've thrown them a curve ball, wasting time, telling them Sophie's the prime suspect. When all along it's obvious who's got Ethan.'

She grabbed a sweater from the back of the door and said from the threshold. 'I'll be downstairs making coffee.'

'Check on Sophie, will you?'

Chapter 54

Diane had woken, very cold, some time in the early hours. She'd taken a moment to work out why she was asleep in a strange armchair instead of her own bed. Then it had all come back to her. And home had seemed so very, very far away.

With a shock she'd remembered the child, last seen mid-tantrum on the kitchen floor. Good Lord, he'd probably died of hypothermia. The heating must have gone off hours ago.

She made for the kitchen door and opened it gently, dreading what she might find. Wondering which would be the worse discovery – the kid dead or the kid alive.

She'd found him on the floor, exactly where she'd left him, curled up like a baby in a womb, preserving his body heat by some ancient instinct of self-preservation.

She'd scooped him up into her arms, registering how heavy he felt for such a little boy. She decided it was better to risk a wet bed than to wake him and so she'd laid him gently down on one side of her double bed. With her raincoat underneath him and the covers over both of them Ethan had slept on and she had eventually fallen asleep again.

Now a faint grey light was coming through the little cottage window. Dawn? Surely too late for that? She checked the time. It was almost nine. It should be daylight outside. She rose and went to the window. Rain was falling. A steady drizzle dropping from a leaden sky that looked far closer to the ground than any sky she'd ever seen.

She looked at the child, his little face smeared with last night's tears and vomit. She felt a rush of emotions that she couldn't begin to disentangle. Guilt, sure. Concern, yes. Affection? She hoped not.

She must be careful not to be brusque with the child today. She must be gentle and kind. It wasn't his fault he was in this situation. So far he was coping remarkably well for such a young child taken from his family.

She watched Ethan's eyelids begin to tremble, frail as butterfly wings. Then slowly he opened his eyes. Diane held her breath, waiting for the inevitable tears. Who could blame the child if he started to scream and didn't stop till he was reunited with his mommy.

His eyes widened. Diane felt her fingers crossing themselves, unbidden. Then, suddenly, Ethan smiled at her. 'Mawmaw?'

'Yes, sweetie. It's Mawmaw. Good morning.'

'Potty, Mawmaw.'

'Come on then, let's go potty. Quick, quick, quick.'

Hand in hand they dashed to the toilet and Ethan let go the longest stream Diane had ever seen.

'What a clever boy,' she said, genuine delight making her want to hug the child. She resisted, but kept her voice light and bright. 'Now, how about a nice bath full of bubbles to play in?' She hoped he was too small to have any set bath routine and it seemed she got lucky. Ethan started to strip off his clothes, chanting, 'Bubbles, bubbles, bubbles, bubbles.'

Before she knew what she was doing, Diane found herself singing. The song was a favourite from her own childhood. She could hear Emmeline's rich voice as she and Ethan waited for the bath to fill.

'I'm forever blowing bubbles,' she sang. 'Pretty bubbles in the air. They fly so high, up to the sky.' She scooped a pile of bubbles onto the palm of her hand and blew hard so they rose in the air and came down around Ethan's head like confetti on a bride.

The little boy laughed. 'More, Mawmaw,' he cried. 'More bubbles.'

The bath was a great success with lots of splashing and laughter. The trouble started when Diane tried to get Ethan out of the bath. He wanted more fun. She wanted him dried and dressed so they could have some breakfast. He must be starving too, she reckoned, but the kid refused to be tempted by offers of food. When she ran out of patience, Diane grabbed him under the arms and lifted him out of the water. As she tried to wrap him in a towel, Ethan fought her, slithering from her grasp time and again.

Was this what lay ahead of her? A constant battle of wills with a two-year-old? It was too ridiculous for words. Diane simply would not have it.

She carried him swaddled in the towel to the bedroom and dumped him, none too gently, on top of the bed. 'Okay, Ethan,' she said, 'Mawmaw's gonna wait right here till you decide to be a good boy and get your clothes on. Then we can go and find some sausages. Ethan likes sausages.'

Ethan refused to be coaxed out of his cocoon. She was trying to decide whether he might smother if she left him wrapped up when she heard a phone ring.

'You wait here, Ethan, while I get this.'

Diane ran for the stairs and dashed to the chair where she'd dumped her bag last night. She fumbled around inside till she found her phone. There was a signal, not strong, but a signal.

'Sophie,' she said. 'At last. I've been getting worried.'

No response.

'Sophie? You there?'

Still no answer, but she could hear nasal breathing. Not very ladylike. She'd have to have a word.

'Sophie? Please don't play silly games with me, my dear. I am *not* in the mood.'

A thought occurred to her. What if this wasn't Sophie on the other end of the line? Say she'd lost her phone? Or, Lord forbid, the police had confiscated it? Diane hung up.

She put her head on one side, listening for Ethan. He wasn't crying.

Diane redialled. 'Hello?' she said, when the phone was answered. 'May I speak to Sophie?'

'Sophie isn't here right now.'

The voice was male, American, and sounded young. She didn't recognise it, but she was pretty sure it wasn't the French police.

'Who is this, please? And would you mind telling me why you have my niece's phone?'

'I'm sorry. My name's Marc. There's been a misunderstanding. I have Sophie's phone because she asked me to keep it for her.'

'Now, why in heaven's name would she do that?'

The young man didn't answer right away, making Diane think he wasn't sure what to say. 'I guess she just wanted me to keep it safe for her.'

'Why couldn't she keep it safe herself?'

Again, hesitation before he answered. 'I'm not sure. The trouble is, she promised to be back within an hour. When she didn't turn up, well, I had a train to catch that I couldn't afford to miss.'

'So you just went off with her phone?'

'Sorry, I couldn't think of anything else to do. Don't worry, she'll get it back.'

'And how, pray tell, will she do that, if you've left town?'

'Well, I was thinking you could give me your address and I'll post the phone to you. Maybe you can give it back to Sophie when you see her?'

'I'm afraid that won't be possible.'

'No worries. I'll hand it in to the police later today.'

'Don't you dare!' The words were out before Diane could stop them. 'Sorry, I mean, there's no need for you to do that. Oh, my goodness, I'm sure the police won't be interested in a silly old phone that has lost its owner.' Diane gave a trill of girlish laughter, conscious that she'd turned up the wattage on her Southern Belle routine. 'Now, why don't you just send it back to Sophie like the gentleman I'm sure you are.'

'I've no idea where she is. It will be a lot easier for me to just hand it over and let the cops sort it out.'

'Please don't do that, Marc. I'm sure we can come to some arrangement.'

'You both seem very keen that the police don't get this phone.'

'Both? Is that what Sophie said?'

Diane heard a sigh, as if the young man was getting fed up with the conversation. 'Okay, there's no other way to put this. Sophie asked me to keep her phone for her while she went to speak to the police. She didn't want them taking it as evidence.'

'Oh, my good lord! Evidence? What on earth's happened?'

'Sorry, I wasn't sure if you knew about any of this. Did you know she was looking after a little boy who has disappeared?'

'Disappeared? How, disappeared?'

'He was snatched when Sophie went into a shop and no one has seen him since.'

'Oh, those poor, poor parents. How awful. And you say the police are blaming Sophie for this child going missing?'

'No, not at all. It's just that she was worried they'd take her phone for investigation and so she left it with me.'

'And she didn't come back for it?'

'I don't know. I told her I only had an hour, and I waited as long as I could. Almost made me miss my train, in fact. And sorry, before you ask, I *had* to get to Paris. I'm flying home to California tomorrow. My dad set up the flights and paid for them. He'd be really pissed if I'd missed the connection because some girl I hardly knew gave me her phone to hold.'

'I can certainly see your father's point of view.'

'Look, I'd really like to hand over this phone before I go. If you can't help then the police are my only option.'

She tried for a light, carefree tone of voice. 'Oh, I'm sure we can think of some other solution. You know how it is. Once the police get a hold of something, you can have the very devil of a time getting it back. Especially in France. Did you know it was the French who invented the word bureaucracy? Please don't misunderstand me, they are lovely people, but oh, my goodness me, they do love their paperwork.'

'I get that, ma'am, but I don't feel comfortable keeping Sophie's phone. I'm going to hand it in.'

'Please don't do that. Say, why don't you throw it away? Yes, that's what to do. Just drop it in a trash can and forget all about it. And don't worry your head about Sophie. I'll buy her a new phone the minute I see her. My goodness, I know I spoil that girl, but why not? She's the only family I've got.'

Diane had the disconcerting feeling she was talking to herself. 'Hello?' she said. 'Hello, are you still there?'

He'd rung off. Freaked by her instruction to throw a six-hundred-dollar phone in the trash, no doubt. She must have sounded like a madwoman. He was probably on his way to the nearest police station right now.

The house was too quiet. Not a sound from Ethan. She shouldn't have left him on his own. She ran for the stairs, praying he was okay.

The bedroom was empty, the towel trailing off the end of the bed.

Chapter 55

The pink washbasin, like the rest of the rented room, had surely seen cleaner, if not better, days. Sophie stood on tiptoe to see in the little mirror. Her face, obscured by brown liver spots in the glass, looked like an old lady's. She raised the scissors.

'You're a fool, Sophie,' she said. 'Why the hell don't you just run for the airport? You could be on a plane out of here before anyone knows you've skipped town.' She put the scissors down on the edge of the basin and thought about reaching for her phone. Then remembered she no longer had one.

Even if she could still get a ticket, the nearest airport that handled transatlantic flights was miles away. And anyway, how could she buy a ticket without touching the money? Fugitives are rarely innocent. Why run and hide if you've done nothing wrong?

'You're hiding in this dump,' she accused herself. 'Does that make you guilty?'

She *felt* innocent. But it wouldn't look that way to Ethan's parents or the public. She'd get torn limb from limb in the street if people knew she'd helped a woman steal Penny's child.

She grabbed the scissors and screwed her eyes tightly shut. No going back. Guilty or innocent, her only choice was to disappear for a while.

Keeping the blades close to her scalp and her fingers out of harm's way, she grabbed handfuls of hair and hacked them off. Each time she closed the blades she cringed at the whisper of steel and imagined how hellish she was going to look. When she could find no more stray strands, she dared to open her eyes. The woman who stared back reminded her of concentration camp images she'd been shown once by a high school history teacher. Patches of scalp, sickly pale, lay exposed to light for the first time since babyhood. Her face seemed ridiculously tanned in comparison, although she'd been diligent in her use of factor thirty. Dark shadows underlined each eye socket and her eyes were red from crying and brimful of fear.

She snipped at escapee tufts that stood up like marram grass on a sand dune, clipping and clipping till the basin and the floor were covered in hair and her head was almost bald. She put down the scissors and, avoiding her reflection, gathered the sheets of newspaper that she'd spread around and crushed them into a tight bundle. She unwrapped the razor she'd bought and removed the lid from the can of shaving foam. She had no idea how to do this. She'd never shaved anything more than an armpit in her life, preferring wax to blade. What if she slashed her head and bled out in this sorry little room? No one in the world knew where she was. She'd be identified by her passport, and her mom informed, eventually.

Sophie had often been alone, but she'd never felt this lonely. How could she have been so stupid?

'Right, kid,' she said, looking her reflection straight in the eye. 'You got yourself into this mess. Now it's up to you, nobody else, to get yourself out of it.'

She covered her head in lather and tentatively drew the blade across her head from one ear to the other. She rinsed the razor under the hot tap and shaved again. Gradually the white foam disappeared and her scalp revealed itself, ghoulish in its nudity. She filled the basin with warm water and tipped her head towards it. Scooping handfuls from the basin to pour on her head, she felt like she was baptising herself.

She reached for the one threadbare towel provided and wrapped her head in it, turban-style, the way she always did. Her reflection looked familiar again and she smiled, briefly. 'Well, Sophie, at least you'll save money on shampoo.'

She'd planned to stride out on to the streets of Narbonne, staring down any interested looks, shaming the curious into looking away. But when she opened the door to the stairs she could hear her landlady's voice floating down from an upper landing. Sophie stuck on the beanie hat she'd worn when she arrived. She locked her door and gave the handle a shake. It felt like it might fall off and she feared for her security, till she remembered she'd nothing to steal. And there was nothing in the room to identify her or connect her to the little boy who'd gone missing in a town forty miles away. She tucked the carrier bag of newspaper-wrapped hair tightly under her arm and headed for the street door.

The sun was warm and her head felt strangely hot under the woollen hat. Sophie resisted the urge to scratch. When she'd gone far enough from her lodgings she dumped the bag in a bin and pulled off the beanie, shivering as fresh air hit shaved skin. She couldn't resist touching and stroked her bald scalp, feeling mildly nauseated by the lumps and bumps of her skull. Her brain seemed closer to the surface without hair, much more vulnerable than before. For a bizarre moment she wondered if passers-by could read her thoughts. She told herself to wise up. Lose the negatives and think how gorgeous Sinead O' Connor looked with a shaven head.

A woman passed with a little boy who pointed and said, 'Why has that lady got no hair?' His mom gave Sophie an apologetic smile as she whispered something to the child and dragged him away. What had she said, Sophie wondered. 'Don't stare, the poor lady's ill.' Or 'Don't point. She might be dangerous.'

As Sophie got closer to town, the pavements became busier and the inquisitive glances increased. Perhaps it was her clothes? Jeans and Converse were too conventional for the Hare Krishna hairdo. She needed to look more 'hippy-dippy' as her mom would say. Maybe she should do something about that? Find a charity shop and buy something a bit less conventional? Sophie dismissed the thought. She'd have to watch every single cent from now on. Try to live on the little she'd saved from her legitimately earned wages. Make sure she didn't take one dollar of Miss L's money.

Sophie was hungry and on the lookout for a little mini-grocery when she came upon a newsagent's. The papers, local and national, lay spread out on shelves. She could have a quick scan of one or two front pages, see if her disappearance had been reported yet.

She was thinking about flicking through a *Midi Libre* when she became aware of someone by her side. The newsagent stood watching. Looking as if he'd be disappointed if she didn't try to steal something.

Life with her new hairstyle was going to be very different.

Chapter 56

Penny blinked into a bank of TV cameras and dazzling lights. She looked at Seth for encouragement. He was always pale, but in the white glare his face looked ghostly. He gave her a tight smile.

She looked down at the furry toy in her hands. It looked like Hoppy, but of course it wasn't. This rabbit was brand new, unloved. He'd been rushed across the Atlantic, like a celebrity, to make a special television appearance. He had never been freed from his box and looked exactly like Hoppy did when Ethan ripped the paper off his birthday present last year. A glove puppet was probably too advanced for a two-year-old, but the truth was, Penny hadn't been able to resist the soft golden fur and floppy ears. Angel had named the toy Hoppy. She'd stuck her little hand inside the puppet and made it 'hop' towards her brother. 'Look, Ethan. Hop, hop, hop!'

Ethan had fallen in love, adopting the bunny as a mascot and taking him everywhere. Hoppy and Ethan were inseparable. At least he wouldn't feel totally alone with his little rabbit tucked under his arm. Scant comfort, but better than none.

She forced herself to take a deep breath and think of Angel. This was the coping strategy she had adopted, telling herself: I've got one perfect child, safe and sound. Focus on her.

Penny worried what kind of a life Angel would have from now on. Even if Ethan came back to them, things would never be the same. How could she let her children out of her sight, leave them with a sitter, send them to summer camp?

Penny noticed dark shadows moving behind the lamps as cameramen took up their positions. A door at the far end of the room opened and a stampede of men and women raced towards her. She let out a little cry and Seth touched her arm. 'It's only the journalists, Penny. We knew they'd be here. They can't hurt you. Don't worry.'

She watched them jostle for position, vying with photographers for the best place from which to observe her. She felt like an exhibit, a zoo animal, a lab rat. She noticed flashes of white, like moths caught in the light, as notebooks were produced and pages flicked over.

She sensed movement beside her and looked round to see the lead cop take his seat. His face was grim and serious.

The room fell silent. Penny had never felt more exposed and self-conscious in her life. Or more nervous.

The policeman cleared his throat. 'Ladies and gentlemen of the media, thank you for coming. We hope that, with your help, we can find little Ethan Gates and get him back to his family as soon as possible.' He paused while the interpreter, a different one from yesterday, translated his words. She noticed the woman spoke with an American accent and wondered if that were deliberate.

'Ethan was last seen by the family au pair near the Porte Narbonnaise in Carcassonne Cité. She left him in his stroller while she went to buy a toy.'

Penny heard a gasp of shock or disbelief, perhaps both, from some of the journalists. Hearing it made her insides curl up. How could Sophie have let this happen? They'd trusted her and now Ethan was gone. Please God, let him be happy somewhere with a new mommy. Penny tried hard to imagine this best-case scenario.

She became aware of her name being repeated and realised she had zoned out. Was it the lights, the heat, the stress? She prayed that she hadn't just fallen asleep on international television.

'Mrs Gates, I wonder if you could tell us a little about Ethan's favourite soft toy which you believe he had with him when he went missing?'

Penny looked down at the rabbit in her hands and clasped it to her chest. Then, realising the viewers needed to see it, she held it out towards the cameras, like a little girl showing off a new dolly. She said nothing, her voice having deserted her. For a second her memory flashed back to the street on 9/11 when her throat was so coated in dust she couldn't utter a word.

Seth seemed to understand. He reached for a glass of water and put it into her hand. 'Take a drink, sweetheart,' he whispered, 'then tell them about Hoppy.'

She swallowed hard and reminded herself she had do her best for Ethan. 'This isn't Hoppy. It looks like Hoppy, but it isn't. Hoppy isn't new, you see. He's not old, Ethan only got him for his second birthday and he hasn't had his third, yet.' She paused, needing a moment to compose herself, and heard sympathetic murmurs from behind the lights. 'Hoppy's fur is worn away from being cuddled so much. In fact, he has a little bald patch, right here.' She pointed to a spot behind the rabbit's ear, which Ethan liked to rub with his thumb before he went to sleep each night. She turned the rabbit around so that its rear was showing to the cameras. 'And Hoppy's butt doesn't look like this.' She was aware of someone giggling, as if she'd said something funny. 'Because he doesn't have a tail. It came loose and fell off. Ethan was very upset. Do you remember, Seth?'

Seth nodded, his face sad as a tragedy mask.

'Ethan can't go to sleep without Hoppy. One time we lost him. We thought he'd fallen out of the car. Hoppy I mean, not Ethan. We were all so upset. Ethan refused to sleep that night. Then Daddy, our hero, found Hoppy under the front seat. What a relief.' She laughed at the memory and several cameras flashed.

'Can you tell us about Ethan?'

'He's a wonderful little boy. Perfect in every way. Please look after him, whoever you are, and give him lots of hugs. Show him endless love – that's what he's used to. Don't forget to kiss him goodnight and please tuck the duvet tight under his chin, so he'll feel secure.'

'Penny.'

Seth was shaking his head at her. Was she talking too much? Saying the wrong things? What was she supposed to say? Appeal to whoever took him, they said, and that's what she was doing.

Seth cleared his throat and leaned in to the microphone on the table in front of him. 'What we want to say is, please don't hurt him. Bring him back to his family. He has a sister who is distraught. She's not eating, she's not sleeping, she cries constantly. She can't understand what's happening. Someone tell me how I'm supposed to make a six-year-old understand the reason she can't see her brother. How do I find the right words to say Ethan has been taken by a stranger? How do you explain that to a kid without making her terrified the same thing's gonna happen to her? Tell me how I look her in the eye when she says, "Daddy, is Ethan coming home soon?" What am I supposed to do, for chrissakes? Lie to her and she'll never trust me again for the rest of her life? Or tell her the truth? "I don't know, baby. Maybe not." Is that what I'm supposed to say to my kid, you sonofabitch?' Seth rubbed at his eyes as if he hadn't slept for a lifetime. Penny knew he was fighting back tears and touched his shoulder.

'Please let Ethan go,' she said, her voice catching. She knew tears were coming. 'Drop him off at a safe place. Anywhere. We'll come and pick him up. And we won't press charges. I promise.'

To her left she felt the policeman move towards his mike. 'If you have any information about the disappearance of this little boy with the rabbit, please contact your nearest police station or call the number at the bottom of the screen. No matter how trivial you think that information may be, it could help us find Ethan and bring him back safely to his family. Thank you very much for your cooperation.'

Suddenly the room was filled with noise as the journalists all seemed to start shouting at the same time.

'Where's the au pair now?'

'Is it true the au pair's under arrest?'

'Will you stay in France till Ethan's found?'

'Mrs Gates?'

'Look here, Mrs Gates.'

Penny put her hand over her ears, like Angel did when she was being told off for doing something naughty. She felt the policeman's hand on her elbow, lifting her from her seat. 'This way, Mrs Gates,' he said, shielding her from the cameras.

'Any last message, Mrs Gates?'

Penny pushed the cop aside and stared out into the crowd, looking away only when the flashing affected her sight.

'Yes,' she said. 'I have a message.'

The room fell silent.

'Mrs Gates,' said the policeman, 'please.'

'Tell Scott Millburn I'm sorry and can I have Ethan back.'

'Who's Scott Millburn?' A chorus of voices asked the question in unison.

'Why are you sorry?'

'What did you do?'

'You know who has your child, Mrs Gates?'

Penny felt a tug on her arm. Seth, shaking his head as if he couldn't believe what she'd just done, pulled her towards the door. 'What the hell, Penny?' he said, low and angry.

The door closed behind them and the corridor felt like a cool, quiet sanctuary.

Seth leaned against the wall, his head hanging. 'Oh, Penny,' he said. 'What have you done? You just gave them a whole different story to chase. This won't be about Ethan any more. What the fuck were you thinking?'

Penny couldn't answer. She didn't know what to say. She had no idea why she'd blurted that out. How could she explain that suddenly she'd lost the image of Ethan smiling at some surrogate mother who was showering him with love and kindness.

All she could see was Scott Millburn's face as he threatened, 'This isn't over, Lucie. We have unfinished business.'

'Seth, I didn't mean to.'

'You didn't mean to? Jesus! Just when I thought this nightmare couldn't get any worse.' Seth dragged a hand through his hair, viciously, as if he wanted to pull it out by the roots.

Penny looked to the policeman, as if for reassurance. The look on his face gave her none. He turned away, saying, 'This way, please.'

Seth, who would normally step aside and wait for her to pass and walk ahead of him, stormed off behind the cop, leaving her to follow on. His disapproval trailed after him like smoke.

'Seth, wait. There's something I've got to tell you.'

Chapter 57

A s Diane approached the bathroom door she caught sight of the soles of Ethan's feet amongst the few remaining bubbles.

'Please, Lord, no,' she whispered as she stood in the hallway, afraid to go any further. A drowned child was not part of her plan. She willed herself to take a step, then another. She pushed the door wide. The floor was soaked. He was on his tummy, dark hair floating around his head. She knelt beside the bath and put a hand on his shoulder. His skin was cold to her touch.

His head bobbed up.

'Swimming,' he shouted and stuck his face back in the water. His legs kicked, splashing furiously.

Diane sat back on her heels, limp with relief. She flopped to the side and toppled. She made no effort to right herself, just straightened her legs and lay flat out on the floor of the little bathroom.

'Mawmaw, look,' demanded Ethan. 'I swimming.' His little face, wet and soapy, appeared at the rim of the bath. He beamed at her, clearly not concerned by her prone position. 'Ethan swimming.'

She'd dodged a whole gun full of bullets. More than she deserved. She reminded herself she must not take her fear out on the child. He didn't know what had been going through her mind. She was the idiot who left him unattended near a bath of water. She tried not to think of what might have happened. Or how she'd have dealt with the consequences.

'My goodness me,' she said, hoping she sounded enthusiastic. 'Swimming. What a clever boy. But isn't that water getting a little cold now? Why don't we go get our clothes on and then Mawmaw can fix us some nice warm breakfast?'

'Sossy?'

She laughed. 'Yes, a sausage for Ethan. And maybe one for Mawmaw too. Shall we go?'

She lumbered to her knees then, holding on to the side of the bath she rose to her feet. She was too old for this, really she was. 'Coming?' she asked.

The little boy raised his arms to her.

'Let me grab a towel,' she said, then scooped him up and over the rim and into her arms. She was soaking wet but she didn't care. She hugged him tightly then wrapped him in the towel and hugged him again. 'Thank goodness you're safe,' she murmured.

As Ethan tucked into his sausage and some milk, Diane tried to connect her phone to the Wi-Fi she had been promised.

Nothing. No connection whatsoever.

Now they were going to have to leave the cottage. Much sooner than she had intended.

She needed internet access. Without it, she had no way of following the story of Ethan's disappearance, now her connection to Sophie was severed. Whatever was that girl thinking about, handing her phone to a perfect stranger? It was unlikely the young man had thrown it in the nearest trash can, but it was the best she could hope for.

Diane checked her settings. Her phone was state of the art. It should be perfectly capable of connecting with 3G and yet that too was failing. She felt a surge of anger at Sophie. Why had the girl been so stupid? All Diane needed to know at this stage was what was happening in Ethan's family. Specifically, how was Lucie Jardine reacting? Diane wanted to hear that the woman was tearing her hair out, going mad with worry. A bit like she herself had felt when the news came through about Scott's crimes.

News. Of course. Television news. Now why didn't she think of that before? She checked on Ethan, who was sitting on a cushion on the floor, a stump of sausage clutched in his little fist. 'Okay, Ethan?' she asked. 'Good sossy?'

The little boy nodded and continued to chew noisily.

She half closed the kitchen door and switched on the flat-screen TV in the corner of the living room. It looked out of place with its DVD player and sat box and Diane wondered for a moment what the cottage's former dwellers would make of such things.

She selected Sky News, her best hope of international coverage.

Scenes of continuing devastation as the people of New Zealand tried to recover from a major earthquake on their South Island. Some boring stuff about the G20 summit that was due to take place in Seoul and more on the Wikileaks story about the involvement of her country in Afghanistan. All pretty big issues compared to one small boy kidnapped in France. Diane was about to give up and switch off when the face she'd come to hate most in the world filled the screen. The banner running along the bottom read *American child snatch – parents make television appeal.*

Diane waited. And waited. 'I need more,' she muttered, but of course that didn't help.

Ethan appeared in the doorway. Diane switched off the television.

'Want my mommy,' he said.

Had he seen his mother's face on TV? For even one second? Enough to remind him that, while Mawmaw might be fun for a little while, he hadn't seen his mother for several days.

'Want Mommy.'

Oh dear, this wasn't good. She needed to distract him. And fast.

Gambling that his mom's face wouldn't appear on the screen, Diane switched the TV back on, hoping for Sesame Street. Every kid loved Sesame Street.

CBeebies? Diane didn't recognise the channel but the screen was filled with bright colours and Ethan seemed drawn to it. Trying to avoid his sausage-greased fingers, she lifted him onto the sofa nearest the television and tucked a couple of cushions around him.

Then she went to the kitchen and filled the plastic washing up bowl with hot soapy water. A basket under the sink provided some rubber gloves and a spray bottle that smelt vaguely of lemon. A large sponge and dry cloth completed her armoury. She carried the basin to the front door and set it down while she found the car keys and a jacket.

The little hire car was still parked on the grass verge outside the gate. Neither safe nor discreet. She manoeuvred it into the tiny drive, grateful she hadn't gone for a station wagon or a huge four-by-four.

She was collecting the basin of water and wondering if she ought to try to cover up the French number plates in some way, when a beat-up old van stopped in front of the cottage. Diane, bowl in hand, moved towards the gate.

A grey-haired woman was clambering, with some difficulty, out of the vehicle. 'Bloody arthritis,' she muttered, apparently to herself. When she noticed Diane, her ruddy face beamed a welcome. 'Oh, you're here?' she shouted. 'Great stuff.' She pointed to the van. 'See that? It'll be the death of me yet.' She rubbed at her back with both hands. 'Far too old to be driving that round …' She seemed to remember herself. 'Sorry,' she said, wiping her hands down the front of a thick tweed skirt. She held one out for Diane to take in hers. 'Hello. I'm Mary Thomson. From the farm.' She pointed across the fields to some white buildings in the distance. 'I keep an eye on the cottage for Mrs Ramage.'

'Pleased to meet you,' said Diane, shaking the woman's hand. It felt surprisingly soft. She had expected callouses.

'You American?' Her head cocked to one side, bird-like. 'Mrs Ramage never said. What brings you to Auchinleck? Most folk cannae get away fast enough.' The woman chortled at her own joke.

Diane had no idea what was so funny but she laughed anyway. 'This cottage brought me here. Isn't it just darling?'

'Aye, it's a nice wee place. She has it done up lovely.' Mary reached into the car and brought out a box of eggs. 'There you go. Fresh this morning.'

'Perfect, thank you,' said Diane, catching herself just in time before she told the story of Ethan and the broken eggs. Ethan. What if he wandered out? Diane crossed her fingers that he'd find CBeebies too enthralling to leave. 'I was wondering, Mary. Did Mrs Ramage ever mention having trouble with the internet?'

The woman guffawed. 'The internet? I don't know the first thing about it. Our James would be the man to talk to. He's never off the internet.'

'Do you get it at the farm?'

'Oh aye, even in the cowshed. You're very welcome to drop in any time. The house I mean. Kettle's never off.'

'No, no. I'll be fine. But thank you.' The last thing she wanted was this woman getting too familiar. 'I don't mean to trouble you. Thank you for the eggs. These will keep me going for ages. I don't eat much and the fridge was very well stocked.'

'Aye, that was me.'

'Thank you so much. And thank you for dropping by. What I need right now is some peace and quiet.'

Diane saw the woman take the hint, her offence as obvious as if she'd been handed a dog turd. Fine. Diane wasn't here to make new best friends.

Without a word, Mary clambered into her van. She gunned the engine and drove off, leaving a belch of blue smoke that hung in the air like an accusation.

Diane turned away, smiling to herself.

Only when she tried to lift the basin of soapy water did she realise her hands were shaking. Suds cascaded over the side and dropped like snowfall on the path at her feet. 'Come on, Diane,' she said, 'time to get this car cleaned up. While Ethan is occupied. Then you need to go and find some internet access.'

The original plan had not involved taking the child anywhere until the grand finale. She'd imagined, as she'd sat there at her rococo desk, scheming, that she would keep him sedated most of the time. She'd planned on knocking him out if she needed to leave the cottage, but that option had become unacceptable to her. She didn't care to consider the reason for her change of heart. Instead she told herself that her supply of the sleeping potion was running low and she had to keep some in reserve. Who knew when she might need to keep Ethan silent and hidden?

Chapter 58

Sophie threw herself onto the single bed. For the first time since she'd left Carcassonne she allowed the tears to come. She'd been holding them back until she got off the street but they'd been threatening all morning. The final straw on her breaking back had been the owner of a little back street bistro whose door carried an ad looking for waiting staff. The woman's haughty demeanour was more suited to a five-star Parisian restaurant than a pretentious little café in a tiny Narbonne lane. She was dressed head to toe in black, her mouth a cruel slash of red in a face too pale to be healthy. In response to Sophie's polite enquiry she had looked down her long thin nose and asked, 'What on earth gave you the idea I might have a job for you?' Sophie had pointed to the sign and explained that she had experience as well as complete fluency in both French and English. The woman had raised one crimson-tipped talon and circled it around Sophie's shaven head. 'And this?' she asked. 'You really expect my diners to look at your bare skull while they eat? It's enough to spoil anyone's appetite. Please go away.'

Sophie had nodded sadly and left, her dignity intact, her self-confidence in shatters. Cruella's was the least pleasant rejection but it was identical to all the others in outcome. There were no jobs to be found.

Despite hours of trudging around she'd had only one offer of the chance to make some money. On the way back to her lodgings a man had stepped into her path and suggested she go with him. He'd said he had customers who liked her look and would pay extra for such a 'special girl'. Sophie had pushed past him and run faster than she had since high school, desperate to reach the busy main thoroughfare with lots of people to protect her.

His audacity had shocked her and she'd been shaken, quite literally, by her own vulnerability. Sophie had always thought prostitution was a lifestyle choice, an easy way to make money for women who were prepared to sell their bodies. For the first time in her sheltered life she was forced to face the truth that some women become prostitutes not through choice, but because they'd run out of options. If she couldn't find work soon, she could be one of them.

As she lay on the bed, her face buried in the not-too-clean cover, Sophie was forced to ask herself some questions. How hungry would she have to be, or how desperate to keep a roof over her head, before she'd have sex with a stranger? What if she had children to feed, or a drug habit? And what if that guy had grabbed her, instead of asking in his sleazy, flirty way? She could be lying on a bed that made this one look spotless, drugged senseless and forced to spread her legs for any creep that walked in the door. With no money coming her way at the end of the day.

Sophie made a silent vow to never again criticise those whose lifestyle 'choices' she knew nothing about. She could hear Mom's voice quoting Mother Theresa: 'If you judge people, you have no time to love them.' A surge of homesickness made her long for her mom.

She swung her legs off the bed and shoved her feet into her sneakers. She had to go find a phone. Before she lost her nerve.

'Sophie! Honeybunch, how you doin'?'

Sophie felt like her voice box had got jammed somewhere in her stomach. No words would come and when she tried to say, 'Hi, Mom,' all that came out was an enormous sob.

'Honey? What is it? Are you hurt?'

The sympathy in her mom's voice was too much. All the hurt she'd been holding in, all the guilt she'd felt since Ethan's disappearance, all the fear she'd encountered since the police had told her to stay in Carcassonne erupted from her in a howl.

'Baby, tell me what's happened to you. Has someone hurt you? John! Can you come in here please?'

Sophie sobbed into the phone. She knew she was making her mother upset and frightened but there was nothing she could do about that.

She listened to her mom talking to her husband. 'It's Sophie. Something awful must have happened. She can't even speak to me. Oh, my good God. We need to help her.'

'Try to stay calm, sweetheart. Let me talk to her, please.'

'Find out if she's hurt. I need to know if someone's hurt her.'

'Sophie, it's John. Your momma is worried, honey. Can you tell me if you've been injured in some way? Has there been some sort of an accident?'

Sophie took a deep breath that sounded like a wet snort. 'I'm okay,' she slurred, between sobs.

'Not hurt? You sure?'

'Sure. Just scared.'

'You still in Europe? France?'

'Yeah.' She was battling to keep her voice, and her tears, under control. She owed them that much. Being hysterical wouldn't help. 'Yes, I'm in France and I'm okay. Please put Mom back on. Tell her I'm okay.'

'She's right here, waiting. Say, Sophie, you want me to catch a plane and come bring you home? I can do that, you know. No problem.'

The kindness in John's words made her regret all the times she'd been rude, completely lacking in gratitude and grace. She wished she could turn the clock back. With that thought came more tears, just as her mom came on the line.

'Sophie, John says he'll come get you. You want he should do that, honeybunch?'

'No, Mom, it's okay. I just needed to hear your voice.'

A long pause told Sophie her mother was struggling to speak. Finally, 'Well, that's okay. Everyone gets a little homesick, once in a while. Even a brave girl like you. I'm so proud of you, you know that?'

Sophie knew her mother's pride, however genuine, would evaporate the minute she heard the reason for this call. Perhaps hanging up would be the kindest option.

'You said you were scared, baby. What are you scared of?'

Sophie couldn't find the words. Where did you start with a story as unbelievable as this shit she'd got herself into?

'Go ahead and tell me, honey. I can't promise to make it better, but they say a trouble shared is a trouble halved, so why don't you try me?'

'Oh, Momma. I've made a mistake. I've done something really stupid.'

'Sweetie. We all make mistakes. That's how we learn. Why don't you tell me what's troubling you?'

Sophie's nerve deserted her. Maybe Mom would find it easy to forgive her, but what about John? What if he wasn't so understanding? Sophie could find herself without the support she so badly needed right now. She had to reveal the absolute minimum. There would be time enough to tell all once she got home safely.

'I've run out of money. Like totally.'

'I thought you had a job.'

'I did. A dream job, I thought. A once in a lifetime chance to see Europe. But I was wrong.'

'Well, sweetie, you know what I always say, ain't no such thing …'

'I know. And it turns out you were right. Momma, I want to come home.'

'Well, what's stopping you? You come right on home, baby girl.'

Sophie said nothing.

'Ah, I see. You've got no money.'

'Barely enough for my next meal and I can't afford to pay for this grotty little room beyond Friday.'

'Sophie?'

She could tell her mother was dying to ask questions. 'Yes?'

'Oh, shoot. It can keep till you get home.' To her credit, Sophie's mom had never been the nosy type and, at this moment, Sophie felt thankful.

'Could you please wire me some money. I'll pay you back, promise.'

Her mother laughed. 'Yeah, sure you will. As if that matters. All we care about is getting you home.'

'Ain't that the truth,' said John, somewhere in the background.

'See? Did you hear that, Sophie?'

Sophie nodded her head. Then, aware they couldn't see her, she tried to say yes. It came out like a baby's cry.

'Where is she? Carcassonne?'

'What's that you say, Johnny?'

'I said, can you ask her if she can get to Toulouse Airport?'

Sophie gave an enormous sniff and wiped her face on the edge of the coverlet. She sat up, the better to hear what was being said. 'I could get there, but I doubt I have enough money for the train fare.'

'That's not a problem. Could we wire her some cash, do you think, John?'

'I'm in Narbonne.'

'May I speak to her, please? Hi, kiddo, John here.'

Kiddo. The word had annoyed her so much when she was younger. John had moved in and tried his best to father her and she'd been ungrateful and obnoxious. Now, far too late, she could see that this man was kind and had her interests at heart all along. Kiddo. Seemed like the most endearing term she'd ever heard.

'You still there, Soph?'

'I'm here, John, and thank you.'

'Listen up. Does the name Boulevard Gambetta mean anything to you?'

'Sure. I know where that is. It's about a twenty-minute walk from here.'

'Well, there's a Western Union at number nineteen and it's open right now. I reckon your cash will be there before you are.

You'll need your password and the answer to a security question but I'm gonna tell you all that stuff in a minute, so don't you hang up. What say I transfer a couple hundred dollars for now, girls?'

'I need to buy a new phone. Someone took mine. I'm calling from a public phone right now.

Sophie's mother said, 'Better make it three, John.'

'Okay, three hundred it is. I'm on it. Meanwhile, your momma will go online and pay for your flights home. I reckon if you can get yourself to Toulouse, the rest is plain sailing. Or plane flying.'

He chuckled to himself. Sophie remembered how that too had got on her nerves in the past.

'Sophie?'

'Yes, Mom?' Sophie was pleased to find her tears had suddenly dried up and she could speak like a normal human being again.

'Looks like the airport you need is called Blagnac. From there you can get a flight to Paris and then good old American Airlines will bring you on home. We'll be right there at the airport waiting for you.'

It was too much. The tears were back. 'Mom, I'm so sorry. I don't deserve this.' Sophie was tempted to come clean and tell her mother what she'd got into. Fear kept her silent. What if John, a very moral man, decided to withdraw his help?

Mom, sounding emotional too, became businesslike and brisk. Sophie remembered the same sharpness from the days before John and understood how hard it must have been for her mother. 'Come on, Sophie. None of that silly talk now,' she said. 'Time to spring into action and get out of there.'

'Money's sent,' said John. 'Should be there in a few minutes. The wonders of technology. Now, they're gonna ask you for a password which is louisianagal, all lower case, and the question you need the answer to is this: New Orleans acronym.'

'NOLA?'

'That's the one, kiddo. They won't ask you the question, mind. Just expect you to offer the right answer, you understand?'

'Thank you, John. louisianagal and NOLA.'

'Lower case for one and upper case for the other. You got that, Sophie?'

'I sure have. What about the tickets?'

'We'll send you those by email. Can you find somewhere to print them off?'

'No problem. Mom?'

'Yes, honey?'

'I've cut my hair. All of it. It looks horrific.'

'One thing you need to know about hair, Sophie. You may not like it, but it grows on you.'

Again, that chuckle. Sophie thought no love song ever sounded so sweet.

She was going home.

Chapter 59

Seth set the bag of croissants on the kitchen table and threw the small pile of newspapers after them. Even from the foot of the stairs Penny could see her own face on the front page. 'Are they awful?'

'I haven't looked inside, but hey, no need. The headlines say it all really.'

'I can't bear to look, Seth. Just tell me. What do they say?'

He took off his jacket and slung it over the back of a chair. He made her wait while he filled the kettle and put it on to boil. Finally, he lifted the first newspaper and waved it in the air. '*Midi Libre*,' he said. 'Covers pretty much most of the south of France. It's one of the kinder ones. "*Laughter through the tears*". The gist of it seems to be astonishment that you should be able to summon a smile while appealing for the return of your kidnapped child.'

Penny felt more stung by his tone than by the article. She'd been aware of the cameras flashing when she'd laughed at the memory of finding Hoppy that time. She'd known it would be used against her. This was just the kind of shit she'd been expecting to follow a TV appeal.

'What about the others?'

Seth sifted through the papers. 'Much the same, I guess. My French isn't good enough to read the full articles.'

'They were like a bunch of hyenas, ready to jump on me and tear me to shreds. Am I smiling in every one?'

'No.' Seth lifted another red-topped paper. '*La Dépêche* is more interested in knowing "*Who is Scott Millburn?*"'

'Have they found out?'

'What do you think? Any junior journalist on his first assignment could find out who Scott Millburn is. It's his connection to Penelope Gates and her family that's the big story. How long till someone works that one out?'

'They can't. We're protected.'

'You think?' Seth spooned coffee into the filter and topped it with boiling water. 'You want coffee?'

His coldness was so alien to her, Penny felt as if some stranger had walked into her kitchen. She went to him and wrapped her arms round his waist. He indicated the hot kettle, using it as an excuse to move away from her. 'Let's get some breakfast,' he said. 'Can you call Angel down, please? Tell her there's a choco for her.'

'Not yet. We can't speak in front of Angel.' He'd refused to talk to her in bed, claiming they both needed to get some sleep.

'Yeah, well, I think you've said enough. Don't you?' He moved to the foot of the stairs. 'Angel?' he shouted. 'Breakfast. With a pain au chocolat, specially for you.'

Penny watched her daughter clatter down the stairs, all arms and legs. 'Mommy?' she said. 'Is this the day Ethan comes home?'

Penny hugged her. 'I hope so, baby. I sure hope so.'

Angel snatched one of the papers off the table. 'Look, Mommy. You're in the newspapers. And Hoppy. Did you find Ethan already?'

'Not yet, honey. But soon.'

Angel pointed to the photo. 'But how did you find Hoppy if Ethan is still borrowed? He never lets go of Hoppy. Not ever.'

Penny was about to explain when Angel said, 'You're smiling in all these photos, Mommy. Why aren't you sad, like me and Daddy?'

Seth looked at her over his coffee cup, his eyebrows raised. Answer that one, why don't you?

Penny was glad to hear a phone ring. She couldn't bear Seth's silent accusations or wait to hear how he'd explain her smiling face to Angeline. 'That's your phone, Seth. Shall I get it?' She was already halfway up the stairs before he could rise from his seat.

His phone still lay where it spent each night. By his bed, so he could answer the moment any news came in. Surprising that he'd gone out without it this morning. Another sign of how wound up he'd been since the TV appearance.

Penny checked the caller ID. 'Seth,' she called as she ran for the stairs. 'It's the police.'

She watched her husband, desperate for any sign that this nightmare might be drawing to a close.

Seth's face gave away nothing then suddenly his eyes lit up.

'Have they found him?' she asked, tugging on his arm like a child.

Seth shook his head, his eyes sad again. 'No,' he said, 'but they've found Hoppy.'

Chapter 60

Sophie hurried along the side street where she'd seen an Internet café, praying it would be open.

As she approached the threshold a bunch of lycée students piled out past her, on their way to school. 'Cool hairstyle,' she heard one girl say. Her friend's reply was less of a compliment.

Still, ugly as it was, Sophie's shorn head seemed to be doing the trick. Most people looked away when she noticed them watching. Embarrassed to be seen staring at a freak, she assumed. The exception were small children and old people, who stared openly. After she overheard one elderly lady mutter something about cancer, Sophie had shaved her head a second time. Her guilt about exploiting the sick was less than her fear of being recognised and arrested.

Ethan's story was headline news in the regionals. *Couple sought in connection with Carcassonne child snatch.* She'd read it again, thinking, wait a minute, *couple*? Sophie could only assume Seth had told the police about the guy from the pizza place. After all he'd been suspicious of Marc from the start. When the police found out that Marc left town the same time as she did, they'd added two and two and got the wrong answer. Works for me, thought Sophie. If everyone was on the lookout for a nice respectable young American couple, the girl with thick, dark, shoulder-length hair, no one would spare a glance at a French-speaking, shaven-headed freak like her.

Sophie ran a hand over her scalp then gestured to the café owner as she sat down at a computer. She noticed him check the time and write it on a clipboard. She didn't plan to take too long, but even if she stayed a while, she didn't have to worry about the cost. Thanks to John and Mom, she had a pile of euros in her pocket. She called for a coffee and asked if they had an almond pastry. It felt so good to have some cash. Sophie promised herself she'd never again take money or food for granted. She'd always remember her relief as the Western Union teller counted out and handed over the bright notes. The spectre of having to starve or start spending Miss L's money was gone. She no longer needed to even think about the 'very last resort' for raising a few bucks. She still believed she'd prefer to go hungry but her few days of near destitution had broadened her outlook on many things and she now knew better than to judge.

Her plan had been to access her tickets, get them printed and go, but the temptation of internet news was too great to resist. She typed in Ethan Gates and got more than two hundred thousand results.

She selected one and there, in front of her eyes was a beautiful, smiling Penny. Sophie felt doused in adrenaline. Ethan was home! 'Thank you, thank you, thank you, God,' she said, sensing other users looking at her. She nodded to the guy next to her and said, 'Good news,' but his eyes returned to his screen.

Sophie read the headline above Penny's photo. *Breakthrough in Ethan Gates disappearance. Could 'Hoppy' hold the clue?*

It looked like Penny had gone ahead with the TV appearance after all. Sophie read as quickly as she could. Hoppy, Ethan's rabbit, authenticated by the worn patch on his fur, had been found on the car deck of a ferry.

Sophie's adrenaline rush waned as fast as it came, leaving her sick. What the hell was Hoppy doing on a ferry bound for England? Had she delivered this innocent child into the hands of a madwoman?

The report went on to say that, whilst Hoppy had been found aboard the ferry, there was no mention of Ethan on the ship's passenger list. Or any two-year-old. Nevertheless, the police were convinced that Ethan had been aboard the ferry bound from Santander in the north of Spain to Portsmouth in the south of

England. The ship had sailed the night of Ethan's disappearance and the journey from Carcassonne was feasible, making it look likely that Ethan was aboard.

Sophie counted back the hours on her fingers. When she thought Miss L was feeding bread to the ducks with an excited Ethan by her side, she was hightailing it across France. What about that conversation when Miss L had claimed they were enjoying an ice cream on the Place Carnot? Sophie *had* heard traffic. She knew it. But she'd believed what her brain told her made sense. And at that point, there was no reason for Sophie to suspect Miss L of lying to her. What a naïve, trusting idiot she'd been.

Now Ethan was the subject of an international police search. British Immigration officials were looking closely at the details of every passenger who had disembarked the ferry. No child of Ethan's age had passed through. Officially. Enquiries were 'ongoing'.

Please God the little boy was unharmed. Ethan was so sweet. How could anyone ever willingly hurt him?

Sophie found Penny's TV interview and pressed play then slid the volume control to almost zero and leaned in close to the screen.

She half listened to the cop's introduction then watched Seth hand his wife a glass of water and encourage her to speak. Sitting there looking at a video of people she'd grown close to, Sophie wondered how it had come to this. She hung her head, truly ashamed. She had betrayed those kind, trusting people. For money.

Penny showed Hoppy to the camera, telling some story of how he'd got lost, one time. Sophie cringed as Penny described their sadness at losing a toy rabbit and their joy when he was found.

The screen froze on Penny's laughing face and right there was the image being used by the world's media. Penny, a bereft, distraught mother looked deliriously happy. It was a gift to the gutter press.

Another video offered itself to her. This time with the banner, 'Who is Scott Millburn?' Sophie hit play.

'Tell Scott Millburn I'm sorry and can I have Ethan back.'

Sophie played it again. 'Tell Scott Millburn I'm sorry and can I have Ethan back.'

Whoever this Scott Millburn was, Penny was backing the wrong horse.

Unless.

Sophie checked the time. Her priority was to get those travel documents printed and get out of there. She had a train and two planes to catch.

Still. How long would it take to Google this guy Millburn?

Chapter 61

Diane did her best on the car but despite several changes of water and many squirts of lemon cleaner, it still reeked. That was unfortunate. They had to go out this afternoon so they'd just have to put up with the smell of vomit. The rain had gone off, perhaps not for long, and the sky was a pale watery blue. Diane opened all the windows and left the car to air in the cool breeze.

Ethan had hardly moved from where she'd left him. He looked up when she came in and pointed to the screen. A fat little figure in overalls and a checked shirt was strutting about.

'Who's this?' she asked.

'Bob a Builder,' said Ethan, 'an Scoop an Tavis an Woly.'

Diane had no idea what the child was talking about but he seemed to be enjoying himself. And not fretting for his mother, which was the main thing. Diane wondered if this would be a good time for her to make the next move.

'You okay there, Ethan?'

The little boy appeared too engrossed to respond.

Up in the bedroom, Diane dug deep into her suitcase and retrieved a phone. It looked unused but she had already set it up with a sim card and charged the battery.

Having learned her lesson about leaving a small kid alone for too long, she hurried downstairs. Ethan looked perfectly contented, eyes fixed on the screen. It sounded as if the episode was winding up. Bob had solved some problem or other and made everyone smile happily. If only real life were so simple.

Being careful not to block his view, Diane knelt on the carpet in front of the child and raised the phone, in video camera mode.

Ethan's little face, cheery and engaged, filled the viewfinder. She pressed the button and watched as the child clapped his hands, clearly delighted at whatever was unfolding on the screen. He glanced in her direction and smiled as if he wanted her to share his fun. Then, cherry on the cake, as the title music began to play, he sang his own version of the words. Diane stopped the recording. Heart in her mouth, she played it back. It was even better than she'd dared hope. Ethan looked adorable, healthy and very, very happy.

'What a good boy you are, Ethan,' she said, meaning every word. 'May I sit beside you?' She took his little hand in hers and joined him in the chorus.

The next programme didn't seem to interest Ethan at all. Or maybe he'd just had enough TV for one morning. He climbed down off the sofa and wandered off to the kitchen. 'Drink, peese, Mawmaw,' he said, standing by the fridge and pointing to the door.

'One moment. Mawmaw is busy.'

'Drink, peese!'

'I'll be right there. I'm trying to get on this damn internet.'

'Daminternet!' said Ethan and laughed as if he knew he was being naughty.

Diane threw her phone at the sofa. 'No signal. Now what do we do?'

'Drink of milk?'

'Good idea. I think I'll join you.' She gave Ethan his drinking cup and raised her own glass. 'Cheers,' she said. The milk was cool and creamy, full fat and sweet. 'Well, young man, I can't tell you the last time I drank milk. It's delicious.'

'Dee-iss-uss,' Ethan agreed, nodding like a wine connoisseur.

'Shall we go get some nice clothes on and then we'll go out in the car?'

'No like car.'

'I know. That's how I feel too after our crazy journey, but we've got a little job to do that's very important. Then we'll go to the supermarket and you can ride in the trolley. If you're a very good boy, we might even buy some sweeties. How about that?'

'Omnom. Don't tell Mommy.'

Diane laughed, wondering where he'd heard that remark. 'Okay, we won't tell Mommy.'

As if the mention of his mother had reminded him, Ethan started to cry. Very quietly at first but getting louder. 'Want Mommy,' he wailed.

'Dang it. Just when we were getting along so well. Don't you go wasting your tears on that silly old mom of yours. If she'd been taking good care of you, we wouldn't be here right now. And if she hadn't stuck her nose in my business, *I'd* be living happily ever after with my lovely husband. But oh no, your mommy had to go and tell the police all those lies, didn't she? She's a bad lady, your mom, so don't you go crying for her.'

Her tirade seemed to shock Ethan into silence. He took her hand when she offered it and they went slowly upstairs, Ethan giving all his attention to counting the treads.

Once he was dressed, in pink cords and a cute white parka with a big furry hood, she carried him to the car and strapped him in.

'Yuck! Stinky!'

'Yes, it is, but we'll just need to hold our noses.' She demonstrated and the child copied her. 'We have to go to Ayr,' she sang in a nasal whine that made Ethan smile and try to copy her.

'Go to Ayr. Go to Ayr.'

'That's right. Mawmaw needs to find a Wi-Fi hotspot. Now, be a good boy while I fetch my bag and lock the door.'

She was closing the cottage door when Mary Thomson's old green van pulled up.

Could she jump in the car and race away before Mary clambered out? Diane rejected the idea. It would look very suspicious and Mary might still spot Ethan.

They could hide here in the drive, but then Mary would definitely see the child, if she cared to look.

Diane would have to brazen it out. She walked quickly to the van, giving Mary a friendly wave, and opened the driver's door, hoping to prevent the woman from exiting her car.

'Hello, Mary,' she said, as if greeting a long-lost girlfriend. 'How nice to see you again.'

Mary sniffed, still offended by their last encounter, apparently.

'It was so kind of you to drop by earlier,' Diane gushed. 'Sorry I couldn't chat. I was exhausted. I find driving so tiring, don't you?'

Mary's round face brightened. 'Aye. Ochiltree's about my limit.'

Diane had no idea what that meant, so she put on her most engaging smile and waited for Mary to speak.

'Don't you give it another thought, dear. I've been sent to ask if your internet's working yet.'

'No, it isn't, I'm afraid.'

'Well, our Jim says it should be easy to fix.'

'Oh, that's kind. Trouble is, I'm not so good with technology.'

'It's easy. Two simple steps, our Jim says.'

'Only two? Well, I could manage that, I dare say.'

'Did anybody ever tell you that you sound just like Scarlett O'Hara? Her in *Gone with the Wind*? Oh my, what a film. And see that Clark Gable?'

Diane turned on her Southern Belle charm, anything to distract the woman from noticing Ethan. 'Well, I do declare, Mrs Thomson, your son James sounds like a mighty fine young man.'

Mary giggled like a schoolgirl, her chins wobbling with mirth.

'Our Jimmy? A young man? He'll be fifty-one on his next birthday. Never married, you see.' Mary lowered her voice as if to share a confidence. 'Not that he didn't have his chances. A very eligible bachelor he was. Still is.'

Diane touched her hair, hoping the grey wig would put paid to any ideas of matchmaking. 'I dare say he is. And he knows how I can fix this dang internet?'

'Oh, aye. No bother. Step one, switch off the rooster.'

'You mean the router?'

'Aye, that'll be it.'

'Step two?'

'Switch it back on.'

'O-kay,' said Diane slowly, trying to keep her voice and face serious. 'Will you be so kind as to tell Jimmy thank you from me? I shall certainly try that trick. But right now, I'm dashing off to Ayr for a few things.'

'Oh, very good. Ayr's nice, so it is. Well, remember, if you're still having trouble later on, just come over. Cheerio now.'

With a crunch of gears and a belch of blue from the exhaust pipe, Mary was gone.

Diane let out a long breath and muttered, 'Fiddle-dee-dee!'

Ethan was waiting patiently, although he had managed to remove both scrunchies from his hair and was chewing one of them. Feeling grateful he hadn't choked to death, and wondering how any mother of a small child ever relaxed, Diane leaned into the car and coaxed Ethan to spit out the pink elastic.

She was tying his curls up in two bunches, singing their bubbles song to stop him squirming, when she became aware of someone behind her.

Mary said, 'Oh my, what a lovely wee lassie.' She bent down and stuck her head in the car. Her face close to the child's, she said in a loud, jolly voice, 'And what's *your* name?'

'She's shy,' said Diane, desperately trying to think of a cover story. 'Won't speak to strangers.'

'Och, I'm not a stranger. I'm your neighbour.' She chucked the little boy under his chin. 'Come on,' she said, 'tell Mary. What's your name?'

'Ethan.'

'Ethan?'

'Bethan,' said Diane, almost too quickly.

'Bethan? Oh my, that's a lovely name, so it is.' She straightened and looked at Diane. 'Mrs Ramage never mentioned a wee lassie.'

'Last minute thing. Her mom is expecting number two and confined to bed till the birth. I had this trip planned so we thought ...'

'You'd just bring her. That's great. Well, you're a lucky woman, so you are. I don't see me with wee ones. Our Jimmy has missed that boat. Mind you, you'll not get much peace and quiet with this one running about, eh?'

Diane laughed. 'That's the truth.'

'She's a wee pet. What age is she?'

Before Diane could answer, Mary was poking Ethan with her finger, trying to tickle him through the thick anorak. 'What age are you?' she demanded.

'Six,' said Ethan.

Mary laughed. 'Och, you're kidding Mary on. You're not six.'

'She's two,' said Diane.

'Two? Oh my, that's lovely.'

She poked again, 'Are you tickly, eh?'

Ethan wriggled in his seat.

'Sorry, Mary. I think Bethan needs to go potty.'

'Right, I must go too. I'm getting my hair done. Yours is awful nice, by the way. Is that your own colour?'

Diane rushed towards the house, Ethan in her arms. 'Sorry, potty time.' She slammed the door and leaned against it, cursing Mary Thomson, who would probably be on the phone to her cronies already, gossiping about the 'lovely wee lassie' in Burn House.

Diane was tempted to stay put, batten down the hatches and wait for developments, but she needed access to the internet. And she didn't think switching a router on and off was the solution to her connectivity problem.

Ayr public library was easy enough to find and would be a good place to ask about internet. As she and Ethan entered the imposing sandstone building, gifted by Carnegie, Diane recalled the philanthropist's words: 'The man who dies thus rich dies disgraced.' She wished, not for the first time, that Scott had paid attention to such wisdom. How different their lives might have been if he'd decided to dispense their wealth rather than accumulate more.

Ethan settled on the floor with some Bob the Builder books from the children's section, and sat turning the pages. He seemed to know the characters already and was saying their names aloud. Diane logged on and uploaded the video she'd made earlier. It was quick and easy. She had set up a YouTube account before she left the States and it was all good to go. The video was short and would be processed fast.

Time for a quick check of how the media were covering Ethan's story. She silently cursed Sophie's stupidity. The girl should have been keeping her posted. Daily updates had been the plan, increasing to hourly if necessary. This feeling of disconnection was adding stress to an already crazy situation. Diane picked up the headphones provided and wondered for a moment how hygienic they were before sticking them on her head and turning up the volume.

Diane's gut clenched. A toy rabbit had been found aboard the Santander ferry. Her hands covered her mouth as she read. There was no evidence of any child passenger fitting Ethan's description. She glanced down at the pretty child sitting at her feet. No one would mistake 'Bethan' for the missing boy.

Relaxing a little, she watched the Gates in their TV appeal and smiled at Lucie Jardine's obvious discomfort. The woman looked awful. Good, Diane thought, I hope you're dying inside. Now you'll know how I feel. Suddenly, talking about the toy rabbit, Lucie Jardine beamed at the camera, flashes lighting up the space around her. How could the woman smile? Her toddler had just been kidnapped. Diane hadn't smiled or laughed for months after Scott was taken away.

'Tell us about Ethan,' someone asked and the face Diane hated so much became serious again.

'He's a wonderful little boy,' said Lucie. 'Perfect in every way.'

Diane had to agree.

'Please look after him, whoever you are, and give him lots of hugs. Show him endless love – that's what he's used to. Don't forget to kiss him goodnight and tuck the duvet tight under his chin, so he'll feel secure.'

For a moment Diane regretted posting her video of a robust, smiling Ethan. It would be better if Lucie Jardine was forced to imagine her child suffering. The woman seemed almost resigned to the idea of someone else having her child, as long as he was being loved and looked after. What was that about? She should be screaming hysterically and ripping her hair out.

Diane searched for YouTube. Maybe it wasn't too late to take it down.

It was. The video had already been viewed. There were even some comments.

'Too cute.'

'Tweeted this.'

'Hey, isn't this the American kid that's been snatched?'

Diane leaned back in her seat. Too late now. Ethan was already on his way to going viral.

Diane logged out and shut down the computer. She looked over at the man behind the desk. He was busy helping someone else. She'd paid for an hour and used much less, so she was free to go.

She prised Bob the Builder from a protesting Ethan. His face puckered in disappointment. She dumped Bob with the other books and made for the door to the street. 'Come on, let's go get some sweeties,' she said, in the hope of cajoling the child into silence.

It didn't work. Ethan's howls echoed up the staircase, even as the big glass doors swung closed behind them.

Chapter 62

Sophie made the train with only minutes to spare. She found her reserved seat and heaved her luggage up onto the rack. She took a swig of mineral water from the bottle she always carried and looked out of the window as Narbonne faded into the distance. She had half an hour to make up her mind.

In two hours, she'd be in Toulouse airport. In four she'd be in Paris, waiting to board her American Airlines flight direct to Louis Armstrong International. This time tomorrow, she'd be home. Home and dry, wasn't that the saying? She could put all this behind her. Learn from her mistake, be less trusting and naïve in future. Get a job to pay Mom and John back then save some for graduate school. Get her teaching qualification and get on with her life.

Or she could do the decent thing.

But then there would be no teaching job. Ever. Even if she was lucky enough to avoid prison, she'd never be allowed to work with kids.

Sophie deeply regretted having no one to ask for advice. She ought to have confided in her mom when she had the chance. Mom was always going on about unconditional love. 'No matter what you do, Sophie, I'll always love you.' She said it so often that Sophie began to challenge its truth.

'Unreservedly?' Sophie would ask. 'Even if I commit murder?'

'Yes, even then.'

'What if I murdered John or one of my *brothers*?' She had sneered at the word, repulsive as only a teenage girl can be.

'Now you're being silly.'

'Answer the question, Mom. You're the one that started this. Would you still love me if I killed John?'

'I'm not having this conversation, Sophie. It's upsetting and pointless.'

So she'd never got the answer and now, when she had a real need to find out, she was scared to ask, in case Mom's love came with conditions after all. Conditions like stay on the right side of the law. Don't get involved in dodgy deals with strangers. Try not to aid and abet a kidnapper.

For that's what Miss L was. A kidnapper. Not a sad, lonely grandma. She was a cold-hearted criminal. A child-snatcher. And Sophie was her accomplice and had been paid handsomely for playing her part.

When she'd found out Miss L's true identity, Sophie had run to the grotty, unisex toilet of the cybercafé and fallen to her knees by the toilet pan. She hadn't much in her stomach to throw up, having gone short on food for a few days, but it still took a long time for her guts to stop heaving.

Miss Louise Mouche-Chamier, aka Mrs Diane Millburn, had been photographed, many times, by the side of her handsome husband, Scott Millburn. They were quite the society couple, it seemed. Thousands of results on Google images, not counting the ones of Mr Millburn once he became Public Enemy Number One.

Scott Millburn, the man who tried to make billions out of the 9/11 tragedy. The man who killed two people, trying to make sure he wouldn't be found out.

September 11, 2001 was vague in Sophie's memory. She remembered seeing her mom become very upset about something on TV. She remembered John trying to protect her and his sons by preventing them from watching. Of course, the scenes had become so iconic since then that everyone knew them well.

It had been a long time since Sophie had given much thought to that important and very sad part of American history. She'd been involved in some sort of study project back in high school and she remembered the opening of the 9/11 memorial clearly because that was much more recent. She could picture Barack Obama, Michelle at his side, stunning in a black dress.

It was hard to imagine Miss L being married for years to a scumbag like Millburn. According to what Sophie had read on the internet, the man had sacrificed his workforce so that he could make obscene amounts of money. A lot of it was hearsay, rumour, conspiracy theory, some said, but there was no doubt Millburn was guilty of something heinous, including the death of his lover and the hitman he hired to kill her.

The part Sophie didn't get was how Penny and Seth were connected to Millburn. Why did Penny think Scott Millburn had taken her child? And why on earth was she sorry? 'Tell Scott Millburn I'm sorry.' Those were her exact words before she was hustled away from the TV cameras.

There was much speculation. All over the internet. Sophie wasn't the only one keen to work out the connection.

A uniformed guy pushing a trolley came along the carriage, offering sandwiches and snacks for sale.

'Excuse me,' she said, as he passed. 'How long to Carcassonne?'

The guy took out his phone and checked. 'About fifteen minutes.'

She rewarded him with a smile. A quarter of an hour to decide her fate, maybe her whole future.

Chapter 63

Penny had insisted on taking the newspapers, every one of them, to the recycling container that sat at the end of their street. As she dropped the lid she blew out a breath so long she wondered how she could have held it in without suffocating.

Penny collapsed against the bin and howled. The sound of her suffering echoed in the narrow street and rose to its rooftops. She raised her eyes, as if following the noise, and saw the turrets of the Cité against the blue sky. How much heartache and bloodshed had those turrets witnessed? How many baby boys had died inside the walls of that fortress? Lost in childbirth or to childhood diseases. Slaughtered by men claiming religion gave them the right, in mediaeval times, to kill children. Not much had changed, it seemed. There were still those prepared to harm and hurt the innocent. Penny said a prayer through her tears.

She implored God to watch over Ethan, wherever he was, and bring him back to her. Even as she spoke the words, she remembered the photos of those sixteen lost children and knew that the likelihood of her baby being spared was remote. Why should hers be the one, of all the missing kids in the world, that made it back home?

She stood up straight, dried her tears and wiped the red, tender skin of her nose and cheeks. They felt like they'd been sandpapered but Penny welcomed the pain. It was no less than she deserved for allowing her child to be taken from her.

As she turned towards the house, she saw him. He was being led by the hand, away from her, in the direction of the Cité. Penny stopped walking and shouted his name. 'Ethan!'

She ran a few steps. It was important that she keep him in her sight. 'Ethan,' she called again. This time the man with the child looked round, but seeing no one he recognised, turned away and walked on.

'Hey, you! Stop!' she shouted and ran after them. As she caught up she said, 'Ethan, it's Mommy.'

She grabbed the guy by the arm.

'What the hell do you think you're doing?' he said, pushing her away.

Ethan started to cry and Penny knelt to comfort him. The moment she looked into the child's face she knew her mistake. 'You're not Ethan.'

The man picked up his child and hugged him close. 'You're mad!' he said, hurrying away.

'Yeah, I think I might be,' she said. 'Or I'm heading that way.'

Seth appeared at her side. 'Oh, my love,' he said, gathering her into his arms. 'Come inside.'

'I saw Ethan. With a man. I was so sure it was him, Seth. From behind, you know, the way he walks, holding on to your hand, kind of lopsided. And his hair, those amazing curls. I was so sure it was him.'

'But it wasn't, was it, honey?'

She shook her head, slowly and sadly, not stopping till Seth took her face between his hands and kissed her forehead. 'You don't deserve any of this. I'm hurting too and I'm so angry at myself, I don't know how to deal with it. I'm trying to be brave for you and for Angel, but I'm terrified of what will happen to us if we don't get him back.'

'I'm scared too, Seth. Scared this will destroy us. I know I'm going to spend the rest of my life looking for him. Right now, I'm watching every toddler with brown curly hair. Soon I'll have to guess what he'll look like at three and four, then five. How pathetic will it be when I start walking up to every handsome, dark-haired young man I see, calling him Ethan and watching for some reaction to a name he's never heard before?'

'Don't talk like that, Penny. We'll find him. I know we will. And we'll get through this. Together.'

'Will we? Tell me you weren't embarrassed to see me knelt in the street, upsetting a complete stranger and his child? I was so sure it was Ethan, I couldn't help myself. I had to go and find out. I actually grabbed the guy by the arm. In some places that's assault. I could end up getting myself arrested.'

Seth tried to laugh. It didn't come out right and he disguised it with a cough.

'Seth, I have to tell you something I've never shared before. You know I lost a baby?'

'I was there, remember?'

'Yeah, in another life, sorry. Well, I never told Curtis this, because he'd have called me stupid. Anyway, I never forgot the loss of that child, and she never even made it into the world. Sometimes my arms ache with the lack of her, can you believe that?'

'Even after Angeline and Ethan, you still feel that way?'

She nodded. 'I do. And the reason I'm telling you now is to try to make you understand that, if we lose Ethan, even though we've got Angel, I don't think I'll make it.'

Seth grabbed her roughly. 'You will. You're strong. Look at everything you've come through already.'

'It's not the same, Seth. I feel like I'm standing at the edge of an abyss and the ground is crumbling under my feet. If Ethan isn't found, I'm going over, I know I am, and I'll never climb out of that darkness again.'

'Penny, please don't say that. You sound like you're giving up hope. You just told me you'll never stop looking for Ethan.' He stood and helped her to her feet. 'Let's get you inside. Angel will be getting worried about us. Come on.'

Angel met them at the door. She was jumping up and down, shouting. 'I saw Ethan, Mommy. I saw him.'

'I know, sweetie. In the street? I thought I saw him too. With his daddy? That's not Ethan. Just a little boy who looked a bit like ours.'

'No, Mommy, not in the street. In here. Ethan's on television.'

Chapter 64

On her way out of Ayr, Diane pulled up beside a red pillar box. She took a padded envelope from her bag, slid the new iPhone in, sealed it and dropped the slim package into the slot. She had prepared the envelope ahead of time, addressed to Apple customer services in London. She had no idea how much the postage costs would be so she'd used every stamp in the little book she'd bought at a service station a lifetime ago. Diane didn't know if the police had the technology to trace the phone that made Ethan's video but if they had, they'd be following a mail train in the wrong direction.

When she was stopped at some traffic lights outside a large supermarket she said to Ethan, 'Let's go in here and get your sweeties, shall we?' She could use a few provisions and it made more sense to shop here, where no one would pay her any attention, than in a village where strangers would be sure to prompt speculation and curiosity.

With Ethan by the hand Diane walked across the car park towards the store entrance. When they were safely away from any moving vehicles she let his hand go for a moment, so she could check she had her pocketbook. She heard him say, 'Doggy.' When he toddled off, his hand stretched out, she grabbed for him. Too slow. The dog lurched and the next thing Diane knew, Ethan was screaming hysterically and a small crowd had gathered. Everybody seemed to talk at once.

'Did you see that? A dug just bit that wee lassie.'

'Phone the polis. That dug needs to get put down.'

'Somebody help the woman.'

Diane pulled up Ethan's sleeve and inspected his forearm. He'd been lucky. There was nothing to see, apart from a couple of surface scratches.

'Can I take a wee look, dear?'

'She'll be fine,' said Diane, scooping Ethan into her arms. 'I'll just take her home to her mom.'

'You should really take her to A and E.'

'I'm sure she'll be fine, it's just a scratch. I'll put some antiseptic on it.'

'Don't you want to report it?'

Diane looked at the dog for the first time. It was cowering away, quivering. Probably as shocked as she was. 'No, I don't. The child approached the dog. It was my fault, not the dog's.'

All she wanted was to get out of there, before any more nosy parkers turned up. Before someone said, 'Hang on, isn't that the kid everyone's looking for?'

'Come on, Bethan,' she said, stressing the name. 'Let's get you home, sweetie.' She turned away.

'Excuse me, madam. Would you like to come with me?'

Diane stopped, feet frozen to the spot. She'd been dreading this moment for what seemed like weeks. Should she hand over the kid without argument or fake outrage, protesting her innocence? She turned slowly, still undecided.

'Hi, I'm Karen, the duty manager. Would you like to come inside and let our first aider take a look? I'm very sorry about this. We ask customers not to leave dogs tied up at the store entrance. Can I get you a wee coffee or something? You look a bit shocked.'

Shocked, thought Diane. You have no idea. 'I'm fine, thank you. I don't hold you responsible in any way. We'd just like to go home.'

'This is for the little girl.' She handed over a doll in a garish pink frock. 'It might cheer her up.'

'You're far too kind. I'm sure we'll be just fine, but thank you. Look, Bethan, the nice lady gave you a dolly.'

Ethan looked for a second then buried his face in Diane's shoulder.

The little crowd was dispersing. Only a few lingered to watch Diane walking away. She took a circuitous route back to her car, keen to avoid prying eyes that might notice the foreign car and start wondering why an American would be driving around Scotland in a French hire car.

Ethan fretted for a couple of miles then fell asleep. He woke when the car stopped, but he didn't mention his sore arm. She didn't remind him about it. Surely if it was a problem he'd be fussing. What was bothering her more was the possibility that someone in the small crowd might, right this minute, be calling the police helpline.

Diane switched on the TV and there it was, her video of Ethan singing. With the helpline number at the bottom of the screen.

Ethan stood leaning on the sofa, rapt. Did he know his own voice? Could two-year-olds recognise their own faces?

Diane had no idea. 'Come on, young man,' she said, realising he was still dressed as a girl. 'Shall we get you into some better clothes?'

'No.'

'Okay, buddy. You sound as if your mind is well made up. Who am I to argue?'

'Bob a Builder.'

'Okay, let's see if we can find Bob. And how about a snack?'

'Ess, peese.'

Bob wasn't airing at that time of day, but there was no shortage of entertainment on CBeebies and soon Ethan was engrossed. Diane was surveying the contents of the fridge when she heard her phone ringing.

Only one person had her number. Sophie.

Chapter 65

As the train slowed, passengers collected their belongings and rose to their feet. A man with a large suitcase and many bags blocked the aisle beside Sophie. Even if she wanted to get off, she couldn't. Perhaps that was the sign she'd been waiting for. She could tell herself that she *did* intend to get off, but it wasn't possible.

She could tell her mom the same story. She might believe it. Sophie wondered how convincing her excuse would sound to the police, if they caught up with her. 'I meant to get off in Carcassonne, but see, this guy was in my way.'

Sophie got to her feet, excusing herself as she nudged the man to the side so she could reach for her bags. To her surprise the guy put down his own case and lifted her heavy suitcase from the overhead rail. He set it on the floor then moved out of the way to allow her to step into the aisle behind him.

Sophie climbed down the steep steps of the carriage and followed the crowd along the platform. A set of stairs led down into a short tunnel. She remembered it from her last train ride only a few days ago. The last thing she'd ever expected was to be back here. But here she was. Doing the right thing. She hoped.

As she rose to daylight at the other end of the underpass she saw the Toulouse train, her train, snake out of the station. Her fate was sealed. Even if she were to change her mind she wouldn't make it to Toulouse in time for her flight.

Might as well let Mom know. Sophie dragged her luggage over to the coffee stall in the corner of the station and asked for a double espresso to calm her nerves. She took a sip of the near boiling liquid and grimaced at the strength of the coffee hit.

Mom answered on the first ring.

'Sophie, I was hoping you'd call. You at the airport? Good to go?'

'Mom?'

'Yes, honey?'

'I can't come home.'

'Didn't you get the tickets?'

'Yes, I did. Say thanks to John for me, please.'

'Why can't you come home if you've got the tickets?'

'There's something I've got to do. First. Then I'll be able to come home. I hope.'

'I don't understand.'

'Mom, remember you always said you'd love me no matter what? Did you mean that?'

'Now you're worrying me, Sophie. What's going on?'

'Did you, Mom?'

'Of course I did.'

'No matter what? Unconditional love?'

'It's the only kind I know. Tell me what's happened, darling girl.'

'I'm in trouble, Mom. Maybe big, big trouble.'

'Is it drugs? Please tell me it's not drugs.'

'No, Mom. It's not drugs.'

'Well, praise be.'

'It's much worse.'

Chapter 66

Playing for time, Diane said, 'And that's where you got this number, you say?'

'Yes, madame, yours is the only number in the phone's contacts list.'

'Well, I do declare.' Diane wondered frantically how she should play it. Could the French police have made a connection between a piece of 'lost' property and the American child who was also 'lost'? She thought not.

She had seconds to decide. She chose to play dumb. Always a safe bet.

'And you say this phone's been found in Paris? That's Paris, France. Am I right?'

'Yes, that's right. The phone was found in a bin in Charles de Gaulle airport.'

'In a bin, you say? Now why would anyone throw away a perfectly good phone?' Diane knew the answer. Marc had done as she'd asked and put the phone in the trash. Diane hoped it hadn't triggered a major security alert.

'Would you have any idea whose phone this might be, madame? Perhaps a friend of yours recently flew in or out of Paris?'

'Well, my goodness me, I have no idea. Would you oblige me by telling me the number of that phone you have?'

The number was quoted and, to sound convincing, Diane asked for it to be repeated twice before saying, 'I declare, I don't recall that number.'

'Several calls have been made to you from this phone, madame, some of them quite long. It has also received quite a few more, all from your number.'

This was getting serious. Diane decided it was time to quit while she was ahead.

'Now, that sure *is* a mystery to me. Let me just check something. Would you be so kind as to hang on one second while I try to look at my call log without cutting you off?'

She pressed on the red circle to terminate the call and waited.

The phone vibrated in her hand and rang out. Diane touched Reject. And sat down to think.

She had to hope the cop, or whoever she was, who just rang was far too busy to follow up on a lost phone. How many mobile phones are lost in a day? Must be millions. No way would the police try to trace every owner.

Unless it was an extremely quiet day in the airport cop shop. So why did they call her number? Because she was the only contact in the phone? Did that mean they were already suspicious? Or was she overthinking things? Maybe some minion had been told to give her a call and see if she could let the owner know the phone had been found.

Under normal circumstances, someone taking a call like that would be delighted. 'Oh, that's my friend Jo-Jo's phone. She'll be so upset she's lost it. Let me give you her address. Lordy, she's going to be pleased to get that phone back. It's almost new.' That's the sort of reaction any cop would be expecting.

Had she screwed up? Would her weird denial make the caller curious?

She sat for a few minutes, waiting to see if the policewoman would call back.

It was time to scope out the place she'd come all this way to see. It seemed to tick every one of her boxes when she was searching on the internet many months ago. But sometimes places looked entirely different in reality. Also, she had to work out the logistics of getting there with a two-year-old.

Chapter 67

Seth was still on the laptop. He'd hardly taken his eyes off the screen since Angel had spotted Ethan on TV. Every so often he would give Penny an update on how many views the video had on YouTube or how many times it had been retweeted.

'This is good, Penny,' he'd say from time to time. 'Real good.'

'You think so?'

'The eyes of the world are definitely on Ethan now. He's become a real little boy for people. Everyone will want to help find him.'

'Apart from the ones on Twitter who are saying how happy he looks and let's leave him with the kind folks who have him because any mother must be better than me?'

'They're morons. What do they know?'

'They know I handed over his care to a girl we barely knew who had no qualifications to look after children. They know we went off to Toulouse and left them overnight with this person. Who has now disappeared, don't forget. And they know I'm some screwball who laughs in the middle of a TV appeal. Who can blame them for thinking Ethan might be better off where he is? Maybe they're right.'

'Stop it, Penny. I'm not having any more of that talk, especially with you know who around. How do you think that stuff will sound to her if she overhears you? You're *her* mom too, don't forget.'

'I haven't forgotten, but maybe these tweeters or whatever you call them have a point.'

'I'm sorry I ever let you see that stuff, Penny. It's the opinion of a few idiots. Most people are right behind us and want to do all they can to help bring Ethan home.'

'There's another thing. Does he even know where home is? Does Angeline?'

'Well, Penny. You're the one who thought this was such a good idea, coming here. You still so certain we were right to leave Texas?'

Penny couldn't believe her ears. Seth, who'd hardly uttered a word of criticism in all the years she'd known him, was having a go at her.

'I thought we were a team, Seth? We talked about it and you agreed to come here. You even said it would be good for your promotion prospects to work with the Toulouse development team.'

'Maybe I did. But I wasn't expecting something like this, was I?'

'Oh, Seth, how could anyone ever expect something like this?' Even as she spoke the words, Penny knew she was being a liar and a hypocrite. And a coward. When was she ever going to tell him? Each time she tried, something got in the way. And now he seemed angry most of the time. She wasn't used to seeing Seth angry and she didn't know how to handle it. Curtis was always angry so she'd learned how to deal with him. She had a whole list of rules she'd recite in her head.

Respect his personal space.

Use non-aggressive body language

Take time to think before I speak.

Be calm and talk in a lower tone than his. That one was always easy.

Focus on the future instead of the past.

That was the kicker, right there, hearing Seth hark back to the past. Hearing him blame her. It was alarming to see such a change in him. She'd waited too long to tell Seth her real reason for wanting to leave the States. To tell him now would only make him angrier and she couldn't bear that.

'I'm gonna take Angeline out,' said Penny. 'Maybe buy her an ice cream in the square, if that's okay?'

Seth's eyes were back on the screen. 'Sure,' he said, without looking up. 'Good idea.'

'You want anything?'

This time he looked straight at her before he spoke. 'Only one thing, but I doubt you'll find him in the Place Carnot.'

'That was cruel, Seth. And unworthy.'

When he didn't reply, she told herself he hadn't heard, but it didn't make her feel any better.

Angeline loved sitting in the pretty square. The waitress brought her two balls of ice cream in a stemmed glass bowl. 'With a paper parasol,' she said, 'because little girls all love parasols.'

'Thank you,' said Angeline. 'And thank you, Mommy.'

'That's okay. You deserve a treat. You've been such a good girl. I know this is horrible for you, Angel.'

'You know the person that borrowed Ethan?' Angel had never abandoned her original explanation for her brother's disappearance.

'Yeah?'

'Do you think they might come and borrow me too?'

'That's not going to happen. I promise you.'

'But that's not fair.' Angel folded her arms and scowled. 'Ethan's having fun. And he got to be on TV.'

Penny sighed. She was all out of answers. The best she could think of to say was, 'Eat up your ice cream, please, before it melts.'

Angel fiddled with the tiny parasol, opening and closing it over and over. 'It's not nice, you know, when you and Daddy fight.'

Penny reached for her daughter's cheek and touched it with the back of her fingers. 'Oh, sweetie,' she said, trying to sound upbeat, 'we're not really fighting.'

'It sounds like it to me, Mommy. Daddy sounds angry.'

'He's not angry with you. You know that, don't you? Daddy loves you so much.'

'Is Daddy mad at you, Mommy?'

What to say? It was important to make this child feel as secure as possible right now and if that involved lying to her, so be it. 'No, silly. Daddy's not mad at Mommy. He loves Mommy. He's angry at the person who borrowed Ethan. Daddy wants his L'il Buddy back now. That's all.'

Angel licked her spoon. 'So do I, Mommy.'

'Me too. Hey, when you've finished up there, why don't we go and see if we can pick you out a nice new jacket for school. It's getting chilly in the mornings. Shall we do that?'

Angel nodded enthusiastically.

'Oops, hang on. My phone's ringing. Let me get this. It's Daddy.'

'Penny, the police just rang. They've got Sophie.'

Chapter 68

Sophie knew she'd made a mistake the moment she'd asked to see Inspector Morand.

Mom had been one hundred per cent behind her decision to go to the police, once she'd heard the full story. Apart from a sharp intake of breath when Sophie told her how much money Miss L had deposited in the bank account, Mom had been calm, reassuring and non-judgmental. If this was unconditional love in action, Sophie wanted more. She could use some right now, in fact. Whatever emotion the three police officers in the room felt for her, she wasn't getting any love.

They had listened patiently to her story, recording every word, which was unnerving. She'd gone right back to the beginning, telling them about Miss L's ad and how she had beaten the other candidates. And been delighted at the prospect of coming to France.

'Did you find your father?'

'I regret to say, no, I didn't get the chance before all this happened.'

'Tell us more about this Miss Mouche-Chamier.' He turned to his colleague. 'Can we run a check on that name?'

'I think I've pretty much told you all I know,' said Sophie, hoping they couldn't tell she was lying.

'And you are adamant you don't know where this woman is now?'

Sophie nodded.

'Please, miss, for the tape.'

'No, I have no idea where she is.' That, at least, was the truth.

'Didn't you think to ask where she planned to go with someone else's child?'

'Of course I asked.'

'And? Did she tell you?'

'Yes.' Sophie knew how ridiculous her next words were going to sound, but she had to say them. 'To, like, feed the ducks.'

'French ducks? Spanish ducks? English ducks?'

'Please believe me when I say I had no idea she was, like, planning on taking Ethan out of the country. They were going to feed the ducks here, by the river, in Carcassonne. That's what we agreed.'

'And you didn't ever think it odd that a woman would pay all that money to feed ducks?'

'I didn't know anything about the money at that stage.'

'You knew she was planning on paying you. Didn't you just tell us that?'

'Yes, but I'd no idea she meant that much.'

'Tell us again how much you "found" in your bank account.' His eyebrows rose at the same time as his fingertips waggled up and down in mid-air.

'A hundred thousand dollars.'

'Sorry, could you repeat that, please?'

Sophie knew they'd all heard first time but she cleared her throat and said, 'One hundred thousand US dollars.'

The cop whistled.

'I promise you I haven't touched a cent of it. You can check.'

'Oh, we will. You can count on it. Sorry, no pun intended.'

Sophie smiled, out of politeness.

'And this was on top of a monthly salary, you say?'

'I wouldn't call it a salary. It was more like an allowance.'

'As you wish. Why was she paying you an allowance?'

'So I had something to live on.'

'But weren't you working for the Gates family?'

'Yes, Penny and Seth were giving me a little pocket money each week, plus food and lodgings.'

'Tell us again how you came to get the job with the Gates family, if you will.'

When Sophie had repeated the story, the cops conferred and then Youngcop asked, 'What was the contingency plan?'

'Sorry?'

'Well, say they hadn't wanted an au pair. Or they were looking to hire someone qualified?'

'They didn't have the money for that.'

'And Miss L, as you call her, knew all about their financial situation, did she?'

'She seemed to.'

'That didn't strike you as odd? This stranger knowing so much about them?'

'No, because as far as I knew, she wasn't a stranger. She was family. Ethan's grandmother.'

'Ah, yes, the estranged grandmother who isn't allowed to see the kids in the States so she pays for you and her to fly all the way to France so she can spend one afternoon feeding the ducks?'

'I guess it sounds crazy when you put it like that.'

'What other way can one put it?'

'But it was never meant to be simply one outing to the ducks. She arranged to see Ethan that day and the following day she was supposed to be meeting Angel.'

The cop pounced like a snake. 'So you aided and abetted the abduction of two children?'

'No! It wasn't like that. She was supposed to take Angeline to buy scrunchies.'

'To buy what?'

'Scrunchies. For her hair. Never mind. The plan was, once she got to know Angel and Ethan, she'd meet Penny and Seth and show them how well they all got along. She was planning to plead with them to reconsider their decision to stop her seeing her grandchildren. That's all she wanted, don't you see? I felt sorry for her.' Sophie let her voice peter out.

'None of that is true, is it?'

Sophie shook her head.

'For the tape, please?'

'No, it turned out not to be true, but I had no idea at the time. I had no way of knowing her true intentions. I believed her.'

'With regrettable consequences. Let us hope, not tragic.'

There was a pause. If it was designed to give her time to feel even more of a shit human being, it worked.

'Now, could you please tell us about the phone you mentioned earlier?'

'What would you like to know?'

'The make and model and perhaps some of the phone numbers that might be in your contacts.'

'It was the latest iPhone. Four? I don't know. I'm not really interested in that geeky stuff.'

'And whose numbers did you have in it?'

'That's easy. There was only one. And you know whose that is.'

Inspector Morand turned to his colleague and spoke quietly.

'Please, can I go now? I've told you everything I know.'

'Unfortunately for you, mademoiselle, that's what you said the last time. We will be keeping you here, I'm afraid, for the moment.'

Sophie wished with all her heart she had stayed on that train. She'd be waiting to board her transatlantic flight by now.

As if he had read her mind, the cop said, 'By the way, it's just as well you did decide to break your journey here instead of going to Toulouse for your flight. Even with your new hairstyle, you wouldn't have got out of the country. Every airport in France is on the lookout for you.'

'I'd have been arrested?'

'But of course. You did the right thing, mademoiselle. It would not have looked good if you'd been caught trying to flee the country. But please, tell me, why the change of heart?'

'I've worked out who Miss L is.'

Chapter 69

Ethan was worn out by their walk. Walk was hardly the word for it. Trek was more appropriate. It was certainly too much for little legs like Ethan's. Diane was glad she had taken the stroller. She'd not have managed otherwise. As it was, she had to carry Ethan for the last stretch. Fortunately, access to the spot was fairly straightforward, give or take a few low branches. And it had not been as difficult to find as she'd anticipated. The directions on the local website were excellent. The setting was exactly as she'd imagined it. Perfect for her needs.

It was getting dark when they finally made it back to the cottage. Diane was relieved to close the door behind her and lock it for the night. She'd had a bit of a scary moment, at one point, when she thought she'd lost her way. Faced with the choice of a night spent outdoors or calling the emergency services, Diane wasn't sure which way she'd have gone. She preferred not to think about it. They'd made it and that was all that mattered.

Dinner was some toasted bread with beans on the top. Ethan was grumpy and insisted on picking up each individual bean between his tiny finger and thumb and popping it in his mouth. As a result, the meal took a while and they were both nodding by the time he'd had enough.

She'd have liked to skip bath time but she wanted to check Ethan's arm and the bath seemed the easiest place to get a good look. The skin around the bite was a bit pinker than the rest of his forearm and she could see a mark where he'd been bitten. He wouldn't let her examine it closely but he seemed happy enough, so Diane decided not to bother him with the antiseptic cream she'd found in the bathroom cabinet.

'A good night's sleep for you, young man, and in the morning you'll be right as rain.'

'Wight as wain,' Ethan repeated, as she got him ready for bed.

Diane yawned, exhausted by her hike and shaken by the events of the day. Still, with the video posted and the perfect spot found, it had been worthwhile. She hoped the footage would cost Lucie Jardine another night's sleep.

As she tucked the duvet tight under his chin, Ethan said, 'Mommy?'

'You'll see Mommy soon. I promise.'

And he would. All Diane had to work out was how to get her there.

She cursed Sophie for losing that phone and wondered what the police had done with it. Was it sitting in a forensics lab somewhere waiting to be examined? Was it speeding its way to Carcassonne by special courier? She hoped it was languishing forgotten on a shelf in airport lost property.

When she woke in the morning she was surprised to see how long she'd slept. There was no sound from the child.

She pulled on her dressing gown and padded barefoot to Ethan's tiny bedroom, planning to say, 'Boo!' and surprise him. He was still asleep, worn out by their hike. Diane tiptoed out and went to the bathroom, grateful for the chance to shower in peace.

Once dressed she headed along the little corridor, singing, 'Wakey, wakey, Ethan.'

The little boy had not stirred since she'd last looked in on him. Fear made her push him, a bit roughly, but she'd heard of tragedies happening while small children slept.

Ethan stirred but did not wake.

She leaned over him saying, 'Come on, sleepyhead. It's morning. Time to get up.' She caught his arm and gave it a little shake. Ethan screamed. His eyes shot open and he burst into tears.

'Oh, I'm so sorry, little one. I forgot the doggy had bitten your poor arm. Will you let Mawmaw see?'

But Ethan was too distraught to listen. He crawled into the corner and protected his sore arm with the other. The sight tugged at her heart.

'Let me see please, Ethan. Is it very sore? Shall we put some nice ointment on it to make it feel better?'

'No,' he shouted and backed further away from her.

Reverse psychology needed here. She'd leave him alone and he'd come to her. Maybe she could nip downstairs and get a drink of juice to entice him from his corner. The sight of him cowering there like some beaten puppy was too heart-wrenching for words.

It crossed her mind that now would be a good time to make a video for his mother. She despised herself for the thought.

'I'll go and fetch some yummy juice. You must be thirsty after that long sleep. Would you like to go potty, Ethan?'

She predicted the answer and she wasn't wrong. She left to fetch the juice.

When she came back, Ethan had slumped over. She ran to him and grabbed his arm, pushing up his pyjama sleeve before he could protest. His skin had turned red, not pink, and it felt hot to the touch. He pulled his arm away before she could inspect the wound, but she caught sight of some yellowish matter where the dog's tooth had caught him.

Diane was no nurse, but she knew an infection when she saw one. Why hadn't she listened to those people who told her to go straight to hospital yesterday? She'd given the infection almost twenty-four hours to get a hold.

'Look, Ethan, would you like a drink of apple juice?' She held the cup to his lips but he turned his face away. She seemed to remember hearing somewhere it was important to keep people hydrated if they had a fever. She touched his forehead. It was hot, like his arm. What was she going to do? She couldn't call a doctor, even if she knew where to phone.

Aspirin was recommended for lowering a temperature. She'd give him some aspirin and wait a while. It was less than a day since the bite. That wasn't long enough to heal, even for a kid.

'You stay here, Ethan, while Mawmaw fetches something to make you feel better.' Ethan looked like he was going nowhere.

The bathroom cabinet had no aspirin. Paracetamol? Was that the same thing? Oh, Lord, why hadn't she thought to bring her own kit, filled with child remedies? How naïve of her to think she could look after such a small child without something going wrong. She spotted a pack of sticking plasters. Maybe he'd like one of those. Kids liked sticking plasters, didn't they?

Ethan was having none of it. He wouldn't swallow the pill and he refused to let her touch his arm with ointment. Not even a large sticking plaster would encourage him out of his corner.

'Would you like to come downstairs with Mawmaw and we'll see if *Bob the Builder* is on TV?'

No reaction. His little eyelids drooped as if he was still sleepy and yet that wasn't possible. He'd already slept for more than thirteen hours. Perhaps the elixir was still in his bloodstream.

She was way out of her depth here. Maybe she should run to the farm and fetch Mary. She must have seen a few bites in her time, living among dogs and cats. She'd know what to do. Or her son, the internet expert, would.

The internet. Of course.

Diane tried for a Wi-Fi signal and this time, glory be, she got on. Turning that router on and off last night had done the trick after all.

Diane keyed in 'dog bite' and got five million results. She clicked on the first, then the second and a third. All bore the same message. Seek medical advice as soon as possible, ideally immediately. There was further information about washing the wound, etcetera, but Diane could read no more. She was already panicking. She'd got this so wrong. How could she have been so careless with this little boy's health?

She fetched her bag and the car keys, took a woolly throw from the back of the sofa and went into Ethan's room saying, 'Sorry Ethan, we need to go to the hospital.' She threw the blanket around him and picked him up, ignoring his cries. This was a case of being cruel to be kind.

In the car he wriggled a bit when she tried to strap him in his seat, but only for a moment, then he went limp and compliant as if he couldn't be bothered fighting her. 'That's a good boy,' she said. 'Now, let's get you to a doctor. Mawmaw's sorry she didn't take you yesterday, but we'll be there soon.'

She headed for Ayr, vaguely aware of having seen signs for a hospital yesterday. She got lucky and found it easily, a sprawling modern building perched high on a hillside looking out to sea. Finding a space in the car park was more difficult. Diane cruised lane after lane. Finally she abandoned the car on the end of a row near the entrance, gathered Ethan and ran.

A dark-haired woman in a suit sat behind glass. She looked up as Diane approached, her face concerned.

'This child's been bitten by a dog.'

'Right along there to the end. Accident and Emergency. Someone will help you.'

She was right. Within minutes a nurse came and ushered them through to an area of curtained bays.

'Doctor will be right with you,' she said, and whisked the curtain closed behind her.

Ethan lay like a baby in her arms. For the first time she realised how young he was. And how small and vulnerable. Diane thought through her options and decided to play it by ear, not make any rash decisions. She might be panicking about nothing.

The curtain opened and a young man came in, sleeves rolled up and a stethoscope round his neck. 'Hi,' he said. 'I'm Greg, one of the junior doctors. Can you tell me what happened?'

Diane explained as quickly as she could and answered the doctor's questions. Or as many as she could, given how little she knew about the child in her arms.

'Let's have a wee look, shall we? Would you like to lay little Bethan on the trolley? That might make it easier for me to examine her.'

Diane said, 'I'll hang on to her for the moment, if you don't mind.'

The young doctor knelt at her feet and said, 'Okay. Now, Bethan, how about showing me your arm? Let me see where the doggy bit you.' He looked up at Diane. 'Did you report the matter to the police?'

She shook her head.

He took a little toy from his shirt pocket and distracted Ethan long enough to get a look at the wound. 'Oh dear,' he said, 'poor Bethan. No wonder that's sore. I'm pretty sure the bite's become infected. We could have done with seeing her sooner.'

'I didn't think it was serious at the time.'

'That's unfortunate. But don't worry, she's here now. We'll get her up to Crosshouse, get her on some antibiotics and she'll soon be good as new.'

'What do you mean by "up to Crosshouse", Doctor?'

'Sorry, we'll need to find her a bed for the night, maybe a couple of nights. We don't have a paediatric department here, I'm afraid. She'll need to be taken to Crosshouse Hospital in Kilmarnock.'

'You're admitting her? I thought you said she just needed some antibiotics and she'll be fine.'

'She will, but we'd prefer to keep her in hospital so we can administer the drug and get her fixed as quickly as possible.'

She read his name badge. 'Doctor Egelton,' she said. 'I feel awful about this. What would have happened if I hadn't brought her in when I did?'

'Well, she may have got better by herself, that sometimes happens, but if the infection doesn't get nipped in the bud, as it were, a child this young could become very unwell and in say, forty-eight, seventy-two hours the situation could become quite grave.' He touched Diane's shoulder and said kindly, 'But please don't worry. Your wee granddaughter will be a lot better by morning. I'm sure of it. Now I'll just leave you for a moment while I see how soon we can get an ambulance organised. Is that okay?'

Diane waited till she heard his footsteps recede then rose to her feet. With Ethan in her arms and a smile on her face that suggested all was well, she walked quickly out of the nearest door and straight to her car.

'Right, Ethan,' she said, 'Looks like you're going to see your mommy much sooner than we all expected.'

Chapter 70

Seth was pacing the floor like a caged beast. 'I knew it,' he said. 'Didn't I tell you Sophie was involved? I could tell by the look on her face when she came out of that shop. She didn't look shocked enough. Didn't I say that at the time, Penny?'

'You did, honey, and I'm sorry I doubted you. She had me taken in. No two ways about it.'

He stopped, as if he'd suddenly realised he was pacing, and sat down by her side. He took her hand, the first show of affection for days. 'Yeah, but she was good. I'll give her that. She had me fooled for a while too.'

'So, let me get this right, officer. Sophie claims some random woman offers her a job in France, because she's from New Orleans and she speaks fluent French? She wants to find her long-lost French father so she says yes. The woman spins her some yarn about being our kids' grandmother but we don't allow her to see them. Sophie's told to befriend us at the first opportunity, which, thanks to the delays, happened to be at the airport. Dammit, we let her reel us in, didn't we?'

Morand nodded.

'I can't believe it,' said Penny. 'We invited her into our lives, our home, trusted her with our children and all along she was working some scam for this woman?' Penny covered her face with her hands. 'God, Seth, I am *so* sorry. This is all my fault.'

'It's not all your fault, Penny. I was taken in by her too.'

'No, you don't understand. It's my fault we ever came on this exchange.'

'How can it be your fault? We're here because my job gave us the opportunity and you wanted to come live in Europe.' Seth shrugged his shoulders as if to say, period, end of story.

'That's not the entire picture.'

'What do you mean, Penny?'

'It wasn't so much that I wanted to come to France. It's more that I wanted to get away from Texas.'

'I know, you fancied an adventure before Ethan started preschool. You explained it all to me at the time.'

'Seth, I *lied* to you at the time. It was nothing to do with Ethan, or adventures in Europe. I was running away.'

'From what? You've lost me.'

'There was someone watching us.'

'What?' Seth's voice was a whisper.

'I was being watched. I was terrified.'

'Why didn't you say?'

'I did. I told WITSEC. That new guy who took over from Janey.'

'And?'

'He wasn't really interested because I didn't have "specifics". I couldn't give him details or descriptions or anything.'

'You decided to run? Without telling me any of this?'

Penny looked her husband in the eye and nodded.

'We got into all of this because you were afraid of someone, but you didn't tell me?'

'I was going to tell you and then I saw a guy in the airport – watching me, I thought. Turned out he was waiting for his wife. I felt stupid. Decided to stop worrying all the time and start trusting people.'

'People like Sophie?'

Inspector Morand's phone rang, shattering the tension in the room.

'Morand.'

After a few rapid words in French, the inspector pressed a button on his phone and a woman's voice, American, filled the space.

'I'm told you're in charge of the Ethan Gates case?'

'That is correct.'

'Well, I'd like you to listen very carefully. I assume you speak English?'

Morand nodded to his young colleague, making sure he was ready to take over.

'How can I help you, madame?'

'I think you will find it is I who can help you. Are you in direct contact with the Gates family?'

Penny made a grab for the phone. Seth caught her arm.

The inspector saw her move and put his finger to his lips.

'We are.'

'Well, please be so kind as to pass on this message. Tell Ethan's mother there is a flight to Glasgow leaving this afternoon. There are still seats available. When she arrives she is to look out for a man with a sign bearing her name. He is a taxi driver who will bring her to meet me. She is to come alone. If anyone else comes with her, I've instructed the driver to leave immediately. She will be given a set of instructions. She is to follow them to the letter. If she doesn't, Ethan will never see his family again. Do you understand?'

'One moment, please. I would like to make sure I have understood and noted everything correctly.'

Penny had seen enough movies to know this tactic. Keep them on the line while you trace the call. She crossed her fingers.

'The plane leaves in less than two hours.'

Penny started to nod wildly. 'Anything,' she mouthed. 'I'll do anything.'

'I will pass this information on to Mr and Mrs Gates.'

'You weren't listening. Not Mr Gates. This has nothing to do with him. Mrs Gates is the only one who is to get off that plane. Do I make myself clear?'

'Perfectly. And if Mrs Gates refuses?'

The woman laughed. Penny thought it was the scariest sound she'd ever heard.

'Mrs Gates won't refuse. But she'd better not think of trying to outsmart me. You tell her that.'

'Madame, please, won't you consider handing over the child to the nearest police station? That is the simplest solution.'

As if he hadn't spoken the woman said, 'Tell Mrs Gates that although Ethan looked healthy on the video I posted, the situation has changed. He was bitten by a dog and has become unwell. He should, in fact, be in hospital. The doctor said he has about forty-eight hours before it gets life threatening. Make sure she doesn't miss that flight.'

A click as loud as a gunshot told them the conversation was over. Everyone in the room started talking at once.

'I'm coming with you,' said Seth.

'You must not go, Mrs Gates,' said Morand. 'Leave this to the police. We are tracing her call right now. We will pick her up. There is no need for you to go.'

'I'm going. Right now.'

'Mrs Gates. Please listen to me. One call from us and police at Glasgow Airport will be on alert.'

Seth said, 'He's right, Penny. The minute that taxi driver holds up a card with your name on it, they'll nail him. Isn't that right, Inspector?'

'Absolutely.'

'And what happens if the guy doesn't talk right away? You heard her. Ethan's ill. She said life threatening.'

'I don't believe that. She's putting a gun against your head to make sure you'll go.'

'It's worked. I'm going.'

'Mrs Gates. I strongly advise you to leave it to the professionals. Please. Take a moment. Think about it.'

'I've thought about it. I'm going. And if you interfere and something goes wrong, I promise I'll sue your ass.'

'Penny!'

'I'm going and I'm going alone. Just as she asked. That is my express wish, as the parent of this child.'

Penny turned to Seth, took both his hands in hers. 'Please, let me do this. I have to.'

'You heard the lady,' said Seth. 'Now let's not waste any more time.'

'Someone get me booked on that flight. Seth, you explain to Angel, please.' She turned to the young cop. 'Do you still have that toy rabbit? Hoppy Two is going to Glasgow.'

'Mrs Gates, wait. We know who has Ethan.'

'Yeah, some crazy woman.'

'Does the name Diane Millburn mean anything?'

Chapter 71

Ethan had fallen asleep again. Before she lifted him out of the car, she went into the house and fetched some antiseptic cream and the sticking plasters. She opened the biggest she could find and smeared it liberally with the white cream. In one swift movement, she pulled up his sleeve and stuck the plaster over the wound. When she pressed it to make sure the cream was in contact with his skin, he startled awake with a yelp.

'Sorry, baby,' she said. 'Mawmaw didn't mean to hurt you. I'm trying to make your sore arm better. Shall we go inside and get something to eat?'

He shook his head. He hadn't eaten for almost twenty-four hours.

'A drink of milk then? And a cookie?'

'No, thank you.'

His polite little voice was too much for her and Diane had to swallow a lump in her throat before she could speak.

'Come on, then. Let's have a little rest before we have to go back out.'

Diane reckoned she had three hours at the most before she had to get into position. If she were Lucie Jardine, she'd be informing the police the minute she knew the meeting place. It was vital that Diane got there first, otherwise they'd block her access.

She laid Ethan on the sofa with the soft blanket over him and turned on the TV. Despite feeling unwell his little face lit up when she switched channels to find CBeebies. She found herself hoping for *Bob the Builder*, a treat for him, like a prisoner's last meal. It wasn't to be. Some cartoon girl with a backpack appeared.

'Dora,' said Ethan, like he was greeting his best friend. 'Look, Dora Explora.'

'You like this one, Ethan?'

'Angel like Dora.'

Diane expected tears at the mention of his sister, but Ethan lay back and concentrated on the television. He'd be okay while she got her stuff sorted out.

First warm clothes for Ethan. Boys' colours this time. His days as a little girl were over. Then some snacks and drinks in case he felt well enough to eat. She looked at the elixir and wondered about giving him some, as per her plan. It was important he didn't struggle at the important moment, but Diane reckoned another few hours would make him even more lethargic and he was already pretty docile. Besides, if he wouldn't take a drink she had no way of doping him.

Then her own gear. Stout walking boots with a good grip. Warm clothing too and waterproofs, of course; this was the west of Scotland, after all. Even the nicest day can turn nasty. A rug to sit on. She could be in for a long wait.

She checked the time. Lucie Jardine's flight would be leaving soon. Would she be on it? Diane would bet her last dollar. Would she come alone? Not such a certainty.

Diane looked around the cottage. She wouldn't be back. It had served its purpose. She went to the kitchen and made herself a sandwich and cut up a banana in the hope of tempting Ethan. She laid a tray with a pretty embroidered cloth she found in a drawer and carried her lunch into the living room where she sat at the child's feet. She couldn't help pulling the cover up and tucking it under his chin, making sure he felt the love.

Her lunch gone, she put the tray down and leaned back against the sofa. It would be nice to watch TV with him one last time.

Chapter 72

'Please may I call my mother?' Sophie asked, when Youngcop came to see her in the cells. To make sure she was 'comfortable'. What a joke.

'I'll check with Inspector Morand,' he said. 'He may not want you to communicate with the outside world.'

'Why not? In the States you're allowed, like, one phone call.'

'This isn't the States.'

'I know, but I've done everything I can to help you. Haven't I?'

'I hope so, but don't you think it would have been better to stay in Carcassonne like we asked you?'

'I was terrified. I thought you were going to arrest me. I don't know if you're aware, but you guys have got, like, quite a bad reputation with the public.'

He laughed. 'You think we don't know? Someone once told me the French language has more slang words for cops than any other. And none of them are complimentary.'

'They also say you're harsh on foreigners. I was scared stiff you'd find that money in my bank account and I'd never be able to, like, prove my innocence. You believe I didn't know what she had planned, don't you?'

He shook his head, but with a smile on his lips. 'I really can't comment.'

'*Sub judice*, I suppose? Anyway, *can* I talk to my mom, please? You can stay and listen to every word I say. I'll even put it on speakerphone.'

'Do you have a phone?'

'I was hoping to borrow yours.'

'Now you *are* pushing your luck.'

The call rang out so long Sophie was sure there was no one home. Finally, when she was about to hang up, her mother came on the line.

'Mom, it's me.'

'Sophie, darling. We were just getting in a cab when John heard the phone. I ran back in. I had a feeling it might be you.'

'Where are you? Is everything alright?'

'I'm, like, in the cells, Mom. So, no, everything is clearly not alright.'

'Oh, my poor baby. Is it okay to talk to me?'

'It's okay, as long as we don't discuss what's been happening.'

'Sure. We can do that. But I don't have too long to chat. We have a plane to catch.'

Sophie felt disappointment like a kick in the stomach. So much for unconditional love. 'You're going on vacation?'

'We're coming to France. Dad, the boys and the best damn lawyer in Louisiana. *She* says you'll be fine. You did the right thing and the fact that you didn't touch a cent of that money proves you had no evil intent.'

Sophie became aware of loud coughing behind her. When she looked round Youngcop was staring at her, eyebrows raised.

'Okay, okay, I get it,' she said. 'Change the subject.'

Youngcop smiled.

'Mom, I have to go. I'll see you tomorrow?'

'You'll see me tomorrow. I love you. Never forget that.'

Sophie clasped her hand over her mouth as she handed the policeman his phone. She wouldn't let him see her blubber like a baby.

'Did you hear that?' she said. 'You better watch out. My mom will be here tomorrow. With the best damn lawyer in Louisiana.'

Chapter 73

Seth had been determined to come with her. Had even bought himself a ticket, in case she changed her mind before the gate closed. But she'd been equally adamant she was going alone and used Angeline as justification for Seth staying behind.

'I'll be okay, Seth. You stay with Angel and I'll come back with Ethan. I promise you.'

'How can you promise that? You've no idea what that woman has planned. She's deranged. Got to be. No sane person would steal a kid and set up such a complicated way to give him back. There's got to be more to it. Why Scotland, for example?'

'She's found out I'm Scottish. Scott must have told her. Or somebody has.' She shook her head. 'Millburn. I knew he was behind this all along.'

'I still don't understand how the hell he was able to find out we'd gone to Texas. That information was classified.'

'Lots of stuff is classified. Doesn't mean it can't get out there.'

'You're thinking of 9/11?'

'Yep. Scott Millburn knew all about that classified information.'

'All in the past. Let's focus on right now, on getting our son back. You sure you can do this?'

'I'm sure. I've learned that bravery is a state of mind. After Curtis I swore I'd never be afraid again. That didn't last. And then when I saw that guy watching me I was terrified, not only for me, but for the kids. Being scared for yourself is one thing. When your child is at risk that's a whole different ball game.'

He hugged her. 'I get that.'

She whispered into his shoulder, 'Seth, I'm so sorry I was too scared to tell you about the guy when Ethan went missing.

I wasn't really *frightened* of you, it was just, well, I *wanted* to tell you but the situation got so crazy and then I couldn't tell you because I'd put it off for too long.'

'I promise you will never ever need to be afraid of me. Anyway, none of that stuff matters right now.'

'All that matters is I find Ethan and he's not been harmed.'

'Please tell me you'll call the local police the minute you know where the driver is taking you.'

'Yeah, I'd thought of that.'

'Dial 999. That's the emergency number.'

'I've known that since I was five years old.'

'Promise me you won't do anything crazy?'

She shook her head. 'I can't promise that. I'll do anything to save our son. I'd lay down my life for you and my children.'

Chapter 74

Diane woke to *Bob the Builder* music. She looked at the screen. The closing credits! How long had she been asleep?

Beside her, Ethan looked settled but sleepy. She touched his forehead. He was burning up. 'Drink of juice, Ethan?'

He shook his head.

She had to move fast. If she didn't get onto the path behind the big house before the plane landed, she was running the risk of Lucie Jardine calling the cops and sending them to the Boswell Estate.

She got herself ready and then zipped Ethan, against his will, into a warm outdoor jacket that was at least two sizes too big. The effect was to make him look even more pathetic and vulnerable. The dark material seemed to rob his face of all colour leaving the unhealthy pallor of a very sick child. Ethan should be in hospital, no doubt about it, but too bad. She wasn't giving up now. She'd come too far and anyway, what difference did it make? Sick kid, healthy kid? He was still Lucie Jardine's kid.

'Come on, Ethan. We're going in the car.'

'No.'

'Oh, but yes.' She caught him under the arms and lifted him. He kicked and struggled and she thought about the sleeping elixir. It was tempting. Then suddenly Ethan wilted and put up no more of a fight.

She decided to dispense with his car seat and plopped him in the front, beside her. They only had about two hundred yards to drive to the gates of the estate and then they'd be on private roads and tracks. What was the worst that could happen, anyway?

313

She drove off remembering she hadn't locked the cottage door, but that too was unimportant now.

She took the car as far as she could. First on the surfaced road that led up to the big manor house. It was unoccupied most of the time, so no one was there to see them drive by. Then onto the little track that led towards the Dipple Burn where it cut through a deep gorge. When the track petered out and she could feel the weeds and grass snagging on the underside of the car, she stopped and said, 'Okay, Ethan. We're walking from here.'

'No!'

'Sorry, kid. I know you're sleepy but we've got no choice.'

He started to cry.

'Come on, Ethan,' she said brightly. 'We're going to see Mommy.' She knew she was being cruel, given what was about to happen, but desperate times and all that.

'Mommy?'

'Yes, if you're a good boy. Let's go, we'll take the stroller.'

Ethan did his best to climb in, but she could see he was getting weak. She lifted him and fastened the straps. She hung her bags round her shoulders and set off, pushing. It was hard work and she knew there was no way the stroller would go much further. Should she leave the kid here and go on ahead with the blanket and supplies? Come back for him later. She checked her watch. That sleep had cost her precious time.

'Ethan, can you walk just a little bit, if Mawmaw takes your hand?'

He didn't even answer this time. She hoped Lucie Jardine hadn't missed that plane. A dead kid was not much of a bargaining chip. She shunned the idea, but at this stage there was no room for tenderness. She knew she had to harden her heart if she wanted to achieve her goal. Once or twice she'd come far too close to getting attached to this kid, something she'd never envisaged when she was hatching her plans. She had to stay strong.

'Come on, then.' She hoisted him into her arms. Could he have lost weight already? Even with the big jacket he felt lighter.

She set off and within moments realised that Ethan was no lighter – he was a dead weight in her arms. Perish the thought.

Finally, her chosen spot became visible through the trees and bushes. When she'd done her research she'd expected the place to be more accessible, but given it was on private land she shouldn't be surprised that the path was not well trodden or marked. Anyway, lack of footfall meant less chance of being disturbed.

The sandstone at the edge of the gorge was wet from a recent shower and, even with boots on, felt slippery. Diane set Ethan down but held him tightly by the hand as she led him back into the undergrowth where she set up a little nest. 'There,' she said gently, 'why don't we have a drink of juice and then a lie-down while we wait for Mommy?' She'd packed some books for him and offered to read a story, but Ethan's eyes were closed by the time she got his bag open. She wished she'd spent more time checking the symptoms of a dog bite and how the sickness progressed. He seemed to be getting sick faster than she'd expected.

She tucked the cover around him and waited. Lucie Jardine should be getting off the plane soon. The driver should be there, waiting, his instructions clear. Ask no questions. Give no replies.

She thought about Scott. Would he be proud of her? It didn't matter, she was doing this for herself. *Because* of Scott and the mess he'd made of their lives. But *for* herself. Maybe she'd go see him once this was all done and the dust had settled.

Chapter 75

Penny had a priority seat which meant she was among the first off the plane. With no luggage to collect she walked through customs ahead of the crowd and towards the arrivals gate. People clustered near the door, their faces expectant. Others were waiting in the hall. She looked around for her driver, crossing her fingers he'd be there. A bald guy leaning against a pillar raised a laminated card above his head. It said Lucie Jardine, not Penelope Gates. First point to Diane then.

She took a step towards him. Four guys suddenly tackled the man, knocking him to the ground. People screamed and darted out of the way.

'Awright, Lucie?' Penny felt a hand gripping her arm, pulling hard, steering her away from the fracas.

'I'm your driver. Quick. This way.' She followed him to the exit and out of the terminal.

The Glasgow air smelt just as she remembered it, cold and damp. The man hurried her across the road and into a multi-storey car park opposite the terminal building. Penny stood by while he fed coins into the payment machine. 'Through here, hen,' he said, and pushed open a heavy door.

He stopped at a vehicle that looked like a normal family car. Penny hesitated. 'Is this a taxi?' she asked.

He indicated a plaque fixed to the bumper. 'Thought you were in a hurry?'

She slid onto the back seat and watched while he joined the M8, heading east, for Glasgow. Could he be taking her home?

Was her dad involved in some way? Did he have Ethan, safe and sound? She dismissed the idea as fantasy.

'Where are we going?' she asked.

The driver put the radio on and turned the volume high. Did he not hear her question?

She leaned forward and tapped his shoulder. 'Excuse me. Can you tell me where you're taking me?'

He kept his eyes on the road but tapped his ear and pointed to the radio, as if to say he couldn't hear her for the music.

Of course, Diane would have told him to reveal nothing. So she couldn't alert the authorities. So much for dialling 999.

She sent Seth a text. *Landed safely. Found driver. He's saying nothing. No idea where he's taking me.*

Seth replied immediately. *Be careful! Love you.*

Penny settled back in her seat and watched the road. Maybe she could guess the destination. Even as she had the thought, she knew it was nonsense.

'Can you turn the music down, please?'

He obliged. Barely.

'Could you please tell me where you've been asked to take me? I need to know where we're going.'

The guy acted as if she hadn't spoken. Penny didn't know what to do. She couldn't force him to talk. Should she tell him about Ethan?

Seth would know. She sent a short message and imagined him, phone in hand at the other end, waiting to hear from her. His reply was instant.

Offer him money to tell you.

I've only got euros and a few dollars. Should I try it?

Yes!

'Excuse me, I know you've probably been told not to tell me where we're going, but believe me, it's really important that I know in advance.'

No response.

317

'I'll give you money?'

He surprised her by replying. 'How much money we talking?'

Penny scrambled quickly for her wallet. She tried to keep him talking while she counted. 'I'm afraid I haven't got any sterling, but I can give you nearly a hundred euros and forty-five dollars.'

'Nae pounds? Nae deal.'

This was hopeless. She had no choice but to sit there and wait.

He won't tell me.

Then watch for place names, road numbers etc and text them to me.

They were still on the M8 but no longer heading into the city. They seemed to be going back the way they had come. Was the guy lost? Had she distracted him by speaking?

They were on the M77 towards the south. Kilmarnock, Ayr, Prestwick – places she used to go as a child to visit aunties or have a day at the seaside.

Over the moor, bleak even in summer, gloomy at this time of the year. The rain came on and the grey-green landscape was blurred to nothing outside her window.

The taxi reached Kilmarnock and turned off the dual carriageway. Onto roads like the ones she remembered from her teens, as different from American highways as it's possible to imagine. They passed a jail and she thought of Scott Millburn. Had he put his wife up to this? She'd find out, and very soon, she hoped. For Ethan's sake.

She'd been trying not to think of her child sick and far from his family. And getting worse, if Diane Millburn was to be believed.

Her phone rang. Seth.

'You okay, honey?'

'I don't have much battery.'

'How come?'

'I was looking at photos of Ethan on the plane. Trying to stay brave. I didn't think.'

'It's okay. Save your battery so you can call the cops when he drops you off. Ask the guy for his phone, if need be. Tell them where you are. Morand has got Strathclyde Police waiting for your call. Good luck. Switch the phone off now. Love you.'

Penny checked. Less than ten per cent battery remaining. How could she have been so stupid? She turned her phone off, feeling as if she was severing her last link.

The countryside was lush and green, unlike anything Penny had seen since she left for the States all those years ago. Cows dotted the fields and the only buildings to be seen were farmhouses, many with modern bungalows alongside. Mauchline. A76. Signposts for Cumnock, Dumfries. The car slowed and turned off to the right, along a narrow, bendy road. She had no idea where they were headed but each turn seemed to take them further from towns and villages. The car slowed again and turned up what looked like a private driveway, lined with tall trees.

'Where is this, please?'

'No far tae go.'

'But where are we?'

The trees were still in full leaf although some were turning golden and with the low light and the overhanging branches, it seemed like twilight had come early. Penny switched on her phone to call the police and when she looked up a big mansion house had appeared on her left-hand side.

'No much sign of a birthday party,' said the driver, pulling up at a wide stone staircase. 'Looks like you're here first. Maybe that's the surprise!' He laughed at his own joke as he reached into the glove compartment and took out an envelope, which he handed over his shoulder. 'You've to take this and read it.'

Penny took it but continued to sit in the cab and stare out of the window. 'I have no idea where I am. Could you not please tell me, for pity's sake.' At that the driver swivelled in his seat and looked at her for the first time.

'Listen, my friend,' she said, sounding as Scottish as she could, 'I'm here to pick up my wee boy. Somebody took him a few days ago. It's been on the television and the internet and everything.

I need to call the police so they can come and arrest the mad bitch that kidnapped him.'

The look on the guy's face changed. She thought she'd got through to him. Then he held up his hand to stop her talking.

'Hey, I don't want any bother wi' the polis. Sorry.'

'Well, will you at least wait here?'

'Sorry, hen.' He shook his head. 'I've got to get this cab back to Glesga. Another hire on. Cannae afford to be late. Time's money.' He got out and opened her door, chauffeur-style, and waited. When she climbed out, he jumped back in behind the wheel and, with a gravelly skid, he was gone.

Penny looked around. She had never felt so alone in her life. She stared at the envelope in her hand. Pretty writing on the front asked her to please open and follow the instructions.

They were brief.

Make sure you are alone.

Walk to the right-hand side of the building.

Follow the track into the woods.

Take the little trail till it runs out.

Be careful. It is dangerous.

I will be waiting for you.

Hurry.

Penny selected Seth's number and hit call.

'Have you got him?'

'No. I've been dropped off outside this spooky-looking manor house with handwritten directions to follow a path into the woods.'

'Where are you?'

'I have no idea.'

'Is it worth calling the cops and describing the place? Somebody might know it from your description.'

'I doubt it and anyway, I don't want to waste any more time. The last instruction was to hurry.'

'You'd better go then. Shit, Penny, I wish you'd let me come.'

'I do too.'

'Penny? Don't …'

The screen went black. The last of the battery was gone. And so was Seth.

The light drizzle had turned to serious rain. She took the toy rabbit out of her pocket and gave him a quick hug.

'Come on, Hoppy,' she whispered. 'Let's go find Ethan.'

Chapter 76

Diane was about to give up and head for the hospital when she heard rustling and the bushes parted to reveal a young woman. She looked nothing like the confident, yummy-mummy type from the 9/11 Memorial a few weeks ago. This woman was soaked, her hair sticking to her face and scalp like wet wool. She looked grey and haggard, much older and more careworn than Diane had anticipated. And yet what could she expect of a woman who had spent days believing her child was gone for ever? Diane looked at Ethan. He was sound asleep, his cheeks flushed bright and burning hot.

'Sorry, L'il Buddy,' she whispered, 'but it's probably best if you don't see Mommy after all.' She stood up and stepped out from her shelter.

Lucie Jardine spotted her. She gasped, 'Jesus,' closing her eyes as if in prayer.

Diane stepped to the edge of the sandstone cliff and set her feet apart to give her a solid grip. The light was failing fast, something she hadn't expected, and the rain made it hard to see.

'Well, Lucie,' she said, 'we meet at last.'

'Mrs Millburn.'

'Oh, please, call me Diane, why don't you? This is pretty intimate, don't you think? Come a bit closer, so we don't have to shout at each other.'

Diane could see the woman was unsure and a glance at her footwear explained her caution. She was wearing normal shoes like she might wear to the office.

'Where is he?' she demanded.

'First things first. Did you come alone?'

'Yes, I did.'

'Has the driver gone?'

The woman nodded, her hair swinging in wet hanks. 'Please, where is he?'

'Ethan? He's right here.'

'Let me see him. Is he okay? If you've harmed him, I swear,'

'You swear what, Lucie? What will you do? That's what I'm keen to find out.'

'You're crazy.'

'I'm not crazy. I admit, I did need a little help, both professional and pharmaceutical, when you first robbed me of my husband. And my life. But now I am medication-free. As sane as the next person.'

'Can I see Ethan, please? You said he was ill?'

'He has a fever. It would be wise to get him to a hospital as soon as possible.'

'What do you want me to do? Tell me.'

'I want you to prove to me how much you love your child because, you see, I don't feel you love him enough.'

'How can you say that? You know nothing about me.'

'Oh, that's not true, Mrs Gates. I know a whole lot about you.'

'You don't know anything. You're bluffing.'

'You think so? Then why did I bring you here?'

'I've no idea. Because I'm Scottish? So what? It's no secret.'

'Do something for me, my dear. Would you take two steps to your left, please?'

She counted seconds in her head, waiting for the young woman to move. 'Thought not,' she said.

'What do you think that proves?'

'It proves what I just said. I know everything about you, Penny Gates.'

'You're lying.'

'How do you think I found you? I know where you live.'

She watched the woman process the information.

'You were having me watched.'

'Indeed I was. For quite some time.'

'But we were protected by WITSEC.'

Diane laughed. 'Clearly, my dear, you weren't. Or at least, not well enough.'

'How did you find us?'

'You remember my brother-in-law, Bill, don't you?'

'The one who leaked information to Scott? Surely he's locked up, too?'

'Oh no, no, no. The politicians couldn't let that happen. That would have made public things they wanted to keep under wraps.'

'Like secrets about national security that he shared with his brother, you mean?'

'Scott was Bill's only brother, Lucie. He'd pledged to always protect him. Bill saved Scott's life. Some might say Bill was the injured party in all of this. He certainly felt that way. He didn't lose his job, but he was downgraded in his post and despised by his colleagues. Fortunately, not all of them. It would have been fairer to let him go, but that would have stoked the fires of the conspiracy theorists.'

'I don't understand. What's Bill got to do with me?'

'I needed some information. Bill had contacts who could get it for me. For a price.'

'Information about me? I don't believe you.'

Diane laughed and heard the sound echo deep in the gorge. 'Still so naïve.'

'But there's no way anyone in WITSEC would sell our secret.'

'Lucie, everything's for sale. If the price is right. I offered Bill a mouth-watering sum of money. Enough to allow him and his source at WITSEC to walk off into the sunset to a very comfortable retirement. His employers put up no fight.'

'Who sold my details?' The young woman's face suddenly crumpled. Like her son's when he was about to weep. 'Please tell me it wasn't Janey.'

'Oh, fiddlesticks, how would I know? Someone who'd had enough stress and was ready to walk away. All she needed, was, how shall I put it, some financial assistance to make retirement possible. Anyway, none of that matters.'

'What matters is Ethan.'

'I couldn't agree more. But it also matters to me that you know how I felt when my world fell apart. When I lost the person I loved most. When he was taken from me unexpectedly and through no fault of my own, other than misplaced trust.'

'But your husband did wrong. Poor little Ethan is innocent.'

'I didn't plan this to hurt Ethan. He's a lovely child. Almost makes me regret never having one of my own. But then, that's difficult when your husband is in a high-security prison. Sure, we might have left it a little late, but we'll never know now, will we? All thanks to you.'

'What was I supposed to do? Your husband was going to kill me. Like he killed Charlotte and the other guy. He said I was a loose end, just like Charlotte.'

'Oh, come on. You could have talked him out of it. But oh, no, you had to bring in the FBI, didn't you? Quite the hero of the hour, as it turns out. Miss Patriot of America, 2001.'

'Okay, you've made your point. What do you want of me?'

'I want to see how far you'll go to save your child.'

'I'd do anything to save my child. Any mother would.'

'Would you die for him?'

'Of course I would.'

'Ah, you say that, but what if I were to put you to the test? Would you lay down your life to save your child's? Now think about it, no glib answers. This could be the most important question you've ever been asked in your life.'

'How do I know Ethan's safe? You say he's here, but I haven't seen him.'

'You haven't answered my question.'

'What do you want me to say?'

'Tell me the truth. Are you prepared to give up your life in exchange for Ethan's? Yes or no?'

Lucie stared at her. Finally, she said, 'If I say yes, how do I know Ethan will be safe?'

'You'd have to trust him to me. Like you trusted him to Sophie, a complete stranger. If you'd turned Sophie down, I'd have left you alone, do you know that? I was testing you.'

'And I failed. Do you think I'm ever gonna forget that? I will torture myself for the rest of my life.'

'I'm offering you the chance to forget it all. A simple bargain, your life for Ethan's. Step off the edge there and I promise you, I'll get Ethan straight to hospital and let his Daddy know where to come get him. By the time he arrives, Ethan will be on the mend. He'll be "good as new", to quote the lovely young doctor, once he gets some antibiotics.'

'You took him to a doctor but denied him treatment? How could you do that?'

'Simple. It's called self-preservation. The survival instinct. Very difficult to overcome, I understand. As you may be about to find out.'

'What happens if I say no?'

Diane pointed to the gorge at her feet. 'Simple. Ethan goes over.'

'You wouldn't do that.'

'You have no idea what I'd do. But please don't try me. I have so very little to lose.'

She let Lucie think for a moment then said, 'So, what's it to be? You or Ethan?'

The little boy emerged from the bushes. Maybe he'd woken and heard his name. Maybe he'd recognised his mother's voice.

'Stay there, Ethan,' said Diane. 'Don't move.'

'Ethan?' said Lucie, her voice calm and gentle. She held something out towards the child. 'Look Ethan, it's Hoppy!'

The little boy took a few steps then stumbled, his feet slipping or his legs tired. Both women lunged for him. Grabbed his sleeves.

He was hauled to his feet and stood stretched between them like a tiny scarecrow.

'Let him go,' screamed Lucie, tugging hard on his jacket.

Diane's feet moved on the slippery stone. She couldn't let him go. She wouldn't let Lucie Jardine win. Again.

Diane hauled the child towards her, wrenching him out of his mother's grip. As his weight came her way, Diane's balance was lost and suddenly the world was tilting.

Chapter 77

Diane dropped him, her arms flailing at the air. Ethan tumbled backwards, Penny watching in slow motion. Somewhere, a scream faded into silence.

Ethan fell, his little body rolling like a discarded doll. All she could do was wait. He lost momentum and came to rest on his back with one arm hanging out over the edge.

Penny stopped breathing and fell to her knees, focusing on her child, willing him not to move. She took a breath and spoke his name, gently, for fear of startling him. She prayed he'd hear and turn towards her voice, but there was no reaction. He appeared to be unconscious. Stunned from the fall, perhaps, or fevered from the dog bite.

Penny edged across the flat, sandstone rock. She tried not to look beyond Ethan. Did not want to see the depth of the gorge.

The abyss she feared so much.

It seemed to draw her, a magnetic force stronger than her willpower. She stared, mesmerised, then reared back, every instinct telling her to save herself.

That was why Diane Millburn had sought out this place. She knew Penny's fear of heights and had brought her here to see if was prepared to die for her child. She was being tested, only Diane was no longer around to gloat and punish her if she failed.

Taking the deepest breath of her life, Penny moved one limb at a time, stealthy as a stalking cat. Though she barely advanced, every inch felt like an invitation to death. She kept her eyes fixed on Ethan, praying for the slightest sign of life.

She reached out and her fingertip grazed the side of his shoe. Found his laces, undone. That's dangerous, she thought stupidly.

His trouser leg had ridden up, showing a stripe of pale skin above his sock. She wanted to stroke it, comfort him, but he was too far away. If she caught his foot, maybe she could stay where she was, safe. And drag him towards her. She pictured his poor little head bumping across the stone. And couldn't do it.

Penny transferred her weight to her outstretched hand and moved one knee forward. She froze, too frightened to move her other arm. Her heart slammed a rhythm in her chest and she cursed herself and her pathetic fears.

If Diane hadn't released her grip on him at the last second, he'd be gone. If he woke and moved an inch in the wrong direction, he'd be gone. If Penny couldn't overcome her fear, and fast, Ethan would join Diane, just as she'd promised, at the foot of the gorge.

She'd thought he was destined to be one of the lost children. She'd thought he was going over the edge with Diane. Now he was right there, within touching distance, waiting for her to do something.

She inched forward, limb by limb, worrying about how she'd lift him. That would mean taking both hands off the ground. She couldn't do it. One hand, yes. Two, impossible. She began to cry, trembling with fear and frustration. The tears passed, having served no purpose.

'Ethan,' she whispered, 'Ethan, it's Mommy. Can you hear me?' Did she really think he was going to wake up and crawl over to her?

She pawed at his sleeve, trying to catch his arm. Some self-protecting instinct curled him like a babe in the womb. He rolled away from her. And was gone.

A heartbeat too late, Penny stretched out both arms, as if begging. She crashed onto her chest, her chin hitting the stone. Her teeth slammed shut on her tongue and she tasted blood. She lay panting, unbelieving, her hands dangling, empty, over the edge. If she'd moved sooner, closer. If she'd been braver.

Diane was right. Penny was too big a coward to save her son's life. Even given that second chance, she'd hesitated. Too paralysed by fear to move fast enough or close enough to rescue him.

Birds chirped in the trees, their last joyous song of the day. Far below, water rushed over rocks. And whatever else lay down there. Penny had to look, and yet she didn't want to see. And looking meant moving even closer to the edge. Did she care anymore? Would it matter if she fell?

Like a baby on its belly, she slithered forward, her fingers gripping the edge. The stone cut into her hands but the pain didn't matter. She moved her hips, one side at a time till the top of her face jutted out and she could see a shape far below. Diane. Spreadeagled on the rocks. Penny closed her eyes.

Where was Ethan? Had he dropped into the water, been swept away? He was too little to save himself. The river would take him. Perhaps he'd landed on Diane and she, in a last unwitting act of kindness, had broken his fall. Maybe he was down there, stumbling, lost, by the side of the water.

She opened her eyes and searched. 'Ethan,' she shouted. 'Ethan?'

The gorge echoed her little boy's name back to her, over and over. She called out, the echo replied, but there was no sound from Ethan.

Chapter 78

Penny moved her hips and wriggled forward, eyes closed. She breathed in and opened them on the exhale. And there he was, only inches away. Directly below her a bush clung defiantly to the rock and there, cradled in its branches, lay her son. She flashed back to Ethan as a newborn, his proud big sister singing 'Rock-a-bye Baby, on the treetop.'

Penny let go of the stone edge and reached, her arms yearning for him. He was still out of reach. His forehead was bleeding, the blood startling in its redness. She moved her hips again, first the left one, then the right and felt her centre of gravity shifting.

Panicked, Penny struggled back to a kneeling position. 'Think,' she said, thumping her forehead as if that would speed up her thoughts. Could she climb down to him? There was no point even considering that option.

She needed help. She couldn't do this on her own. But the only way she could get help was by leaving Ethan. And that was never going to happen. She'd perish on this rock before she'd leave him.

She had to save him. There was no one else.

Maybe she could find a stick or break one off a tree, something for Ethan to catch hold of. She got to her feet and started to haul and twist at a branch in the thicket. It turned and flexed in her hand but refused to break. When she let go, it swung back and slapped her across the face. No more than she deserved for wasting time on such a ridiculous idea. Even if he were conscious, Ethan was far too small and weak to hold on to a stick.

Under the bush, Diane had set up camp with a blanket spread out as if for a picnic. Ethan's drinking cup lay on its side by a neat pile of children's books. The striped bag they'd used since Angel was a baby sat in the middle of the blanket, its strap coiled like a bright snake.

Penny grabbed the strap and unclipped it from the bag. She made a loop and wrapped the other end round and round her hand. This time she dropped easily onto her belly and commando-crawled her way to the edge. One elbow, one hip, repeat. Her arms felt like the skin was being ripped off and her stomach heaved with fear. Not of falling anymore, but of failing.

Leaning as far as she dared she let out the strap. It dangled in the breeze.

'When the wind blows, the cradle will rock.' She needed to hurry; not only was it getting windy, it was getting cold.

She waved the strap back and forward, cringing each time it swung near his face. She tried again, hoping to loop the strap over his foot, like a lasso. Each time she was about to snag him, the strap twirled away. She was reminded of a fairground game she'd loved as a child. She would stand, as long as her pocket money allowed, trying to grab a cuddly toy with metal pincers. At the last breath-holding moment, they would slide to the side, leaving the teddy bear safe and her disappointed.

This wasn't working. She dropped the strap and watched it disappear. She had to think of something else. Fast. She couldn't expect those willowy branches to support Ethan's weight for ever. *What happens when the bough breaks?*

And what about that head wound? How long would it take for a toddler to bleed out? A sick toddler like Ethan.

She edged forward till her head, shoulders and chest hung in mid-air. Her elbows ran out of rock to lean on and nausea hit her in waves. 'Focus on Ethan,' she told herself.

He looked paler than before. His bleeding forehead was a shocking contrast to his white face. The blood looked wet and sticky. As if it hadn't yet clotted to a stop.

She moved again, arms reaching for her child. He seemed further away than before. Was the bush parting from the rock, its roots tiring, its branches weary of Ethan's weight?

She looked down at Diane. Pictured Ethan sprawled beside her.

Penny shook her head to dislodge the image. The movement disturbed her balance. She felt herself begin to tip. She slapped her hands onto the wall of rock and pushed back, clenching every muscle in her body.

Seconds passed, several heartbeats at a time. Penny concentrated on breathing, settling, taking control.

Now she knew her tipping point. Go beyond it and she'd fall, dislodging Ethan as she went. Move back to safety and she'd never reach her child.

With one arm rigid to keep her in position she reached out with the other, caught the collar of Ethan's jacket and pulled. He started to rise towards her, heavy for a moment then suddenly weightless. She watched in horror as the zipper of his coat slid slowly open and the jacket parted, threatening to tip Ethan out. She let go and tried to control the rush of panic. He settled on the branches and lay still.

She dared to reach a little further and caught his arm. She felt it move inside the sleeve and grabbed again, relieved to feel flesh and bone through the padded material.

'You've got him,' she said, as if providing a running commentary for herself. 'Now lift him up.'

She tried. He was too heavy. Her mind searched for facts. His last health check, at two and a half, he'd weighed thirty pounds. The same, she'd thought, as a fat Thanksgiving turkey. She could lift a turkey, couldn't she? She loaded more than a fifteen-pound plate on each end of the bar when she went to the gym, didn't she? She could easily raise that above her head and squat. How hard could it be to haul her child to safety.

Very hard, seemed to be the answer. Especially with one arm. And she didn't trust his too-large jacket. She gently let him go, holding her breath till she saw the branches take his weight and hold him there. She adjusted her position, swapped arms and reached out with her other hand till she caught Ethan's leg. It felt slighter and thinner than her own puny wrist. She moved her hips, one then the other, just a fraction, and felt Ethan come with her. She saw the branches wave as they gave up his weight. He dangled, upside down, from her fist, like a rabbit fresh from a trap. As she edged back to safety, she knew his little face was hitting the rock but there was not a thing she could do to prevent it. Better a broken nose than a broken body, she told herself, so she would carry on.

He hung there, pulling her arm out of its socket. Ignoring the shards of pain, she moved back till she could move no further.

She'd heard of women outsprinting a car, lifting a fallen tree, taking the weight of a concrete beam. Impossible tasks made possible by the need to save a child. Penny had always thought that stuff a bunch of sensationalist lies but, now she was being put to the test, she wanted to believe it.

'Believe you can and you're halfway there, Lucie.' Granny used to say that to her when she was wee, sitting at the top of the slide, too scared to let go, the other kids impatient on the metal steps behind her. She could hear Granny's voice as clearly as if she was right there at her side. 'Listen, lass, it's not who you are that'll hold you back. It's who you think you're not. You think you're not strong, but you are. Trust me.'

Penny trusted. 'Granny, I can do it,' she shouted.

The echo replied, or maybe it was Granny, 'Do it, do it, do it.'

She felt invincible. With a surge of strength she didn't believe she had, Penny hefted her child up over the edge and rolled onto her back. Ethan landed on her chest like a newly delivered baby and she clasped him to her. She sat up and cradled him in her aching arms, whispering, 'It's alright, baby. Mommy's got you. You're safe.' His skin was cold to her touch.

As she struggled to her feet she grabbed the blanket, damp now, but better than none. She wrapped Ethan tightly, saying his name over and over. His little face was bloodied and bashed and it tore at her very heart to think she had caused his pain. She felt for a pulse. Her sore, numb fingers found none.

Hoppy lay, a forlorn bundle, where she'd dropped him earlier. Ethan would want Hoppy with him. Whatever happened. She picked up the rabbit and tucked him in the blanket too.

Then she ran, crashing through the bushes, keeping the gorge behind them. The light was fading fast and the tree cover made it all the darker. She found what must have been Diane's abandoned car and opened the door, praying for a miracle. The keys hung there, dangling from the dash.

Penny laid Ethan's little blanket-wrapped body on the back seat, handling him as gently as she could. She knew he was feeling no pain, but still, she couldn't bear to hurt him. She started the car and shoved it into reverse, muttering a prayer of thanks when it lurched backwards. She accelerated, not caring how much the car snaked around, as long as it took them away from the abyss. When she found space to turn, she shot off towards the big house and skidded over the gravel. At the end of the long drive she stopped, no idea where to go, what to do. Race to a hospital or find a phone?

The taxi had turned in from the left so she accelerated in that direction. A large farm sat off to the right, its buildings glowing white in the dying light.

Penny shot up the narrow lane and screeched into the yard. A woman climbing out of a van glared at her as if she'd no business there.

'We need an ambulance.'

'Jim!' yelled the woman as she ran to Penny's side. She touched her shoulder. 'What's happened, hen?'

Penny pointed to Ethan.

'Oh my, it's wee Bethan.'

A middle-aged man appeared, his red-cheeked face concerned. 'Phone an ambulance, son. Quick.'

The man took out a phone and dialled. 'Who's it for?' he asked, looking at Penny.

'My son. He's only two. Unconscious.'

'Ambulance. Berryhill Farm, Auchinleck. Hurry, it's a wee boy.'

Chapter 79

Penny felt someone touch her shoulder.

'Mrs Gates?'

Penny startled awake.

'I fell asleep! Is Ethan okay?'

The nurse nodded. 'He's fine, don't worry. And, he's got another visitor.'

Penny looked up. 'Seth, oh, thank God you're here.'

Seth hugged her quickly, saying, 'How's he doing?'

Penny pointed to Ethan, connected up to tubes and machines. 'It's not as scary as it looks. Intravenous antibiotics, fluids and some monitors.'

'What the hell happened to his face? He looks like he's gone twelve rounds with Rocky.'

'Funny you should say that. Rock was what happened to his face. The dressings are a precaution. His nose will be okay. No lasting damage.'

'And the head injury?'

'All the scans are clear. They say he'll be fine. Once the antibiotics really kick in, he should get well fast, but another few hours and it could have been serious. But wait till you hear this. There were drugs in his bloodstream.'

'Drugs? What kind of drugs?'

'Something to make him sleepy. Well, to knock him out, basically.'

'Do the police know?'

'Yes, they were in last night. The doctors gave them a full report on Ethan and I told them absolutely everything. No secrets this time. What's happening with the French cops?'

'International cooperation.'

'What does that mean?'

'It means Youngcop gets a free trip to Scotland. We flew over together.'

'He'll want to speak to me, I expect.'

'He will, but he says you don't have anything to be scared about. It's all over.'

'Thank God.'

'I can't believe she drugged our kid. That's how she got him on and off a boat without anyone noticing?'

'And it means he didn't go off willingly with some stranger and forget all about me.'

'Have you been worrying about that?'

She nodded, suddenly too emotional to speak. She pointed to Ethan again, wanting his daddy to talk to him.

Seth took Ethan's hand in his. It looked tiny in his father's palm. 'Hey, L'il Buddy, you doing okay there?'

Ethan's eyes flickered open. Penny felt like the sun had come out on a grey winter's day.

'Daddy,' he said.

'Hi, Bud.'

'Angel?'

'She'll be here soon. We'll all be together again.'

Ethan closed his eyes and went back to sleep.

'Seth?' whispered Penny.

'Yes, honey?'

'I've been doing a lot of thinking while I was sitting at this little guy's bedside. I don't want to go back to France.'

'Me neither.'

'Or Texas.'

'Seriously?'

Penny nodded. 'It feels pretty good being back in Scotland.'

'That's natural, I guess. It's your home.'

'No, my home is where you and the kids are. But I was thinking, I'd kinda like to stick around here for a wee while.'

'A wee while?' Seth laughed. 'Listen to you. You're sounding Scotch already.'

'Now that's the first thing you've got to learn. We're not Scotch. Whisky is Scotch.'

'Sorry ma'am. I'm hearing you.'

'You're not saying no to my suggestion?'

'I'm saying yes, to whatever you want. Within reason, of course. I'm just thankful to see you both safe.'

'Dylan? There's one more thing.'

'Dylan?'

'Yes. No more hiding. No more fear. From now on, it's Dylan and Lucie, okay?'

'Won't that be weird for the kids?'

'Legally and officially, we'll still be Penny and Seth, Angeline and Ethan. The Gates family. But I want us to call each other by our real names again. Starting right now.'

'And what if people ask why you call me Dylan, Lucie?'

'Then we'll tell them it's a long story.'

Acknowledgments

My first thank you must go to the many readers who, in telling us how much they enjoyed *Till the Dust Settles*, requested a follow-up and to Betsy Reavley, my wonderful publisher, for trusting me to go ahead and write *I know where you live*, with the contract safely in my pocket. Betsy, I'm thankful, as always, for your faith, advice and patience. Thanks, Alexina Golding, for loving my first story and setting this whole crazy ball rolling.

Till the Dust Settles was read by many before it was published. This, its sequel, had a much shorter and faster journey to publication. I'm grateful to my critical friends Grant Young, Caren Young and June Bone for feedback, and particularly to Winnie Goodwin for her insights and honesty.

I owe a huge debt of gratitude to Sarah Hardy for publicity and to the army of book bloggers who wrote reviews of *Till the Dust Settles* that enticed many others to read it. Thank you, Sharon Bairden, for naming it as one of your top ten reads of 2017. What a compliment! Thanks to the huge crowd who turned up to my first ever book launch and to Michael J Malone for interviewing me and tolerating my surplus excitement. I was quite overwhelmed by the love in the room that night.

Thank you, Fred Freeman of Bloodhound Books for taking care of business and for helping me so generously, whether with books to replace stolen ones, a donation to my charity fundraising or with emails of explanation and reassurance. Thanks to Sumaira Wilson for looking after my 'second baby' with such care. It was also great to work again with Lesley Jones, my editor, whose knowledge and eye for detail identifies things I miss.

For advice on matters medical and for not batting an eyelid when suddenly asked, 'Can a wee kid die from a dog bite?' I want to thank my pet medics, Dr Gregor Young and Dr Jessica Taube.

Finally, for this stunning cover I'm indebted to Betsy for design, Caren for suggesting Carcassonne and the amazingly talented Joan Bobet of Barcelona, whose beautiful photo I found by chance. I hunted Joan down, seeking his permission which he gave wholeheartedly, at no charge. Muchas gracias, Joan, mi amigo.